Praise for Tim Powers

"It would be a serious mistake to dism *the Graves* as something less than art. It's literary fiction in tv ——————————————————nat-ing fictionalized look at some of En ————————————————————ust Polidori and the Rossettis, but also th ——————————————————nd, it's written impeccably. Powers is a ——————————————————de-scriptions of the gaslighted streets ————————————————————ury London are awesomely creepy. . . . Above an, ——————————————————aves is just pure fun. Powers knows how to temper terror with humor, and he knows something that a lot of adventure writers never learn: Without well-rounded, fully realized characters, it doesn't matter how good your concept is. It's a smart, exciting and perfectly constructed novel, and it's hard as hell to put down. Let the kids have their overwrought, sullen romances—*Hide Me Among the Graves* is a vampire novel for readers who still believe in the power, and the joy, of great literature."
　　　　　　　　　　　　　　　　　　　　　　　　　　　　　—NPR.org

"[A] fine example of the work of a much-beloved author, and a spooky ride through Victorian London to boot. . . . Powers's work engages with something prerational that is buried deep, deep in our brains, and that won't be bullied into submission by mere reason."
　　　　　　　—Cory Doctorow, boingboing.com, on *Hide Me Among the Graves*

"[*Three Days to Never*] contains so many genuine pleasures . . . plenty of action, humor and unexpectedly touching human drama. . . . [A] welcoming entry point to [Powers's] singular fictional universe."　　　　—*San Francisco Chronicle*

"Endlessly inventive. . . . You might finish this overstuffed novel still unsure about the connection between Einstein and astral projection, but if you give in to Powers's imaginative leaps and relentless pacing you may find that a mere quibble."　　　　　　　—*New York Times Book Review*, on *Three Days to Never*

"Tim Powers has long been one of my absolutely favorite writers, those whose new books I snatch up as soon as they appear, and *Three Days to Never* puts on dis-play all the qualities I most admire in him: intelligence, narrative sparkle, great dialogue, speculative imagination, and emotional power. This is a wonderful novel."
　　　　　　　　　　　　　　　　　　　　　　　　　　　　　—Peter Straub

"Powers has forged a style of narrative uniquely his own, one filled with sharply drawn characters, fully imagined settings, elaborate underpinnings that pull all rugs out from under us and let us glimpse terrible, ragged floors beneath."
　　　　　　　　　　　　　　—*Los Angeles Times Book Review*, on *Last Call*

"[Powers] orchestrates reality and fantasy so artfully that the reader is not al-lowed a moment's doubt throughout this tall tale."　　—*The New Yorker*, on *Declare*

"Dazzling . . . a tour de force, a brilliant blend of John le Carré spy fiction with the otherworldly."
　　　　　　　　　　　　　　　　　　　　　　　　—Dean Koontz, on *Declare*

ALSO BY TIM POWERS

HIDE ME AMONG THE GRAVES

Tim Powers

WILLIAM MORROW

An Imprint of HarperCollins*Publishers*

P.S.™ is a trademark of HarperCollins Publishers.

HarperCollins books may be purchased for educational, business, or sales promotional use. For information please write: Special Markets Department, HarperCollins Publishers, 10 East 53rd Street, New York, NY 10022.

A hardcover edition of this book was published in 2012 by William Morrow, an imprint of Harper-Collins Publishers.

FIRST WILLIAM MORROW PAPERBACK EDITION PUBLISHED 2013.

Library of Congress Cataloging-in-Publication Data has been applied for.

ISBN 978-0-06-221080-7

13 14 15 16 17 OV/RRD 10 9 8 7 6 5 4 3 2 1

To Joe Stefko and Thérèse DePrez

Acknowledgments

With thanks to Father Chrysostom Baer, O. Praem; John Berlyne; Jim Blaylock; Russell Galen; M. L. Konett; Barry Levin; Andreas Misera; Father Jerome Molokie, O. Praem; Chris Powers; Serena Powers; and Joe Stefko.

And mother dear, when the sun has set
And the pale kirk grass waves,
Then carry me through the dim twilight
And hide me among the graves.

—*Elizabeth Siddal Rossetti, "At Last"*

HIDE ME AMONG
THE GRAVES

PROLOGUE

1845: *The Bedbug*

I.

So I grew half delirious and quite sick,
And thro' the darkness saw strange faces grin
Of monsters at me. One put forth a fin,
And touched me clammily: I could not pick
A quarrel with it: it began to lick
My hand, making meanwhile a piteous din
And shedding human tears: it would begin
To near me, then retreat. I heard the quick
Pulsation of my heart, I marked the fight
Of life and death within me; then sleep threw
Her veil around me; but this thing is true:
When I awoke, the sun was at his height,
And I wept sadly, knowing that one new
Creature had love for me, and others spite.

—*Christina Rossetti*

T HE FELT-PADDED BASE of the ivory bishop thumped faintly on the marble chessboard.

"Check," said the girl.

The face of the old man across the table from her was in shadow—the curtains were drawn across the street-side windows, and the chandelier overhead hung crookedly because of the gas-saving mantle screwed onto it—and all she could see under the visor of his black cap was the gleam of his thick spectacles as he peered at the chess pieces.

Both of them hated to lose.

"And mate in . . . two," he said. He sat back, blinking owlishly at the girl.

She sighed and spread her hands. "I believe so, Papa."

The old man thoughtfully lifted the ebony king from the board and looked toward the fireplace, as if considering throwing the piece onto the coals. Instead he put it into the pocket of his robe, and when his hand reemerged it was holding instead a thumb-sized black stone statue.

Christina raised her eyebrows.

Old Gabriele's answering smile was wry. "I carry it around with me now," he said, "very close. Not that it does me any good anymore. Nothing does."

He put it down onto the square where his king had stood, and it clicked against the marble.

Wanting to head off yet another melodramatic elaboration along the lines of his *Nothing does*, Christina quickly asked, "What sort of good did it once do? You've said it's *buona fortuna*."

She and her sister and two brothers had seen the little statue on a high shelf in their parents' bedroom ever since they could remember, and they had even taken it down and incorporated the stumpy little stone man into their games when they were alone, but this was the first time in her fourteen years that she had ever seen it downstairs.

"It led me to your mother," he said softly, "all the way from Italy to England, and I thought it might keep us healthy and prosperous, not—not destitute and losing my sight—'And that one talent which is death to hide, lodged with me useless . . .'"

Christina could see him blinking behind the thick lenses, and saw the glint of the tears that were always embarrassingly ready these days, especially when he quoted Milton's sonnet about going blind. She wished she had let him win the chess game.

Adopting a manner that reminded her of someone, Christina lightly quoted a later line from the same sonnet as she stood up and began to pick the chess pieces from the board: "'Doth God exact day-labor, light denied?'" And she smiled at him and went on, "'I fondly ask.'"

"Yes, you foolishly ask," he snapped. "Where is your mother, tell me that! Embroidering in the drawing room, could it be? *Corpo di Bacho*, where is the drawing room?"

It occurred to Christina who it was that her own indulgently dismissive manner reminded her of—her mother, comforting Christina or one of her siblings when they used to wake up from nightmares.

And she remembered that when they had been troubled by nightmares, her father had always dropped the little stone statue into a glass of salted water. She couldn't recall now whether it had ever helped.

Her mother at the moment was out at work as a day governess, and this rented house on Charlotte Street had no drawing room.

Christina had laid all the chessmen except the black king into the wooden box, and now, leaving the statue alone on the board, she knelt by her father's blanketed knees and took his cold, dry, wrinkled hand.

"How did it lead you to Mother?"

He was frowning. "'Light denied,'" he said. "I should destroy the damned thing. This is my last summer. Italy never again."

She blew a strand of hair back from her forehead. "I won't listen to you when you talk like that." Again she reminded herself of her mother, as if she were the parent now, and her father had become a petulant child.

"Is it a compass?" she asked.

After a moment his scowl relaxed into a grudging smile. "You were always a contrary little beast. Tantrums. Cut yourself with scissors once when your mother corrected you! I should never have told you about it."

"Tell me about it."

He sighed. "No, child, it's not a compass. Am I being selfish? It gives you dreams . . . that are not really dreams."

"Like second sight?"

"Yes. I knew about . . . statues, from my days as curator of ancient statuary at the Museum of Napoli—some of them are not entirely lifeless. And I belonged to the Carbonari there, who also know more than a little about such things."

Christina nodded, noting the black spot on his palm—he had often told the children that it was the mark of Carbonari membership.

"And then King Ferdinand outlawed the Carbonari, and I fled to Malta—but in '22, when I was thirty-five, there was an earthquake, and I," he said, scratching his palm, "sensed this little stone, north of me. A summoning compass, if you like! I sailed east of Sicily, past the Gulf of Taranto and Apuleia, many perils, all the way up the east coast of Italy to Venice, following the, the dream-song that led me to find *him*"—he nodded toward the tiny lone figure on the chessboard—"in the possession of an ignorant Austrian soldier."

" . . . Led you to find *him*." Not *it*, she thought.

He freed his hand to ruffle her brown hair. "Understand, child, I had at that point nothing to lose. The Pope had already excommunicated the Carbonari."

Christina was momentarily glad that her sister, Maria, was living with another family as a governess, for Maria was virtuous and devout; and that her brother William was at work at the government tax office in Old Broad Street, for at the age of fifteen William was already a mocking skeptic.

Her brother Gabriel, though, who was off at Sass's art academy in Bedford Square, would be intrigued. Christina wished he were here.

She nodded. "I understand."

Hesitantly she reached her hand across toward the statue, giving her father time to tell her not to; but he made no objection, and her fingers closed around the cold thing.

Into her mind sprang the last line of the Milton sonnet: *I also serve who only stand and wait.* But that wasn't right—it was supposed to be *They,* not *I.*

"You shouldn't touch it," he said, now that she already had.

She let go of it and drew her hand away. "Did you buy . . . it, from the Austrian soldier?"

Her father waved his hand in front of his spectacles. "In a sense, child."

Christina nodded. "And this little stone man gave you a—a vision of Mother? Here in England?"

"That it did, though I'd never been to England, and I fell in love with her image—and set out to find her and marry her." He nodded firmly. "And I did."

Christina smiled. "Love at first second sight."

But her father's face sagged in renewed self-pity, the vertical lines around his mouth making him look like a ventriloquist's dummy. "Poor Frances Polidori! Working for wages in strangers' houses now! It was a bad day for her when she became Frances Rossetti, married to this half-blind wretch who earns nothing anymore—whose only hope now is to . . . to move on, and join so many of our old friends!"

He cast a theatrical glance at the framed portrait on the far wall. It was a picture of his wife's brother, John Polidori.

Christina recalled that her uncle had committed suicide in 1821—

four years before her father found her mother. Her father couldn't ever have met the man.

"Did you put it under your pillow, like a piece of wedding cake?" she asked, springing to her feet and crossing to the street-side window.

The rings hissed on the rod as she pulled the curtains aside, letting in afternoon sunlight reflected from the row of tan-colored houses on the other side of the Charlotte Street pavement. She glanced left and right through the glass, hoping her brother Gabriel might be coming home early from the art academy, as he often did, but she didn't see his slim, striding figure among the weaving hedge of horses and carriage wheels.

From behind her came her father's frail voice: "Turn off the gas, if you're going to scorch us with sunlight! What pillow?"

She turned back to her father, and the sun glare from the windows across the street now made momentary dark webs in her vision, connecting everything in the parlor.

"In Malta," she said. "Did you put the little man under your pillow?"

"Don't touch it again, Christina," he said quietly. "I shouldn't—I should have thrown him into the sea. Yes, under my pillow, on Midsummer's Eve."

Christina recalled that today was Midsummer's Eve—June 23. Was that why her father had brought the thing downstairs and shown it to her?

He was shaking his head, and strands of his sparse white hair were falling over his glasses. "It's a wicked trick, no good from it—you children, Hearts, Clubs, Diamonds, and Spades! Where did *that* come from? Eh?"

Christina smiled as she walked back across the old carpet to the table and stood on a chair to reach the stopcock at the base of the chandelier. When she and her brothers and sister had been children, they had played endless games of whist and Beggar My Neighbor in the nursery, and at some point they had each adopted one of the suits of cards: Gabriel was hearts; William, spades; Maria, clubs; and Christina was diamonds.

"I think several of us dreamed it," she said, hopping back down to the floor, "and it was fun to have . . . secret identifications."

"Not in a house with children!" muttered the old man. "And even now, you're only fourteen! I've been a terrible father."

Christina paused, staring at him. She and her siblings had read Maturin's eerie *Melmoth the Wanderer* and *The Arabian Nights,* and their mother often read to them from the Bible. William would scoff, but William was at work.

"Just," she said, "with it under your pillow? No . . . special rhyme to say?"

"Prayers, you should say! With a rosary under your pillow! Not what I did . . ."

"What did *you* do, Papa?" she asked softly. "Confess." His mention of rosaries had reminded her that he was at least nominally Catholic, though her mother and her sister were devout Anglicans.

"Promise me you'll destroy it when I'm gone—crush it and scatter the powder into the sea. Promise."

Not destroy it now? she thought. "I promise."

"I—God help me. I bled on it. I rubbed some of my blood on it, first. Promise!—but where would you children be, if I had not? Is it a sin to have sired the four of you? What would have become of Frances, as she was—a governess and still unmarried at twenty-six? Now she's the wife of a professor of Italian at King's College!"

A retired professor, thought Christina, with no pension. But, "Just so," she said.

He had begun coughing piteously, and it probably wasn't all for show—he did have bronchitis again.

"Stir up the fire, *vivace mia,*" he quavered.

Christina slid the fire screen aside and reached into the fireplace with the shovel and pushed the gray coals into a pile to make a bed for a handful of fresh lumps of coal from the iron basket on the hearth.

Then she heard her brother Gabriel's boots tapping up the steps, and a moment later heard the hallway door unlatch and swing open. The air in the parlor shifted and abruptly seemed stuffy when Gabriel strode into the room with a few whirls of the outside summer breeze still at his back.

"Salve, buona sera!" he said with cautiously preemptive cheer, tossing a couple of books onto a chair by the door and shrugging out of his coat.

Christina knew he was apprehensive about having left school early—their father often complained that Gabriel was wasting the tuition money—but her brother's first words had made her realize that she and her father had been speaking in English. Everyone in the family was fluent in both English and Italian, but old Gabriele nearly never spoke English in his home.

Her father closed his hand over the little statue and returned it to his pocket.

Christina glanced at the old man, and he very slightly shook his head. Do you mean stop speaking English now, she wondered, or stop talking about the statue?

Either way, her brother's jarring entrance—he was riffling through the mail beside the empty chessboard now, looking very much the man of the house in his shirtsleeves and waistcoat, though he was only two years older than Christina—had broken the morbid, secretive mood. Gabriel's ostentatious youth, his clear blue eyes and his untidy auburn hair, made her father seem decrepit and almost senile by comparison.

"Buona sera, Gabriel," she said, and added, still in Italian, "Would you like some tea?"

BY SEVEN O'CLOCK WILLIAM and their mother had come home from their jobs, and after the family had dispatched a platter of pasta primavera, three elderly Italian men came calling and sat with Christina's father on chairs dragged up by the fire.

Christina and her brothers sat at the window-side table, sketching and composing rhymes by lamplight while the old men argued politics in histrionic Italian on the other side of the room, airing their eternal grievances against the Pope, and the kings of France and Napoli, and the Austrians who controlled Italy.

Christina and her brothers half listened to the familiar talk, and their mother sat at the cleared dining table in the next room with a stack of clothes, stitching up frayed sleeves and darning stockings.

The daylight on the bricks and windows across the street slowly faded from gold to gray, and then the curtains were pulled across and the chandelier was relit, and eventually the clatter of hooves and wheels on the pavement outside became just the fast snare-drum approach and diminishment of individual hansom cabs.

At one point Christina heard the old men talking about the Carbonari, and she looked up from her sketch of a rabbit.

Her father might have been watching her for several seconds, for immediately he beckoned to her; and when she had got up and walked across to his chair, he pulled a folded handkerchief from his robe pocket and handed it to her.

"Hold it for me," he said quietly, in English.

Christina knew that her mother couldn't see them from the other room—and she didn't need to unfold the handkerchief to know that it was wrapped around the little statue, for she could feel the cold of the stone through the linen.

She gave him a quizzical glance, for earlier he had said that he carried the thing around with him now—and he had told her not to touch it. His expression was impossible to read behind his thick lenses, though, so she nodded and tucked it into the pocket of her frock and went back to her sketching.

But her rabbit began to go wrong under her darting pencil—the hind legs and back seemed broken now, and the creature's face began to take on a human-like expression that somehow expressed both scorn and pleading—and when she heard her brother Gabriel gasp at the sight of it, she crumpled the paper.

"I think I'll go up to bed," she said. She curtsied toward the blinking old men but avoided looking at her father, and she hurried from the parlor to say good night to her mother and to light a candle to guide her up the stairs.

UNTIL FOUR MONTHS AGO Christina had shared the slant-ceilinged bedroom on the third floor with her older sister, Maria, but Maria had left home on her seventeenth birthday to work as a governess for the children of a family in the country. Maria was the one who always remembered to say her prayers, and Christina, now alone, often forgot.

Tonight she forgot. She lit a pair of candles that stood on a niche in the chimney bricks, washed her face in the basin and brushed her teeth, but as she climbed into the bed in the corner and blew out the candles and pulled the bed curtain across, her thoughts were of her father's little statue. It still sat rolled in the handkerchief in her frock, which hung now from a hook by the door.

The window overlooking Charlotte Street was outside the tent made by the bed curtain, so she sat up and pulled the heavy fabric aside—drafts or no drafts—and stared at the dimly glowing east-facing square in the wall. She was seeing it nearly end on, and couldn't hope to glimpse stars through the sooty glass, but she was vividly aware of the volume of space outside, all the tangled streets sloping down to the dark moving river, and the vast breathing sea out beyond all the bridges and docks—and then she was dreaming, for under the moon the river and the sea were alive with hundreds, thousands of pale figures waving jointless arms, dark spots intermittently appearing on their distant faces as eyes and mouths opened and closed.

The window rattled, and she was fully awake again. She and her siblings called that dream the Sea-People Chorus, and she hoped it wouldn't persist all night, as it sometimes did.

She preferred it to the visions of the creature she called Mouth Boy, though—an apparition who never appeared to the others, and whose head was flat because it was just an enormous mouth, with no eyes above or behind it. And even as she thought of him she thought she heard his characteristic harsh bellow's breath all the way up from the pavement below the window; it might have been an exhalation of his that had made the window rattle.

It was unpleasant to have such dreams when Maria wasn't in bed beside her! Often Christina and Maria would have had the same nightmare, and been able to hold each other in the darkness and reassure each other that the visions were imaginary.

This night seemed full of ghosts and monsters impatient to command her helpless attention—and her eyes darted to the faint outline of the door across the room, beside which hung her frock.

The window rattled again, and her resolve was instant. She bounded out of bed in her nightgown and groped her way to that corner and patted her hung frock till she felt the lump that was the handkerchief, and in a moment she had fumbled it out, shaken the little stone figure free, and hurried back to bed with the cold thing in her fist.

Blood, she thought—and she bit her finger, chewing beside the nail and ignoring the pain, until she could feel slickness there with her thumb. She rubbed the wet ball of her thumb over the tiny face of the stone figure, feeling the points that were the crude nose and chin of it.

Her father claimed it had given him a prophetic vision of her mother.

She tucked it under her pillow and pulled the bed curtain closed again, and she lay down and snuggled herself under the blankets, hopeful that she had banished the old nightmares and would instead dream of the man she would one day marry.

AT FIRST THE FIGURE seemed to be Mouth Boy after all, for the thing's lips were grossly swollen, as if from an injury—in the dream it limped from darkness into the ring of light below a streetlamp—but when she focused more closely, she saw that the effect must have been a momentary exaggeration of the shadows, for its lips were simply wide and prominent below a pug nose and two enormous eyes. Its hair was an untidy tangle, and somehow it seemed to bear a caricature resemblance to her brother Gabriel.

This wasn't the Mouth Boy phantasm, which always looked more like a wide-snouted crocodile with no eyes at all.

This figure in the street waved both arms upward, and she saw that its coat sleeves hung over its hands, and from the steamy puffing of its breath it seemed to be speaking rhythmically, or singing, though she couldn't hear any sound.

It was standing at the steps of a house, and in a moment Christina recognized the house in the dream—it was her own house, her own front door at the top of the steps.

The flabby white cheeks glistened, as if this thing that resembled her brother were weeping at being locked outside.

"Wait," she said, and she realized that she had sat up in bed and was awake, and speaking out loud in the close darkness. "I'll let you in."

Her heart was pounding and her pulse thudded in her temples, and she wasn't able to take a deep breath, but she stepped out of bed straight toward the bedroom door, letting the curtain slide over her head till the hem of it fell off behind her like a discarded shawl, and she opened the door and stole down the stairs to the street door.

II.

So in these grounds, perhaps in the orchard, I lighted upon
a dead mouse. The dead mouse moved my sympathy: I took
him up, buried him comfortably in a mossy bed, and bore the
spot in mind.

It may have been a day or two afterward that I returned,
removed the moss coverlet, and looked . . . a black insect
emerged. I fled in horror, and for long years ensuing I never
mentioned this ghastly adventure to anyone.

—*Christina Rossetti,* Time Flies: A Reading Diary

That September the summer twilight still extended past supper and the hour for the Read girls to go to bed, and so Maria and her visiting sister were permitted to take horses from the stable and ride as far as the family chapel and back.

The rosemary-scented breeze fluttered the girls' skirts as they rode slowly along the dirt path between the shadow-streaked grassy hills. Maria wore a long black riding habit loaned to her by Mrs. Read, and in spite of her stoutness she rode comfortably sidesaddle on a chestnut mare, but Christina, though she was riding more securely astride a man's saddle, was terrified whenever her gray gelding broke into a trot.

"He's a gentle old thing," Maria called to her. "You can simply relax and move with him."

"I feel like a tennis ball," said Christina breathlessly, "being bounced up and down on a racket. One time I'll—miss the racket when I come down, and I—*don't see any* way to fall off which doesn't—involve landing on my head." She smiled, but her face was misted with sweat and she felt as though her teeth might at any moment start chattering.

Maria reined in her own mount so that Christina's would subside to a steady walk.

"You'll be returning to London with a much rosier complexion than you left with," Maria observed. "Sun and fresh air have done it."

"Possibly." Christina knew that she had not regained any weight during this week in the country at the house of Maria's employers, and on the few occasions when she had ventured out into the sunlight she had been wearing a hat. Her forehead was always damp with perspiration. "I certainly like your cure better than iron filings steeped in beer."

"You don't swallow the iron filings, do you? Is that a cure for angina pectoris?"

"For anemia, actually. No, they decant the beer off them."

Maria was looking at her, but Christina couldn't make out the expression on her sister's round face against the glowing western sky.

Perhaps she was disapproving of anyone giving quantities of beer to a fourteen-year-old girl, even as medicine.

"You must be a very good teacher," Christina said quickly, "to be a live-in governess for such a well-to-do family."

"They rejected another girl," said Maria, "because Mrs. Read felt she was too pretty to be in the house with Mr. Read. I'm employed because I'm not comely. I'd like to have the girls learn Greek and Latin, but I'm only to teach them from the *Historical and Miscellaneous Questions*— from it they learn things like, oh, when the Diet of Worms occurred, but not a bit of what it was."

"They must wonder what other diets were tried before it," said Christina, smiling. "The Diet of Dirt, the Diet of—"

"Anemia," Maria interrupted flatly, "angina pectoris, palpitations, shortness of breath." They were in the long shadow of a western hill now, and the northern breeze from the Chiltern Hills was cooler. "What is it?"

"Doctor Latham says that puberty is often—"

"Not what Doctor Latham says it is. What do *you* say it is?"

Christina opened her mouth, and then after a moment closed it again. "Oh, Maria," she whispered finally, "pray for me!"

"I do. And I hope you pray for yourself."

The dark spire of the Read family chapel was visible now ahead on their left, beyond the tall black cypresses and the iron fence of the family churchyard, and it occurred to Christina that it might not have been entirely the chapel's convenient distance from the house that had led Maria to choose it as their goal.

"I try to pray," she said. "I can't go to Confession anymore." She spread the fingers of one hand without releasing the rein. "What would I—*say?*"

Maria's voice was gentle. "Say it to me."

"I—Maria, I think—I'm ruined!"

Maria rocked back in her saddle, and her mare clopped to a halt.

"Ach, 'Stina!" Maria whispered. "You *think* so? Are you—to be sent away?"

"I don't know. Can ghosts father children?"

Her horse had stopped too, and she could see the silhouette of Maria's head shaking slowly.

"It was a ghost?" asked Maria.

Christina nodded.

"I want to understand. You're saying it was the spirit of a dead man."

"*Yes.*"

"If you've been feverish—"

"Maria, I didn't *dream* it! Well, I did at first—I saw it outside the house, but then I woke up and went downstairs and let it in—"

"Why on earth would you let it *in*?"

"It was in already, really—its body, in any case, petrified. Aren't ghosts supposed to sit by their graves? And it was sick, and weeping, and looked like Gabriel! And you and William too. It looked like family—I felt as if I were letting it back into its own house. *And* I—oh, I thought it would show me visions of my future spouse, guide me there, as it did for Papa."

Maria glanced at her. "Really? I never knew."

Christina just shook her head, biting her lip.

"Er . . . *did* it? Show you a vision of that?"

"No. It only showed me itself."

For a few moments there was no sound but the wind that shook the grasses and tossed stray strands of Christina's fair hair across her face.

At last Maria said, "Was it . . . substantial, your ghost?" She waved one hand. "Did it have weight, did the floorboards creak?"

"Weight? Not at first," said Christina bleakly. "Later, yes. Yes." She sighed. "As I diminished."

Maria was deep in thought and absently said, "I don't think anybody would say a *ghost* can ruin a girl." She looked up. "I thought Papa—"

"But *I* know." Christina's face was damp and chilly as she made herself speak. "Oh God. It wasn't—he, it, didn't *force* itself on me."

After a pause, Maria nudged her horse into a walk with her left heel, and Christina's moved forward to keep pace.

Maria said, "I thought Papa kept that damned thing on a special shelf in his room." She looked at Christina and shrugged. "Of course I know. What other ghost could it be?"

"Oh. Yes. Papa was keeping it in the pocket of his robe, lately. He thought it helped his vision. But then he gave it to me, three months ago."

"And where—" Maria's head whipped around to face Christina. "Jesus save us! You didn't bring it *here,* did you?"

"I'm sorry! I thought you'd know how to . . . make it stop, free his soul from the statue, lay him to final rest! You've read so many—"

Maria's eyes darted over Christina's long coat and bunched-up skirt. "Do you have it with you *now?*"

Christina nodded miserably. "I carry it around with me, very close. Not that it does me any good."

"I cannot believe you had it in the house with Lucy and Bessie!" Maria peered at the open gate of the cypress-shadowed churchyard, only a dozen yards ahead now along the rutted dirt path. "We could bury it in consecrated ground."

"I don't think it would lie . . . inertly, in peace. And Papa entrusted it to me—I know he'll want it back, sooner or later. Oh, Maria, I don't want to hate him for this!"

"Hate which?"

Christina blinked at her sister, then answered softly, "Well—either of them."

"You say he led Papa to our mother." Maria's voice was flat. "And he resembled Gabriel and William and me. And Mama and you too, I imagine. I think I know who your ghost must be." She shook her head. "Have *been.* And you—you're *fond* of him."

"I—try not to be. I do want to send him away."

"Exorcise him? To Hell? That's where he belongs—he committed suicide, remember, in 1821."

"No—I know, but Mama—"

"He's what's made you sick. Does he keep you from eating, sleeping, to make you so pale and thin?"

"No," said Christina. She laughed briefly, a sound like dry sticks knocked together. "He's more like a—a bedbug."

"He, what, he *bites* you?"

"It doesn't hurt. It did at first, but now it—doesn't hurt."

The horses had rocked and plodded up to the arched wrought-iron gate of the churchyard, and Maria unhooked her right leg from the fixed saddle pommel and slid down to thump her boots on the dusty ground.

"We might be able do something here," she said.

Christina, up on her own conventional saddle, hadn't shifted. "Maria, you've read, oh, Homer and Euripides and Ovid! I don't want to exorcise him to Hell. Isn't there some *pagan* ritual we could do?"

"We're Christians, and this is a Christian church; I don't—"

"Mama loves him still! He's her brother! What if it were a brother of yours—Gabriel or William?"

"Any such 'ritual' would . . . compromise our *souls,* Christina, yours and mine." She squinted up at her sister. "Our Savior mercifully put an end—and an interdict!—to the old pagan tricks."

"Can we at least give him some sort of pagan burial, so he might dissipate into the dirt and the grass? Then tomorrow I could dig him—it—up again, once the spirit was gone, and take the emptied statue back to Papa."

"Christina, this is a job for a priest, not two girls! A *Catholic* priest, really—they're more familiar with devils."

"I *won't* send him to Hell. I'll let him drain me to a husk, sooner." She shuddered and hugged herself with her thin arms. "I'm glad he didn't do this to Papa. But, Maria, why *didn't* he do this to Papa, who found him and woke him?"

"Papa married into the Polidori family; he's not a blood relation. You are. Do you need help getting down?"

After a moment of puzzlement, Christina shook her head and pulled her right foot free of the stirrup, and when she swung her leg over the horse's back, Maria caught her by the waist and steadied her to the ground.

"You don't weigh anything," said Maria, brushing her sister's skirt out straight.

Christina took a hasty step to catch her balance and said, breathlessly, "Help me down—from this precipice!—Maria."

For several seconds neither girl spoke, and Christina's panting gradually subsided.

"Can he hear us?" asked Maria finally. "Now?"

"No—he's *aware* of me—I can feel his attention like spiderwebs—but—" Christina looked up at the fading blue sky and then looked around nervously at the chapel and the grassy hills. "We'd see him, if he could hear us. Why?"

"I can think of a couple of things we might try," said Maria gruffly. "One, out of Papa's old Hebrew books, would surely damn our souls."

Out of consideration for her sister, Christina asked, "What's the other?"

"Well—Mama was a Polidori. She said the family, Grandpa and all of them, liked to think they were descended from Polydorus, in the *Iliad* and the *Aeneid*."

"That's right." Christina crouched beside her horse's front legs, for she still felt dizzy. "You wanted to call Grandpa's house in Park Village 'Myrtle Cottage' because of something to do with Polydorus."

Maria nodded and cast a long look at the churchyard gate, and at the dozen headstones standing up in the shadowed grass beyond it, then sighed and led her horse away, across the road to a ditch and a low fieldstone wall. Beyond the wall a wide field sloped up to a hedge, still brushed with gold sunlight, on the crest of the hill.

Christina straightened up and followed, scuffing her shoes in the dust as she pulled her own horse clopping along after her.

"What did Polydorus do, again?"

"Die, mainly," said Maria over her shoulder. "In the *Aeneid* they find his body, his unrestful murdered body, tangled up in the roots of a myrtle bush on the island of Thrace, and they give it proper honors and—and it's implied that the ghost lies quiet after that."

"Can we give—*him*—those 'proper honors'?"

Maria muttered some Latin hexameters under her breath, then said, "Milk and blood, and dirt piled on him. And black fillets, like hair ribbons—and the Trojan women let down their hair in grief."

Christina was leaning forward to rest her elbows on the waist-high stone wall and looking away, up the hill. The stone was still warm, though the breeze was now uncomfortably chilly.

"The question is," Maria went on, "will he recognize it as a fitting *au revoir* for a Polidori? Not just fitting, in fact, but compelling?"

Christina said, "*I don't know,*" in a weary exhalation. "Can you ride back and get milk? And black ribbons?"

"Surely. Er . . . what will we do for blood?"

"He's had enough of mine." Christina waved back toward the chapel without looking at it. "Would there be sacramental wine?"

She heard Maria gasp. "That would be sacrilege!"

"It's only wine, Maria—we're not Catholics! But he was raised Catholic, he might *believe* it's blood." Their grandparents had raised their mother and aunts Anglican and their uncles Catholic, and Christina supposed that the beliefs would have been deeply implanted into her uncle John, even if he later rejected them.

She looked up at the darkening sky. "I think he's . . . not far off." Her voice was unsteady.

"I'll hurry," said Maria, stepping up into the saddle and settling her right leg over the fixed pommel. She deftly reined the horse around and set off at a trot back toward the Read house.

⚘

THE SKY WAS MUCH darker by the time Maria came riding back less than ten minutes later, and the hill beyond the low wall was a patchwork of grays shifting in the chilling wind. Christina was standing in the road by the wall, facing the hill.

"This is a bad idea," Maria said, lowering herself carefully from the saddle while clutching a screw-top glass jar in one hand. "'If 'twere done, 'twere best done quickly.'"

Christina nodded and touched the gold chalice that now stood on the rough top edge of the wall, but she didn't take her eyes from the hillside.

"I fetched this from across the road," she said quietly. "And we're all here."

She was staring at a hunched silhouette that stood halfway up the shadowed slope, and a moment later she heard Maria gasp and scuffle backward.

"Is that . . . *him?*" Maria whispered.

Christina's breath caught in her throat when she tried to answer, but she managed to nod.

The ashy figure up on the slope seemed to sway and flutter in the breeze, but it didn't shift its position.

After a long, strained moment, "Back to the house!" said Maria breathlessly, grabbing Christina's shoulder; "or no—into the chapel!"

"He's blind," said Christina, "no eyes. And he can't hurt you without you inviting him." She looked away from the distant figure to face her sister. "As I invited him, Maria! And he's . . . our uncle."

"He's—he doesn't look anything like—any of us!" Maria was still gripping her sister's shoulder. "He looks like—some kind of shark!"

"He hasn't been well. And he's more Mouth Boy now than our uncle John."

Maria let go of her sister's shoulder. "*Mouth* Boy?" she said in a wailing whisper. "What, from your old nightmares?"

Christina nodded. "I suppose I've always been waiting for him, and that's the—the sketch I did in advance. He's partly assumed it now, out of economy."

Maria took a deep breath and let it out shakily. "I said I'd do this, and I will. But God help us."

Christina reached a trembling hand into the pocket of her jacket and pulled out the little black stone figure. "Tell me what to do."

"I don't want to get on the same side of the wall as him," Maria said. "Stop looking at him! Yes, you invited him, and we've got to uninvite him, surely. Ach, but I think it should be in the grass, on that side. The road dirt's packed too hard to dig anyway. And the milk and—and *blood* wouldn't sink in. I should have fetched a trowel. Maybe the—"

Christina was looking at her sister, and now reached out to touch her lips to stop her talking. "In the grass it is," she said, and she turned away from the hill to hike herself up onto the wall, then swung her legs around and hopped down into the calf-high grass. "Thank you for doing this," she said over her shoulder, trying to sound more resolute than she felt. "For saving me."

"If I'm not damning us both."

Maria clambered over the wall herself and immediately crouched to begin pulling up clumps of long grass and then scooping out the warm black loam underneath. "You watch him!" she said in a shrill whisper. "If he comes this way, run for the chapel!" She glanced up at her sister, and then hissed, "Jesus save us, are you *smiling* at him?"

"I'm the last sight he'll see, God willing."

"That's right, that's right. Kneel down here—and let down your hair. We're supposed to be mourning."

"I think," said Christina, reaching behind her head as she knelt in the grass, "I am."

Maria pulled clips from her own black hair and shook it out. Both girls were shivering. "I can mourn for our uncle," Maria said, "dead these twenty-four years."

Christina kissed the stone before laying it into the shallow hole Maria had dug. Maria frowned but didn't say anything and began piling the damp earth onto it.

"More," she said. "We want a mound."

Christina pulled up some more sheaves of grass and gouged up handfuls of dirt from underneath and added them to the pile.

From her pocket Maria pulled three black ribbons, and after a moment's hesitation she laid them crossed in a star pattern over the little mound.

Then she shook the jar she'd brought from the house—"It's supposed to be foaming," she said—and poured milk over the mound. In the gathering darkness the milk hardly showed on the black mound, and in a moment it had disappeared.

"Now the blood," she said.

Christina reached behind her and lifted the chalice from the wall top and handed it to Maria.

"Rest in peace, Uncle John," said Maria softly as she poured the wine over the dirt. "Please."

Christina nodded and managed to say, "Go."

She glanced up quickly, and Maria flinched back with a gasp, for a deeper shadow had seemed to fall across them from only a yard away—and then it was gone, and the grass was rippling in waves away from the raw mound.

Christina was reminded of having once at twilight walked through a field of tall grass and disturbed sleeping birds, who darted short distances away without appearing above the grass tops, so that her passage had seemed to cause ripples, as if she were wading through a pond instead of grass.

She thought she caught a whiff of the sea, or gunpowder, and the metallic smell of blood.

She rubbed her hand over her face, and there was no more sensation of clinging spiderwebs. "He's gone," she whispered, feeling empty.

"Thank God." Maria got laboriously to her feet, brushing off the front of her riding habit. "We must return the chalice."

"Tomorrow I'll dig the statue up again," said Christina. "Papa will be relieved to have it back, even inert."

Maria started to speak, then just shook her head.

The two girls led the horses back across the road, and within minutes they were mounted and trotting away through the deepening gloom toward the lights of the Read house.

THE WIND FROM THE north swept the grass in even waves across the slope in the darkness, but in the patch of grass by the wall, the waves converged in on the mounded pile of fresh-turned dirt and combed the grass into a spiral, and then the grass blades and the mound flattened, as if under a weight.

By morning the grass had straightened up again, as if the weight had joined the milk and wine in soaking into the ground, or as if it had risen and moved away.

BOOK I

Hope to Die

February 1862

CHAPTER ONE

I shall go my ways, tread out my measure,
Fill the days of my daily breath
With fugitive things not good to treasure . . .

—*Algernon Swinburne, "The Triumph of Time"*

WYCH STREET WAS two rows of tall old houses facing each other across a narrow pavement now dusted with snow, just north of the broad lanes of the Strand and only a few streets from the line of arches along the land-facing side of Somerset House. The cold morning sun silhouetted the steeple of St. Clement Danes to the east and lanced down the street—here glaring from the panes of a bay window on an upper floor, there glittering in the frost crystals on a drainpipe slanting across a still-shadowed wall—and a woman in a blue coat was walking slowly down the middle of the pavement with the sun at her back.

Her hands were hidden in an oversized white ermine muff, and her breath was puffs of steam whisked away on the breeze as she peered at the variously shaped dark doorways she passed on either side. Finally she halted, and for nearly a minute just stared at a brass plaque beside the door of an otherwise unremarkable house:

The plaque read: JOHN CRAWFORD, M.R.C.V.S. SURGERY FROM 9 TO 11 O'CLOCK.

The knocker was a wrought-iron cat's head, hinged at the top.

A bigger plume of steam blew away from under her bonnet, and then she stepped to the door and carefully freed one gloved hand to give the knocker two sharp clanks.

"In sunshine or in sha-adow," she sang softly to herself; then she smiled and touched the ermine muff. "And kneel and say an ave there for me."

She heard steps from inside, and a curtain twitched in the frosted window at her left, and then a bolt rattled and the door swung inward.

The man who had opened the door blinked out at her without recognition. "Is it an emergency?" he asked. "The surgery isn't open for hours yet."

He wore a brown sack-coat with an outmoded plaid shawl over his shoulders, and she noted that his beard was still dark brown.

"Come in," he added, stepping aside.

She walked past him into the hallway's warm smells of bacon and garlic and tobacco as he closed the door behind her and asked, "Can I take your coat?"

She laid the muff on a table and pulled off her muddy boots and her gloves; then she shrugged out of her blue velveteen coat, and as she handed it to him, the muff on the table squeaked and chirped.

He paused, looking from it to her, and raised his eyebrows.

"Er . . . do you," she asked with a tight smile, "minister to birds?"

"I really only ever go as small as chickens, and that sounded like a songbird. My main customers are cab horses, and I do *pro bono publico* work for stray cats." He smiled. "But I suppose I can advise, if you'll bring the patient in." He waved toward an open doorway, and the woman retrieved the muff and stepped through into a parlor with framed hunting prints on the green-papered walls. The ivory-colored curtains over the front windows had probably been white originally.

A cold fireplace gaped below a marble mantelpiece that was still hung with tinsel and wilted holly. A dozen wooden chairs were ranked closely along two of the walls, and a long couch hid the sills of the street-side windows. Half a dozen cats were sprawled on the couch and the low table.

"Do sit," said Crawford. "I'll fetch in some tea."

He disappeared through an inner door, and the woman pushed several of the cats off the couch onto the carpet—one had only three legs, and another appeared to have no eyes, though they all scampered away energetically—and sat down on the cleared cushion. She carefully slid a small cylindrical birdcage no bigger than a pint-pot out of the ermine muff and set it upright on the table. The tiny brown bird within peered around the room, paying no evident attention to the retreating cats.

This room was chillier than the entry hall, and, in addition to the apparently constant whiff of garlic, smelled of dogs and spirits of camphor. A framed notice between two pictures of leaping horses listed prices of various operations and remedies.

Crawford came pushing back in through the door carrying a tray, and as he set it on the table he said, "And what ails your bird, Miss . . . ?"

"McKee," she said. "Adelaide McKee." He had poured steaming tea into a cup, and she accepted it with a nod, ignoring the pots of sugar and milk. "Who is Mister C.V.S.? I didn't notice the sign the last time I was here."

"Mister . . . ? Oh! That's me, I suppose. The whole thing stands for Member of the Royal College of Veterinary Surgeons." He pulled up one of the wooden chairs and sat down across the table from her. "You've been here before? Was it another case of bird malaise?"

"I gave you a different name then." She untied the strings of her bonnet and pulled it off, shaking out her shoulder-length chestnut curls. "And it was seven years ago." She glanced around the room. "Frankly, I'm surprised to find you still here."

Crawford had poured himself a cup too, and started to raise it, but now he clanked it back down onto the saucer. His face was chilly with a sudden dew of sweat, and two full seconds later his ribs and the backs of his hands tingled with remembered fright and enormous present embarrassment.

HE HAD STILL BEEN drunk most of the time in that summer of 1855, and on many nights memories of his wife and two sons had kept him from sleeping; on those nights he had sat up drinking and trying to lose himself in cheap novels or, giving up on that, gone for long walks along the banks of the Thames.

And on one such rainy summer midnight, he had found himself drawn toward the lights along the south shore of the river—but when he had paid his ha'penny at the Strand-side turnstile of Waterloo Bridge and walked out as far as a recessed stone seat above the third of the bridge's nine arches over the river, he stopped there with such deliberateness that he wondered for a moment if he had had some now-forgotten purpose in coming out here.

There were no lamps on the bridge, and he had been able dimly to see the silhouette of St. Paul's Cathedral a mile away to the east, and strings of yellow and orange lights on the south shore flickering through the veils of rain. Occasional patches of moonlight shone on the rain-dulled water below him.

His wife and sons had died on the Thames two years earlier, in a boating accident, and he wondered, with some alarm, if his purpose in coming out here had been to throw himself into that same water, perhaps maudlinly inspired by Thomas Hood's poem about a prostitute who had committed suicide off this bridge.

His wife's name had been Veronica. His sons had been Girard and Richard. He stood there for several minutes, while rain washed away the tears on his cheeks, and told himself, They're gone. They're gone.

Over the hiss of the rain and the constant hoarse whisper of the river shifting around the bridge pilings below, he became aware of a metronomic clinking getting louder. A woman was walking toward him from the Blackfriars side of the bridge, and she evidently had metal pattens on her shoes to protect them from puddles. The round bulge at the top of her silhouette was certainly an umbrella. Embarrassed at being caught weeping, even though it would not be evident, Crawford straightened and wearily got ready to lift his hat as she passed him.

His hand was on the brim of his bowler hat, and the silhouette of the umbrella became wider as she presumably glanced toward him—

—And then for a frozen instant it seemed that a piece of the umbrella broke free and hung in the night air, swelling rapidly in size—

But it was something rushing down at the two of them out of the charcoal sky, something alive and churning and savage, and at the sudden roaring of it the woman glanced up and then leaped backward, colliding with Crawford and spinning him half around.

The harsh bass noise of the thing was like a locomotive about to hit them, compressing the air, and a sharp machine-oil smell like ozone was harsh in Crawford's nostrils. In a convulsion of total panic, he seized the woman around the waist, boosted her right over the stone railing, and pitched her away from the bridge—she had been too breathless even to scream—and in the same motion he slapped one boot onto the wet stone bench and sprang over the railing after her.

Then he was plummeting through yards and yards of empty rushing air, and he crashed into the cold water before he had thought to take a breath; he might even have been screaming.

When he thrashed back up to the surface, gasping, he could see the woman flailing in the water near him, her billowing crinoline at once keeping her afloat and impeding her efforts to swim, but before struggling out of his heavy coat and starting through the water toward her, he threw a fearful glance up at the bridge high overhead. For a moment there might have been a flexing, spiky bulk visible at the railing, but if so, it had withdrawn by the time he had blinked water out of his eyes for a clearer look.

He swam to the struggling woman and grasped her upper arm,

then began kicking through the frigid salt water toward the shore. The current swept them east, past the arches and water gates of Somerset House, and he managed to slant in at the steps below Temple Place. The woman had also lost or shed her jacket in the river, and both of them were shaking as they climbed on their hands and knees up the steps to the narrow river-side pavement.

Looking back fearfully, Crawford couldn't make out the bridge at all in the darkness. From very far away he thought he caught a slow bass thrumming under the percussion of the storm.

His hand slapped his waistcoat pocket, but the little jar he sometimes remembered to carry wasn't there.

Cold rain clattered around him, and river water dripped from his beard. "*What,*" he choked, "the bloody *hell*—was—"

She put her cold palm across his mouth so quickly that it was almost a slap, and water flew from her stringy wet hair. "Don't . . . give words," she panted. "Don't . . . *draw, attract.*" She lowered her hand to grip the edge of the pavement. "We need to get indoors. Walls, a roof."

He was panting too. "I—live near here. Five-minute walk."

She nodded. "Good—but first—" She rolled over and sat up, apparently to untie one of her shoes. A moment later she handed him the metal frame that had been strapped to the bottom of it.

"Strap that over the sole of one of your boots," she said. "Quickly— even with this change in our silhouettes, we've got to be inside before the rain washes the salty river water off us."

He didn't argue. He was still breathing rapidly, and when his shaking fingers discovered that the straps wouldn't fit over the instep of his boot, he impatiently pulled his sopping scarf from around his neck and tore it lengthwise in half. He used the narrower strip to tie the metal sole onto his left boot, with a big wet knot over his instep.

The woman had got to her feet. "Come on," she whispered. "You go, lead the way—I'll follow about twenty feet behind you. We've got to stop our auras overlapping."

"Auras." Crawford stood up unsteadily on the wobbly metal sole. "We're," he said to her, "safe? For now?"

"Safe?" The streetlamps of Arundel Street ahead of them threw enough light for him to see her wondering frown. "Go. I'll follow."

The two of them weren't much wetter than the few other pedestrians they passed, as first Crawford and then the woman crossed the muddy gravel lanes of the Strand, and the one cabbie that reined in his horse for a moment just shrugged and sped up again when Crawford waved him off. The unsynchronized crunch of the shared pair of pattens sounded like the footsteps of a drunk repeatedly attempting and then abandoning a difficult dance step.

When he had walked quickly down the narrow lane that was Wych Street to his own front door, he looked back as he dug the key from his pocket. The woman had stepped in under the overhanging upper floor of an old house a dozen yards behind him.

His hands were shaking but he was careful to twist the bolt back as quietly as possible, and then he paused to reach down and push the knotted strip of scarf forward off his boot; ordinarily he would have stepped straight into the parlor and yanked the bell-pull to summon Mrs. Middleditch from her little top-floor bedroom, but tonight he wanted to recover from whatever it was that he had just participated in, without extra witnesses.

He swung the door open, lifting its weight against the hinges, and stepped into the unlit entry hall. He waited until the woman had hurried in past him, then shut the door and rotated the bolt knob. The rattle of the rain on gravel was shut out, and the only sound was panting breath and the dripping of water on the waxed wooden floor.

The woman was carrying her shoes now, and laid them carefully on the hall table.

"This way," he whispered, and stepped into the parlor.

The fire in the grate was just glowing coals, but he propped a couple of fresh logs in there and tucked some crumpled newspapers under them, and after he had fetched a decanter and two glasses, he and his unknown companion sat on the carpet in front of the reviving fire and took the first, restorative gulps of whisky. The warm liquor burned its way down his throat and began to loosen his tensed muscles.

The fire was flickering brightly now, and he pressed water from his hair and beard and then held his chilled palms out toward the heat. He exhaled, and for the first time looked squarely at his companion. She was younger than he had assumed, perhaps twenty. She had pushed her dark hair back from her forehead, and her face was pale and narrow.

The windows rattled, and the woman's head whipped around—the noise wasn't repeated, and after a few seconds, she slowly turned back toward the fire.

"Wind funnels down this street," Crawford said. That was true, and probably it had been the wind. But he sighed and glanced at the clock on the mantel and saw that it was well after one in the morning. "I have a guest room, here, with a bath," he said. "My housekeeper can show you where it is."

She nodded. "Thank you."

"What," he began at last, giving her time to stop him; but the wide dark eyes simply held his, so he went on: "was that?"

Her abrupt laugh was quiet but jarring. "The gentleman wants to know what it was," she said. "This *isn't* your first drink of the evening, is it? Let's see, it appeared when you and I were close enough that we could have touched each other, and you knew to get us into the river, and—and your parlor reeks of garlic! What do *you*, now that you can ponder it, *imagine* that it was?"

Crawford drained his glass and refilled it. "The garlic," he said weakly, "is a disinfectant. Prevents mortification. I'm a veterinary surgeon."

"A veterinary surgeon." She looked around at the tidy room by the flickering firelight: the framed prints, the old-fashioned vine-patterned

wallpaper, the street-side curtains. "Smells like you treat a lot of morti-
fied horses right in here."

What he smelled was river water, and it occurred to him that his
watch was probably ruined. "You can't expect me to explain medical—"

"A waste of time, I'm sure. Let's talk about what happened just now.
The thing on the bridge, the river—"

"Listen." He shifted around on the carpet to face her more squarely.
"Two years ago," he said. He noticed that he was still shaking, and he
took another swallow of the whisky. "Two years ago I was drunk. Not
like this—*really* drunk. And I thought I saw a—a ghost, and it attacked
me. I—hid from it—" He gave a hitching gasp and realized to his embarrassment that he was on the verge of sobbing again, as he had been on
the bridge before this woman had appeared. He shook his head and
stared blindly into the fire.

After a moment she asked quietly, "Why were you so drunk, before
you saw the ghost?"

"Why," he countered dully, "should it make a difference that we
were close together, on the bridge?"

"Close together and out in the open, under the nighttime sky. Oh—"
She shrugged. "I think it's like . . . two candle flames are more visible if
they're held together, overlapping. Those things ordinarily don't see us
very well, thank God."

"What . . . *are* they? The g-ghost, two years ago, I used garlic and the
river to hide from it."

"Didn't you have any garlic tonight?"

He shook his head and again touched his damp waistcoat pocket.
"Evidently not. My housekeeper is punctual about renewing the disinfectant garlic wash on the windowsills, but—these days I'm sometimes
careless about carrying it with me."

"Disinfectant garlic wash," she said, apparently savoring the jargon.
"Well, I should have been carrying some myself. But you never invited
one of those things in here, I hope?"

"No." He yawned, more from tension than fatigue. "I would have, this ghost, before it attacked me—but I was outdoors, by the river. And in any case I've moved since."

"Ah." She reached out and took his hand. Her hand was warm from the fire, but he still didn't look at her. "Why were you so drunk?"

He was increasingly uncomfortable, with this conversation and also with the fact that he was alone here at this hour with this woman. Really he should summon Mrs. Middleditch.

"Drunks have hallucinations," he said, more to himself than to her. "It *might* have been a hallucination, the ghost; this thing tonight doesn't prove . . ."

She was still holding his hand. He glanced at her, and she was staring at him, her eyebrows raised.

Crawford took a deep gulp of the whisky and sighed. "Oh hell. The reason I was drunk was because my wife, and my two sons, had died the night before. They said, witnesses said, that lightning struck the ferryboat they were on." He freed his hand to refill his glass, and he gave her a haggard caricature of a smile. "What of yourself? Do *you* have a family?"

"My husband died—uh, six months ago. We didn't have any children." She stretched her arms over her head and then sat forward, staring into the fire. "But you carried garlic with you, after. And you knew to get us both into the river tonight. How is it that you know these things?"

"I hate all this filthy stuff," he said absently; then he frowned into the fire. "My parents had a history with creatures like that thing on the bridge, and they managed to elude them. They told me how. They were old and eccentric, and I didn't entirely believe them."

She stared at him with no expression. "Who was the ghost? The one that you would have invited in, but it attacked you?"

"It was—it was probably a hallucination."

She didn't look away.

He pressed his palms flat into the carpet but still felt as if he were losing his balance at the top of a high precipice.

But it was easier to go on than to stop now. "The witnesses—one of them said that my eldest son, Girard, was helping some person or— helping some person, onto the ferry from a boat that had drawn up alongside, in the moments before . . . before the vessel was struck."

"The witness didn't know it was your eldest son," she said gently. "You knew it, later. When Girard's ghost appeared to you. And attacked you."

The ferry deck had been shattered but not scorched, he recalled, and the only reason the other passengers guessed that it had been lightning was because of the deafening, echoing roar that had shaken the boat in the moment of impact.

Why did I go walking on the bridge tonight? he asked himself. I don't usually go out onto any of the bridges in my midnight walks. Why did I neglect to bring any garlic? Was I drunkenly hoping that Girard would come again, and finish me off?

Was that Girard?

"Attacked me, yes," he said, almost matter-of-factly. "And I broke the garlic jar and ran into the river. I *hid* from him."

"Lucky thing for you that you did."

"Girard was my son, and he came back to me—and I hid from him."

"I'm sorry," she said. "But it wasn't really *him,* you know, anymore. Not *mostly.*"

"I'd like to believe you're right." He thought of asking about her husband, then realized that he didn't need to.

"'The many men so beautiful,'" she said quietly, "'and they all dead did lie, / and a thousand thousand slimy things / lived on, and so did I.'"

He recognized it as a line from Coleridge's *Rime of the Ancient Mariner.*

The woman beside him shivered. "Thank you for rescuing me," she whispered. "And taking me in like a hurt cat."

"All the cats I take in," he said, "are hurt cats."

"I—I don't even know your name."

"John Crawford."

"I'm Lisa Griffin." She got lithely to her feet, but when he had stood up beside her, she swayed against him and he caught her elbow to keep her from falling. "I'm afraid the whisky has rather got on top of me," she said with an awkward laugh. "Could you . . . escort me to this spare room?"

Mrs. Middleditch should escort her, he thought.

But he glanced at the curtained window and thought of the turbulent sky and all the lightless alleys out there in the cold rain, and he didn't want to let go of this woman's elbow.

"This way," he said unsteadily, starting toward the stairs. He forced the thought of Veronica out of his mind.

NOW, SEVEN YEARS LATER, Crawford again picked up his teacup, and his hand didn't shake.

"I—" he began hoarsely; then he cleared his throat and said, carefully, "I tried to find you, afterward." He realized that he was stroking his beard as if miming deep thought and stopped.

The bird in the little cage on the table whistled several notes.

The woman nodded. "I believe you. But as I said, I gave you a false name that night. Griffin, wasn't it? That was the street I was—living on. And I never had a husband." She gulped some of the tea in her own cup, then abruptly set it down and whispered, "Of all the times I could ever have used a glass of whisky."

It was only an hour or two after dawn, but Crawford said, "Would you like some? I might join you."

"I gave it up." She exhaled and stared squarely at him. "I was a prostitute, in those days. 'Living upon the farm of my person,' as the law has it. I'm not any longer."

The little bird was darting glances from one of them to the other.

"Oh," said Crawford blankly. "Good. That you—stopped."

Over the years he had wondered about that, a woman walking alone on Waterloo Bridge after midnight, but it was still a shock to hear it confirmed.

"I enrolled myself in the Magdalen Penitentiary for Fallen Women, on Highgate Hill, and I spent two years there. Thanks to the sisters there, I was able to change my ways."

"Oh."

"And—before that"—she took a deep breath—"we had a daughter, you and I."

CRAWFORD HELD UP HIS hand to stop her, then stood up and crossed to the mantel and poured several inches of whisky into a glass, from, he realized, the same decanter he had poured from seven years earlier. He drained half of it and then clicked the glass down on the mantel, and for several seconds he kept his hand on the glass and squinted at it. Finally he let go of it and turned toward her.

"How can you be—if you were—"

"I used what they call prophylactic measures when I was on the job," she said flatly. "That night seven years ago was . . . spontaneous."

Crawford wished he had not drunk the scotch, for he was dizzy and nauseated now, and his heart was pounding.

She glanced toward the inner door, behind which he could hear Mrs. Middleditch ascending the steps from the below-stairs kitchen.

"Let's go for a walk," McKee said, picking up her gloves from the table.

But Crawford sat down again. "The last time you and I were together, we got into trouble."

She opened her mouth as if to say something, then apparently thought better of it.

"I mean *outdoors,*" he added, feeling his face heat up. "Overlapping candle flames, you said. We were more visible, to"—he waved vaguely—"things."

"That was at night. They don't generally travel abroad during the day."

He shrugged and nodded. He recalled his parents telling him that. And Mrs. Middleditch was now audibly bustling around in the little dining room behind him.

He got to his feet again, reluctantly. "Very well. Let me get a hat and coat. And—" He stepped to the mantel and found the little bottle of ground garlic and slipped it into his waistcoat pocket.

She smiled. "In case we're out past sunset?"

He ignored that and waved distractedly at the little cage on the table. "I can put the bird somewhere the cats can't get to."

"He can come along with us."

CHAPTER TWO

✶∻◈∻✶

She sleepeth: would ye wake her if you could?
Is her face sad that ye should pity her?
Did Death come to her like a messenger
From a far land where is not any good?

—*Christina Rossetti,*
"O Death, Where Is Thy Sting?"

MCKEE LOOKED LEFT and right at the brick and wood houses along the narrow street as Crawford pulled the door closed behind them, and then she peered up at the variety of snow-capped roofs and gables and projecting upper floors.

Her fur-trimmed bonnet hid her face. "This is an old street," she said, her breath wisping away on the breeze like tobacco smoke.

"These are mostly Tudor houses," he said gruffly. The air was so cold that it hurt his teeth to talk. "The Great Fire missed this area. I moved here nine years ago. Which way?"

The bird in her ermine muff chirped several notes, and she said, "East, I think—through the Temple Gate. Where did you live before?"

"Clerkenwell. But I wanted to be closer to the river, after—"

"After Girard," she said, nodding.

He was startled, and even almost pleased, that she remembered the name after all these years. "And the next street toward the river is Holywell, and the story is that there was a holy well there once. It's said to be under an inn now—still, a nice thing to have nearby."

"Yes, it is," she said. "I don't know how *holy* it is anymore."

Crawford blew away a cloud of his own. They were walking past the dark windows of the Angel pub, and the tall spire of St. Clement Danes stood on its island in the lanes of the Strand ahead.

McKee nodded. "Oranges and lemons, say the bells of St. Clement's."

Crawford frowned impatiently. "'Had a daughter,' you said. Not 'have.'"

McKee wasn't wearing the metal pattens now; her boot soles just scuffed on the old cobblestones under the swirls of snow.

"Her name," she said, "was Johanna. She died. The woman who . . . housed and fed us, an old witch called Carpace who maintained a number of girls in a bawdy house in Southwark, she took Johanna away from me and then let her die, of neglect. Cold and starvation."

They had emerged from the shadowy defile that was Wych Street into the crowded open square around St. Clement Danes, and the sky was a bright blue behind the smoke-stained spires and cupolas and chimney clusters of London's skyline. Below that close horizon, pedestrians strode along in hats and overcoats, mostly clerks who lived out in suburbs like Hanwell or Dulwich and every morning walked to their jobs in shops and factories and inns of court, their boots now adding a tympanic rattle to London's perpetual background rumble.

And already the broad lanes of the Strand were crowded with wheeled traffic. Crawford found himself squinting at the horses that pulled the tall omnibuses and cabs and barrel-laden carts, and he was cautiously pleased to see glossy coats, clear eyes, and firm steps.

HIDE ME AMONG THE GRAVES

I may well have treated some of these, he thought, for dysentery or mange or bronchitis. I can't save people—especially the ones I've loved—but I can help animals. It's God's job, His neglected job, to save people.

But McKee's words echoed in his head: *cold and starvation.*

If this woman hoped to wring money from him with her sordid tale, surely she would have claimed that the daughter was still alive.

"Was she," he asked, "baptized?"

McKee was looking away, toward the columned gray front of the Provident Institution on the far side of the street, but he heard her say, "I try not to lie to people anymore."

Ah, thought Crawford bleakly.

Then God had not claimed the child as His own—any more than He claimed all the blameless suffering animals.

"When?" he asked.

McKee looked back at him, her face pale in the ring of white fur. "In March of '58. She was just two years old."

Nearly four years ago. Crawford shook his head.

Children were dodging between the carts and carriages in the street, some of the ragged little figures seeming scarcely older than this alleged daughter would be if she had lived; they might have been playing some game this morning—they were singing some nursery rhyme that mingled in the chilly air with the clatter of hooves and the textured whir of metal wheel rims on frozen gravel.

Crawford looked back at McKee and spread his gloved hands. "I don't see what I can do. What anyone can do."

"You can get an invitation to a salon," said McKee, "is what you can do, and bring me as your guest."

Crawford lowered his arms. "A . . . salon."

"Poets," she said absently, watching the street children. Their narrow faces and bare arms and legs were darkened as if with soot, Crawford noticed, and though they were scampering back and forth in the street, none of the faces he glimpsed held any expression. "Artists," McKee added.

"No, that's quite—I'm sorry, but that sort of thing isn't—"

Under the fur that covered her hands, the tiny bird squeaked four quick notes.

"Well, let's consider," McKee remarked quietly, perhaps talking to herself. "It's not a day for boating."

"No, it certainly is not," exclaimed Crawford in alarm. "Around the church, and back, is enough of a—a stroll this morning. Really, Miss McKee—"

"Call me Addie," she said, leaning forward on the pavement to look intently at the passing vehicles. "I think we can consider ourselves amply introduced."

Crawford winced.

She bit one of her gloves and pulled it off, then stuck two bare fingers into her mouth and whistled four piercing notes very like the bird's. Several men hurrying past looked back at her in surprise.

Crawford grimaced in embarrassment. "I really need to get back to my practice—"

"We're bound that way," she assured him, "just a bit roundabout. I think I may have attracted attention, forgive me."

"Well—whistling—!"

The high-perched driver of a shiny two-wheeled hansom cab reined his horse in toward them, but McKee shook her head and waved him past, then after a moment whistled again in the same way.

This time it was a shabby old hackney coach that wobbled toward them, its two horses contradicting Crawford's estimate a moment earlier of the evident health of London horses; the nostrils of the curbside mare were widely dilated and her flanks were twitching, and she was exhaling twice for every inhalation.

McKee stepped off the curb to nod and wave, and then she turned back toward Crawford.

He stared at the vehicle—the yellow paint on its bodywork was faded and chipped, and the door still carried the crest of whatever aristocratic family had long ago sold it.

"I am *not*—" he began.

But McKee had grabbed the arm of a man on the pavement, a nervous-looking young fellow with sparse muttonchop whiskers.

"Where are you walking to?" she asked him quickly.

"W-well," the fellow stammered, "the—the Royal Exchange, ma'am, on Threadneedle Street—"

"We're going that way, save some shoe leather and join us as a chaperone, no charge." And as the young man was nodding eagerly and taking off his hat, she tossed a half-crown coin up to the driver and called, "Threadneedle Street."

The hackney cab's door was open and the young clerk was already climbing inside. Crawford stepped back, but McKee caught his gloved hand with her bare one.

He started to yank his hand away, then paused when he saw the intensity in her eyes.

"I don't lie to people anymore," she whispered rapidly to him. "We're in danger if we stay here—those Mud Larks are beginning to bracket us. In their dim way, I think they've sensed what we are, and there's a man they report to. *Get in,* for the love of God."

Crawford opened his mouth, then closed it and obediently stepped up into the coach. The young clerk had thoughtlessly settled himself on the forward-facing seat, where good manners dictated that the lady should sit, and Crawford hesitated, momentarily unsure of where he should seat himself.

McKee poked him in the back.

Even as he made up his mind and sat down beside the clerk on the cracked leather upholstery, Crawford was regretting this whole enterprise. It occurred to him that this woman might well be insane.

Then McKee had got in and pulled the door closed and shaken it until it latched, sitting down across from him as the coach lurched forward. She didn't seem to mind the seating arrangement. The upholstery and the cloth paneling exhaled smells of old tobacco and stale cooking oil.

"Mud Larks?" asked Crawford in a neutral tone.

"Those children." McKee was leaning back in the seat and peering slantwise through the window. "The tide's low right now, they *should* all be out in the mud, harvesting." She shook her head. "A boat would have been better than this cab, but I had no warning—we'd have had to get past them to reach the water, and God knows where we would have found a boat for hire."

"Thieving little gypsies," put in the young man beside Crawford.

"But I don't think they can have picked us out," McKee went on, "especially now, in a coach with so much old emotional cross-stitching in it, and a random stranger's janglings." She pulled the little birdcage free with her ungloved hand and peered at the bright-eyed bird, who just blinked around the interior of the coach. "Evidently not."

"And is that a . . . Mud Lark?" ventured the young man.

McKee stared across at him. "This is a linnet. Who are you?"

"My name's Tilling, ma'am, Arnold—"

"Excellent. I'm Lady Wishfort and this is Mr. Petulant." Crawford recognized the names as characters from Congreve's play *The Way of the World,* but he was embarrassed that she had chosen the names of villains.

"Actually," he said hastily, "my name is"—he couldn't remember the first name of the play's hero—"is Mr. Mirabell." He added, "And this is Lady Millamant," giving McKee the name of the heroine.

But this wasn't a time for nonsense. He cleared his throat and looked across at McKee. "You said they might . . . sense what we are? Er . . . what are we?"

The windows were in shadow for a few seconds, and the knocking and rattling of the coach was louder, and Crawford realized that they were passing under the Temple Bar arch.

McKee seemed to relax. "Were you too drunk to remember that thing you saved us from, on Waterloo Bridge seven years ago? It was . . . angry seems too pale a word, too *human* . . . about our relations with members of its family. Well, jealous, in your case. Girard presumably loved you."

Crawford winced. In spite of himself, he was remembering things his parents had told him. "My mother and father," he said hesitantly, "were kin by marriage, or said they were, to . . ." He laughed uneasily. "Well, they said it was to a species of *vampire,* actually. I don't think—"

"That would have been before about 1820?"

He nodded, feeling nauseated again with the smell and motion of the carriage. He was peripherally aware of Arnold Tilling's stare.

"That's likely why the creature found your family," said McKee. "The vampires were gone for about thirty years, and then about fifteen years ago somebody must have invited one back and blooded it." She gave him an appraising look. "You probably resemble your parents in some way these things sense and remember, like the smell of your soul or something."

What she was saying fit in with things he recalled his parents saying, and in spite of her outlandish statements, Crawford heard the quiet assurance of sincerity in her voice, and he gave a sigh that seemed to deflate him. He was looking away from her at the bird as he asked her, "And they hate us?"

Arnold Tilling apparently took him to be addressing the bird, for he raised his eyebrows and stared with some evident anxiety at the little cage.

McKee said, "They hate us because the ones they adopt loved us—if only in a brief, token way sometimes! They see the ones they adopt as having been part of *our* families, and these things don't want them to be part of any family but their own. So they kill as many members of the plain human family as they can reach. You and I added to their burdens, with Johanna." She laughed bleakly. "It would powerfully inconvenience them, Mr. Mirabell, if you and I were to marry and have lots more children."

Crawford could feel his face stiffen, and he kept his eyes on the caged bird.

"Not," added McKee after a pause, "of course, that you'd ever consider marrying a onetime prostitute." Crawford heard her shift on the seat, and then she went on brightly, "Have your wife and the *other* son come back, ever, since their deaths? Have you seen them again? It would be at night."

"No," whispered Crawford.

"Well, they *did* die on the river, after all, so their ghosts are probably safe in the common crowd that infests the water. Mr. Tilling, you remember how bad the river smelled four years ago? The Great Stink?"

Crawford, still staring at the bird, felt the young man beside him nod jerkily.

"A saturation of ghosts, that was. More the *result* of cholera than the cause of it! They seem to decay in an organic way, you see, and if the concentration of them is high enough—"

Arnold Tilling lunged half out of his seat and yanked on the cord that rang the bell beside the driver. "I've only just," he babbled, "only just remembered!" He was already gripping the inner door handle as the coach rocked and slowed. "I need to—business at . . ."—he crouched to peer out the grimy window—"at the Old Bailey this morning. It's been lovely spending time with—"

Then he had got the door open and was already leaning out over the pavement. Cold river-scented air whisked through the coach.

A front wheel grated against the curb, and Tilling evidently decided that the vehicle had slowed enough for jumping.

When he was gone—perhaps falling, from the clattering sound of it—McKee gripped the door lintel and leaned out, squinting up toward the driver. "Carry on!" she called, and the coach wobbled and lurched forward again.

"Did he," Crawford asked when she had pulled the door closed and sat down again, "break his leg?"

"Why, do you treat humans too?"

"Never. *God* looks after them, or claims to."

"Ultimately, I suppose. Are you and God—at odds?"

"Yes."

They stared at each other for several seconds, and then Crawford said, "Have *you* seen your daughter—"

"Our daughter."

"Our daughter, since her death?"

McKee opened her mouth—then closed it and shook her head, scowling. "I'm sorry," she said. "I shouldn't have got—it was unreasonable of me to get angry. I'm glad your wife and younger son are apparently resting in peace. No, I haven't seen Johanna, since. Most people just die, and stay dead."

Crawford nodded several times and looked out the window at the Romanesque spire of St. Bride's. He had to remind himself that all this distressing business really might be true. He had seen what he'd seen, done what he'd done.

"Why have *you* caught their attentions?" he asked. "I suppose I can see now why the—the thing on the bridge recognized *me,* but why did it recognize you?"

"Oh, why do you suppose?" He was surprised to see a glint of tears in her eyes a moment before she angrily cuffed them away.

"Girls in that trade," she went on, "may sometimes unknowingly have congress with adopted human members of that terrible family. Even a . . . brief connection of that sort looks like trespass to those creatures, suffices to rouse their jealousy." Crawford glanced at her, but she was avoiding his eyes. "A month or so before you and I . . . met," she said, "there was a young man, at an accommodation house in Mayfair. Afterward, he seemed ill at ease, more than the ordinary, and he urged me to enroll at the Magdalen Penitentiary in Highgate;

he said the priests and sisters there could help me *undo bad connections* I'd made. I thought he was just another guilty Christian trying to salve his conscience after the fact, after the act . . . until I walked outside again."

She shivered. "Right away, as soon as I was out under the night sky again, there was . . . webs in the air, and a smell like rainy streets, or broken stone, very strong. Old Carpace had made sure all the girls knew what to do when that happened, and she always made us wear some metal on our shoe soles at night—sometimes pattens, otherwise anything wired on—holed coins, spoons, eyeglasses."

"Really. And what were you—" Crawford began, but the caged bird began chirping rapidly, and McKee pulled a tiny cloth bag from a pocket in her coat, dug a pinch of what appeared to be white sand from it and sprinkled it through the cage bars onto the bird's tail.

"Salt?" said Crawford. "But you've already caught it."

"Don't want anyone else to," she said. "He senses a ghost—it happens from time to time—and the salt keeps the bird's spirit too heavy to catch it." She managed to smile at him, though squinting. "This ave is for me."

Crawford blinked. "I'm sure. So what were you supposed to do?— when the webs and smells happened?"

"Oh—run, get away from the spot they're focusing on, cross the river if possible and hope the metal on your shoes makes a kaleidoscope of your identity and location. Dive into the river if you have to." She sighed. "I got away, but it—they, it—knows my spirit silhouette now. It was another three years before I finally took that fellow's advice and checked in at Magdalen."

"And you still have to . . . take precautions?" He waved at the bird, which was huffing and squeaking.

"They're still *aware* of me. That's why I need the help of someone"— she made a tossing motion toward him—"who has a stake in this."

"Agh." Crawford thought of the half glass of whisky he had left on the mantel in his parlor. It didn't seem so repulsive now; he had been mad not to finish it. "Help to do what?"

"Everybody said Carpace died of consumption two years ago, while I was in Magdalen, but just yesterday I learned that she's alive, monstrously fat now and under a different name, and she's coming out socially *tonight,* hosting a salon for artists and writers in Bedford Square. I need, you and I need, to get in there. One of the women who's going to be there is a musician, and—she has a dog that you've treated! For an infected eye!"

McKee thrust a folded piece of paper at him. "I have the musician's name here—if you tell her you write poems, she can surely get you an invitation. We need to confront Carpace, find out from her where our daughter is buried."

Crawford groaned and reached past her to pull the bell rope. "Listen," he said. "Miss McKee. We don't. Wha—write *poems?* That was tragic, criminal, what happened to the child, and it may be that you can interest the law courts, but what good is there in finding a *grave?* *Poems?* You can't possibly—" The carriage was slowing again, and he half knelt on the crackling seat to fish some coins from his pocket. "I'll walk back."

McKee grabbed his arm. "What if there *is* no grave? Or only an empty one? Listen to me! They say now that old Carpace didn't just tell us how to protect ourselves from the—the things, but every year offered *tribute* to them—put out a child for them to take, as they took your son. I'm sure Carpace had a lot of children to choose the tribute from, in any year, but—I need to *know* that Johanna is safely dead. *You* need to know it."

Crawford had hold of the door handle. "You said she was." He was sweating in spite of the chilly air.

"She probably is. Is that enough?"

Humans aren't my concern, thought Crawford desperately. They're God's lookout.

But this child had not been baptized—God wouldn't have claimed her. *Cold and starvation.*

"She's our daughter," said McKee. "It's what we can do for her."

"*What* is what we can do?"

"If she's truly and ordinarily dead, nothing. But if she's not, if she's come back from the dead, like Girard . . . we can put her to rest."

Crawford was thinking of his son. "By what means?"

Tears were running down McKee's cheeks, but her eyes were steady. "What do you think? What did your parents tell you? Silver bullets, a wooden stake through her heart—we can free her, let her ghost sink down into the Thames to oblivion with all the rest of London's peaceful dead."

The cab had squeaked and shuddered to a halt, not to let its passengers out but because the traffic through Ludgate Circus was for the moment a solid forest of stamping horses and vehicles with halted, dripping wheel rims.

Crawford pushed the door open and stepped out onto the iron footrest above the mud. The cold morning air was cacophonous with the yells of frustrated cab men and the monotonous cries of street vendors, and the dome of St. Paul's Cathedral stood in black silhouette directly east of him, blocking the sun, framed by the receding rooftops and spires of lesser buildings.

Crawford took a deep breath of the cold sausage-and-horse-dung breeze. It was real with Girard, Crawford thought—why shouldn't it be real with this child? *Can* you walk away from this?

He imagined hopping down from the carriage, threading his way through the stopped vehicles to the curb and walking back to Wych Street, leaving this woman to pursue her phantom alone.

This woman, he thought—the mother of my child; her phantom—our daughter.

He would need the half glass of whisky when he got home. Another glass too, probably. *Another and another cup to drown / The memory of this impertinence,* as Omar Khayyam had written.

Hardly impertinence, though.

He was still holding the slip of paper McKee had handed to him, and he glanced at it. It was an address in Wardour Street, back the way they had come; and he recognized the woman's name and remembered her dog.

The driver was squinting down at him, and Crawford sighed and handed the paper and another half crown up to the man.

"This address," he called, speaking loudly to be heard over all the impatient shouting in the street. Concerned about the right-side mare, he pointed at her and added, "Broken-winded! Give her soft food and raw pork fat!" He waited until the driver nodded, then he folded himself back into the cab and pulled the door closed.

"What time tonight?" he asked McKee.

"Eight." She was peering out the window at the irregularly shifting tide of horses and vehicles. "Good thing we got an early start."

"I'm not going to write any poetry."

Still looking out at the crowded street, she shook her head impatiently. "Once we're in there it won't matter. And in any case you could copy out some lines from the middle of a Southey epic, nobody alive has read those."

CHAPTER THREE

Six days I rest, and do all that I have to do on the seventh,
because it is forbidden.

—*Edward John Trelawny, in a letter to Mary Shelley, 1835*

SIX MILES NORTHWEST of the Fleet Street traffic and the long blue
shadow of the St. Paul's dome, up among the woods and country
roads north of Hampstead Heath, the cold eastern wind swept through
the bare yew branches and over the snow-drifted lawns of Highgate
Cemetery and down the white lanes on the west slope of Highgate Hill.
It blew pennants of snow from the roof of the three-story Magdalen Penitentiary for Fallen Women at the south end of Grove Lane and whistled in
through the one-inch opening of a window on the ground floor.

The breeze lifted a sheet of paper from the desk by the window and
spun it away, and when it hit the wooden floor with a sharp tap, the
woman at the desk looked up.

Momentarily disoriented, she blinked around at the narrow room—
the bed, the bookcase, the cold gas jet, the print of Jesus hung on the
plaster wall. She dropped the pen she'd been holding and moved some

papers aside in order to touch the Bible on the desk, and then her hand
fell to the crucifix hanging from the narrow rope at her waist.

She knew she was supposed to be correcting proofs here, but her
mind must have wandered. Had she been writing? The brass pen nib
gleamed with fresh ink.

She sighed shakily and pushed the chair back and stood up, more
comfortable in this black dress and white muslin cap than in the
necessarily-more-frivolous dresses she wore when she wasn't on residence duty, and before picking up the sheet of paper on the floor she
stepped to the door and looked through the little window into the
empty dormitory. Sunlight slanted in through the tall eastern windows
and lit the neatly made beds between the low partitions. The girls had all
attended the Sunday service in the chapel at dawn and were now having
breakfast in the refectory, soon to start their daily tasks in the laundry
and kitchen. Thirty-seven girls were in residence at the moment, the
youngest sixteen and the oldest twenty-four.

Three of them would soon have completed their two-year stay, during which time they would have learned household skills that would
qualify them for domestic positions in the colonies or in distant parts
of England.

On the desk behind Sister Christina lay the neglected galley proofs
of a collection of her poetry, soon to be published by Macmillan—but
it was her reluctant duty to confiscate from the new girls the books of
poetry that they frequently arrived with. The books were often gifts
from former clients, and therefore considered dangerous reminders,
and in any case the romantic fancies of modern verse seemed likely to
be lures back into sin. But the girls nevertheless often quoted poets like
Byron and Coleridge and Browning, and, when they were invited to
choose new names for themselves, regularly chose names like Haidee
or Juliet or Christabel. A few, like Adelaide McKee two years ago, resolutely kept their old names and stayed in London, and Sister Christina
worried and prayed for them—especially Adelaide.

The literacy of many of these ex-prostitutes had surprised Christina when she began volunteering here four years ago. She had assumed that London's population of streetwalkers was exclusively drawn from the lowest levels of poverty and ignorance, but she had discovered that this was by no means always the case; the girls weren't encouraged to talk about their pasts, but their accents and table manners often hinted at respectable middle-class origins, as did the clue—gathered from their admittance forms—that many of them had more than one baptismal name.

Christina turned and looked warily at the sheet of paper lying on the worn floor. She could see from here that it was covered with lines in her own handwriting, but she had no memory of writing it. She shivered.

She was still unmarried at the age of thirty-one, living with her mother and two of her three siblings in a house in Albany Street just two streets from Regent's Park, and some of her friends thought this work was perilous to her own innocence and virtue; her brother Gabriel had written a poem in which a prostitute was described as: *a rose shut in a book / In which pure women may not look / For its base pages claim control / To crush the flower within the soul . . .*

If she was feeling facetious, she would sometimes reply to their misgivings with a quote from Emma Shepherd's *An Outstretched Hand to the Fallen*—"the purer, the more ignorant of vice the lady is who seeks them, the greater the influence she has"—but to herself she could admit that there probably wasn't an inmate in the house as much in need of redemption as herself.

She had found a refuge in her volunteer residency work here, at least for one fortnight every two or three months, and Reverend Oliver, the warden, had shown her some tricks for "keeping the devils out," as he put it—the iron-barred decorative openings in the garden wall, the mirrors in the entry hall, the garlic in all the window boxes.

Her sister, Maria, was doing work for the All Saints Sisters of the Poor, and possibly finding similar protections there. Christina hoped so—Maria would never discuss such things, and in fact had never referred to that evening seventeen years ago in a twilit field, when the two of them had given Greek funeral honors to their father's temporarily buried little black statue.

Christina had lately written a long poem about a girl who surrenders to supernatural temptation, to her ruin, and her sister who rescues her by exposing herself to the same perils. The poem was called "Goblin Market," and the book whose proof pages were on the desk was titled *Goblin Market and Other Poems.*

Christina had restored the little statue—rendered inert, she had believed then—to its usual perch on her father's shelf when she had returned from her visit to Maria in the country, and her father had never mentioned the thing again. He had died nine years later, and his last words before he hiccuped into his handkerchief and choked and expired had been *Ah Dio, ajuatami Tu!* Which meant, roughly, *God help me!* Their mother, though grieving, had gathered up all the copies in the house of his book, *Amor Platonica,* and burned them, along with the unpublished notes he'd made on the Kabalistic idea of the transmigration of souls. Nobody, not even Christina's skeptical brother William, had asked why.

Christina had dreamed of her father since his death: always in the dream he was sitting across a table from her in a small room lit by candles, talking earnestly; but she couldn't make out the words in his droning monologue. After a few minutes, she would lean forward and watch his lips intently and concentrate, and he would become visibly alarmed—apparently at the prospect of her comprehending his speech, which she realized he was unable to halt—and he would lean across the table and stick his fingers into her ears, so that she could no longer hear his voice, though she could see his lips still moving helplessly.

Always she lived with a conviction that at the age of fourteen she had brought a curse on her family by quickening that little statue with her blood.

Neither Christina nor Maria had married; their brother Gabriel was more stubborn and had married two years ago, at the age of thirty-two—his wife had borne him a dead daughter shortly afterward and was now, God help her, very ill herself. William had been engaged, in spite of Christina's oblique warnings—and Gabriel's too, she suspected—but he had canceled the engagement in bewilderment when the young lady insisted that it should be an entirely celibate marriage.

Amor Platonica indeed, thought Christina now as at last she crouched to pick up the sheet of paper. The young lady had not perhaps been as unreasonable as William had thought.

The paper was a page from a story she recognized. She had written it out last year and had submitted it to Thackeray's *Cornhill* magazine, but after it was rejected, and she reread it, she had found herself sickened by William's comment that it was the best story she'd ever written—because, though it had been her hand that had held the pen, she was now convinced that she was not the one who had conceived and composed it.

She had burned it—but since late December she had found her hand writing it out again, in moments when her mind strayed from whatever she'd meant to write.

Its title was "Folio Q," and she suspected the Q was meant to indicate the German word *quelle,* source. It was about a man who didn't dare look into mirrors, and instead imposed his own face onto the people he loved.

She suspected that the actual author was her uncle, John Polidori, who had killed himself in 1821, forty-one years ago. It was clear that he had not, after all, been laid to rest when she and Maria had temporarily buried the little statue.

She glanced at the handwritten page—then stepped to the window for better light, her heart beating more rapidly, for this newest page was a scene that had not been in the story as she had originally written it.

When she finished reading the page, she stepped to the desk and slapped around among the long galley proof sheets, for the handwritten page ended in midsentence—there was, though, no subsequent page.

But she needed to find out how the scene ended. Gabriel needed to know.

I could sit down and hold a pen over a blank sheet, she thought, and open my mind to *him,* deliberately this time, instead of inadvertently. He could write another page, or several.

All at once her heart was pounding and her mouth was dry. Yes, she thought excitedly, I'll give him my hand, let him in just to that extent, just for a little while . . .

Then she clutched the crucifix on the rope around her waist, and for a moment she wished she were Catholic instead of Anglican, and that the rope was a rosary, so that she could pray to the Virgin for help—for she had sensed that her sinful eagerness was reciprocated from some direction, requited. She couldn't say an Our Father right now—ever since the age of fourteen she had instinctively feared the all-seeing God of the Old Testament—and even Christ would not shelter a soul who couldn't bear to entirely relinquish its one most precious sin . . . but the Virgin Mary might understand . . .

She shook off the thought—heretical Papist superstition!—and tore the handwritten page into strips and then into tiny fragments and tossed them into the cold fireplace.

She gathered the galley proofs into a stack, the corrected pages facedown on top of the uncorrected ones, then folded the stack and tucked it into the valise beside the desk. She would have to get another of the sisters to assume her duties today and find someone to take the last few days of her scheduled residence—but she needed to see Gabriel immediately.

She glanced at the closet where her street clothes were hung, then impatiently shook her head. There wasn't time. She hefted the valise, opened the door, and her heels echoed in the empty dormitory as she hurried past the rows of empty beds on her way out to the carriage lane by the stables.

IN THE WEST END, northwest of Waterloo Bridge and the open market at Covent Garden, seven narrow streets met from all directions in a confusion of carriages and wagons and omnibuses below the wedge-shaped buildings that framed an irregular open space. Earl Street stretched east and west, and its balconies and awnings and the hats of the pedestrians on the pavement were lit with the morning sun, while only the chimney pots and roofs of the other streets stood free of the chilly shadows that made the old women around the bakery shops below pull their shawls more tightly around their shoulders. A smoky beam of sunlight crossed the crowded square, occasionally reaching through gaps in the traffic to touch the stone circle where there had once stood a pillar with six sundials on it. The junction had long been known as Seven Dials, for the streets and buildings themselves were said to make a seventh sundial for those who could read it.

Through the crowds of cartwheeling children and adolescent thieves in corduroy trousers and black caps, a peculiar couple shuffled to a corner on the west side. Though the man's hair and beard were gray as ashes, his shoulders were broad under his flannel coat, and his step was springy—but when his dwarfish companion hesitated at a wide curbside puddle, he crouched and braced himself and lifted it with both hands, then shuffled carefully through the puddle to put the burden down on the pavement with a *whoosh* of exhaled steam.

The little person was draped in a voluminous Chesterfield overcoat and a baggy slouch hat, with a scarf wrapped around its neck and face, and though now it hopped out of the way of a couple of sprinting boys, its eyes weren't visible. Long shirtsleeves covered its hands, but in its right hand, half hidden behind the curtain of a lapel, it gripped a violin with a bow clipped to the neck.

Now with its sleeve-shrouded left hand the little figure plucked the bow free, and raised the violin and tucked the chin rest into its scarf and skated the bow over the strings—the hidden fingers of its right hand slid up and down the neck, and the instrument produced a hoarse seesawing note.

The gray-haired man nodded impatiently. "What does it look like?" he snapped. His lip was curled into a perpetual sneer by a scar that ran down his jaw.

He was squinting around at the people hurrying past or slouched against the buildings, and at last he saw the person he was looking for—an old man in a floppy hat and a formal but tattered black coat on the far side of Monmouth Street, his gloved hands holding a broom as if it were a drum major's baton.

"This way," said the gray-haired man, starting forward.

The violin emitted a downward-sliding note, but the little person holding it scuttled along after him.

At the corner the old man with the broom had stepped out onto the crushed gravel of the street, waving his broom to halt the horses of an approaching beer wagon, and then he proceeded to sweep the slushy top layer of gravel aside so that three businessmen in bowler hats could cross the street without getting their shoes too muddy. On the far side they paused to give him money, and then, visibly surprised, paused for a little longer while the old man reached into a pocket and gave them change.

He dodged and splashed his way back to the corner where the mismatched couple waited, and he didn't look at the short figure but grinned at the gray-bearded man.

"Stepping out, Mr. Trelawny?" he said.

Trelawny nodded and handed him a gold sovereign. "I want it all back," he said.

The crossing sweeper nodded judiciously as if this was an uncommon but not unheard-of transaction, and from his pocket produced two ten-shilling pieces. "There you go, a pound for a pound. I'll just switch brooms."

He hobbled to a nearby druggist's shop with red and purple glass jars in the window; a boy crouched in the recessed entryway beside another broom, and the old man took it and left the one he'd been using.

"A new broom sweeps clean," said Trelawny dutifully when the old fellow had returned.

"But the old broom knows all the coroners," returned the old crossing sweeper with a cackle.

Trelawny's scarred lip kinked in a tired smile at the exchange.

Trelawny glanced left and right at the coaches rattling past on the street, then suddenly darted out in the wake of a fast-moving hansom cab. The old crossing sweeper followed him nimbly, sweeping Trelawny's boot prints out of the wet road surface.

On the pavement behind them, the dwarf in the slouch hat and overcoat swiveled its covered head in all directions and sawed shrill notes on the violin.

On the far side of the street, Trelawny looked back and couldn't even see his diminutive onetime companion.

"Well done," he said to the old man. "You . . . don't get into trouble over this?"

The crossing sweeper laughed. "I may be a prodigal son, but I'm still a son. And how should I refuse crossing to," he added, pointing at his own throat and then at Trelawny's, "the bridge himself?"

Trelawny pursed his lips irritably at the reminder, but he nodded and hurried away up Queen Street, the narrowest of the streets that met at the Seven Dials.

He remembered this area of the City as it had been in the late 1830s, before the track for New Oxford Street had been leveled through the tangled courts and densely packed houses of the St. Giles rookery. He smiled and softly hummed an old song as he hurried along the crowded pavement, thinking of streets and houses that were just memories now—Carrier Street, with Mother Dowling's undiscriminating lodging house . . . Buckeridge Street, where lords and vagabonds mingled in Joe Banks's Hare and Hounds public house . . . Jones Court off Bainbridge Street, where Trelawny had once drunkenly surprised a roomful of his enemies by riding a donkey into their midst . . .

Trelawny's eyes were relaxed in a wide-focus stare, and his hands swung loosely at his sides, the fingers slightly spread. He stepped into an alley on his right, and though there was scarcely six feet of pavement between the windows and doors of the buildings on either side, dozens of figures moved in the shadows. Many were young children huddled around adults who might be their parents and who appeared to be offering broken trinkets for sale on tables set up against the black brick walls, but most of the inhabitants of the alley seemed to be idlers, men who were of working age but who had no evident occupation.

As Trelawny strode toward a door at the far end of the alley, two of these men stepped into his way.

"Ho, Mahomet," drawled the shorter one, "first visit was free." His gray felt top hat might have been salvaged from the river, and his blackened toes stuck out from the ragged edge of his pavement-length coat. "Second visit costs money."

His companion, skeletally thin in the remains of a frock coat, exposed toothless gums in a grin. "Fork over your purse, Ahmed."

The man opened his coat with one hand to show a long knife in the other.

On his previous visit to this place, Trelawny had asked directions in Turkish from one of the immigrant residents; and though he had been born in Cornwall, his face and hands were indelibly tanned by years of Mediterranean sun, and the local residents had evidently concluded that he was some species of Arab.

Trelawny took an apparently inadvertent half step forward, his open hands raised in front of his shoulders as if to assure the men of his passivity—he was nearly seventy years old, and he let his lined face sag in an expression of senile dismay—

—And then his right arm straightened in an instantaneous blow that drove the heel of his hand into the thin man's shoulder; the collarbone broke with an audible click and the man dropped to the pavement as if shot.

In the same motion, Trelawny dove forward in a fencer's lunge and slammed his right fist into the shorter man's belly; as the man doubled over, Trelawny recovered forward and gave him a slap across the ear that sent him spinning into the wall. Muffled laughter or coughing sounded from the people in the shadows around the combatants.

Swearing in Turkish just because of the reminder, Trelawny hurried to the door at the end of the alley and drew a knife of his own, and he slipped the blade between the door and the jamb to lift the inner bar.

When he had stepped into the low-ceilinged room beyond and pushed the door closed and latched behind him, a black-bearded man in an interior archway lowered a pistol. Daylight, reflected down through holes in several overhead ceilings and the roof, glittered on gold teeth as the man smiled.

"You come unseen?" he said, speaking English with a Turkish accent.

Trelawny was still holding the knife. "Yes, Abbas. Well, a couple of your hooligans out front are hurting, but I left Miss B. in the Seven Dials."

"Ah. Blinded by the crossing sweeper who gives change and keeps only a ha'penny."

"Blinded on the occasions when he gives back the payment entire," said Trelawny, "and then uses his Lady Godiva broom, his Rapunzel broom."

These references were clearly lost on the other man, but his smile widened. "I will not give back payment for the Greek boat, beyond doubt."

It was clearly a hint. Trelawny nodded and with his left hand fetched a purse from his waistcoat pocket. He tossed it to Abbas, who caught it in a hand missing several fingers.

The Turk hefted it, then turned and spoke to someone behind him; a moment later Trelawny heard footsteps pounding away up wooden stairs, and he knew that a semaphore signal would be sent from the rooftop of this house, relayed by flags waved on other rooftops across the City, to a man on London Bridge, who would signal a crewman on a cargo boat now laboring up the Thames. The crewman would shortly be diving overboard and swimming to the docks by the Billingsgate fish market.

Abbas sat down on the damp boards of the floor and picked up a bottle. "You wait so long until perhaps it is too late."

Trelawny sat down cross-legged near the door and stuck his knife upright in the floor beside him. The house smelled of mildew and olive oil and spinach cooking. "I wanted to be sure this was the right boat. I don't kill innocent people."

"Anymore."

"Anymore," Trelawny agreed.

"Betrayal, in the other hand," said his companion as he twisted the cork from the bottle, "is good, eh? These in the boat are your—your *allies* long ago." He took a deep gulp of the liquor and smiled as he held the bottle out toward Trelawny. "For them you killed . . . how many Turkish peoples on Euboea, in the Greeks' revolution? Children and women too?"

Trelawny took a mouthful of the liquor—it was arrack, harsh and warming. "Many," he said after he had swallowed it. "As many, probably, as you killed Greek women and children in the Morea. But I have renounced the gods I sought then, to whom I made that blood sacrifice. Now," he said, waving in the direction of the river, "I hinder them."

Remembering the man he had hit outside, he rubbed his own crooked collarbone, wondering if the stony knot in his throat next to it was bigger than it used to be. It did seem to be. Nevertheless, he thought uneasily, I do hinder them.

Abbas nodded several times cheerfully. "And we help, when you pay us. But why, old enemy, do you not work with the Carbonari? They would fight these old gods for nothing, for even paying *you*."

"Oh, I don't know," said Trelawny, rocking his knife free. He tucked it back into his sleeve and lithely straightened his legs and stood up. "Maybe I just don't like Italians."

Abbas tapped his own chest. "And you like Turks?"

"I suppose I don't really like anybody. Do you mind if I vacate your premises by the back way? Your injured neighbors out front may have found reinforcements."

"You leave peace in your wake, now, always. Yes, go away by the back."

Trelawny nodded and stepped past the sitting man and, skirting a kitchen in which several robed women huddled over a smoking black stove, climbed through a glassless window in the hallway. He was now in a long unroofed space too narrow even to be called an alley—a gap where two crumbling buildings didn't quite meet—and short boards were wedged everywhere between the walls like rungs of a three-dimensional ladder. Any number of destinations could be reached by climbing in one direction or another, even downward into ancient ruptured cellars, and Trelawny began pulling himself up toward the right, toward the shingle eaves and rain gutters that were in sunlight far overhead, knowing that he could get to a rooftop in Earl Street this way, and from there to a flight of lodging house stairs that would lead him down to the Earl Street pavement and the Seven Dials, where the diminutive Miss B. was undoubtedly waiting for him in front of the druggist's shop where he had left her.

She would be angry. It wouldn't matter much now, while the sun was up, but he wasn't looking forward to the night, when she would be . . . bigger.

CHAPTER FOUR

[O]ne feels again within the accursed circle. The skulls &
bones rattle, the goblins keep mumbling, & the owls beat their
obscene wings again . . . Meanwhile, to step out of the ring is
death & damnation.

—*Dante Gabriel Rossetti, in a letter to William Bell Scott, 1853*

A T LOW TIDE there was a narrow sandy beach between the
embankment wall and the river in the shadow of Blackfriars
Bridge, and a gang of ragged children had somehow found it and were
wading out into the icy water and bending to sift the sand through their
blackened fingers.

Standing on an iron balcony a hundred feet above, shaded from
the bright winter sun by an overhanging roof, Dante Gabriel Rossetti
puffed on a cigar and stoically watched several large sheets of paper,
bobbing on the ripples out of reach of the scavenging children, as they
were swept out of the sunlight and into the shadows under the bridge.

He was wearing baggy houndstooth check trousers and a buttoned-
up waistcoat under a black wool coat, but the wind—which had carried

the drawings so far out over the river to the west that they had only
now disappeared from sight—seemed to be finding the gaps between
all the buttons.

And in spite of the cold, the Thames here smelled like a cesspool,
largely because the ancient Fleet Ditch, a subterranean channel now,
flowed into the river beside Blackfriars Bridge. God only knew how
those little street Arabs in the shallows below kept from being poisoned
by the sewage—They must build up an immunity gradually, he thought,
like Mithridates of Pontus who was said to have deliberately acquired a
cumulative tolerance to all the poisons of his day.

The thought made him shift around to look over his shoulder back
into the parlor, and in fact he didn't see the slim figure of his wife on the
couch. Probably she had gone back to bed with the laudanum bottle.
They were to go out to dinner with a friend tomorrow night, and she
would conserve her meager strength for that.

Their bedroom was always foul with the metallic reek of laudanum. Since her miscarriage in May of last year, Lizzie had needed
ever-increasing doses of the opium-in-alcohol medicine to fight her
fevers and insomnia. Already today she had taken twenty drops of it,
to counter the fit that had shaken both of them awake at the ungodly
hour of six this morning. The medicine had worked, and it was now
presumably helping her back to sleep, but Gabriel was irremediably
wide awake.

Lizzie would be awake again in a few hours. He wondered if she
would remember throwing his drawings off the balcony.

He pitched the cigar out toward the river and shuffled back through
the French doors into the relative dimness inside, and, before stepping
to the bedroom to check on her, he looked at the framed watercolors
hung around the blue-tile-fronted fireplace. They were all Lizzie's—his
own work was in the studio down the hall—and on this cold malodorous morning he saw her pictures as lifeless, the figures blank faced and
awkwardly proportioned.

From across many years he remembered a disturbing pencil sketch of a rabbit, drawn by his sister when she'd have been about fourteen, and he absently touched the revolver he always carried in a holster on his right hip.

Flickers of reflected sunlight from the river played across the high blue-painted plaster ceiling, making Lizzie's pictures look as drowned as his drawings of Miss Herbert and Annie Miller would soon be.

The room smelled of cigar, the Fleet Ditch, and garlic.

He crossed to the bedroom door and opened it quietly, but Lizzie was not in the big four-poster bed—she was sitting at the desk by the open river-facing window, hunched so closely over whatever she was doing that her wavy red hair lay tumbled across the desk and hid her face and hands.

"Guggums," he began, using his pet name for her, but he stepped back when she gave a kind of whispered inhaled shriek and tore a paper she'd apparently been writing on.

Her face when she looked up was pale and thin, but her eyes on him were enormous.

"I'm sorry!" she said hoarsely; then she added, "Walter says your sisters are on their way over here."

Clearly it wasn't a visit from Christina and Maria that she was sorry about—though this was an inconsiderately early hour—and he was careful not to seem to be hurrying as he moved to the desk.

She had laid out a large page torn from a sketch pad, and it was covered with lines of penciled writing—passages of her own neat hand-writing alternating with a wavering loopy script, the source of which, Gabriel soon realized, must be the pencil that stood upright in a little disk that sat on the paper. Gabriel reached out slowly—Lizzie didn't stop him—and pushed the disk, and it slid smoothly across the paper, leaving a penciled line. Apparently the disk rolled on confined ball bearings.

"You promised Doctor Acland that you'd give this up. He says it makes you sicker."

"Séances," said Lizzie weakly, throwing herself back in the chair. "This isn't—"

"Oh, *don't*, Gug—you know he didn't mean the groups, the hand-holding! You *know* he meant—talking to dead people!"

She gripped the arms of the chair and got halfway to her feet, then collapsed back, panting.

Her eyes were closed, and her eyelids were wrinkled. "Who can I trust," she whispered, "besides dead people?"

He opened and closed his mouth several times before he spoke. "I've done everything I—we're practically *on* the river—and—"

"And the garlic and the mirrors," she said, "and your gun. I know."

Gabriel looked around the musty room in frustration, then snapped, "You're too weak to go out to La Sablonniere tomorrow night. I'll call on Swinburne and tell him it's off. Mrs. Birrell can make us some soup."

"I'll be rested. I should go out sometimes." Her fingers touched the torn paper, then quickly retreated. "Please."

Gabriel exhaled and shook his head in reluctant acquiescence. "If you're better by then. If! But no more of this—this *necromancy*." He picked up the paper and the pencil disk. "Let poor Walter rest in peace. You owe him that." He turned on his heel and left the room, ignoring her weak protests and kicking the door shut behind him.

He tucked the pencil disk into his pocket and squinted at the paper.

Walter was Walter Deverell, who had died eight years earlier. Deverell had been a close friend, a year older than Gabriel and a teacher at the Government School of Design, and it had been he who discovered Lizzie in a milliner's shop near Leicester Square. Deverell had immediately hired her as a model, and Gabriel and his group of young painters—who called themselves, a bit self-consciously, the Pre-Raphaelite Brotherhood—had all soon hired her too, to model for various of their paintings.

Gabriel had long suspected that Lizzie would rather have married

Deverell than himself, and when he thought about Deverell—which he tried not to do—he had to suppress a nasty satisfaction that the man had died when he did, at the age of twenty-six.

Since Deverell's death Lizzie had two or three times contacted his ghost at séances, or claimed that she had. But—Gabriel hooked his reading glasses out of his breast pocket and sat down on the couch—Gabriel had never until now seen a transcript of any of those conversations.

At the top of the sheet of paper, *Walter, are you there?* was written three times in her clear hand. Below the last one was a meandering and unbroken pencil line; Gabriel managed to decipher it as,

there fair ne'er

Well, thought Gabriel sourly, that's well said.

Lizzie's handwriting followed it with, *What shook me awake this morning?*

Gabriel could only read the next line as,

parnassus has its flowers

Very poetical, Walter, he thought. The flowers on Mount Parnassus woke her up, of course.

Lizzie had followed it with, *Where can we be safe?*

And the pencil oracle had scrawled,

dark river you come soon

Gabriel scowled through his glasses. Why were ghosts such imbeciles? Who could be blamed for striving, at any cost, to avoid forever the decay-of-self that death was?

Below that Lizzie had written, *Must I die soon?*

—to which the meandering line replied,

or never

Lizzie countered, *You know why I can't.*

—and Deverell's faint handwriting followed with,

worse for both you if you stay

Gabriel started to get to his feet, then slumped back. It would do no good to try to reason with Lizzie right now.

"Damn you, Walter," he whispered furiously, "you want her with you *still*?"

Lizzie's next line was, *I can't.*

And the last line on the sheet was Deverell's:

ask his sisters are there in your soon

Gabriel tossed the paper away; it swooped back and forth and settled on the carpet.

According to spiritualist lore, a ghost could only be invited to reach up from the river and participate in this sort of written communication—they couldn't be compelled; it had to be voluntary. Walter was apparently as poisonously eager to converse as she was.

If *converse* was the proper word. Morbid malignant gibberish. And Gabriel couldn't see that the ghost had said that Maria and Christina were coming here.

He got to his feet and walked down the hall to his studio, stepping around stacks of books along the way. When he had married Lizzie almost two years ago—after so long an engagement that everyone, including her, had assumed he didn't mean to go through with it—he had got the landlord to cut a door through to the next house in the row, connecting Gabriel's old bachelor rooms on the first floor of Number 13 Chatham Place to the corresponding floor of Number 14. He had moved his bed—the bed he had been born in—to the newly acquired bedroom where Lizzie now sat, but he hadn't shifted his studio.

Stepping now into the wide, high-ceilinged room, he let his eyes play over the canvases leaning in stacks and the sketches tacked to the walls.

He owed three paintings to the estate of a deceased patron—three paintings or the return of the 714 pounds the patron had advanced to him—but all he had been doing was portraits of Lizzie. It was Lizzie's sad face in every picture, looking in every direction but straight at the viewer.

How could she still be in love with a man who was dead, and who furthermore could no longer frame a coherent sentence? But Deverell was fixed forever in her memory as he had been in 1854, young and almost ridiculously handsome—while Gabriel's hair, though still curly and black, had begun to recede, and he wasn't as slim as he had been in 1854, and he believed his trim goatee gave him dignity, but his youthful Byronic looks were gone.

He inhaled the smells of linseed oil and turpentine and crossed the bare wood floor to the window wall, where he stared out at a string of barges moving downstream, and a low-in-the-water sloop with filled sails moving slowly the opposite way, and the smokestacks of the iron foundry on the river's south shore. At least, he thought with a wry smile, I have the advantage of being alive.

But if she had married Deverell, came a sudden and unwelcome thought, while she was still a virgin, Deverell would still be alive, and she wouldn't be dying.

The doorbell in the hall clanged then, and he was grateful for the interruption as he hurried to the stairs; already he could hear Christina's voice below, and he pulled out his handkerchief and wiped the sweat from his forehead.

Now both of his sisters were clumping up the stairs, stout Maria in the rear—and he frowned in irritation and mild alarm to see that they were somehow both dressed as nuns.

"Sisters!" he called down in greeting—adding, with somewhat forced cheer, "Have you come to save our souls?"

"Not primarily yours," said Christina.

In the shadows of the stairwell she was backlit from below, and not for the first time he noted the planes of her narrow face, framed by the dark hair parted in the middle and swept back. He had twice used her as a model for the Virgin Mary, and her present expression made him wish he could stop her right now and sketch her for a painting of Mary ascending to the upper room in Jerusalem to meet with the apostles after the Crucifixion.

"Where is Lizzie?" asked Christina quietly when she had stepped up beside him.

"In the bedroom," said Gabriel, "sleeping at last, I hope—she had a fit at dawn, then threw a dozen of my drawings into the river. We can talk in the studio without . . . disturbing her."

Maria had made it to the top of the stairs, puffing, and now sidled around the couch to pick up the sheet Gabriel had tossed down.

"Automatic writing?" she asked.

"Ah—she does it with a sort of sliding pencil device—"

"Bring it along," said Christina, starting down the hall.

GABRIEL CLEARED BOXES AND brushes off a couple of stools for his sisters, but he remained standing, hoping the light from the glass window-wall at his back would make any facial expressions harder to see.

Both women were studying the pencil lines on the sheet.

"Walter Deverell said you'd be dropping by," Gabriel remarked lightly, waving at the paper. "Why are you two dressed for the convent?"

"I came straight home from the Magdalen Penitentiary," said Christina, "and Maria was on her way to All Saints. I suppose you understood Walter to be referring to you and Lizzie, here, where he writes, 'worse for both you if you stay.'"

"I suppose I did, if indeed that's Walter, and not just Lizzie's imagination. I thought you were scheduled at Magdalen for another . . . two days, was it?"

"Yes." Christina took a deep breath and exhaled. "But I seem to have done a bit of automatic writing myself. 'Folio Q' won't stop writing itself."

Maria closed her eyes and shook her head.

Gabriel raised his eyebrows at Christina and made a beckoning motion with his hand.

There were tears in Christina's eyes. "It's Uncle John who's writing it, I'm nearly sure, and I don't think it's voluntary on his part. I think it's his—his dreams, if such creatures dream. And he says—" Her voice faltered.

Maria spoke up. "*Sembra che Lizzie sia di nuovo in dolce attesa,*" which was Italian for *Apparently Lizzie is expecting again.*

Gabriel was glad that he had chosen to stand against the light, for he could feel his face chill and he assumed he had gone pale.

"That's not possible," he said. "Do you think I didn't learn, from the first one? I've admitted you were right, and—since May, we haven't—"

Christina started to say something, but Maria interrupted: "Why did she throw your pictures into the river?"

Gabriel was still frowning. "Jealousy. Baseless. Old pictures of models I don't use anymore."

"Stunners," said Maria with a wan smile, using Gabriel's term for beautiful women.

Gabriel nodded in dismissal of the brief diversion and turned to Christina. "Uncle John," he said clearly, "and poor old Walter too, if that's what he meant there, are wrong. The dead chaps are, in this, unreliable."

Lizzie's recent words came back to him—*Who can I trust besides dead people?*

"I'm sorry," whispered Christina, staring at the paint-dappled wooden floor.

Gabriel understood that she wasn't apologizing for anything she'd said or done today.

So did Maria. "You were only fourteen," she said. "And Papa, God rest his soul, deliberately led you into it."

Gabriel wavered, then stepped forward and briefly gripped Christina's shoulder. "I would have done the same," he said. "I *did,* eventually."

And so did my poor Lizzie, he thought.

"If we could *find* it," said Christina, without looking up, "and destroy it—I promised him I would grind it to powder and sift it into the sea—"

Gabriel stared at his sister with mingled sympathy and cynicism—after their father's death, the three of them had searched every corner of the old house in Charlotte Street, but they had not found the tiny black statue; and Gabriel wondered if Christina would be so resolute to destroy the thing if she were actually to have it again.

"Prayer," said Maria, "is our only hope now."

"And the temporal measures," said Christina with a sigh. "Garlic, mirrors, and celibacy."

Gabriel was still angry that his resolve—his selfless resolve!—had been called into question, and by dead men. "Well, if Uncle John thinks—"

"He isn't really our mother's brother," said Maria. "Poor damned John Polidori is just the latest mask—a suffering, half-alive mask!—that this thing is currently wearing. It's Gog and Magog, the eternal enemy of God's kingdom, from the prophecies in the books of Ezekiel and Revelation."

Gabriel saw Christina's face go blank, and he quickly said, "No doubt, no doubt! Or something of that general description, I'm sure." Maria looked away, so he was able to send a warning frown to Christina.

"If we'd see you in church occasionally—" began Maria, but Christina interrupted her.

"We could be sure it *was* you," she said, "since I don't believe Uncle John would venture into a church. You remember the drawing you did when you and poor Lizzie were in Paris on your honeymoon? The two couples in the forest?"

Gabriel did indeed remember it. It was a pen-and-ink drawing of a man and a woman in medieval clothing, visibly astonished at coming face-to-face with exact duplicates of themselves.

"I called it *How They Met Themselves*," he said cautiously. "It was a study in—"

"It was a prophecy," said Christina. "Forgive me, Gabriel, but I wonder if Lizzie would agree that the two of you have been celibate since May."

Gabriel stepped back toward the window, perhaps to keep from raising his hand to his sister.

"I," he said hoarsely, "know you've never approved of her—but she would not ever—"

"She would have thought it was *you*," wailed Maria, raising her hands halfway to her face as if she meant to cover her eyes. "You knew—when you drew that picture!—that creatures of our uncle's sort can take on the appearance of their hosts."

Gabriel was shaking his head and had started to speak, when the window glass rattled and the timbers creaked as a reverberating boom rolled over the house.

His sisters had both stood up and were staring past him out the window, so he spun around—a plume of black smoke was churning and swelling over the water of the Thames a hundred yards out from the shore, and pieces of debris were spinning upward across the view of the buildings on the opposite shore.

"Was that a boat?" asked Maria breathlessly.

Gabriel shrugged. "What else?" He wondered if it had been the heavy-laden sloop he had noticed a couple of minutes earlier. "Nobody on board will have survived that."

Down the hall they could hear Lizzie weeping now.

Gabriel turned toward the doorway and hesitated, his teeth bared in indecision. At last, "Help me with her," he said to his sisters.

Maria nodded and hurried past him, her long black sleeves flapping.

Christina took Gabriel's arm as they strode behind her, and Christina whispered, "At the Lord Mayor's Show that time—"

"Hush. You'll upset them both."

He should never have told Christina what Lizzie had said then—it had been a little more than nine years ago, in November of '52, shortly after he and Lizzie had become lovers. They had gone to see the Lord Mayor's parade in New Oxford Street, and a deformed dwarf beggar had been lurching alongside the parade, pacing the traditional giant wicker figures of Gog and Magog that were being ceremoniously carried down the street, and when the dwarf stumbled and fell near where Lizzie stood, she had run to the little figure and in pity taken it right into her arms—invited it into her bosom!—and even though its face was entirely wrapped in a scarf, the dwarf had somehow managed to *bite* Lizzie. When Gabriel had pushed the malignant thing away and pulled Lizzie to her feet and said, "Let's get that bite attended to, Lizzie," she had shuddered and said to him hoarsely, "Call me Gogmagog." A moment later she had claimed not to remember having said it—and when he asked her if she knew of the sinister "Goemagot" giant in Geoffrey of Monmouth's *Historia Regnum Britanniae,* who was called Goemagog in Milton's *History of Britain* and Gogmagog in Midlands devil legends, she had responded with genuine bafflement—but he had called her Gogmagog for the rest of that day, and the name had soon become the affectionate nickname Guggums.

And now, for the first time, it occurred to Gabriel that Lizzie might have acquired a *second* vampiric patron, on that day, in addition to his uncle. Her unspecific infirmities had started around then. Could *two* of the damnable things be *sharing* her? Uncle John *and* this Gogmagog thing?

Which of the two might it have been who, in his sisters' repellent speculation, had congress with Lizzie in Gabriel's form?

He shuddered and forcefully dismissed the thought and took Christina's arm to hurry her along.

When Gabriel and Christina arrived at the bedroom doorway, Lizzie and Maria were huddled in the far corner over the crib Gabriel had bought last year in anticipation of the baby who had been stillborn. Lizzie had never let him get rid of it. Maria had one arm around Lizzie and was murmuring.

Lizzie was sobbing and shaking her head. "Did you *shoot* at him, Gabriel?" she whined. "Look, you woke the baby!"

And for just a flickering split second, Gabriel thought he saw a tiny figure in the crib, a dark little thing with long fingers and enormous eyes; then, even before he could shake his head or blink, it was gone.

Maria didn't move, but she had gone quiet; and beside Gabriel, Christina had audibly caught her breath.

Gabriel swallowed, then managed to say, "The baby's quiet, now, G—darling. See? Take some more medicine, if you need to, and you should be back in bed."

Lizzie's urgency seemed to have evaporated—she stared at the empty crib and then nodded and let Maria help her back to the bed. She sighed and lay back across it, and Gabriel stepped forward and pulled the sheet up to her shoulders, and she closed her eyes. Her eyelids looked like an old man's knuckles.

Gabriel jerked his head toward the hallway, and his sisters followed him back to the studio. Maria was visibly shaking.

The cloud of black smoke over the river had thinned and drifted west almost out of sight beyond the brick wall of the next house, and several rowboats and a steam launch were arrowing toward the arches of the bridge, no doubt heading for whatever floating debris the river had carried to the east side of it.

Gabriel crossed to a cabinet and reached down a bottle. He waved it at his sisters—Christina nodded energetically and Maria shook her head.

As he carried two filled glasses back to where the women had resumed their seats, he handed one to Christina and asked in a defeated tone, "Very well, who did she imagine I was shooting at?"

Christina gulped the brandy to avoid replying and Maria just stared out the window, but Gabriel knew what the answer was: their uncle. Or conceivably the Gogmagog thing. Lizzie might have mistaken the apparition for her husband the first time—or two—but had apparently not been fooled forever.

Jealous husband, he thought bitterly, shoots at immortal vampire rival.

And then he drained his glass in several eye-watering swallows and went back to refill it, for the thought had occurred to him that the apparition might have taken the form of Walter Deverell.

Christina finished her own glass and, staring out the window, seemed to brace herself. "Soon," she said levelly, "there may be two phantom infants in that crib."

For a moment Gabriel wasn't able to take a deep breath, and then he was panting. "Yes, probably!" he burst out. "But I *will* shoot him, if I get the chance. I've got silver bullets."

"I wish you didn't carry that firearm about," said Maria.

He drew his hand back as if to throw his refilled glass, then just set it down carefully beside the bottle. "William will marry eventually," he said in a quieter tone. "He'll try to have children—he doesn't believe any of this."

"Not even in God," said Maria sadly, shaking her head, "who is our only hope."

"And an unhelpfully remote and theoretical hope, at that," Gabriel snapped. "He *was* shot once, though, wasn't he? Our monstrous uncle, not God. In your story, Christina, your 'Folio Q.'"

Christina rocked her head back and stared at the high plaster ceiling. "The story took place in Italy, and it concerned a man who didn't dare look in a mirror. He was threatened by a rival in love, but he let down his guard, and his rival shot him, in the mouth, and yes, it was with a silver bullet; he never really recovered. He died not long afterward, in Venice." She lowered her head and looked at her siblings. "Papa told me once that he got the little petrified statue in Venice, before he came to England—he said it showed him visions of Mama. And he implied . . . that the acquiring of it put his soul in peril."

Maria muttered something doleful in Italian.

Christina went on, "I seem to be—our uncle seems to be—writing a sequel now, in which he's alive again, in London."

"We need to read this sequel," said Gabriel. "I wish you hadn't burned 'Folio Q.'"

Christina gave him a stricken look. "I'm sorry, I—I've destroyed the new page too! I didn't think—"

For several long seconds none of them spoke.

At last Gabriel said, gently, "You remember it, though."

"Yes—yes."

"And if you write more—if *he* does, that is—you can save it." When Christina nodded, he fished Lizzie's automatic-writing pencil disk out of his pocket and tossed it to her. She caught it deftly. "Use this," he said, "if it will help. I don't want it in the house."

Maria frowned, but Christina nodded and gingerly put the thing into the side pocket of her habit.

"And," Gabriel went on, though it actually made his forehead sweat to say it, "he claims that my wife is with child by . . . by a vampire wearing my appearance, is that right? Does he actually . . . mention Lizzie by name?"

Christina sighed and nodded. "Lizzie Siddal."

"Damn him, her name is *Rossetti* now, Elizabeth *Rossetti*." Gabriel jammed his fists in his coat pockets and paced to the far wall and back, staring around at all the portraits of his wife.

"If she is with child," he asked finally, "as the ghosts and devils claim—who is the father?"

"You are," said Christina. She too was pointedly looking at the pictures, not at him. "There's no other human, no other male, really, in the picture. He took your—when you invited him in, in whatever form he was wearing—along with your blood—" She was blushing, and Maria had turned to face the wall. "'The expense of spirit in a waste of shame,'" Christina finished quickly, quoting Shakespeare's sonnet about the effects of lust.

"Er, yes." Gabriel was blushing himself. "Quite so. Well! In that case we need to catch him and kill him, don't we? Shoot him with a silver bullet again." He patted the bulk of the revolver under his waistcoat.

"Catch him?" cried Maria. "You'll damn your soul simply doing that! And silver bullets will only injure him—you need to find the statue too and destroy that. At *least*."

Gabriel flinched at *damn your soul*, for he had not entirely shed the Catholic beliefs of his youth; but he nodded grimly and went on, "If we—if I—can catch him, injure him, bind him somehow—he's weak in daylight, according to what I recall of your story, Christina!—we can make him tell us where the statue is."

He looked squarely at Maria. "How do we catch him, Moony?" he asked, using the nickname she had been given in childhood because of her round face.

"Why do you imagine I would know?"

"You seem to know the cost of it. And you read all of Papa's manuscripts, burned now, even the ones in Greek and Hebrew—all his occult interpretations of Dante and Pythagoras and the Jewish mystics."

"It's ridiculous to think that—"

"Do you know a way, Moony?"

Maria got to her feet and smoothed out the apron of her black habit. "Consider it, Gabriel," she said earnestly as she moved to step past him. "If Papa knew anything about—"

He stepped in front of her. "But do you know a way?"

Her round face looked up at him from under her folded-back veil. "Gabriel," she said, "I am a lay member of the All Saints Sisters of the Poor, soon to be undertaking my novitiate. I love you, and through you I love Lizzie and any children you have. But if I know a way to catch *him,* it would be a mortal sin, for all of us, to use it, and therefore I would not reveal it. You *know* me." After staring into his eyes for another couple of seconds, she said, "I'll just go look in on Lizzie," and again stepped around him.

This time he didn't block her.

As Maria clumped away down the hall, Gabriel said to Christina, "A clear yes."

"And a clear no." She shivered, but Gabriel couldn't tell what emotion it sprang from. "I believe I could *summon* him," she said. "I don't know about restraining him."

Gabriel nodded. I imagine I could summon him too, he thought—but in my case it would be the form of a woman who answered the summons.

As before, it would be the image of Lizzie. I wonder if I *could* shoot a creature wearing that image.

CHAPTER FIVE

She loved the games men played with death,
Where death must win . . .

—*Algernon Swinburne, "Faustine"*

B Y NOON THE unseasonal east wind had died. With sunset came
clouds from the west that hid the rising full moon, and the
streetlamps of London were lit early because of a heavy fog that was as
much coal smoke as dampness.

Cabs and coaches moved slowly down the streets from one patch
of lamplight to the next, the creak and clatter of their passage seeming
to echo back more clearly from the housefronts in the opaque night air
than they did by daylight.

A slow-moving clarence cab made a wide right turn from Charing
Cross Road into New Oxford Street, its two lanterns lighting the driver's hat and turned-up coat collar and the horse's flexing back and not
much else. A hansom cab would have been faster, but McKee had said
that if they were to travel together at night, they must have a vehicle
with four walls as well as a roof, and hansom cabs didn't have a partition in front. Crawford had been happy with the choice, for it let him

sit across from her with his silk hat beside him—and he was facing the rear, this time, as good manners dictated.

"I believe the British Museum is ahead of us," McKee remarked now, peering out at the vague shapes of the buildings looming past on either side. Windows of houses were luminous yellow smears in the angular black silhouettes.

The cab's windows rattled and the wheels made a loud grinding sound on the crushed stone of the street surface, and Crawford had to lean forward in the dimness of the interior to hear her.

"I don't know where we are," he said, trying to remember precisely why he had agreed to this. "Talk louder."

"My father took me to the British Museum when I was eleven," she said. He cupped a hand to his ear, and she added, "Oh, for God's sake, sit over here beside me so I won't have to shout."

It seemed, on the whole, ridiculous not to. He nodded and stood up in a crouch and sat down on the forward-facing seat, of which McKee's crinoline dress occupied more than half. He smelled lavender with the faintest undertone of garlic.

"The, uh, British Museum," he said.

"Yes. I mainly remember being scared by the Egyptian mummies— I was afraid we might happen to be in there in the moment when the General Resurrection took place, and they'd start to come to life all around us."

Crawford realized that he was smiling in spite of himself. "Well— on the whole, that would be a festive moment, wouldn't it? The Second Coming, Jesus arriving to judge the living and the dead? You couldn't have been much of a sinner at the age of eleven."

"As opposed to later, you mean. Shall I tell you how I came to be ruined, eight years after that?"

Crawford's smile had disappeared. "Certainly not, Miss McKee. I think we're almost at our destination. Do you suppose there'll be a dinner?"

He had obtained with no trouble from his dog-owning client a note of invitation to the salon, but the note, written on the back of her calling card, simply said, *Please welcome into your company John Crawford, a poet, and his guest.* No reference to dinner. He had taken McKee's advice and copied out twenty lines from a middle canto of Southey's *Thalaba the Destroyer,* just in case.

She shrugged. "This isn't my pasture any more than it's yours. It sounded like more talking than eating—which ought to mean beer, at least. I grew up in the country, in Sudbury. You know it?"

"Certainly."

"In '54, when I was nineteen, I was visiting cousins in London; one night we got separated in the crowd in Mayfair. I was dazzled by all the bright gas jets and music and the fine-dressed ladies and gentlemen . . . as I thought at the time. The *elegant scene.* And I got lost, and found myself in a dark street with the crowds all somehow gone, and an old woman in an open doorway spoke to me. I told her I'd lost my way and asked her how to get back to Langham Street, where my aunt and cousins lived, though I didn't know if it was in Soho or Fitzrovia or St. Pancras or what—I've heard it's in Fitzrovia—"

"Yes," said Crawford.

"—but she swore she knew it and would have her groom escort me back, but first I must come in and have a cup of coffee to take the chill off. I did. The coffee was drugged. When I woke up after noon the next day, I learned that at least one man had visited me. I was kept prisoner for a week and then wholesaled with two other girls to Carpace across the river." In the dimness he saw her raise one hand and let it fall. "There's no going back."

"I'm sorry," Crawford said stiffly, squinting through the front window into the light-stained fog ahead of the driver. Then he glanced at the pale oval of her face and said, "And . . . and I'm sorry."

"Do you have siblings? I don't remember."

"No."

"If I were—your sister, say—what would your feelings be?"

"I'd want to find that old woman who drugged you. I'd want to kill her." He sat back, wishing he'd brought a flask. "I want to kill her now."

"That's something."

Crawford was startled then by a squeak from her purse—she had evidently brought her bird along. She went on, "I imagine there'll be sandwiches or relish trays or things of that sort—artistic folk won't stay if there's no food or drink at all."

"Stands to reason," he agreed. "Haven't you—sorry, I ought not to ask you personal questions."

"'Ought not'?" she said sharply. "'Personal questions'? Why are we in this cab?"

Crawford inhaled through his teeth and nodded, conceding the point. "To find out what became of our daughter," he said. "Fair enough. So—haven't you, now that you're free of the Carpace woman, tried to contact your family? How many years has it been?"

"It's been eight years. I ran away from Carpace's house to the Magdalen Penitentiary four years ago, and I've been out of there for two years, in the Hail Mary trade. No, I haven't tried to approach them. My father is a curate and my mother teaches at the church school . . . if they're still alive." She gave a hitching laugh. "That *was* a personal question, wasn't it?"

"They wouldn't . . . *blame* you, surely, for having simply stumbled into a trap."

"I hope no reasonable person would blame me. No, they'd be saddened by it but overjoyed to see me alive and restored. And I would dearly love to see them again, before they die." She glanced at Crawford and then away. "But I love them, you see—I think they're safe from the devil I've acquired, as long as I don't go near them."

Several seconds went by with just the noise of the cab and the passing blurs of light outside the window glass. "The, uh, Hail Mary trade?" he said finally.

"A veterinarian, and you don't know the term? Aves." She sang three lines from the Irish song "Danny Boy": "'And if I'm dead, as dead

I well may be, / You'll come and find the place where I am lying, / And kneel and say an ave there for me.'"

"Avis, aves," said Crawford, nodding. "Birds. The bird business?"

"Exactly. Songbirds. It overlaps with some other trades—gypsy soul-catchers, absinthe-sellers, the eyeglasses men."

Crawford was curious about these, and about how they overlapped with the songbird trade, but the cab had pulled up in front of one of a row of tall narrow houses; a gas lamp shone beside the door at the top of the steps, and the curtained windows glowed upstairs and downstairs.

"You pay the cabbie and go to the door first," said McKee. "When they open the door, I'll join you as you go in." Seeing his puzzled look, she added, "You and I ought not to be together under a naked night sky."

"I take your meaning," said Crawford slowly, remembering their calamitous meeting seven years ago on Waterloo Bridge. What the hell am I doing here, he thought bleakly—but just see it through, see it through. "I'd forgotten."

McKee caught his arm. "Now I think of it—once we've been admitted, let's stay on opposite sides of the room."

"What—why? Who am I to talk to?"

"We don't know who or what might have been invited inside. Did you bring your garlic?"

Crawford touched his waistcoat pocket. "I did, but—"

"So did I. I think we'd be well advised to play this as if we were outdoors. Might be nothing would happen, but just in—"

"Why am I even *here?*" demanded Crawford—quietly, for the cabbie had stepped down from his perch and was standing outside the door now. "If I'm not to be anywhere near whatever you're doing?"

"Watch me—if it goes wrong, barge in, devils or no devils."

Crawford nodded tightly. "Garlic flying. Aye aye." He picked up his hat and opened the door, wincing at the cold night air, and stepped down to the gritty pavement. He paid the cabbie and then tapped quickly up the steps to the house door.

His knock was answered by a middle-aged man whose old-fashioned knee breeches and stockings indicated that he was a servant; Crawford handed him his hat and the dog owner's calling card.

The man glanced at the card and looked down the steps to the cab. "And guest, sir?"

Crawford stepped past him into the entry hall and nodded, hearing the cab door slam below. "She, uh, catches cold easily," he said. "I didn't want her to stand in the chilly air."

"Of course, sir. Guests are in the library and sitting room, through those doors."

Crawford strode toward the indicated doors, and another servant pulled them open. Crawford stepped through, moving quickly to maintain a distance between himself and McKee; and he found that dozens of people in a dimly lit room all now seemed to be staring at him. He nodded vaguely and shuffled away from the clear area of carpet in front of the doors.

It was certainly a large room, with a very high ceiling, though its dimensions were hard to guess since the only illumination was dozens of candles; no, there were several gas jets too, but they were enclosed in thick red glass shades. He could smell coffee and vanilla under a haze of cigar smoke, and he hoped there would be more substantial fare than just coffee and cakes.

An unguessable number of people were sitting in clusters of chairs or standing beside a long table to his left. There were no white ties on the visible gentlemen, and his fretfulness about his own frock coat and cravat abated; but McKee would be coming in behind him in a moment, so he hurried to the farthest ring of chairs. Long curtains indicated tall windows at intervals along the length of the room, and dark paintings were hung with their frames nearly edge to edge all over the walls, extending so high up that surely nobody could ever look at the top several rows, even in daylight.

Looking back, he could see the dim shapes of faces looking after him, but when McKee stepped into the room, they turned toward her. Grateful that he had only momentarily been the object of attention, Crawford sat down in an empty chair in the nearest circle, to the left of a lean, gray-bearded gentleman, on the far side of whom stood a tall woman in what seemed to be a toga.

The old man was staring at him, and Crawford nodded and said quietly, "How do you do?"

"Stupidest question I've ever heard," the old man growled, and he looked away.

On Crawford's left, a young man in a lacy collar giggled softly and whispered, "That's Edward John Trelawny, the great friend of Shelley's."

"Oh." The people in the chairs around him seemed to be looking expectantly toward the long table along the wall opposite the curtained windows, but Crawford glanced curiously at the old man on his right.

He had heard of Trelawny. The man had reportedly been a close friend of the poets Byron and Shelley, and a few years ago he had published a sensational memoir of their last days. And Crawford recalled that the man had published an autobiography some thirty years ago, recounting his bloody adventures as a pirate on the Indian Ocean. Crawford remembered hearing that Trelawny had joined Byron in fighting to free Greece from the Turks, and had married a Greek maiden in a cave on Mount Parnassus—perhaps that's who the tall woman was.

Crawford looked past the young man on his left, peering to see where McKee might have alighted, but he couldn't make her out in the red-tinted dimness. He wondered uneasily if she had found Carpace.

"I am sorry to announce," said a woman's strong voice then from the direction of the table across the room, "that our guest speaker will not be joining us—"

Trelawny snorted, and the woman standing beyond him seemed to stir. Crawford heard exclamations of dismay in German and French from nearby circles. The man to Crawford's left was now peering at the speaker through a pair of opera glasses.

"—because of a sudden illness encountered on the river this morning. We hope to have her back with us soon."

Crawford hiked up in his chair to try to get a better view of the speaker—she appeared to be in charge, and McKee had said Carpace was hosting this affair—but he could only see that she was very wide and wore some sort of tall ornamental headdress.

"Therefore," the woman went on, "we'll proceed directly to individual recitals and political dialogues."

Crawford heard the notes of a flute start up somewhere in the middle of the long room, and farther away a man's voice began singing something dirgelike, and a young woman seated across from Crawford in this ring of chairs waved a sheaf of papers and announced, "If I may, I will read a passage from my *Lunar Encomium*."

A portly man beside her stood up and fetched a candle from a nearby table, and then he knelt by her and solicitously held the candle beside her elbow so that she could see the pages.

Trelawny leaned forward while she read the first several lines of her poem, about which Crawford was only able to discern that it was in iambic pentameter, but Trelawny soon leaned back and yawned audibly. None of the other people in the circle took note of it—apparently Trelawny was expected to be rude.

After perhaps a minute, the young woman stopped reciting, and since it was at the end of a line and the man with the candle had wobbled to his feet, Crawford concluded that it was over, but he didn't clap his hands until several others in the circle did.

The young man to Crawford's left sighed loudly and said, "Isn't she marvelous? So *very* like a gold-lit cloud at dawn." He beamed expectantly at Crawford.

"Incredibly like," said Crawford. The young man apparently expected more, so Crawford added, "It's uncanny."

Behind him, Trelawny laughed, and when Crawford turned around he saw that the old man had stood up and was walking away with his Junoesque robed companion.

Looking back down the room, Crawford saw McKee now—she was walking toward the woman who had addressed the crowd.

"May I borrow your opera glasses?" Crawford said to the young man beside him.

"My dear fellow," the man replied, lifting the ribbon over his head and handing them to him.

"You're very kind." The focus was sharp, and in a moment Crawford was viewing the woman as if up close; she was very fat, with tiny dark eyes that weren't made to seem bigger by the kohl dusted around her eyelids.

He saw the moment when she noticed McKee approaching—the woman's eyes widened and then narrowed, and she turned away, toward the table. From his viewpoint at the end of the room farthest from the doors, Crawford was able to see her poke the fingers of one hand into the neckline of her orange silk dress and lift out some small object. She bent over a row of wine glasses, then replaced the object in her bosom and straightened and turned around.

For several seconds she made a show of looking around at the various groups in the room, and then her gaze fixed on someone closer, and Crawford's view was blocked by the back of McKee's hat.

"Thank you," Crawford said, hastily handing back the opera glasses.

He hesitated for a moment, wondering how he would know if McKee's meeting with Carpace were to "go wrong"—what had that business been with the wine glasses?—and then he decided, a bit breathlessly, that even letting McKee confront the old woman alone would be wrong enough, and he began threading his way rapidly around the chattering groups toward the two women.

He had two fingers in the pocket of his waistcoat, nervously ready to pull out the vial of garlic and bite it open if some roaring monster appeared in the smoky air.

He approached the table from behind Carpace, if that was indeed who the fat woman was, and McKee had not noticed him yet. Carpace had slid two wine glasses forward across the tablecloth, but she was looking at McKee, and so Crawford reached out and reversed the glasses. Then he stepped back and said, "Am I intruding, ladies?"

McKee blinked at him in alarm and glanced around the room, but no devils seemed to be manifesting themselves. Still, he noticed that she stepped back to slightly increase the distance between them—and for just a moment he was distracted by her parted lips and wide eyes and chestnut hair, and the irrelevant realization that she was in fact very pretty.

"Hard to say," she answered. "Mr. Crawford, this is Miss Carpace."

Crawford looked away from McKee to the old woman.

Carpace turned to him with a smile that wrinkled her heavily powdered face. She was holding a decanter of red wine, and now she filled the two glasses and carefully handed one to McKee.

"*Enchante*, Mr. Crawford," she said in a husky voice, "but Miss McKee is a sad hand at foreign names." She waved her glass at the decanter. "Would you care for some wine? You must be the new poet."

"No, thank you," Crawford said, resolving, though, to pour a fresh glass for himself at the first opportunity. He too took a moment to look uneasily up toward the dark moldings in the corners of the vast room.

"Mr. Crawford," said McKee, "is the father of Johanna. He knows my entire history."

"Ah," said Carpace, giving Crawford a reassessing look, "but nothing's to be gained by stirring up our histories at this point, is there?" She lowered her voice and leaned forward. "What could be more dull, really, than an old whore and an old bawd and an old cad reminiscing?" She sipped from her glass. "You have family, friends, business acquaintances, I'm sure, Mr. Crawford. My name is Carpaccio, hmm?"

"Carpaccio," said Crawford, sweating with embarrassment. "Fair enough."

"And you've brought us some verse, I trust!"

Crawford remembered the lines from Southey in his pocket. "I hope not."

McKee touched her lips to the wine in her glass. "We need to know where the baby was buried."

"Well now, I'll tell you," Carpace said. "Miss Thistle, I must hear the newest canto!" she added more loudly to a woman who had bustled up to the table. "But excuse me a moment while I recommend a good book on grammar to these neophytes."

The poetess gave Carpace an amused, pitying glance and retreated into the dimly red-lit crowd.

Carpace drained her glass and put it down, then waved the decanter toward McKee. "Drink up, my dear, I know you love the stuff."

"I've given it up. Where is she buried?"

Carpace frowned, rippling her whitened forehead. "Given it up? Oh dear. Not even just one, for old time's sake? No? I see. Well, I can't really give you adequate directions in the midst of this affair, now can I? You can see that. Let's meet tomorrow, if you choose. Then I can even draw a map."

McKee was frowning too. "Very well, that will have to do. Where shall we—"

But the glasses and decanters on the table rattled as Carpace suddenly leaned her hips back against it, and she dropped her wine glass to claw furrows in the powder on her pendulous cheek.

"You," she whispered, "no, you were—" She turned clumsily toward Crawford. "*You* switched the glasses!"

Crawford just stared at her helplessly as McKee looked down at the dropped glass and then up at him with surprised comprehension.

Carpace's hips slid off the table edge and she sat down heavily on the floor. The bass-drum thud was followed by alarmed cries and hurrying footsteps, but McKee, and then Crawford, knelt on the carpet beside the panting old woman. Crawford's face was cold with sweat.

"Fetch an ave!" gasped Carpace. "Save me from Hell!"

"They don't do that," said McKee impatiently. "*Where is Johanna buried?*"

Carpace's eyes were wide. "Fetch the woman who's with Trelawny!"

"Tell me first."

"Ach, too late, too late, the damned stuff works fast." Her words were slurring. She bared her yellow teeth and squinted at McKee. "I'll leave the world with truth on my lips. Johanna is alive." She was barely able to articulate syllables now. "She—dith—did not—die."

Carpace sneezed, inhaled deeply, and expelled her breath in a sigh that seemed to go on far too long, and then toppled sideways against Crawford's quickly extended arm. Her head lolled loosely on his elbow, and her feathered headdress fell off her artificially darkened curls.

Crawford looked up in horrified bewilderment at the people who were now crowded around, and the first pair of eyes he met were those of the tall woman who had been with Trelawny—and he instinctively recoiled back from her, letting Carpace's head fall to the floor. As a boy he had once awakened to see a leggy black wasp on his pillow, and this reflex now brought that icy moment forcefully to mind.

Now the woman had glided closer, or else had got bigger. The chattering of the crowd seemed to slow and fall in pitch until it was isolated clicks in total silence.

The woman was taller now, with a stark red light on the vast marble planes of her face like sunset on the highest of the Alps, and the intelligence in her glittering eyes was alien and old, older than organic life. The mouth opened like a rift in clouds, and suddenly he was profoundly cold. The whole world seemed to tilt toward her.

When he had moved—when he had still been able to move—there had been the faintest tug against his cheek and forehead, as if he had blundered into a cobweb, and now his nostrils stung with the acid scent of freshly broken stone . . .

But it was immediately subsumed in a sulfury reek of garlic; and the rapid exclamations and questions all around crashed back in his ears, and the dimensions of the room and the people in it seemed to fall back to their normal proportions. Warm air tingled on his cheeks and forehead. Able to move again, Crawford glanced at McKee and saw that she had unstoppered a vial and spilled the mushy yellow contents into her hand and on the carpet.

Crawford's hand darted to the little bottle in his waistcoat, but the robed woman, once again just a tall woman, had flinched back, and her place at the front of the crowd was taken by ordinary people with anxious faces, and he decided to save it.

But the tall, gray-bearded figure of Trelawny pushed through the press of people then and knelt beside Crawford and McKee to peer at Carpace's limp body where it lay in dimness half under the tablecloth hem.

"You two glow," he growled. His lips were distorted by old scars into a snarl. "Did you come here to do this? You must be mad to come here, even with garlic."

"I needed to find out something from her," said McKee. Her lips were firm, but tears glittered in her eyes.

"Did you learn it?"

McKee shook her head.

Trelawny glanced sharply at her purse, though in the babel of querulous questions and shrill advice any noise her linnet made would surely have been drowned out. "You know Chichuwee?" asked Trelawny. "The Hail Mary man?"

"Of him," said McKee.

"See him." Trelawny glanced over his shoulder—Crawford followed his look, but didn't see the tall, robed woman in the jabbering crowd.

"Get out of here," said Trelawny. "Separately." Looking up, he said, loudly, "Apoplectic fit. Fetch a physician."

The crowd broke up then, some people hurrying away and some rushing forward to elbow Crawford and McKee out of the way, though no one jostled Trelawny.

McKee grabbed Crawford's lapel and pulled his head to hers. "Your house," she whispered, and then she had released him and disappeared in the dim light among the dozens of agitated poets.

Crawford stood up, and a woman caught his wrist—he jumped in alarm, but it was his client, the woman who had got him the invitation.

"Mr. Crawford, can you do something? You're a medical man!"

Crawford had the impression that Trelawny looked up at that remark, but he said to the woman, "I'm afraid she's gone. I believe it was her heart."

"Oh! How horrible!" She shook her head and stepped back, then went on distractedly, "Old Mr. Figgins is well, by the way."

Crawford had no idea who she was talking about. "Good, good," he said automatically, wondering where McKee might be, "tell him we must get together for dinner sometime soon. I'm sorry, you'll have to excuse me."

Before starting away he threw one more glance down at Trelawny. The old man met his eye and held up his hands, palms out, and then spread them and raised his eyebrows impatiently.

Baffled, Crawford held up his own hands in the same way.

Trelawny nodded with evident satisfaction and jerked his head toward the door before returning his attention to Carpace's inert body.

CRAWFORD DIDN'T SEE MCKEE on the street, though admittedly she'd have had to be very close for him to see her in the yellow-stained fog, and he flagged down a hansom cab on Bloomsbury Street.

As the cab whirred south through the fog, Crawford huddled on the single seat, squinting into the damp and chilly headwind, and he tried to fit the events of the last fifteen minutes into his experience; they were as vivid and loud in his mind as if they were still happening, all overlapped and at once, and he wished his house was farther away so that he'd have time to relegate them—come to terms, see priorities and comparative magnitudes—before meeting Miss McKee again.

For the moment he simply shied away from thinking about the woman who had been with Trelawny, the woman who had seemed to stop his identity, crush it; to remember the encounter might be to reexperience it.

And the old woman Carpace had *died* there, and he had caused her death—he could simply have knocked both glasses off the table, couldn't he? But that hadn't even occurred to him at the time. Even so, he might have supposed it was opium or some similar drug that would only have made the drinker lose consciousness . . . but in fact, to the extent that he had thought of it at all, he knew he had assumed that one of the glasses had been primed with a lethal poison.

It was to save McKee . . . but he could have broken the glasses. Instead, he had switched them.

Sweat on his face and in his hair made the headwind even more sharply chilling, but he welcomed the immediacy of it.

Apoplectic fit, heart attack, those were plausible—no one had seen him switch the glasses. And even if someone had, what business did Carpace have putting poison in a wine glass? And mightn't Crawford simply have a habit of idly moving objects around . . . ?

Hidden away under layers of cloth, his heart was shaking inside his ribs.

The woman with Trelawny had been like the moon falling out of the sky onto him—

He took a deep breath and held it, and when he exhaled, he told himself that the evening's scenes were falling away behind him with the steam of his breath.

The cab bounced across an intersection that he believed was High Holborn. He was just one anonymous Londoner among—what? a million?—in the foggy night.

He tried to imagine that his part in this entirely calamitous business was at an end. McKee had needed his help to get into that ill-starred salon—fair enough, and she had got it!—and now she could pursue her dubious quest alone.

He shifted uncomfortably on the damp leather seat at the memory of having found McKee attractive.

But her daughter—his daughter—was alive; according to that old dead bawd, at least.

I might have a living child, he told himself, cautiously tasting *that* thought.

Abruptly he remembered that Old Mr. Figgins was the name of his client's dog, and his face burned now as he remembered saying that he and Figgins must get together for dinner. Did his client imagine that Crawford intended to have the dog sit at the table, or that Crawford proposed to crouch on the floor and share the dog's dinner? Tomorrow he must send a note—

But the shallow evasive thought fell apart, leaving him with the weighty knowledge that he had a daughter, somewhere. She would be . . . six or seven years old now.

When the cab drew up in front of his house in the narrow lane that was Wych Street, Crawford had paid the cabbie and started up his steps before he noticed McKee leaning in the recessed doorway, out of the wind.

Thinking of *overlapping auras,* he quickly unlocked the door and led her into the parlor and turned up the gas jet. Cats, a few of them missing limbs, looked up incuriously from the couch.

"Shall I take your coat?" he asked neutrally, unbuttoning his own. His fingers were still trembling.

But McKee just laid her purse on the table by the couch and pulled the tiny cage out; she peered at the little bird for a moment, then set it down.

"I hope he shook all of this morning's salt out of his tail," she said. "With any luck, he *did* catch that old woman."

The old woman I killed, Crawford thought; and he threw his coat onto a chair and crossed to the mantel. The fire had gone out, and the room was chilly.

"Will it—save her from Hell?" he asked as he poured himself a glass of whisky. He looked from his glass to McKee. "Would you like . . . some tea?"

"No. And no, thank you. We have to be going. No, the bird might have caught her ghost, but her ghost isn't *her.*"

"Going? No, Miss McKee, I've—"

"You and I need to see a man." She was pacing the carpet by the table.

Crawford shook his head in bewilderment. "Who, that Vindaloo fellow that Trelawny mentioned? Fricassee? Look what time it is—he'll be asleep."

McKee frowned and halted. "Trelawny? That old bearded man was Edward John Trelawny?"

"Apparently."

"I think you saw the—the *woman* he was with."

Crawford cleared his throat and nodded, and he took a gulp of the whisky before he dared to speak. "Good thing you were quick with your garlic," he said finally, trying to put a light tone in his voice. "I"—he forced an awkward laugh—"almost tipped over and fell into her eyes."

"It would have been a long fall. And it's a good thing you were quick at switching glasses—I owe you my life, I believe." She blinked at him, then looked away and went on, "But Trelawny didn't . . . oppose us."

"No," said Crawford. He rubbed his free hand over his face. "In fact, before I left, he showed me the empty palms of his hands and made me show him mine. A . . . truce gesture?"

McKee shook her head. "He was establishing that neither of you is a member of the Carbonari. They all have a black brand on one palm. And it's Chichuwee, not Vindaloo." She canted her head and looked at him through narrowed eyes. "We need to go see him now, to save our daughter."

For several seconds neither of them spoke; the only sound was throaty mumbling from the bird. Finally, "We'll go in the morning," Crawford said. "You and I can't travel under a—a naked sky at night, correct?"

"It will be mainly . . . indoors. And she's *alive*! Put your coat back on."

Crawford tried to yell very quietly as he looked around the room and thought of his bed and the oblivion of sleep waiting for him upstairs.

His wife and younger son were dead, and Girard was . . . something like and unlike dead.

But this Johanna was, apparently, still alive.

He drained the whisky and, with huge reluctance, picked up his coat.

MCKEE WHISPERED, "YOU KNOW the Spotted Dog, on the next street?"

She and Crawford were standing in the recessed doorway of his house with the closed door at their backs. The night air was colder than ever, and her little birdcage was wrapped in a cloth in her handbag.

Crawford was hugging his coat around himself and shivering. "Of course."

"Meet me there. I'll walk west, around the old Inn of Chancery, and you go east, as we did this morning." He saw a quick smile on her face in the shadows, and she softly sang a couple of lines from a popular song: "'Meet me by moonlight alone, / And then I will tell you a tale.'"

And something-something at the end of the vale, thought Crawford, remembering the vapid lyrics. And was it, he thought forlornly, only this morning that this woman and I walked down to the Strand and got in an old hackney cab with that clerk? And the day's not done yet.

She had tapped down the steps and was hurrying away to his right, quickly disappearing in the shadows of the old overhanging houses that were now mostly used-clothing shops.

Crawford touched the lump under his coat that was the little bottle of crushed garlic, then sighed and descended the steps and set off to the east.

This end of the street was brighter, for the windows of the Angel public house glowed amber in the fog ahead of him, and, when he had rounded both corners of the place, he could see the blurry lights of the bookshops that had driven the old-clothes business into the next street—though the gigantic masks over the vacated costume warehouse still grimaced down from the murky shadows overhead as he passed by.

The Spotted Dog was at the far end of Holywell Street, almost to Newcastle Street, and Crawford, his gloved hands deep in his overcoat pockets, peered in at the shop windows he passed. Three-volume novels, newspapers, pamphlets denouncing Darwin . . . he wondered if the young authoress of the *Lunar Encomium* was represented by any published books. On the whole, he hoped not.

CHAPTER SIX

"Nay now, of the dead what can you say,
Little brother?"
(*O Mother, Mary Mother,*
What of the dead, between Hell and Heaven?)

—*Dante Gabriel Rossetti, "Sister Helen"*

MCKEE HAD ARRIVED at their rendezvous before he did and pulled the door open for him.

"We'll have to buy two tickets," she said, "even though we're only going downstairs." She had four pennies in her hand, and she pushed the big brown coins across the counter of a little window set into the wooden wall of the entry hall; and a moment later she turned and handed Crawford a dented tin card, keeping another in her gloved hand.

She gestured toward the open doorway beyond the counter, and Crawford shrugged and stepped through into what proved to be a vast kitchen lit by gas jets between the beams of the ceiling, with at least twenty people standing around on the flagstone floor or sitting on a bench that ran like a continuous shelf around the whole room. A big

black iron stove stood in a far corner, and something was cooking that
involved bacon and onions. Some people were lining up with plates.

Crawford looked hopefully at McKee, but she shook her head.
"Downstairs," she said, nodding toward a doorway in the back wall,
which was papered with posters announcing various music-hall per-
formers.

Crawford followed her across the room, promising himself a good
supper when he got back home.

A couple of the men on the bench called, "Addie!" and another said,
"Back in trade, girl?"

"Don't you just wish, Joey," she said to him, not pausing.

Beyond the doorway was a dark hall and a flight of wooden stairs
leading down. A cold draft welled up from below, smelling of wet clay
and wood smoke.

McKee paused at the top of the stairs to shed her coat and bonnet
and hang them on a couple of hooks in the wall. "Leave your hat and
coat here," she said. "And take off your gloves. You'll want to be able to
feel the walls."

Crawford sighed and carefully hung his coat and hat on another
hook and stuffed the gloves in his trousers pocket.

The stairs were unlit, and as McKee and Crawford descended below
the level of the floor, he held the banister rail and felt for each step with
his boot.

He was holding the little tin card in his left hand. "Will we need to
show these to anybody?" he whispered. "The tickets."

"Those are for bed check," came her voice from the darkness below
him. "We're not going to be sleeping here."

"No," he agreed, tucking the thing in his pocket on top of his gloves.
He peered uselessly upward, wondering what sort of beds the Spotted
Dog offered. "Shouldn't we have brought lanterns?"

"It's considered arrogant. There'll be light after a while, farther
down."

Considered arrogant by whom? he wondered. "Shouldn't we be talking in whispers?"

"Not yet. This is still the Spotted Dog basement, really."

The banister ended in a splintery stump, and as they descended farther he had to press his right palm against rough bricks.

Crawford cleared his throat and spoke a little more loudly. "You've been here before?"

"A couple of times. But there are ways down all over the City."

"Are we . . . going into the sewers?" Crawford had heard stories about feral rats and pigs that lived in the London sewers. "What I mean to say is—I'm not going into the sewers." Her definition of *downstairs* was proving to be more far-reaching than he had expected.

"*Old* sewers," she said in what was apparently meant to be a reassuring tone. "Ones that have been cut out of the system by newer ones. Just damp tunnels now, except when it rains. Right below us was a regular Phlegethon a couple of years ago, but the new interceptory Piccadilly Branch drained it."

"Phlegethon," said Crawford, largely to gauge the volume of the unseen space they were in by the way his voice rang in the dark. "Plato's flaming river to the underworld, in *Phaedrus*. You're well-read."

"This one caught fire too, sometimes. Oil and decaying ghosts on the water igniting—smoke coming up out of street gratings—you probably noticed it. I've always been one for having the nose in a book, and at Carpace's there was plenty of spare time for reading." He heard her pause below him. "Steps ending here, flat floor for a while. Not level, but flat."

"I," said Crawford carefully, "killed her. Carpace."

The sound of her steps changed from clumping on wood to tapping on stone, and he stepped carefully down onto the sloping floor.

"If you had not," McKee said, "she would have killed me." He heard her sigh. "I suppose I parade it, sometimes. Quoting things. So people at least won't assume I'm a *typical* ex-whore and Hail Mary dealer."

So much for Carpace, Crawford thought. "Not just one more of that lot," he agreed, and she laughed quietly.

"Your holy well is up ahead," she said. "Roman stonework, I'm told. It was probably on the surface once, along with a lot else—London keeps shifting underground. One day people will—" Her footsteps stopped. "Yes, here it is. One day people will have to go down into tunnels to see St. Paul's."

Crawford could see . . . not a glow, but a lessening in the darkness ahead; and after a few more steps, his outstretched palms collided with a waist-high stone coping. The smoky smell seemed to be rising from beyond it, and now it bore a faint salt-and-rot tang of the river.

Then McKee startled him by saying, loudly, *Origo lemurum.*

He jumped again when McKee's hand touched his face—she brought her head close to his and breathed in his ear, "Whispers from here on, I think. And not loquacious. Feel over the rim—there's rungs, leading down."

He let her carry his hand over the rim of the well and press it against the stones of the curved inner wall, and his fingers brushed an iron bracket.

Downstairs! he thought. "Is this the only way?" he whispered desperately.

"No. Best, for now."

Then she had released his hand, and he heard her long skirt rustle against stone; and when he heard a scuff from down in the well, he realized that she had swung over into the shaft and that one of her shoes was on a lower rung.

He was about to call her back and absolutely refuse to climb down—but the tunnel they were in apparently extended on past the well, and now he heard a sort of whistling moan from far away in that direction.

It was answered by a similar sound, but shriller and perhaps not so far away, from behind him.

He was sweating, and now he had to restrain himself from clambering over the well coping until he heard McKee's shoes on rungs a good distance below. Finally he slid one leg over the edge and scuffed around with his boot until it rested on the iron rung, and, trembling and mouthing frightened curses, he lowered himself into the well until he could feel the next rung down with his other foot. As soon as it seemed possible, he let go of the stone coping with one hand and grabbed the topmost rung, and after that he was able to descend steadily.

He had no idea how far behind his back the opposite wall of the well might be, and soon he had lost count of the rungs he had passed. He wondered vaguely if they were below the level of the river.

There were moths, or some other sort of silent-flying insects, in the shaft—the first one that brushed against his face almost startled him into letting go of his perch, but after several softly fluttering impacts against his face and hands, he was able to ignore them. Apparently they didn't sting.

The repetitive motions of descending the rungs became metronomic and almost mesmerizing, and he found himself imagining, very clearly, wooden forts barely crowding back forests along the Thames, the banks of which were notched in several places where wide fresh streams flowed into it.

His thoughts returned to his present situation when he realized that he could see the iron rungs in front of his face—dimly, but well enough to place a hand firmly on one without pawing at the wall first; though he still couldn't see any of the blundering winged insects. The river smell was stronger on the upward breeze, and it seemed to have a sour tobacco-smoke reek in it.

McKee's whisper sounded loud in the shaft: "Last rung—drop from here."

Drop? he thought. And get back up how?

But a moment later he heard her shoes chuff against something like sand, and soon his foot found no more rungs below to stand on, nor, when he swung it back and forth, any more wall.

He lowered himself to the last rung by the strength of his arms alone, and when he was hanging by both hands from the last rung, he opened his mouth to tell her that he was about to drop, but realized that she could tell where he was just by the noise of his breathing. Vaguely he could see the texture of some motionless surface below him.

He let go. For a dizzying second he was spread-eagled in empty air, and then the sandy surface struck his boot soles and his knee chopped him hard under the jaw, and he was sitting in loose, damp sand. The smell he had thought of as tobacco-like was stronger but now seemed more like sour, crushed seaweed.

McKee was standing, so he got to his feet, rubbing his chin and brushing the seat of his trousers, and he was cautiously pleased that there didn't seem to be any of the flying insects down here. His eyes had grown sufficiently accustomed to the dim glow to see that they were in a circular chamber with archways opening at irregular intervals around its circumference; he counted seven of them, and all of them showed blurs of many-times-reflected light in their farther reaches. The distant airy groaning was audible again, and he glanced around nervously, but he couldn't tell which arch or arches it might be echoing out of.

"What *is* that?" he whispered.

"A noise. Hush."

The caged bird chirped inside its handkerchief several times, and Crawford saw McKee's arm extend toward one of the arches, and then they had stepped through it and he was trudging along after her through the clinging sand, crouching to keep from knocking his head against the wet bricks of the low arched ceiling. To Crawford's relief, the only sound from ahead of them was a muffled chittering like crickets.

This tunnel curved to the left, and kept on curving, and Crawford soon realized that they were tracing an ever-tighter spiral; the light from ahead was brighter and distinctly yellow now, and the cricket sound was recognizable as the cheeping of many birds. A smell like rancid butter reminded him of chicken coops he had visited professionally.

And then McKee's chestnut hair glowed in direct lamplight, and she stepped to the left into a wood-floored circular room no more than fifteen feet across.

Crawford followed her in, and then squinted in the jarring glare of a paraffin lantern—it was mounted on the back railing of a wagon, which was either cut in half and mounted against the brick wall or was completely filling a farther tunnel. Only after he had taken in the cages full of small noisy birds stacked around the walls did Crawford notice the dwarfish, white-bearded figure sitting cross-legged beside the lantern.

"Look at the two of you!" the figure said in a deep voice. "A couple of doomed souls if I ever saw any. Which church did you come down?"

"St. Clement's," said McKee, speaking loudly to be heard over the shrill racket of the birds. "*Origo lemurum,* oranges and lemons. I'm Adelaide McKee—"

The birds all around them were chattering excitedly.

"You're a prostitute," said the dwarf. His lean old face held no evident expression.

McKee shook her head. "That's old news. I've changed careers. I'm a Hail Mary dealer now. Are you Chichuwee?"

"No, child, you've found the chambers of the prime minister. Of course I'm Chichuwee."

The dwarf swept his long white beard over his shoulder and hopped down from the cart, and the boards of the floor shook and boomed hollowly like a drum—apparently it was just a platform mounted over a deep shaft. Crawford eyed the arch they had come in through, ready to grab McKee and dive for it if the boards under their feet should shift.

He thought he could hear, over the incessant cheeping of all the birds, a clicking and rattling from the farther shadows of the cart.

"This," McKee went on, "is John Crawford."

"Husband, brother?"

"Neither one," said McKee hastily. "But he is the father of a child of mine, a little girl."

The dwarf limped forward and gave Crawford a disapproving look from under bushy white eyebrows, and Crawford met the gaze, reluctantly conceding that he deserved the disapproval—though it seemed unlikely that this creature might be a model of virtuous living himself.

A handshake seemed to be unlikely, so Crawford just nodded. After an awkward moment, he ventured, "Is that an Indian name? Chichuwee?"

The old dwarf just spat, and McKee said, "It's a birdcall. All the great old Hail Mary artists are named for birdcalls." To Chichuwee she added, "We need to get an answer from a person."

The dwarf shrugged. "Not difficult."

"It's a person who's dead."

"More difficult. Newly dead, I hope? Not lost beyond recall in the river?"

"Less than an hour ago, and I *may*," she said, "have caught her in my linnet." She held out her little handkerchief-wrapped birdcage. "It's Carpace, the old bawd. John here killed her—tricked her into drinking a glass of poisoned wine she meant for me."

"Carpace!" Chichuwee gave Crawford another look, perhaps more respectful. "She panders to a bigger sort of clients these days—ones that particularly like artists and poets. Even before you were born, she was drinking wine from amethyst cups at the Galatea under London Bridge." He frowned at McKee's bird. "She always loved her own self too much to surrender to that unhuman family, and she was savvy enough with her evasion tricks to keep from getting trapped by them. I bet now, though, she wishes she was due to be climbing up out of a grave, even if she wouldn't really be herself anymore."

The old dwarf now gave Crawford a somehow unflattering wink. "You weren't tempted to just take the ghost yourself?"

"He's not a Neffy!" said McKee, apparently insulted on Crawford's behalf.

Crawford blinked at her. "Take it?" he asked. "Neffy?"

"People who have let themselves be bitten by these devils," explained McKee. "They can sometimes catch a very fresh ghost, ingest it, and it supposedly gives them extra psychic strength—lets them control the people around them for a minute or so."

"Come in then," sighed the old dwarf, turning back toward the wagon, "and we'll see if we can get your answer."

"Will you question the bird?" Crawford asked.

"No," said the old dwarf. "The bird doesn't know anything."

McKee was carefully unwrapping the handkerchief from around the birdcage—Crawford saw that the bird had fouled the cloth square—and, holding it by one corner, she stepped after Chichuwee. As they drew closer to the lantern, they threw huge shadows across the tiers of birdcages on the curved walls.

Crawford reluctantly followed McKee out across the creaking floor toward the wagon, wrinkling his nose at the strong smell from all the birdcages.

"Sam!" called Chichuwee. "Get some river water boiling."

Behind the glare of the lantern Crawford now saw that there was a cabin set back on the bed of the wagon, for a pale child was peeking wide-eyed from a doorway in it. The child tossed two tiny white objects to Chichuwee and disappeared back inside.

The old dwarf tossed the objects to the floor, and Crawford saw that they were dice.

McKee turned and caught Crawford's chin in her hand. "Don't look at the numbers on them," she said. "But if you want to be helpful, you could pick them up and throw them, over and over again. Not looking, remember."

Crawford grimaced in anxious impatience but nodded and crouched; he scooped up the two ivory cubes and dropped them, then did it again.

"I'm going to have to be getting back to . . . streets, again, soon," he said.

"This water boils quick," said Chichuwee. "It's in a pot that's actually up in the Alps, so the air pressure is very low."

Crawford picked up the dice and let them fall. "But the pot is here—too?"

"Enough of it to boil water in," said the dwarf. "Be quiet now."

Crawford scowled at McKee, who just shrugged.

As he dropped the dice one more time onto the floor, it occurred to Crawford that he had been hearing this repetitive rattle ever since they had entered this chamber. Were these dice thrown perpetually, their numbers never read? Chichuwee must employ a relay of children to keep it up.

Three wooden steps beside the far wheel led up to the wagon bed, and Chichuwee and then McKee climbed up, skirted the lantern, and shuffled to the door the child Sam had peeked out of. Even Chichuwee had to crouch to fit through the open door, and McKee had to crawl through on her hands and knees.

"Dice, dice!" she called back over her shoulder, and Crawford hastily dropped the dice and snatched them up; and she added, "Follow."

The finches and larks around the walls seemed to echo the cadence of *"Dice, dice!"* and Crawford tossed the dice up onto the wagon bed and hastily scrambled up after them.

A curtain was sliding over McKee's back as she crept forward, and Crawford could see a glow of candlelight on her hands; then he crawled under the curtain too and found himself in a room he could stand up in. He remembered to toss the dice and scoop them up before getting to his feet.

This room clearly extended beyond the wall of the birdcage chamber, and, between shelves that were crowded with ragged books and obscure brass and crystal instruments, closed curtains implied windows in the varnished wood paneling that gleamed in the light of a dozen candles in glass chimneys.

The boy Sam was crouched over a low iron stove, watching water bubble in a glass pot; but when Crawford looked more closely, he saw that there was apparently no pot at all—the flat-topped ball of bubbling gray water was holding its shape with no visible containment.

Sam straightened and crossed to Crawford with his palm out, and then had to nudge him, for Crawford was gaping at the prodigy on the stove; finally the boy pried the dice from Crawford's limp hand and hurried away to resume throwing them in the corner.

"You know how this is done?" Chichuwee asked McKee.

"Yes." She set the birdcage on a shelf near the impossible volume of water. To Crawford, she said, "This will draw the ghost, if there's a ghost there."

Chichuwee nodded to her, and she dropped the soiled handkerchief into the boiling water. Steam immediately sprang up, and at this point Crawford was hardly surprised to see that the vapor didn't dissipate but instead floated over the water in a distinct wobbly oval.

"Lucky," said Chichuwee, shaking his head. "If it's her."

McKee crouched so that her face was level with the blob of steam while the handkerchief spun in the water below. Crawford noticed that, in spite of her show of confidence, she was trembling.

"Carpace," she said.

A whisper bubbled out of the water in puffs of vapor: "None of the officers wear waistcoats in the mornings . . . I travel with two canes, one for morning and one for evening . . ."

"Damn," said McKee, "it's that ghost that was buzzing around the bird by the Temple Arch this morning. *Carpace!*" Sweat gleamed on her forehead in the candlelight.

" . . . catch me, the ground quakes . . . ! I—*Adelaide.*"

"Got her," said McKee with feral satisfaction; then, to the vapor, she said, "You shouldn't drink."

"Drink," whispered the steam, "the glasses, the man switched them? Am I dead?"

"Yes."

"Ah, don't look at me!" The steam oval wavered. "Back in my ave!"

"Soon," said McKee, "and then you can share all the half-wit gossip of the ghosts. But first—you said my daughter is alive."

"Fly to the rooftops," the steam bubbled, "trade stories with the sparrows. Nobody looking at me."

"Yes," said McKee, "greet every dawn before the people in the streets below see it. Where is my daughter?"

"Her name is Johanna."

"Yes. Where is she?"

"Your man switched the glasses. Ach! I think I puked, in front of everybody."

"No, not a bit," McKee reassured the frail ghost. "It was as dignified a death as I ever saw. Where is Johanna?"

"I told you she died. At a different time than now."

"Yes. But then you said that she is still alive."

"Aye, she's alive, but—"

McKee waved her open hand. "But . . . ?"

"She's not well, to speak of."

"Tell me where she is."

"Why can't I think? Promise you'll put me back in the ave."

"I promise."

"Hope to die?"

"Hope to die."

"Fair enough. She's alive but pledged to death and eventual resurrection." The boiling water emitted several pops that Crawford thought might have indicated laughter. "I . . . adopted her out to the Nephilim."

Even though it was just an inorganic whisper, the last word seemed to concuss the still air.

Crawford gripped his elbows and held his breath so that it wouldn't hitch audibly. His mother and father had used the term *Nephilim* to describe the supernatural tribe they had escaped and spent the rest of their lives hiding from.

And he remembered his encounter with Girard, after Girard's death on the river . . . and the thing he and McKee had encountered seven years ago on Waterloo Bridge.

And, it occurred to him, the woman who had been with Trelawny tonight.

Can we . . . *oppose* those things? he wondered; surely not. But he was surprised at the anxiety and grief he felt for a daughter he had only learned of today and who he had thought was dead until an hour ago.

McKee's face in profile looked older and haggard, but she said, "Where can we find her?"

Crawford shuddered.

"This will be my first dawn, as a bird," babbled the steam.

"Where can we find Johanna?"

"Put me back in my ave and I'll take you there, over the rooftops."

"You'll move too fast. We need to walk where we go. Where can we find her?"

The steam said, "The river, now—it's cold and dark, and full of eely things."

McKee opened her mouth to repeat her question, but the steam went on, "Her father is swallowed in Highgate; she brings him flowers."

"Swallowed," said McKee, frowning, "flowers—is he buried? Is he buried in Highgate Cemetery?"

"Often I've seen Johanna there," whispered the blurry oval over the globe of water, "at night. Perhaps I'll fly to her now."

"Does she . . . *live* at the cemetery?"

"For now she does, I think. Soon she'll be busy being dead there."

McKee nodded at Chichuwee, then straightened up and took her birdcage from the shelf and handed it to Crawford. "Take this into the other room," she told him. "I don't want her getting back in."

Chichuwee was dropping handfuls of rusty nails and screws into the water now, and it stopped boiling.

Crawford nodded and crawled back through the curtain into the shaking cacophony of cheeping birds, and stepped down from the wagon to the creaking wooden floor. He walked quickly to the archway through which they had entered, and looked at the bright-eyed bird in the little cage he was holding.

"I imagine you're glad to be rid of her," he said quietly.

The bird just blinked at him.

A moment later Chichuwee and McKee emerged from the low wagon doorway; the old dwarf sat down on the wagon bed, nearly invisible again below the bright glare of the lantern, and McKee walked down the steps and crossed to where Crawford stood.

"Piping bullfinches," came Chichuwee's deep voice. "Two dozen of 'em."

Crawford saw McKee wince.

"And four dozen miscellaneous," the old dwarf added.

"That'd be larks and linnets, mostly, in winter," McKee said.

"Fine. And scrapings of church bells, Fleetditch or St. Catherine's." He glanced at the excited birds and then looked squarely at Crawford. "Any reason you got *cat* ghosts following you?"

Crawford actually looked behind himself but saw no diaphanous cat forms. "Uh," he said, "I'm an animal doctor. I—"

Chichuwee interrupted with a wave like a benediction. "You're mad if you try to find the girl," he said, "but in any case don't get killed before you pay me. Travel by day, wear metal, and do you know the crossing sweeper who takes only a ha'penny?"

"I know him," said McKee.

"Pass through the eye of his needle when you can."

"And you keep your dice rolling," said McKee.

She turned away and led Crawford back into the spiral tunnel, and the light quickly faded behind them. Crawford couldn't see at all now in the darkness after the hard light of the paraffin lantern. He remembered to keep his head down.

"Carpace won't get a bird to live in," he guessed. "An ave."

"No," came McKee's voice from ahead of him. "She's spilled into the sewers, and good enough for her—she'll wind up in the river with everybody else."

Crawford didn't say anything.

"Promises to ghosts don't count," McKee said. "They're promises to nobody." She plodded through the wet sand for a few moments, then went on, "Piping bullfinches he'll wait for, they need training, but he'll want the miscellaneous pretty quick. I'll have to bring my nets out to Hampstead or Tottenham—used to be I could get hundreds at Primrose Hill, but the railway has frightened them all away. But—" Crawford heard her fist hit the damp brick wall. "But merciful God, how will we get her away from the devils? She was such a sweet-natured baby!"

"I'd—bring a priest," said Crawford helplessly. "Two priests, big ones."

"I'm not sure what side of the line priests would see her on. But at least she hasn't died yet."

"If Carpace was telling the truth, in any of this."

"Ghosts are stupid, but they can't lie."

Crawford could tell by the curve of the brick wall under his sliding hand that the tunnel was straightening, and soon they were able to stand up in what must have been the circular chamber with the seven arches and the hole in the ceiling, though he still couldn't see anything.

From some direction he heard again the gasping, moaning sound he'd heard on the way down, and it seemed louder, or closer, now.

"How do we get back up the well?" he asked, barely remembering to whisper.

"We don't go back up it. Come on." She patted his arm and took hold of his hand and began leading him forward. "Two to the left from Chichuwee's is the way out." They were moving up a slope now.

"What *is* that noise?"

"*Vox cloacarum,* the voice of the sewers. Tide and pressure changes force air through all the clogged channels, and you get that."

The sound trailed off in indistinct syllables this time, though, and Crawford thought he heard sand shifting and rocks grating in the blackness behind and below them. His forehead was cold, and he was suddenly achingly aware of the vast volumes of earth above him, between the windy streets of London and this dark intestine of the earth.

McKee's hand brushed his face, and then one of her fingers pressed firmly against his lips; and she began tugging him along more quickly.

From behind them, echoing, came a woman's voice: *"John."*

Crawford's ribs went tinglingly cold. He didn't stop, but he looked back—a dim blue glow stained the darkness behind them, possibly beyond the curve of the low ceiling.

Veronica! he thought.

"That's my wife's voice," he whispered shakily.

"She's dead, I believe?"

"That's right."

"Keep moving. Don't say her name."

They plodded more quickly up the tunnel, their boots sloshing in muddy sand. Crawford dragged the fingers of his free hand along the wall and trusted that McKee had an arm extended in front of them.

The subterranean breeze was at their backs, and the seaweed-and-rot smell was gone—the air now smelled of mimosa.

"Her perfume?" whispered McKee.

A strangled syllable: "Yes."

"John," came the voice from behind again; Crawford could hear motion back down there, but the grinding sound seemed to imply a very big body moving. *"Be safe. Stay. Forget everything. Never be afraid again."*

The mimosa scent was stronger, cloying. To his surprise, Crawford found himself wanting to obey the voice; he didn't let go of McKee's hand or slacken his trotting pace, but the thing behind them was at least to some extent mimicking Veronica, his wife—wouldn't staying down here with an imitation of her, even a grotesque imitation, be preferable to his empty life in that unroofed world of cold sunlight so far above?

He remembered thinking, at the salon, that McKee was attractive—and now he couldn't understand why he had thought so.

The breeze from behind was coming intermittently now, in puffs—was it breath, her breath?

"Father," came a boy's echoing voice, closer, from back in the darkness. It was the voice of his younger son, Richard. Crawford moaned behind clenched teeth.

"Johanna is still alive," came McKee's breathless whisper.

That was right, he had a daughter up there somewhere.

But *pledged to death and eventual resurrection.*

"I named her," panted McKee, "after you."

John, Johann, Johanna. Six or seven years old now. Unbaptized, like the poor animals he cared for.

McKee pinched his thumb hard, and then gripped his hand tightly. Her hand felt hot.

"Stay with me," she said, quickening their pace still further and pulling him along. "I'm alive."

And so am I, he thought, suddenly very tired. And a thousand, thousand slimy things lived on, and so did I.

The dragging sounds from behind were louder. Crawford's legs were beginning to ache.

McKee said—no whispering now—"Do you have any iron, steel?"

Crawford thought about it as they jogged on upward through the darkness. "My watch," he panted. "The clockwork in it."

"A timepiece! Perfect. Quickly, stop and bash it to pieces against the wall. Don't drop any of the pieces!"

Crawford fished his watch from his waistcoat pocket, then slid to a halt and broke a fingernail prying the back cover open; holding the watch cupped in his hand, he slammed it against the brick wall while pressing the open palm of his other hand against the bricks below it to catch any falling pieces.

"Drop the watch, John," echoed the approaching voices of his wife

and son, *"time doesn't matter here."* He could hear wet sand shifting only yards away, and the mimosa perfume was failing to cover a smell of fermented decay.

After two more rapid spasmodic blows, he had a scant, bristly handful of what felt like tiny gears.

Something webby and wet brushed his face and he convulsively lashed out, flinging the bits of metal in a wide arc behind him.

The clinging membrane was snatched away, and he spun his wrecked watch on its chain and slung that toward the voices too. The air shook with a sound like dozens of castanets.

McKee yanked him back by the collar, and then the two of them were running.

"That's stopped *them* for now," she panted, "and we're nearly out."

Crawford forced himself to look only forward. I'm sorry, Veronica! he thought.

And now he could see a tall, dim, round-topped shape—it was a volume of dimly lit space on the far side of a dark archway, and in moments they had skidded around the left-hand side of the arch; a wide knobby surface slanted up in front of them, and when McKee let go of his hand to begin scrambling up the incline, he followed her and realized that he was climbing up, or rather across, the face of a toppled building. A rounded stone bar across his path was an attached column, and he followed McKee as she skirted a semicircular hole that was the top of an arched doorway.

The faint illumination was coming from above them, and when they had climbed around a wide balcony and were scrambling between the holes of windows, he recognized the white glow as moonlight.

"What—*is* this?" Crawford gasped.

"A first-century Roman building," came McKee's reply, "wrecked when Boadicea destroyed London."

Knocked right over sideways, thought Crawford with some awe as he continued climbing.

At last they came to the highest corner of the building—it was a rounded berm of masonry in front of them, probably the middle of a now-diagonal turret—and the moonlight was slanting in through a rectangular hole some twenty feet overhead.

"It's an easy climb now," said McKee, pausing, "and we should leave separately. We'll come up in a yard off Portugal Street, only a few streets from your house."

"Why didn't we come down this way?" panted Crawford. "It looks easier than that well."

"For getting out, it is. Entering requires protocol, though—those ghost-moths would have been . . . different, if we had tried to avoid the well and the incantation." There was enough moonlight for him to see her brush her dark hair back from her forehead. "Tomorrow we need to visit somebody."

"I've got business, horses to see," said Crawford, standing on the gritty curved surface of the ancient turret wall and staring longingly up at the patch of moonlight. "I'm afraid I won't be—"

"This woman can help us save Johanna," McKee interrupted, "if anybody can. She knows about these things."

"Another of your—your Hail Mary artists?"

"No—she's a poet, actually—though not the sort to have been at that salon tonight. And she's a sister at the Magdalen Penitentiary for Fallen Women . . . which happens to be right near Highgate Cemetery. Her name is Christina Rossetti."

Crawford had never heard of her.

"After my surgery hours, then," he said. "Noon, say." He was still staring up at the moonlight. "Portugal Street? Near St. Clement's?"

"Near enough. Within the *origo lemurum* incantation."

"What's that mean?" he asked. He was squinting at the slope ahead and bracing himself for the last bit of climbing. "You said it, earlier."

"You've got to placate the old . . . gods or devils or whatever they are, who are confined down here. Protocol. *Origo lemurum* is Latin for something like 'maker of ghosts,' I'm told. You remember it by 'oranges and lemons, say the bells of St. Clement's.' The old rhyme gives invocations for other ways down too, near other churches."

Churches, thought Crawford bitterly. No wonder I stay away from them.

McKee waved at the muddy slope that led up to the street. "You go first; I'll follow in a couple of minutes. And I'll be at your door at noon tomorrow."

Crawford was already wondering when he might conveniently get his coat and hat back from the Spotted Dog, but he asked, "You'll be safe here? By yourself?"

He saw her exhausted smile. "Quite safe, thank you for asking."

He hesitated, suddenly reluctant to leave her. "That watch was seven years old," he remarked. "I bought it after ruining my last one when we dove into the river."

She shrugged. "I owe you a lot of time."

He smiled, then turned away and plodded to the embankment; it was in shadow, but it wasn't steep, and the timbers and masonry of buried and long-forgotten buildings made climbing easy enough. Within minutes he had clambered up out of a coal chute in a street he didn't recognize—men were smoking clay pipes on a set of steps nearby, but none of them appeared to see anything odd about Crawford's entrance into the scene—and after he had walked randomly through several sharply turning streets, he found himself at the broad lanes of the Strand, facing the spire of St. Clement Danes.

And this is where you started this morning, he thought bewilderedly, turning his weary steps toward home.

CHAPTER SEVEN

I will keep my soul in a place out of sight,
Far off, where the pulse of it is not heard.

—*Algernon Swinburne, "The Triumph of Time"*

CHRISTINA LOOKED AWAY from her gentleman caller, who sat on the sofa a few yards away across the carpet, but her wandering gaze happened to fall on her mother's treasured portrait of Uncle John Polidori on the wall over the slant-front desk, and so she reluctantly looked back at Charles Cayley, who was leaning forward earnestly.

"They're so . . ." he began.

Seconds ticked by on the old clock on the mantel. Christina remembered her father winding that clock every Sunday, in their old house in Charlotte Street.

She sighed, catching a whiff of Cayley's liberally applied cologne. The tea was getting cold in the pot, and Cayley had eaten all the digestive biscuits. Perhaps his stomach was out of order.

She recalled that she and Cayley had been talking about his recent translation of the Psalms. He had published it at his own expense, and the Rossetti family had charitably subscribed for a dozen copies.

". . . savage!" he finished at last.

"True," she agreed. "God was raising the Jews by steps from barbarism to a state in which they could receive His son, and they *were* still genuine barbarians, in those early steps."

"But to ask a blessing!—in the otherwise sublime 137th Psalm—on anyone who would knock the brains out of a Babylonian infant! I don't—"

He was off in a pause again. Sunlight outside made the lace curtains glow behind Cayley, and all Christina could clearly see of him was his balding head and his ears and the edges of his beard, but she knew he would be faintly, awkwardly, smiling.

Christina's mother was pottering about in the kitchen and would not interrupt what she saw as, what might in fact be, a courtship. But Maria would, mercifully, be home soon.

Christina poured out the last of the tea in the pot into Cayley's cup, and she was about to use the emptied pot as an excuse to join her mother for a few moments in the kitchen when three clanks on the front door knocker made both her and Cayley jump.

Lillibet the housekeeper would answer the door in a few moments, but Christina stood up to answer it herself, glad of the opportunity. "Excuse me a moment, Charles."

She hurried to the hall, and paused to look in the mirror between two potted geraniums to make sure her hair was not pushed up in the back from slouching in her chair. Maria would not have knocked.

When Christina pulled open the front door, squinting in the sunlight and the winter breeze, she smiled at the respectably dressed man and woman who stood on the doorstep. They were probably students from Maria's Sunday Bible class, come to ask a question or return a book.

Then the woman pushed the bonnet back from her brown hair, and Christina recognized her.

"Adelaide!" she exclaimed wonderingly.

Cayley, always socially inept, had shuffled up behind her, his old-fashioned tailcoat flapping in the chilly draft.

"Adelaide *Procter?*" he asked brightly.

Cayley evidently supposed this was the devoutly Christian poetess who did volunteer work for homeless women and children in Bishopsgate.

"Hardly," laughed Christina without thinking, distracted by the uncomfortable sunlight. Then, embarrassed, she smiled and said, "Won't you come in, Adelaide? And—?"

"This is John Crawford," said Adelaide McKee, stepping into the hall and unbuttoning her coat. "You remember I had a daughter? John is the father."

Christina suppressed a frown—at the Magdalen Penitentiary the reformed prostitutes were told that they must not reestablish contact with characters from their degraded pasts, and this was certainly a violation of that rule. And Christina recalled now that McKee had never agreed to leave London either.

But in the heat of embarrassment, Christina had already invited them in. And she could hardly ask poor Cayley to leave.

She introduced the company to one another, and Cayley was blushing behind his beard, and his nervous smile was broad. Clearly he had gathered that this couple was not married.

"Do join us in the parlor," Christina went on bravely. "I was just about to have a fresh pot of tea brought in."

For a moment she thought McKee had tittered at the remark, and she dreaded an uncomfortable conversation, then realized that McKee had a bird in her handbag.

That, at least, was a good sign. "Keeping the Hail Mary dealers busy?" Christina said.

"I am one now," said McKee. "With, in fact," she added, glancing toward her dubious companion, "a tall order at the moment."

"I'm glad to hear it," said Christina sincerely. "Honest work, lots

of fresh air." She led the company back into the parlor, and when all
three of her guests were seated and blinking uneasily at one another,
she leaned through the kitchen door.

"Visitors from the Magdalen," she told her mother. "Could you ask
Lillibet to bring us another pot?"

She sat down beside Cayley and gazed frankly at Adelaide's companion. Mr. Crawford didn't look depraved, sitting beside her with
his bowler hat in his lap—his dark brown hair and beard were neatly
trimmed, and he had the air of a professional man, or a scholar, caught
in embarrassing circumstances.

"What do you do, Mr. Crawford?" she asked.

The man shifted uneasily. "I'm a veterinary surgeon, Miss Rossetti—a horse doctor. I have a surgery in Wych Street."

Emboldened by this sally, Cayley turned his nervous smile on Ade-
laide and said, "Hail Mary dealers?" The presence of strangers made
Christina aware again of how high pitched his voice was. "Are you a
Roman Catholic, Miss McKee?"

Christina knew that Cayley didn't think much of Catholics. "It's slang
for dealers in live songbirds," she said, and blew a stray strand of hair out
of her face. "*Ave,* from *avis,* in Latin—calls to mind *Ave Maria*—hence
Hail Mary. The big markets for them are in Hare Street and Brick Lane."

"And no, I'm not Catholic," said McKee. "Their standards are too
high." She faced Christina. "I'm sorry to burst in on you this way, but
our daughter—well, you remember I thought she was dead? We have
it from a reliable source that she's alive after all. Possibly living around
Highgate."

"Oh, that's wonderful!" exclaimed Christina. "Can you find out
exactly where she's living? Could your 'reliable source' help?"

"Unhappily not." She glanced toward Cayley, then back at Christina, and shrugged. "It was the old bawd Carpace, and she was a ghost
when she told us as much as she did. And now she's—" McKee made a
diving gesture.

"Ah." Christina nodded. "In the river with the rest of them."

Mr. Crawford seemed surprised that Christina knew of such things.

Charles Cayley raised a hand, and Christina turned to him.

"Is—there more tea coming?" he asked.

"Yes, in a moment. Charles, this—"

"Spiritualism?" he said. "I assume? Christina, by the affection which I may be so bold as to say I hold for you—ah—"

McKee caught Christina's eye and raised her eyebrows.

"—I have to remind you," Cayley went on, and then he paused.

After a few seconds, McKee said, "Miss Rossetti, I apologize. John and I shouldn't have interrupted. We can come back—"

"No, no," said Cayley, "it's I who should be—"

The front door latch rattled then, and heavy boots thumped on the hallway carpet.

That must be Gabriel, Christina thought. Maria would have been better.

And a moment later Gabriel appeared in the doorway, tossing aside a broad-brimmed hat and unwinding a straw-colored scarf from around his neck and looking more dissipated than ever—his dark hair was falling down in oily curls over his forehead, his eyes looked pouchy and sunken, and his cheeks around his goatee were bristly.

He cast an incurious glance over Christina's guests, then said to her, "I'm thinking of fetching in a priest, a Catholic one. They're the lads for exorcisms."

"A priest," said Christina, flustered, "might throw out the baby with the baptismal water. Oh dear, this is all so—"

"She's alive, at least," Gabriel went on. "At the moment. She even wants to go out to dinner tonight. But if we can't detach the devil's hooks—"

McKee had stood up, and Gabriel frowned at her.

McKee said, "Excuse me. But—could you—push your hair back?"

Gabriel opened his mouth, then shut it. "No," he said finally.

"No," said McKee, "you don't have to, I know your voice too. I never forget a client. You're the man who advised me to enroll at the Magdalen Penitentiary, one night seven years ago. It was in Mayfair, do you remember? You said the priests and sisters at Magdalen could help me . . . undo the bad connections I'd made."

"Oh, *Gabriel*," said Christina reproachfully. "Mayfair? The Argyle Rooms, the Alhambra? Kate Hamilton's on Prince's Street?"

"No," put in McKee, "I was trolling under Carpace's colors."

Christina turned to McKee. "North of the river in a borrowed dress? She must have trusted you, to let you wander so far from Griffin Street."

Both Cayley and the Crawford fellow were looking from one speaker to the other in evident dismay.

"My young daughter," said McKee, "is in the same peril as this woman you're referring to, I believe. We're talking about the Nephilim? 'The giants that were in the earth in those days'? I agree with Sister Christina about the perils of calling in a priest."

Gabriel was squinting at her. "Daughter?" he asked hollowly.

"By this man," said McKee, waving toward Crawford. "Put your mind at ease—about that, at least."

Crawford was still sitting on the sofa, and he and Gabriel exchanged an embarrassed and unfriendly glance.

The Rossettis' housekeeper bustled in then with a tray on which sat a teapot and four cups.

"Mr. Gabriel!" she said. "I'll fetch another cup." She set the tray down and returned to the kitchen.

"Never mind, Lillibet," Christina called after her. "Charles, I must beg your forgiveness here, I—"

"Yes," said Cayley, getting to his feet. "We can talk another time." His face was red, and his bald scalp was gleaming. "I fear that your volunteer work among the lower—excuse me—among the unfortunate, has—has—"

"Lower—?" began Crawford, getting to his feet; Christina sent him an imploring glance, and he sat down again, grumbling.

Gabriel laughed, and it pained Christina to see her youthful brother for a moment in that prematurely sagging face.

"If you will all forgive me," said Cayley in his piping voice, "it's been a—I certainly never meant to—but I'm afraid I must—" He bowed and scuttled out of the room.

Nobody spoke until they heard the front door click shut and the knock of boots descending the front steps.

"Poor Charles," said Christina.

"The man's an idiot," said Gabriel. He glanced at the clock on the mantel. "Is that right? Half past noon?"

"I wouldn't know," said Crawford sourly. "My watch is in fragments down a well."

Gabriel nodded. "That's the spirit. It's damnably sunny out, but I think we should take this conference to the park, so as not to disturb Lillibet with talk of devils."

"Lucky thing for you that you had that watch," McKee told Crawford as she got to her feet. "Or the devils would be digesting you right now."

Crawford shrugged and nodded. "Both of us," he said.

Christina sighed. "Let me get my coat and a bonnet."

"And a parasol," advised Gabriel, picking up his scarf and hat. "The sun is like a lion."

REGENT'S PARK, TWO STREETS away to the west, was a landscape of black trees and iron fences standing up in a carpet of old snow under a deep blue sky. The road linking the inner and outer circles was marked by a few tracks of hooves and boot prints, but aside from Crawford and McKee and the two Rossettis, the only figure in the landscape was a man walking an ungainly dog a hundred yards away.

As if the dark old houses they had passed had been huge, blank-eyed brickwork heads poked up out of the pavements to spy on them, they had not spoken until they were past even the tall white Cumberland Terrace houses on the park's eastern boundary and had crossed the outer circle and were well out onto the park grounds.

Crawford couldn't even see any birds, and McKee's linnet was silent—the only sounds were the wind in the bare branches and the crunch and slither of boot soles on the snow-drifted gravel.

Finally Christina's brother Gabriel spoke. "It's my wife—she seems to be dying, and I don't want—" He waved helplessly.

"You don't want her to come back," suggested McKee, staring down at the path as she walked. "If she does die."

"What I *want* is for her not to *die*," Gabriel said angrily. "This isn't a—a game, you know—we're talking about a woman's *life*. And an unborn child's too—she's apparently—"

"Believe me," interrupted McKee in a flat voice as cold as the wind, "I know it's not a game. You brought this to me, like a disease, and now my daughter is likely to die of it. I want *her* not to die too—but if she does, I want to see that she stays dead."

"You said," intervened Christina, blinking anxiously in the shadow of her parasol, "that your daughter might be living in Highgate."

McKee nodded. "That's what old Carpace's ghost said. She said she had seen the girl in the cemetery—that the girl's father was buried there."

"*Swallowed* there," Crawford corrected.

"Swallowed, buried," said McKee impatiently. "And she brings him flowers."

"Her father," said Christina. "But I thought you, sir, were the child's father?"

Crawford opened his mouth, intending to say *allegedly*, but instead simply said, "Yes."

"Ghosts don't lie," said Christina thoughtfully, at which Gabriel snorted.

"Adoptive father, I imagine," said McKee. "The . . . the vampire."

"Oh," said Christina. "Of course."

"*Our* father is buried at Highgate," said Gabriel.

"He's safe," said Christina. "He died clean, with God's name on his lips and in the midst of garlic and cold iron."

Crawford glanced at Christina Rossetti—Sister Christina!—and wondered if this serious and respectable young lady might know even more about the occult world than McKee did.

"And we know," said Gabriel, "who the vampire father is." His eyes glittered under the broad brim of his hat.

Christina sighed, blowing away a plume of steamy breath, and Gabriel gave her a look that seemed almost reproachful.

"Over there," said Christina, pointing with her free hand away across the white-dusted dead grass plain to the right, "are the zoo cages."

She stepped off the path and onto the faintly crunching grass. The skirts of her coat flapped around her boots.

"We've got more privacy out here," said Gabriel impatiently, following her.

"There are cages outside the wall," Christina said, "on the west side. They're empty in the winter, nobody'd be out there on a day like this."

McKee and Crawford looked at each other and shrugged, then trudged after the Rossettis.

"Sister Christina," called McKee, "who *is* the vampire father?"

Christina swung her parasol aside and looked back over her shoulder, still walking. "You deserve to know, since one of us woke him and the other brought him to you. It's our uncle, my mother's brother. His name is—"

"Best left unsaid!" interrupted Gabriel. "Even in daylight."

"Your *uncle?*" exclaimed McKee, stopping on the grass.

"Yes." Christina halted too, and she tucked the parasol handle under her arm to take hold of McKee's hand; and with the forefinger of her gloved right hand she began stroking McKee's palm. After a moment Crawford realized that Christina was drawing a series of letters.

"I know you can read, Adelaide," said Christina. "Can you remember that name?"

"Yes," said McKee, frowning down at Christina's scrawling finger, "yes, but if it's—"

"He killed himself in 1821." Christina released McKee's hand and resumed walking, gripping the parasol handle again. "He had tried to enter a monastery, but they wouldn't have him—I can't blame them, since by that time he was—" She waved vaguely.

"Pledged to death and eventual resurrection," suggested McKee with a brittle smile as she stepped after her.

Gabriel was striding along beside Christina, but Crawford took a moment to look around at the desolate park grounds before rejoining his peculiar companions. The man with the dog had passed them, well to the north—Crawford noticed that the dog appeared to be tied up in some sort of flapping shawl against the cold.

Christina was still leading the way across the frostbitten grass, and Crawford saw her bonneted head nod. "Not the resurrection Christ bought for us."

"I knew," began McKee, and Crawford could see that she was speaking carefully, "that Mr. Rossetti here—"

"Call me Gabriel," said Christina's brother in a tight voice; and Crawford remembered, with a surprising surge of jealousy, what McKee had said yesterday morning when she had asked Crawford to call her by her first name: *I think we can consider ourselves amply introduced.* Of course she and this Gabriel fellow with his foolish hat had been similarly . . . *introduced.*

McKee went on in a tight voice, "I knew that Gabriel had brought— your uncle's!—attentions to me, and to my daughter. But do you say *you—woke* him?"

Christina's shoulders rose and fell. "I did. I was fourteen."

"Our father forced it on her," said Gabriel gruffly, taking his sister's arm as they all trudged across the grass.

"At first I thought it was our uncle's *ghost*," said Christina. "Well, it was, in a way. I invited him in because I felt sorry for him, and he *was* family . . . but it wasn't really him, not really."

"Our father," said Gabriel, "had a little statue that he'd acquired in Italy. No bigger than your thumb. We always, even as children, knew it was alive."

"It wore the doomed soul of our uncle," Christina went on, "but it was one of the—a dormant, petrified, *condensed* member of the—well, you know the term that Gabriel would advise me not to say out loud here. The tribe that troubles us, the giants that were in the earth in those days."

The Nephilim, thought Crawford with a shudder. They were mentioned in the Old Testament book of Genesis, and the writer of the book of Numbers described encountering them: *we became like grasshoppers in our own sight, and so we were in their sight.*

The man with the dog had reached the eastern edge of the park, but he had paused in the outer circle road.

"That," said McKee, "would have been in about 1850?"

"1845," said Christina, glancing back at her in evident surprise.

"They had been dormant then for twenty or thirty years," said McKee. "From about 1850 onward, they've been active again." To Gabriel she said, "It was 1855 when you brought your uncle to me." She shook her head and gave Crawford a wide-eyed look. "Was I right about coming here? We've found the monster's very *family!*"

"It's true," said Christina mournfully.

Crawford was looking at her, and so he didn't see why Gabriel had abruptly leaped to one side and drawn a revolver from under his coat and McKee was suddenly crouching and holding a short-bladed knife; both of them were squinting past Crawford to the east.

Crawford spun in that direction, losing his footing and falling to one knee as his left hand tore open his coat so that his right could dive into his waistcoat pocket.

The dog in the shawl was sixty feet away and rushing directly at them, tearing up spurts of snow and dirt—and somehow its lunging head was entirely wrapped in gray cloth—

—Crawford's vision narrowed in shrill shock when he realized that it wasn't a dog at all, but a little misshapen human figure, wrapped in cloth like a mummy, its knees and elbows flexing rapidly like spider limbs as it ate up the intervening ground—

A loud bang like a hammer on stone numbed Crawford's ears, and the rushing figure did a ragged backflip, spasmodically ripping at the ground even as it still slid heavily toward them; Gabriel's second shot stopped its slide, and his third and fourth shots shook the creature violently. Faint echoes of the shots were batted back from the distant Cumberland Terrace housefronts.

Crawford stared, the wind cold on his wide eyes—the thing's limbs were retracting; it was shrinking inside its flapping cloth coverings even as it thrashed furiously.

The frozen ground seemed to shiver, and for a moment the ringing in Crawford's ears seemed to be a remote chorus climbing through impossibly high notes to inaudibility.

Gabriel fired his revolver twice more at the heaving pile of cloth; bits of thread and sprays of black dirt flew away from the ragged holes.

The man who had been walking with the thing was running up now, but he was running a good deal more slowly than the creature had, and he was still twenty yards distant. He was carrying a black angular case, and Crawford wondered if he were a doctor. Far too late, he thought.

Crawford looked back at the women. Both were standing and staring at the subsiding cloth-covered mound. McKee caught his eye and actually grinned, tensely.

Crawford found that he couldn't smile. His face was stinging with sweat, and his hands were shaking.

Gabriel lowered his pistol, panting hoarsely. He glanced at Crawford beside him and nodded. "Garlic in the bottle?"

Crawford could barely hear him over the ringing in his ears, but he nodded.

"Not useless, if you could have got it open in time."

"Is it dead?" Crawford asked, sure that he was speaking too loudly but wanting to hear his own voice.

"No," said Christina, stepping up beside her brother. "It will have burrowed into the earth, I imagine."

"Injured, though, definitely," said Gabriel. He wiped his mouth with his free hand.

"Can you reload?" asked Crawford, nodding toward the man who was striding toward them now. It was, Crawford saw, an old man in a black Chesterfield overcoat and a black silk hat, and the object he was carrying was a violin case. All Crawford could make out of his face was a white beard and dark features—but he recognized him.

Apparently McKee did too. "I don't think you'll need to shoot him," she said, though she had not yet put away her knife.

"It takes me half an hour to reload this," Gabriel muttered. To Christina he added, "I *shot* that thing, did you see?"

The old man paused on the far side of the now-motionless lump of cloth on the frosty grass, and with the toe of his boot he flipped most of the fabrics aside. Underneath was a mound of fresh-churned dirt.

He looked up at the four people on the other side of the mound, and for a moment his scarred lips seemed to be sneering; then his lean brown face flexed in a wolfish smile.

"She'll be a thing like a crab now," he said. "No use digging for her; you won't catch her and she'll still weigh upward of two hundred pounds—you'd never lift her."

"Who the bloody hell are you?" demanded Gabriel, still visibly shaky. "And what *was* that thing?"

Edward Trelawny shook his head impatiently. "Don't waste my time. You know what it was, or you wouldn't have had a gun loaded with silver bullets, now would you? Nothing else could have done that to her. Well, gold may be a better electrical conductor, but I doubt someone like you could afford gold bullets." He laughed. "As to who I am, it's better you don't know, and I don't want to know who you are. Even a captured mind can't reveal what it's never learned, right? If you all have any brains, you don't know each other's names either, but I suppose you haven't any brains, walking around in a damn clump out here like red flags in front of a bull. Are you *surprised* that you drew the bitter attentions of"—he waved back toward the pile of dirt—"*her*?"

He made a tossing motion toward Crawford and McKee. "You two especially! You killed her Judas Goat last night—you might have had the sense to lay low."

"By daylight—" began Crawford weakly.

"I knew you were a fool the first time I laid eyes on you, sitting in that ring of failed poets. Daylight. She's mighty hampered in daylight, but not immobile. She'd have torn *your* empty heads off."

Christina surprised Crawford by stepping forward and saying, "You can call me Diamonds."

"Hah!" said Gabriel. "At that rate I'm Hearts."

Christina gave McKee a frail smile. "A childhood game," she said. "We have a sister we called Clubs and a brother we called Spades."

"You," said Trelawny, pointing at McKee, "I'll call Rahab."

McKee blinked and frowned, and Crawford guessed that she wasn't entirely pleased to be given the name of the Biblical ex-prostitute who betrayed Jericho to the Hebrews; but she nodded.

She pointed at the violin case in the old man's hand. "Are you a musician?"

"Not me, no." Trelawny turned to Crawford and went on, "You're a medical man, I heard, so I'll call you Medicus. In fact, you look uncannily like a medical man I knew in Italy years ago, but we'll let that go."

"If you like," said Crawford. His father *had* been a physician, and *had* been in Italy in the 1820s, but Crawford couldn't recall his parents mentioning Edward Trelawny.

"And call me Samson," Trelawny said. "My spiritual hair has almost completely grown back, I believe. I hope." He glanced at the scattered cloths and the mound of dirt on the grass, and then looked up at all four of them. "You've left me unchaperoned, for a few days at least. It may be that we can help one another. Where were you walking to, so carefree?"

Christina nodded toward the long wall at the north end of the lawn. "The zoo cages outside the wall," she said, "on the north side of the outer circle just below the canal. They're for cassowaries and zebras, and they're empty in the winter. If we could find one around the back where nobody's likely to be, on a day like this, and get into it, with cold iron bars on all sides—"

"Ah!" said Trelawny. "I could see from the start that you're the only one of your lot with any sense, Diamonds. The iron bars, yes, they should hide our auras just as a Faraday cage deflects electric fields—block our radiances, keep the other big one from sniffing us."

"The other big one," said Gabriel.

"We can discuss it when we're caged," said Trelawny, "like a pack of sickly cassowaries."

CHAPTER EIGHT

It was not daring . . . to bring Miss B. to Cefn Ila, and set her up to be worshipped there. But society was justly scandalized by the spectacle of this shaggy Samson carrying the diminutive form of Delilah to and from his carriage at the foot of Shanbadoc Rock—his Delilah was not even pretty, if the memories of my informants are to be trusted.

—M. B. Byrde, "Trelawny at Usk," *Athenaeum, August 1897*

W HAT IS 'THE other big one'?" asked McKee.
They had found a row of empty and unlocked cages well west of the offices of the superintendent and ducked into the farthest one, pulling the barred door nearly closed behind them. Bare trees hid them from most of the park.

"If anyone *should* stroll by," advised Trelawny, "all of us just make hooting sounds and hop up and down. Scratch."

Gabriel giggled. "One of us sh-should—be outside to t-take money," he stammered, and then he coughed and scowled around at the others.

They were shaded from the bright sunlight by a wooden roof that extended out past the rows of vertical bars confining them, and the wind that whistled through seemed much colder than it had outside. The black bars were ornate with stylized ironwork vines and flowers at the tops, but the cage was no more than ten feet square, and though wide shelves had been bolted to the bars at various heights, all five of them remained standing. Any smells the cage might once have had were lost in the stinging astringence of the icy air. Crawford thought of taking off his hat, but neither of the other two men did, so he left it on.

"The other one," said Trelawny, sliding his violin case onto a shelf and pulling a cigar from inside his coat. Crawford noticed that the old man wore no gloves or scarf. "Miss B., who you just now shot, has a *partner*. He was a doctor too," the old man said, nodding to Crawford, "when he was a normally living man. Name of Polidori. I never met him, but we had friends in common."

Christina had collapsed her parasol and laid it on one of the metal shelves, and now leaned back against the shelf and made the sign of the cross. Gabriel rolled his eyes. McKee glanced at the palm of her gloved hand.

"You know of him," said Trelawny, raising his white eyebrows as he struck a match to his cigar.

"He is," said Gabriel, "the one who menaces my wife and unborn child—and the daughter of," he added with a sideways wave, "of Rahab and Medicus here." Then a thought seemed to strike him. "Could they," Gabriel went on quickly, and Crawford was surprised to see sweat on Gabriel's face now, in spite of the freezing breeze, "Miss B. and Polidori—could it ever happen that they might *share* possession of a person?"

Trelawny cocked his head at him. "I suppose so, if the person were so unwise as to welcome one of them and then welcome the other one as well."

Gabriel's expression didn't change, but Crawford got the impression that some effort had been required for it not to.

"Who is this Miss B.?" asked Christina. "How was *she* quickened?"

Trelawny puffed smoke for several seconds, staring at Christina. "You seem to know how the Polidori creature was quickened," he said. "I'll want to hear about that. But—as for Miss B.—I'm afraid it was my fault."

The breeze whistled through the bars, and flurries of snow spun around their boots.

"Your fault," prompted McKee impatiently, hugging herself in her coat.

Trelawny eyed his companions speculatively and spoke around the cigar. "Do you all know about statues? Living statues?"

"A little," said Christina softly.

Trelawny went on, "I have made it possible—well, others forced it on me, actually—I have made it possible again to do what Deucalion and Pyrrha did, in the old Greek stories: establish a link between humans and the stony tribe, those pre-Adamite creatures that the ancient Hebrews called the Nephilim."

A moment went by in which no one spoke.

"Forced it on you," said Crawford, remembering the story his parents had told him.

"I'd say *forced* is too mild a word, to be honest," said Trelawny testily. "A mountain bandit who hoped to establish an alliance with these creatures arranged for me to be shot in the back—and one of the two balls the gun was loaded with was a tiny statue. It broke, bouncing around among my bones, and I spat half of it out, along with several teeth. The other ball was silver, and it's lodged in me somewhere, and it kept me safe for a long time. Balanced. Net zero."

Ash blew away from the tip of his cigar, and the coal glowed as he inhaled. "But—the problem is—the other half of the *stone* ball, the little statue"—he lifted his chin and patted his collar—"is, I'm afraid . . . growing. And as it grows, the Nephilim become stronger." He snapped his fingers. "What's the word? Rosetta!"

"Yes? What word?" said Gabriel. He seemed distracted.

"Rosetta," said Trelawny impatiently. "I just said it. The stone, you know? I'm the Rosetta stone in this—I make translation between the two species possible."

"It could be cut out," said Crawford.

"And pulverized and scattered in the sea!" added Christina.

"You're a good girl," said Trelawny, smiling crookedly at her. "But it's in under the jugular vein, and I haven't yet met a medical man I'd trust to cut it out." He shrugged deprecatingly. "And, to be honest, it gives me a certain immunity, with them."

"You," said Gabriel, "what, accept their amnesty?"

Trelawny gave him a scornful look from under his bushy white eyebrows. "I *use* it, sonny. I've been *making amends* for things I did in Greece, in Euboea and on Mount Parnassus, forty years ago." Trelawny's scarred lips gave him an expression that was only humorously rueful.

Gabriel and Christina glanced at each other, and Gabriel mouthed the word *Parnassus*.

"The Italian Carbonari pursue efforts similar to mine," said Trelawny, "but I'm not a joiner. Any time you work with people, they turn out to be inept clowns." He glanced at Crawford, which Crawford thought was unfair. "I get things done by myself," Trelawny went on. "Your old woman, Carpace or Carpaccio, she hoped to introduce another of these vampires to that sad crowd of poets last night." He laughed. "But a boat carrying a statue from Greece happened to explode on the river yesterday morning, and so Madame Carpaccio's vitreous guest of honor is now on the river bottom. And I maintain a small army of spies—" He paused and laughed again, but to Crawford it seemed forced now, and the old man squinted around at his companions as if regretting his momentary openness. "I try to work them ill in many ways," he said gruffly, "when Miss B. isn't looking." He tapped the sand with his boot toe. "And by now she's probably burrowed right down into the sewers."

"I'm glad we didn't meet her last night," said Crawford to McKee.

"What are you talking about," snapped Trelawny, "you *did* meet her last night. Who the hell do you think that tall woman with me was? As I recall, she nearly lapped up *your* sorry soul like a cat with a bowl of milk."

Christina stepped forward and touched Trelawny's sleeve. "And how is it that she has come to be attached to you, Mr. Samson?"

"Attached to me. Yes. Damn it, I returned to England *clean*, in 1834, after a voyage across the whole Atlantic Ocean, to America, where I baptized myself by swimming the Niagara River, though it nearly killed me to do it—when I really thought I was drowning, I could feel the devil claws pulling out of me, reluctantly! I was as clean as a newborn babe—"

"Except for the half statue in your neck," said Gabriel.

Trelawny scowled at him, then grinned around the cigar in his teeth. "Well, yes, sonny, except for that. But it hadn't started growing yet, you see. Probably wouldn't have. In any case, I became a responsible citizen here, wasted my time with politics, went to a lot of foolish dinners. Scandalized society by not wearing stockings. But there were still people about the place who remembered the old Neffy days, and they could recognize the—the *look*, on me. So I took me a wife and built a house on the cliff at Llanbadoc Rock, in Monmouthshire in eastern Wales. Lived there happily for ten years, had three more children, planted a row of cedars from cones I brought from the poet Shelley's grave in Rome. And I happen to have a piece of Shelley's jawbone—he was a half-breed member of their tribe by birth, and relics of him tend to deflect or refract their attention—"

"You're Shelley's famous friend, you're Edward John Trelawny," said Christina suddenly, and then she covered her mouth.

"Bad luck for me that you know it," said Trelawny. He frowned and rubbed his eyes with a spotted old hand. "Don't tell me who you are."

"Oh, you wouldn't have heard of *me*," said Christina.

Trelawny dropped his hand and glared at her. "Damn it, now I know you're an aspiring poet. Will you *not* speak, please?" His craggy face above the white beard was fierce, his blue eyes glittering. "At any rate!—being remote from London, and with Shelley's jawbone to keep the devils from seeing me, I relaxed. And five years ago I went exploring up the river Severn; and eventually I rowed right up the Birmingham and Worcester Canal and—"

"You *rowed* up the Severn?" interrupted Gabriel.

"Byron once swam from Sestos to Abydos," Trelawny said irritably, "and even in my forties I was in better condition than he ever was. The stories I could tell you about him!"

"Up the canal," prompted McKee.

"Indeed. Well, I could have rowed on to Birmingham, easily, but I went ashore for the night in a little village called King's Norton. Means 'the king's northern settlement' originally. And I couldn't sleep—I could feel someone calling me, in the old melody—so I went for a walk."

"I know that melody," said Christina softly.

Trelawny gave her a relenting, sympathetic look. "I'm afraid your poetry is probably very good, my dear. That's one of their gifts. Byron was a member of the tribe too."

To Crawford's alarm, Christina seemed to conceal satisfaction at the remark. But, "You should have gone to a church," she said.

"Stop it," said Trelawny mildly. "King's Norton lies on what they call Watling Street, the old Roman road that cuts right across Britain. I walked out of the village by moonlight, and out in the fields among the old oak trees I found stones, rounded now by weather but clearly cut by man many centuries ago, and then I was in a narrow defile, and—I met," he said, nodding toward Crawford and McKee, "the woman you saw me with last night. Her husband had died, leaving his lands to her and her daughters, but the Romans annexed them, and flogged her and raped her daughters—"

"The Romans did?" asked Crawford.

"This was a ghost," Gabriel told him shortly.

"Aye, a ghost," said Trelawny, "to the extent that a figurehead is a ship. And so in revenge she led the Iceni and the Trinovantes against the Roman settlement at Colchester, and they damn well leveled the place. Then she led her barbarian army to London, and the Romans simply ran, so she leveled it too, with the help of an accommodating earthquake."

"My God." Christina was pale, and she nodded. "I know *her* name too."

"She told you all this, there?" said Gabriel.

"She was boasting, boy," said Trelawny softly. "Trying to appear substantial. Ghosts are ashamed of being dead."

The cage they were in was west of the zoo wall, and Christina looked out across the grass to the south, toward where the creature had burrowed into the ground, and shook her head unhappily.

"She had sold her soul to get revenge," Trelawny went on, "to a goddess she called Andraste, which was also called Magna Mater, and Goemagot or Gogmagog."

Christina gripped Gabriel's arm; she started to whisper something to him, then shut her mouth and just shook her head.

Trelawny raised an eyebrow. "We're all in the soup, I perceive. Well, the emperor Nero was ready to abandon Britain altogether, but the Roman troops under Suetonius finally caught her on Watling Street, in the very defile I had wandered into. And her army was destroyed, and she drank poison."

"So did Polidori," said Gabriel.

"The last sacrament to the goddess," said Trelawny, nodding. "But by that time she had of course been *bitten* by the stony goddess, and so she was not permitted to lie quiet in the earth. She—came home with me."

"You invited her in," said Christina.

"I couldn't just—*leave* her out there!—somehow. By daylight she's—well, you saw her: dwarfish, imbecilic, has to be covered against the sun. Can't speak, has to wring notes out of that violin, with her hands in quilted mitts or hidden in long sleeves. When we arrived at my house, this was five years ago, I had to carry her up the hill, near bursting my heart with the effort of it. While she's 'alive' she always weighs the same, regardless of her volume. I told my wife she was a long-lost daughter of mine, and she lived with us, even when we moved to a nearby estate, Cefn Ila. I took precautions, you understand, even though I had Shelley's jawbone—garlic and mirrors and wood and silver—she was never free to consummate a link with me or any of my family. *But—*"

He exhaled a cloud of steam and cigar smoke. "My wife was no fool. To make sure of protecting our children, she left me, and I returned to London . . . with my inextricable companion, Miss B."

"Boadicea, queen of the Iceni," said Christina softly. "Was it about A.D. 60 that she . . . died?"

Crawford tried unsuccessfully to catch McKee's eye. We saw some of Boadicea's ancient havoc last night, he thought.

"You're a scholar, Miss Diamonds. And she would dearly love to destroy London again."

"I'm—embarrassed," Christina said, "to have seen her like"—she waved out toward the park—"like that."

Crawford looked out across the desolate park. One solitary walker wearing a very broad-brimmed hat was plodding west among the elm trees on this side of the frozen boating lake, the laboring silhouette merging and separating from the vertical lines of the black tree trunks.

"She's far more dangerous now," Trelawny told Christina, "than she was when she was entirely human." He turned to McKee. "You had an ave with you last night. Did it catch Carpace's ghost?"

"Y-yes," said McKee, "and I went to Chichuwee, as you advised; and I got an answer—"

Trelawny interrupted urgently: "Do you still have the ave?"

"The ghost isn't still in it," she said. "I had got my answer, so—"

"You *dumped* her?" he asked incredulously. "Into the river?"

McKee bit her lip and nodded.

And broke a promise in order to do it, thought Crawford. For revenge.

"Didn't you—" began Trelawny; he took a breath and went on, "She'll never *willingly* answer questions, with a planchette and pencil! Didn't it *occur* to you that she knows—knew!—important things about the Nephilim, things that might help save your—what was it, daughter?"

"She told me where to look for her . . ."

"And she said that the living Polidori statue is in Highgate Cemetery!" burst out Christina. "We can trust Trelawny!" she insisted to her brother, who had grimaced fiercely at her.

"Certainly," agreed Gabriel through his teeth. "He's only got a similar statue *in his damned neck.*"

"Not precisely *similar,*" said Trelawny. "But you can trust my ignorance. I don't know who any of you are, nor where you live. Let's maintain that lack of acquaintance; a good social policy in general, probably." He tossed his cigar cleanly between two of the bars onto the snowy gravel lane. "Highgate Cemetery. She might be breakable through Polidori." He fixed a glare on Christina. "How was he quickened?"

Christina turned away so that all any of them could see was the side of her bonnet. "I, God help me, I rubbed some of my blood on the statue—and then slept with it under my pillow."

"She was only fourteen!" Gabriel burst out.

For a moment Trelawny just smiled gently at her. At last, "A prodigy!" he said. He took his violin case from the shelf and stepped to the cage gate and pulled it open. "I hope you all fare better than you seem likely to do," he said when he was standing in sunlight out on the gravel. "Never speak to me again. Muster what wits you have, and exert them."

"And pray to God for deliverance," said Christina.

Trelawny gave her a withering smile with his scarred mouth. "I like you, Miss Diamonds, so I won't call you a fool." He bowed and turned away, and within moments his long stride had carried him out of the zoo lanes to the west, and soon he was a dwindling figure on the yellow grass, angling north toward the canal.

Crawford looked away from him, to the south, and saw that the person in the broad hat he had seen walking among the trees was, though still fifty yards away, now slowly trudging north, toward the broad lane of the outer circle. If he crossed that, he'd be in among the empty cassowary and zebra cages and could hardly fail to notice the cage on the end that was occupied by four humans.

We should get out of this, Crawford thought in embarrassment, onto the lane, like normal people.

"So that's the infamous Trelawny," said Gabriel, still staring west. "Arrogant ass."

"If you two were *men,*" McKee burst out, "you'd have overpowered him and cut that stone ball out of his neck right here!"

Crawford blinked at her irritably, then forced himself to smile. "Well, I *meant* to," he said, "but the appropriate moment never presented itself."

"Somehow," agreed Gabriel, rocking on his heels.

McKee scowled at both of them, but a reluctant smile was tugging at the corners of her lips. "You could have *interrupted* him to do it."

"You always were headstrong, Adelaide," Christina said with a sigh. "He might be an ally, and his devil isn't the one that threatens us."

Gabriel's face was blank.

"No," said McKee, turning on her, "your uncle is that. And he and my daughter both seem to be connected to Highgate Cemetery. You know more about all this, I see, than you could possibly tell us now— come there with us."

Gabriel blew out a breath and shook his head. "My sister isn't well; it's out of the question."

"I really couldn't do it," said Christina. "But I can tell you any number of—"

Crawford interrupted her with an involuntary gasp. The figure he had been watching was closer now, and there was something wrong with its silhouette.

Its wide leather hat, as wide as a horse collar, had no crown and seemed to rest directly on the figure's neck, with no room for a head in between.

The others had followed his wide-eyed gaze, and now Christina waved urgently.

"He's blind," she whispered. "Complete silence, all of you."

Crawford's ears were ringing shrilly though almost inaudibly, and he could feel his heart thudding in his chest.

Below the impossible hat the figure wore an old brown coat that trailed on the gravel of the outer circle road, and the thing was meandering back and forth in the road like someone looking for a dropped coin, but its random-looking course kept bringing it toward the row of cages. Its harsh breathing was audible already, and soon Crawford could hear it muttering to itself in a hoarse voice as resonant as someone speaking from the bottom of a well, though he couldn't make out words.

McKee's hand was gripping Crawford's upper arm tightly. He glanced at her, but she was staring out white-faced at the advancing thing.

The brim of the hat flapped as the creature spoke, and Crawford's heart seemed to freeze solid when he realized that the thing's mouth was as wide as the hat brim, a yard across at least. He looked away, fearing that it might sense and track his gaze, but not before he had glimpsed two long rows of shadowed teeth and a tongue like a black sunfish.

Its words were audible now: "My darling, my Diamonds! Do you move so fast? My sister is hurt, away under the ground in the dark; help me find her. Touch me—where are you? Take my hand! Don't you hate the sun? You know what those children sing? 'When the sky began to roar, / 'Twas like a lion at the door!'"

Its long arms were extended as its shoes scuffled and scraped across the gravel, and its hands were hidden under the long, flapping sleeves. The breeze seemed to have halted, frozen like glass.

Crawford was watching the thing only from the corner of his eye, and so he saw Christina open her mouth when it became clear that the thing's wobbling course would take it past the cage toward the canal, with yards to spare; but Gabriel gripped her shoulder, and she closed her mouth and gave him a guilty look. Gabriel's free hand was visibly a fist in his coat pocket, no doubt gripping his now-empty revolver.

None of the four moved their booted feet on the sandy cage floor, but their heads slowly turned to watch the thing's hunched back and flopping hat recede in the direction Trelawny had taken.

Several minutes passed before the shambling figure disappeared among the elms to the west, but none of the people in the cage spoke until it was out of sight, though Christina began panting.

"That was your damned—" said Gabriel to Christina, "your—what did you call him?"

"Mouth Boy," said Christina breathlessly. "But it was Uncle Polidori, wearing the form of my childhood nightmare." She rubbed her eyes with trembling hands.

"Yes." Gabriel gave her an angry glance. "I don't know what you see in him."

She squinted at him. "Yes, you do."

"I'd have shot him if I'd had a seventh bullet."

Christina didn't reply. She stretched and retrieved her parasol and stepped to the cage gate. "We should separate, all be indoors by sunset." To McKee she said, "When can we meet at Highgate Cemetery?"

"You can't!" said Gabriel. "You're not strong—"

"Tomorrow," said McKee.

"I will," Christina insisted to Gabriel. "It's because I woke our uncle—and because you . . . brought him to Adelaide—that her daughter's soul is in danger. It may be that we can find his statue, and—"

Gabriel gave her a look that seemed both cynical and pleading.

"—and destroy it, and him," Christina went on firmly, "and free Adelaide's little girl. And you and me." She clasped both hands on the parasol handle, possibly to keep them from shaking. "It doesn't matter if I—what my natural feelings for him still are."

After a grudging pause, Gabriel said, "You don't mention Lizzie."

Christina touched his arm. "And go some way toward saving Lizzie too," she said gently. "You believe she's *shared* by these two devils?"

"I—damn it, *yes*. And either one could have assumed my form and . . . potency. I can't know which of them it was who—"

Crawford thought about his practice and his rent, then sighed and quietly said to McKee, "After noon, please."

McKee nodded.

Christina turned to Gabriel. "I think you'll come too."

Gabriel almost seemed ready to spit; but, "You're my sister," he said, "and their child might just as easily have been my daughter. And it is conceivable we might be able to do something to help Lizzie." He heaved a windy sigh. "Yes, I'll go along."

Crawford forced himself not to scowl. Damn the man, he thought. Might just as easily have been his daughter indeed!

"Get your gun loaded again," McKee told Gabriel. "Load two, if you have them."

CHAPTER NINE

I have a friend in ghostland—
Early found, ah me, how early lost!—
Blood-red seaweeds drip along that coastland
By the strong sea wrenched and tossed.
In every creek there slopes a dead man's inlet,
For there comes neither night nor day.

—*Christina Rossetti, "A Coast-Nightmare"*

THE DINNER AT La Sablonniere in Leicester Square was, Gabriel thought cautiously, going as well as could be expected. He was more comfortable with the informal dinners he served for friends at home—"nothing but oysters and of course the seediest of clothes," as he often specified in his invitations—but this dressing up for an elegant restaurant was what Lizzie had apparently wanted.

It helped that the young poet Swinburne was there. Swinburne was twenty-five but looked a malnourished sixteen, and his wild mane of kinky hair was the same carroty color as Lizzie's, and his twitchy cheerfulness often sparked a like response in Lizzie.

Lizzie had in fact vacillated all evening between giddy hilarity and a wooden silence, and she had drunk several glasses of Haut-Brion Blanc but had eaten only a few bites of her *supreme de volaille,* a chicken breast in a white sauce; Gabriel recognized all this as the effects of her damned laudanum.

Their table for three was beside a window overlooking the streetlamp-dotted darkness of Leicester Square, and now Lizzie had pulled off her shawl to polish the glass, and her bare shoulders glowed too pale in the glare of the restaurant's wall-mounted gas jets.

"There's a . . . new building there," she said. "In the middle of the square."

Swinburne, not entirely sober himself, goggled at the glass but apparently couldn't see beyond his own reflection and the steam of his breath.

Gabriel leaned forward and squinted. The high dome and pillared entrance to the Wyld's Globe exhibit was the only building visible out there in the dark. "Nothing new that I can see," he said.

"That dome," Lizzie said. "Wasn't it grass there . . . ?"

"That's been there for eleven years, Guggums. Ever since the Great Exhibition."

"Is it a church?"

"My sort of church," said Swinburne, slouching back in his upholstered chair and reaching for the decanter of claret. "The world, introverted."

"It's a giant globe," said Gabriel patiently, "turned inside out. You go in and you can see all the seas and continents around you."

"Turned inside out," echoed Lizzie. "I'm turned inside out. Everything around me is my own grief and loss, and inside I'm just an empty street, an empty building."

Gabriel wished she weren't so devoted to poetry; she wrote a lot of it, and it was, frankly, pedestrian stuff, though Swinburne loyally claimed to admire her verses.

"Nonsense, Gug," Gabriel said. "You're ill, it colors your mood. I think a crème brûlée and a glass of sauternes—"

Lizzie was frowning and shaking her head. "If the globe is inside out, where's God? Rise up from one place and soon you'd only bump your head against another! And Hell—under the surface—is infinite! Don't bury me!"

"For God's sake, Gug, pipe down! Nobody's going to bury you, you're not dying. Algy, she listens to you, tell her she's not dying."

Swinburne was a frequent visitor at Chatham Place, and he and Lizzie were forever reading to each other, or playing with the cats, or jointly composing nonsense verses and wrestling for possession of the pen as inspiration struck one or the other of them.

Swinburne blinked at her now over the rim of his wine glass. He lowered it and said, "Don't die, Lizzie darling. Who else could I find who doesn't despise me?"

She sniffed and shook her head. "It's the ones who love us that are the peril. 'And well though love reposes, in the end it is not well.'"

Now she was quoting an unpublished poem of Swinburne's. The young man, whose red hair was now sticking out in all directions, pursed his lips in wry acknowledgment. "But Gabriel and I love you. We're no peril."

"You don't love me as much as two others do," she whispered.

Gabriel shivered. Two, he thought; and he remembered Trelawny's words this afternoon: . . . *if the person were so unwise as to welcome one of them and then welcome the other one as well.*

Lizzie looked back out the window, and tears stood on her eyelashes as she kissed one finger and then stroked it down the glass. "Oh, do you see her? She followed us, but she won't come in where it's warm."

"Who?" asked Swinburne, to Gabriel's alarm.

"Don't let her get started on—" he began, but it was too late.

Lizzie was sobbing, and Gabriel pushed his chair back and stood up, waving to the waiter.

"My daughter," wailed Lizzie, "dead but weeping, immortal but starving!" Gabriel had strode around to her side of the table and was pulling her shawl across her shoulders and shushing her, but she went on, "Is my second child to join her out there?"

Gabriel was peripherally aware of eyeglasses and red lips and mustaches turned toward them from the tables nearby, and for a moment a smell of wet clay seemed to eclipse the aromas of beef and cigar smoke and wine sauces, but he had got Lizzie to her feet and was concentrating on guiding her toward the dining room door; he could hear Swinburne's boots rapping on the polished wood floor behind him.

Gabriel dug a five-pound note out of his pocket and thrust it at the wide-eyed waiter, who hurried to fetch their hats and coats; and after what seemed like an infernal eternity of tugging at sleeves and scarves and glove cuffs, they were at last stepping across the foyer and he was pushing open the heavy front door. Wintry air numbed his cheeks and stung his teeth as he whistled to a cab standing at the curb a dozen yards away, and when the driver shed his blanket and shook the reins, Gabriel turned to Swinburne over Lizzie's shaking shoulder.

"Sorry, Algy," he said, "she's—"

"Take care of her," said Swinburne, shivering in his too-large coat. "And thank you for dinner." Then he nodded and set off walking away down Panton Street.

It was difficult to get Lizzie into the cab, as she kept looking yearningly back at the restaurant. *Probably wanting us to wait for our dead daughter,* thought Gabriel grimly as he pushed her up the step; *either that or she's reconsidering the crème brûlée.*

"WHAT ARE YOU WRITING, Christina?"

"Nothing," snapped Christina crossly, rolling the pen between her fingers. "Nothing!"

The room was too warm and reeked of William's tarry latakia

tobacco. The tassels that dangled from the runner on the fireplace mantel were throwing their usual shadow pattern on the high ceiling, and to Christina, as she looked up in frustration, the little wavering Y-shaped figures looked like tiny men clinging to a cliff edge over an inferno.

Like Catholic souls clutching the last edge of Purgatory, she thought. Filthy Romish superstition!

Her bearded, bald-headed brother blinked at her in surprise but took no offense. He never did. He had only been home for half an hour, his job at the Inland Revenue offices in Somerset House having kept him late, and he had been scribbling busily in a notebook before he had noticed her scowling over her papers at the slant-front desk below the old portrait of their uncle.

"I'm sorry," Christina said. William was the only one of the four siblings who provided any substantial household money—Maria's Bible classes hardly brought in a hundred pounds a year, and Gabriel's income from his paintings was erratic and carelessly spent—and William never complained about the fact that the whole family lived off his salary. He wrote poetry too—he had probably been writing verses just now—though it was all hopelessly pedantic and uninspired.

Christina absentmindedly blew a strand of hair out of her face. "I'm trying to continue the story I burned last year."

" 'Folio Q,' " said William, putting down his notebook and taking off his spectacles. "Continue it? Have you written it out again? I thought it was very good."

"I know you did. But I didn't write it." She took a deep breath. "*He* did," she said, pointing her pen up at the portrait above the desk. "Through me, through my passive hand."

He frowned. "Do you mean you were inspired—"

"I mean *he—wrote—it*. His ghost did. I was in a sort of trance, and I didn't know what I'd written—what my hand had written—until I read it."

"Ah, you mean automatic writing," William said, nodding in sudden comprehension. "Really! That's why you burned it. But that's fascinating! Why didn't you tell me?"

"You? You're so skeptical—"

"Only about obvious superstitions," he protested. Like Christianity, Christina thought sourly. "But," he went on, "never about possibly valid scientific phenomena. Some intriguing work is being done these days in spiritualism."

"Well, he's giving me nothing tonight." She tossed the pen onto the paper and glanced irritably up at the portrait. John Polidori, with his antique collar and his curly black hair and his dark eyes peering off to the side, for once just looked stupid and cunning.

"Was it—important? That he do?"

"Yesterday he was writing about Lizzie, through me. He knew, or said, that she's . . . expecting again. I need to know, from *him,* what her prognosis is."

William tamped the smoldering tobacco in his pipe. "I hope she recovers from this . . . nervous prostration of hers," he said, puffing smoke. "Gabriel loves her."

"So should we all. She's family now."

"Why don't you just visit her? And why would our departed uncle be particularly informed about her condition?"

"He'd know better than anyone," said Christina. "He's what's making her sick." With, she thought, perhaps some assistance from the historical Boadicea, God help us.

William pursed his lips and stroked his beard. "Ghosts, if indeed they exist, aren't supposed to be able to hurt people. All the evidence indicates—"

"There's fresh evidence. Firsthand evidence."

William blinked. "What's—going on?"

"She—he—oh, hang on a moment." Christina stood up and crossed to the mantel, where she had left the rolling pencil disk Gabriel had tossed to her yesterday. She picked it up and hurried back to the desk.

"I forgot about this—Gabriel told me to use it."

"It looks like one of those children's toys that spin," said William.

"Lizzie was using it to communicate with a dead friend," she said without looking up from her paper. "I saw the sheet she used—apparently you write out a question first—I could ask Uncle John to continue—"

But as soon as she set the disk on the paper and laid two fingers on it, it started moving; a tingle passed through her chest, and the fingers of her free hand stretched out and then clenched in a fist. She heard William stand up from his chair, but she didn't look away from the pencil line already being traced.

When the disk paused, it had written,

get it out

"Get it out?" said William, standing now behind her shoulder. "That's not clear."

"Shh." Christina began awkwardly trying to write a question with the upright pencil, but the thing was moving again.

river closest meet tell you

The writing was faint and loopy, and William squinted at it. "Riven closet?" he asked.

"'River closest.' I think he wants me to meet him by the river," said Christina in a quavering voice. "I won't go. I *won't*."

William straightened up. "You believe he would hurt you?"

"Well, no. Not *me*. I believe he loves *me*."

She started to say something else, but the disk was moving again:

need you always

She inhaled sharply, then leaned down and said to the pencil, "*Where* by the river?"

find you I will

Christina let her gaze fall from the paper on the desk to her shoes. She would need to put on boots, and a coat and hat and gloves—at least the hateful sun had set—and find a cab; Gabriel lived right on the river, perhaps he would not mind letting her spend the night there, save her the cold trip home—of course she would want to come home—

The disk jiggled under her fingers and wrote,

my dear ones my francesca

William was peering at it. "I don't think . . ." he began slowly, but the disk was moving again:

christina vivace mia

" . . . that that's our uncle," William finished.

"No," said Christina, careful to keep any disappointment out of her voice or manner. "No, it's . . . Papa."

"Why is he writing in English?"

Christina recalled the conversation she'd had with her father seventeen years ago, when he had let her take the tiny Polidori statue. "I think he uses English when he's—ashamed of himself."

"Wha—why should he be ashamed of himself?"

Because he used me, Christina thought, sacrificed my honor to his devil, in the hope that the devil would . . . restore his sight, his fortune, his youth. A dishonorable bargain, and one in which he was cheated to boot.

And she recalled what Trelawny had said this afternoon. "Ghosts are ashamed of being dead," she said.

William stepped back to the center of the parlor. "I'll go with you."

"No, William, it's—"

William, of course, with his generally mocking attitude, had never been told the story of Christina's catastrophic intimacy with their father's statue, and she didn't want him to learn it tonight.

"It won't happen unless I'm alone," she said. "I'll be safe—I'll go to where they hire boats, by the Adelphi wharfs."

William was frowning. "But I'm one of his children too. Why would he—he didn't *say* that you had to come alone."

"Dear William! I'm sorry. But this time it must be just me. You can contact him afterward, and meet him . . . or his ghost, at any rate."

"But isn't his ghost *him*?"

"Not . . . not much. Most of him will have gone on, though I know what you think about Heaven and Hell. This fraction of him might be—a Catholic might say that it was—his participation in Purgatory."

"I—for God's sake, it's after nine o'clock, Christina! I *insist* on going with you."

"If you do, nothing will happen. We'll take an uneventful walk by the river and come home again. I'll be perfectly safe alone, I promise you." She smiled at him. "You know I'll get my way in this."

After another few seconds of frowning disapprovingly, William looked away. "Do you have money?" he asked in a flat voice. "You'll want a cab both ways."

"Well, if you could," said Christina, mentally adding *as always*, "lend me a pound . . . ?"

William pulled his coin purse from his waistcoat pocket, snapped it open, and handed her several coins.

"Even so," he said gruffly, "tell him, if you would, that I—love him." He grimaced. "If his ghost is there, and even if it's not much of *him*."

"I will!"

Christina kissed him on the cheek and hurried to the hall to get her things.

GABRIEL HAD TO TAKE most of Lizzie's weight as they clumped and scuffled up the dark stairs at Chatham Place, and when he had sat her down on the bed and turned up the gas flame he wiped his face with a handkerchief. Laudanum and the closed windows gave the room a stuffy sickroom smell.

"It's nine thirty," he said breathlessly. "I've got to go." On Monday nights he taught a drawing class at the Working Men's College in Great Titchfield Street. "I'll be back at eleven or so."

"Is that tonight? Miss the class tonight," she said, falling back exhaustedly across the bed. Her closed eyes were smudges of darkness. "I'm afraid he'll come to me, or she will, if you're gone."

He or she, Gabriel thought. How are we to free her from *two* of them?

"I can't," he said. "The students will all be there."

"Gabriel, I don't want to have to—do what I'd have to do, to resist them!"

Gabriel forced himself not to roll his eyes in impatience. "You're safe *here*, indoors in this house, and I'll only be a couple of hours."

"Bloody lot you know," she muttered, turning toward the wall. Her dress was going to need pressing before she could wear it again.

"What was that?"

She rolled around to face him, her eyes wide with apparent fright. "Stay, Gabriel! I don't want to be left with nothing but Walter's counsel."

"Walter! Walter is dead because your—your *new lovers* were jealous! Walter's just a half-wit ghost now." He blinked away tears impatiently. "Walter's not the—*father of your child.*"

Lizzie shook herself and looked around the dim-lit room and absently smoothed out the pleats of her dress. Gabriel wearily recognized one of her abrupt changes of mood.

She muttered something of which he caught only the words *my child.*

"What?" he snapped.

She sighed, calm now. "Nothing. Go to your school. Your students matter more to you than I do."

"Damn it, Guggums—"

"You were perfectly beastly to me at dinner."

"*I* was—? Who was it made such a scene that we had to run out? Algy must think you're insane."

"Algy loves me like a sister. You love me as a model for pictures." Gabriel started to object, but she interrupted, "Give me my laudanum bottle, and then go."

"You've had quite enough of that damned stuff. You hardly know where you are these days. I don't—"

She rolled her eyes and shifted on the bed as if to stand up. "Can't you do even *that* for me? Never mind, I'll get it for myself."

Furiously, Gabriel snatched up the bottle and strode to the bed and shoved it into her hand. "Here," he said, "take the lot!"

She was sobbing weakly behind him as he strode out the bedroom door and down the stairs.

CHRISTINA HAD HAD TO knock at the side window of the hansom cab on the corner, waking the cabbie, and now that she had climbed out at the river end of Villiers Street ten minutes later, he swung down from his perch at the back and stepped up into the cab again to resume his interrupted sleep.

"I'll be right here when you're ready to return," he said gruffly, pocketing her shilling and pulling his collar up and his hat down. "Unless somebody hires me first."

"I shall hope that you remain undiscovered," said Christina, shivering in the chilly fog that swirled up the street from the river.

The cab's right wheel was up over the curb on the pavement, below a dark building with a crane and a wide, shuttered door dimly visible overhead on the second floor, in a shadowed and mist-veiled corner of the street, and it seemed very possible that no late-night revelers would venture beyond the crowded, jostling cab stand under the streetlamp a dozen yards back up the street.

Even on this cold Monday night the fog glowed back there around a place called Gatti's Music Hall, and a man was out front shouting through a speaking trumpet about the musical show inside, which was apparently the source of the occasional spirited chorus of "Hee-haw" that rang between the blurred buildings and out across the river.

Beyond the chest-high brick wall along the river-side lane, the river itself was invisible in what seemed to be a solid cloud descended out of the sky—and she remembered her father once saying that the clouds of night were not the same as the clouds of day.

On the far side of the river, she knew, were warehouses and the ironworks and the tall shot tower, where molten lead was dropped from a height into cold water to make the little balls men shot birds with, but tonight those places all might as well be on the moon—the river of fog seemed to extend out to the sky, and with an odd thrill she remembered her childhood dream of the Sea-People Chorus, the thousands of ghosts in the river waving jointless arms at the night sky.

She straightened her shoulders and began resolutely walking down the street in that direction, away from the lights and the noise.

On clear nights, visitors from the country might be waiting at the stairs by the seventeenth-century water gate, which was all that remained of the old York House, to hire a boat and see the sights along the river, but when Christina walked between the pillars and reached the top of the stairs, she saw only four or five watermen sitting in a half-walled shed down to her left, huddled around a couple of lanterns. Along the narrow, fading pier, their boats sat in the water like sleeping gulls.

The stone steps below the arches of the water gate were wet, and Christina gripped the marble rail with her gloved right hand as she cautiously descended. The night was suddenly quiet down here in the dimness—she could hear a bell ringing faintly out on the river, and she thought she could hear frogs croaking not far away. The fleeting scent of tobacco smoke made the air seem warmer.

"Be you wanting to cross, miss?" called one of the gray-bearded men in the shed. "It's no night for it, even with the purl men still out, mad fools."

Now that she had reached the desolate river shore below the steeply slanted masonry of the City's edge, Christina was not anxious to look for a ghost, even or especially her father's, and the phrase that sounded like "pearl men" had an unwelcomely macabre sound. She imagined pearl-eyed drowned mariners rowing boats out there in the dark, not needing sight on the infinite river.

"Pearl men?" she asked, shivering as she picked her way over half-seen gravel and sand toward the yellow light of the kerosene lanterns. The fog moving in off the river smelled of the sea, though the tide didn't appear to be high.

"Purl men is beer sellers," the man said, to Christina's instant relief. "It's their bells you hear out there, looking to be hailed by sailors on moored ships. Used to be they'd mix wormwood in the beer, called it purl, and the name's stuck." The man stood up from the wooden box he'd been sitting on, took a short clay pipe out of his mouth, and said, "I'm called Hake. Who be you lookin' for, miss?"

She was standing now only a couple of yards from the open side of the shed, and the air on her cheeks was perceptibly warmer there, but the faces of the other watermen, all middle-aged or older, were still just noses and gray beards and wrinkled foreheads picked out against the darkness by the lantern glare.

"My name is . . . Christina." She could see the cloud of her breath now. "Must I be looking for someone?"

"Oh, aye. Your dress and manner are modest, and you're alone. You hear 'em all yonder," he added, waving at the nighted river behind her.

Christina turned to peer uneasily down the invisible shoreline.

"All I hear is frogs."

One of the other men laughed or coughed. "Ain't frogs," he said.

"Nights like this," said old Hake kindly, "fine folk sometimes come down here, not to hire a boat."

"Nobody comes to hire a boat," growled another bony old fellow. "Not since the new London Bridge."

"Sure enough," agreed Hake. "We're well after being ghosts our-selves. The old bridge, gone these thirty years, had nineteen arches, and you needed a licensed waterman to shoot any one of them, but this

new bridge has got only five arches, all very wide—a child could row
you through 'em."

"Almost ghosts yourselves," echoed Christina cautiously.

"Aye," said Hake with a nod, "there's no apprentices to speak of anymore. Soon enough *we'll* be out there in the dark on the other side of the
stairs, with none anymore manning this pier to listen to us." He smiled
at her through his gray beard. "Who were you looking for?"

Feeling dizzy at doing it, Christina answered him honestly. "My
father—he—"

"I'm sorry to hear about it, miss." He stepped past her, his boots
crunching in wet gravel, and beckoned her to follow. "When did he
pass on?"

Christina fell into step beside him as they plodded away from the
lantern light.

"Eight years ago."

Hake stopped. "Did you say eight years? I'm sorry, but it's not likely
that he'd be still—"

"He contacted me, tonight. He asked me to meet him by the river."

Hake shrugged. "Fair enough. I'll stop here, miss, and let you go
farther. Not more than twenty paces past the stairs, mind, or you'll be
in grievous mud."

"In grievous mud," echoed Christina, stepping forward away from
him across the wet sand and gravel, into the dark mist. The light from
the lanterns behind her glittered faintly on the tops of the closest sand
ripples, and she tried to step on those.

When her eyes adjusted to the faint gray luminescence of the fog,
she became aware of several sets of abandoned-looking stairs fretting
the patchwork stone wall to her right, and the river on her left was nothing but remote bells and vague splashing sounds at indeterminate distances; she believed she was somewhere between the Scotland Yard coal
wharf and the Adelphi terrace houses, but the real world seemed to lie
very far away behind her.

Never mind ghosts, she thought—there are probably thieves and footpads along this Godforsaken strip of the bottom of nowhere. I should go back to Hake and his companions, back to the sleepy cabbie, back to poor William with his wretched poetry in the warm parlor at home.

Damn you, Papa, for—but she cut the thought short.

And then she heard a whisper to her left: "Christina!"

She halted, and then gingerly stepped out into the river shallows, hoping her boots were waterproof. "Papa?"

Through the blurring mist she could see that there was something like a small dolphin or huge catfish lying in the shallows, panting visibly. Tentacles growing out of its face curled and splashed.

She heard water trickling, and then saw that the thing had a bony hinged arm too, with wet fingers on the end of it.

"Take my hand," it wheezed.

Christina forced herself not to step back; but in a tight voice she said, "No."

"My fault," whispered the creature that was her father's ghost. The arm fell back into the water with a splash. "Gabriel's daughter—your lives—your *soul*. Looking at me? Don't look. I stay on the bottom most days—all fear one another—river worms now."

"William," she said helplessly, "said to tell you he loves you."

The creature groaned softly.

It occurred to Christina that she would be able to bear this for only a few more seconds.

"What did you want to tell me?" Her mouth was full of saliva, and she swallowed and gagged. "You asked me to meet you here."

"Cut yourself?" said the fish-thing on a rising, whistling note. "On a rock? You could. Give your poor father a few drops of your living blood?"

This time she did step back. "No. Was that all you wanted to say to me?"

"No, no, I'm sorry, forgive me: don't look at me. No, I wanted to say—choke it. It choked me."

Icy water abruptly invaded the toe of Christina's left boot, and her whole body shuddered at the shock. She gasped, "Choke what, Papa?"

"Statue, the uncle, of yours, my Francesca's brother! Moony knows how. Save your souls; undo it all, then I can save mine."

The freezing water quickly spread under the sole of her foot; her toes were already numb. "Papa, where *is* it?"

The fish-thing blew out spray, though its breath didn't steam. "Here," it rasped, "damn you, here! No, not here—in my throat. My heart clenched, I was dying—I thought Polidori would save me, immortal—I meant to swallow it—but—just gasping, choking."

For the moment she forgot about her foot and her lonely and gloomy surroundings. "You *choked* on it?"

"Choke *him*. Moony knows how." The thing thrashed clumsily, rolling out toward deeper water. Its wide ragged mouth was toward the foggy sky, and it wheezed, "Ugly, crushed, blind—I know—sorry—this waits for you all too, remember."

Then it seemed to suffer some sort of fit, and went spasming and splashing out of sight into the fog; and it must have sunk, for the scratching breath and the splashing ceased.

"Papa . . . !" whispered Christina, all alone in the cold on the narrow dark shore.

Then she reminded herself that she was thirty-one now, not fourteen anymore; and she was likely to catch pneumonia if she didn't get into dry slippers soon.

Tears were cold on her cheeks. She turned and began plodding back toward the lights of the watermen.

IT WAS ELEVEN THIRTY when Gabriel unlocked the street door at 14 Chatham Place and began groping and clumping his way up the unlit stairs. He heard furtive rustling and whispering from the floor above, and hoped Lizzie wasn't in communication with dead Walter Deverell again; Gabriel had taken away her pencil planchette, but she could have improvised one with a bent fork or something.

The sitting room above him was unlit, but he could see faint changes in the dimness up there, as if figures were quickly but silently darting about.

"Who's there?" he whispered, not wanting to wake Lizzie if it was someone else. Could Swinburne have come back here?

A draft of chilly air swept down the stairs, and Gabriel's nostrils twitched at the scent of the sea. Christ, she had opened the French doors over the river!

Gabriel took the last steps two at a time, but the sitting room was empty when he stood panting in the dark doorway. Reflections and echoes from the river, he told himself, not intruders. He stepped to the French doors, but before pulling them closed, he looked out at the infinity of fog. A bell sounded out there somewhere, and then after a few seconds another; who would be out on the river tonight? He thought of going out onto the balcony and peering down at the dark shore below—but the sudden, irrational thought that he might see his dead father down there on the sand, blindly gaping upward, made him close the doors with enough force to rattle the glass panes.

He was sweating—because he was still wearing his overcoat. He wrestled it off and threw it, along with his scarf and gloves, onto the couch. And finally he walked across to the hall and the bedroom door.

The door was ajar, and Lizzie was asleep on the bed, lying on top of the blankets and still in the dress she'd worn at dinner. She was snoring deeply.

Gabriel sighed in qualified relief and decided to pour himself a brandy before going to bed.

Then he noticed the piece of paper on the front of her dress. Stepping closer, he saw that it was folded and pinned to the fabric.

Not letting himself think or breathe, he crossed to the bed and tore the note free and opened it.

He read: *This is the only way out that will save us. Preserve my family by avoiding them, especially poor Harry.*

The laudanum bottle was on the bedside table, empty now. She had always been protective of her family, especially her half-wit brother Harry.

"Lizzie!" He took hold of her bare shoulders and shook her, but her head just rolled limply. *"Lizzie!"* he shouted into her face.

She showed no response. He noticed that she was paler than usual, and with a trembling hand he took hold of her wrist. Her pulse, when he found it, was slow and weak.

Take the lot, he had told her when he had thrust the laudanum bottle into her hand. His chest was suddenly empty and cold.

He dropped her hand and for a long moment just stood shaking over her, his hands spread helplessly; then he cried, "I'm sorry, Guggums! Wait for me!" and hurried out of the room and down the stairs and out the street door, straight across the damp pavement of Chatham Place square to the fog-veiled lanes of Bridge Street and the house of a doctor.

CHRISTINA WAS ALREADY AWAKE when Maria came hurrying heavily up the stairs to rap at her door.

Christina had awakened at dawn, splashed her face in the water in the basin on the old birchwood washstand, and then padded barefoot across the rug—it had been the parlor rug in the house back on Charlotte Street, cut up for bedroom rugs now—and stared out through the frosted windowpanes at the bundled-up people who were already out and walking along the pavements this morning. Some were clearly peddlers, and some were probably clerks; but after a few minutes of steaming the glass with her breath, she had had to force down the suspicion that some of them were only pretending not to be scrutinizing this house, perhaps peering right up at her window from under their hat brims. She stood and looked for a while, anxiously watching for a particularly clumsy figure under a very wide hat brim.

But she had stepped back, and then heard Maria on the stairs, and she opened the door at Maria's first knock.

Maria had pulled a robe over her nightdress, and her hair had been hastily brushed. Smells of coffee and bacon from downstairs followed her into the room.

"Lizzie," Maria panted, "has died. I'm sorry to just—I only now heard."

Christina sat down on the bed. "Died? Died how?"

"Laudanum—poisoning. Gabriel is ready to go mad. He had half a dozen doctors there, since midnight—Lucy Brown was at the door just now—of course it was William who spoke to her—I gather Lizzie was pronounced dead only a few minutes ago."

Christina couldn't see in her sister's tear-streaked face any of the relief Christina herself felt—but if this death were a suicide, Lizzie might very well have escaped the gross, physical immortality that Christina's uncle would force on her, and been free to take instead the spiritual immortality offered by Christ. Suicide was a deadly sin, of course, but perhaps Lizzie had done it to save herself and her unborn child from a surer exclusion from Heaven.

And Christina was honest enough to concede, though only ever to herself, that she would be jealous if Lizzie were to become one of her monstrous uncle's vampiric brides.

"Was it," began Christina. She paused, then went on, "Was it, does it seem to have been—an accident?"

"'Stina! Of course it was an accident. Don't be ridiculous!" Maria sat down on the bed beside Christina. She took Christina's hand and said, "Probably it wasn't an accident. Oh, it *might* have been, you know!"

"I don't think it would damn her soul," said Christina, "under the circumstances?"

"True, she was saving her child, and herself—if—if she did it in time."

Christina took a deep breath and squeezed her sister's hand. "Listen, Moony, I know where the statue is. Papa's little black statue."

Maria frowned and shook her head. "What? You know where it is? How long have you—?"

"I only learned last night."

"Oh, 'Stina, if only we had got it and destroyed it as soon as you knew! It might have saved Lizzie. But, but!—if she *was* too late, if she didn't die . . . clean!—we can probably still save her from . . ."

"Premature resurrection."

"Yes, by destroying it! With Uncle John gone, I doubt she'd be sustained. Where is it?"

"It's—awkward. I spoke to Papa last night—his ghost, down by the river."

"Christina, you can't—that's not good. That's witchcraft."

"It's spiritualism, science! I didn't . . . draw a pentagram, or light candles! He was just there in the shallow water, like—like some sick fish."

"And it was cold." Maria shook her head. "Poor Papa." Then she squinted at her sister. "How did you happen to be down by the river last night?"

"He told me to meet him there."

"Told you how?"

"I was—it doesn't matter. He said—"

"You used that pencil thing that Gabriel took from Lizzie, didn't you?"

"Somewhat. Slightly. I wasn't trying to talk to him, but he—"

"Consulting the dead! That's a sin, 'Stina! Who *were* you trying to talk to?" Then she nodded. "Uncle John."

"Not talk to, I simply hoped to get more of the 'Folio Q 'story. But Moony! Will you listen? The statue is apparently *in Papa's throat.* When his heart failed, he put it in his mouth, hoping Uncle John might save him, and in his travail he apparently *inhaled* it—and choked." Christina was horrified to realize that she was close to giggling, and she bit her tongue.

Maria's wide face was blank. "Evidently burial in sanctified ground doesn't stop him," she said slowly.

"No," agreed Christina.

"And our little ritual, at the Read estate seventeen years ago—"

"It kept him away for a while. It let my body expel—" She caught herself and hurried on, "I didn't see him for . . . months, afterward, and I had time to get stronger. I might have died, otherwise."

Maria hadn't been listening closely. "But what can we *do*?" she said. "We can't dig up Papa and—and cut his throat open!"

"He said you would know how to *choke* him, choke Uncle John."

"Choke him? Choke the statue? What would that mean?"

"Well, he didn't say. Ghosts are never *lucid*, Moony! They're shy—ashamed. And not very intelligent. But I think they are more honest, with their souls gone. They've lost all their . . ."

"Scruples."

"Yes. I don't think they remember why they ever kept secrets."

"In his last year," said Maria slowly, "Papa was writing a treatise on transmigration of souls. Mama burned it after he died, but he had me find and translate some Hebrew sources for him, in one of the manuscript collections in the British Museum. I could easily get permission to see those manuscripts again. There was a passage . . . I remember thinking at the time that it would have been helpful if I had read it before you and I did our . . . Grecian burial, seventeen years ago."

"It wouldn't . . . compromise you? Us, I mean? Spiritually?"

"No, as I recall, it didn't involve summoning or confronting anything. I believe it involved mirrors—and, well, blood—but it was like a trap, or a fence; it would stop spirits, but you didn't have to be present."

"How would we arrange it?"

"I—I'd need to reread the old manuscript."

Christina stood up. "When is the funeral to be? Lizzie's, I mean."

Maria shook her head and tried to speak; she cuffed tears from her eyes and hiccuped, then managed to say, "God knows. Apparently Gabriel is not nearly ready to admit that she has actually died."

Christina shivered. "I hope she has. Died for good, that is to say, with no . . . earthly return from it."

"I do too," whispered Maria. "I pray to God that she has."

Christina crossed to the pegs on which her clothes were hung. "I must go to Gabriel. And I need to get a letter to a veterinarian in Wych Street—I've got to cancel an appointment I made for today."

CHAPTER TEN

And watchers out at sea have caught
Glimpse of a pale gleam here or there
Come and gone as quick as thought,
Which might be hand or hair.

—*Christina Rossetti, "Jessie Cameron"*

SHEERNESS WAS AN old garrison town on the coast, at the mouths of the Thames and the river Medway. It was forty-six miles east of London on the London, Chatham and Dover Railway line, and Swinburne had spent two hours and nine shillings to get there in a drafty second-class railway carriage that he had shared with half a dozen women, apparently the wives of laborers in the dockyard. Swinburne had reflected that any one of the women looked capable of throwing him bodily off the train, and he had left his copy of Baudelaire's scandalous *Les Fleurs du mal* in his overcoat pocket and had instead contented himself with reading Dickens's *David Copperfield*. He had even pulled his ridiculous sou'wester hat down at the sides to somewhat conceal his possibly affronting hedge of coppery hair.

He was out in this Godforsaken corner of England because Lizzie had died two days earlier, apparently by her own hand.

A five-minute walk from the Sheerness station had taken him to a railed lane overlooking the shore, and since the sun had only a few minutes ago gone down over the Gravesend hills behind him, and the sky was still pale, he had stood there for a few minutes with the cold sea wind flapping the long back brim of his rubberized hat. A couple of distant figures trudged along the darkening expanse of sand below him, carrying a pole that might have been a mast or some fishing apparatus, and a man on horseback a hundred yards farther away was trotting north along the band of darker damp sand by the gray fringe of surf. Off to his right, near the empty steamboat pier, Swinburne saw a long open shed with what looked like a row of a dozen gypsy wagons in it—and then he recognized these as bathing machines stowed away for the winter. Come June they would be wheeled out, and ladies in street clothes would climb in and pull the doors closed, and then the vehicles would be drawn by horses down the slope and a few yards out into the shallows, where the ladies, having changed into bathing suits, could open the seaside doors and step down to splash about in the water, unobserved from the shore. In spite of the purpose of his quest tonight, Swinburne had forlornly wished that one hardy lady or two might have braved the cold sea this evening; and that, if any had done it, he had brought a telescope.

He had sighed and walked on to the brightly gas-lit Grand Hotel, where he had moodily drunk three brandies before strolling southeast down Broadway, away from the lights of the town. The slow crash of surf against the seawall a mile out to his right was the only punctuation to the steady wind, and the coming night looked likely to be far darker out here than any ever were in London.

Soon the lantern on the pier Chichuwee had told him to watch for stood out clearly ahead of him, and Swinburne trudged up to within a few yards of the foot of the short pier and stood there for a full minute, nerving himself to take the last few steps of this long day's journey. Someone must have lit the lantern and hung it on its pole at the end of the pier, but Swinburne couldn't see anyone.

He took a deep breath now and squeezed Baudelaire in his pocket for luck, then tramped down the booming planks of the pier, threading his way delicately around buckets and lengths of rusty chain.

Several moored boats rocked gently on the black water in the lantern light, but only one seemed occupied. If it were the one Chichuwee had directed him to, it was a fishing boat, and Swinburne couldn't imagine this vessel being anything much else. The grimy, battered vessel was no pleasure craft, certainly.

The boat was about twenty-five feet long. The short mast was bare, and the sail on its tethered boom was furled, but smoke was fluttering up out of a short tin pipe on the deck forward of two wide rectangular holes; stepping closer and peering over the gunwale, Swinburne saw that the rearward hole was partly filled with what appeared to be wet gravel. Perhaps it was some unattractive sort of shellfish. The chilly onshore wind was metallic and sulfurous, with a taint of coal smoke from the little chimney.

"Are you a singer?" came a harsh voice from only a couple of yards away, making Swinburne almost dance in surprise.

A stocky gray-bearded man in a voluminous oilskin coverall was sitting against the far gunwale among untidy heaps of rope, puffing on a short clay pipe.

"No," said Swinburne. He gestured inexpressively. "Uh, no."

The old man waved his pipe. "On your way then. I was informed that I'm waiting for a singer."

Swinburne bit his lip and looked up and down the miles of dark shore under the starry vault of the sky, and then at the three other boats moored here. They looked long abandoned. The wind in the ropes and the textured crash and hiss of the waves emphasized the overall silence.

"Could it," he ventured, "have been 'a poet'?"

For several seconds the old man squinted at him in the lantern's light; then he nodded. "Aye, the relay bird might have meant poet just as well. Are you a poet then?"

"Yes."

The old man's face crinkled with something like disgust, but he got his boots under him and struggled to his feet.

"You're going to find it a cold night," he said. "Your hat and gloves look good enough, and I've got a spare pair of boots and a neck wrap, but in between will suffer."

"Suffering will be helpful, I think," said Swinburne, stepping aboard. "Especially in between."

"I'm Chess," the old man said, and as if to emphasize it, he stamped twice on the rocking deck.

"Algernon," said Swinburne. Apparently they were not to shake hands.

The stamping had evidently been a summons, for in a few seconds two other men appeared, climbing laboriously up out of a previously unnoticed square hole in the deck near the tin chimney. Their beards were if anything whiter than Chess's, and Chess introduced them, perhaps seriously, as his father and grandfather.

"The bait's aboard for our catch tonight," Chess told them, waving at the skinny, top-heavy figure of Swinburne.

The two older men had closed a hatch cover over the opening they had emerged from, and they set about casting off lines and freeing the boom and unfurling the sail. Swinburne stepped cautiously around the open pit full of wet gravel to lean against the front side of the mast and look out over the bow at the black sea.

By his shadow on the raised bow ahead of him he could see that the silent mariners had carried the lantern aboard and fixed it somewhere amidships, and then he felt the deck move as they poled the vessel away from the pier.

When the offshore wind had filled the sail and the boat had begun to tack against it, surging out across the water to the south, Chess stepped up beside Swinburne.

"You've brought payment," the old man said.

Swinburne nodded and with one gloved hand dug a stoppered bottle out of his pocket.

When he had laid it in Chess's palm, the old man held it up, squinted at it, and shook it. "Catholic?" he asked.

"As specified. From St. Ethelreda's in Holborn."

"Cheat me and this enterprise won't work."

"I know," said Swinburne irritably, "the bird man told me that." He waved at the bottle. "It's genuine."

He wondered why, if Catholic holy water was so valuable to Chess, the old man didn't simply go ashore and fetch some on his own. Perhaps these three never did go ashore, Swinburne thought fancifully—perhaps they were a trinity that was somehow not able to.

The wind was already achingly cold on his face as he squinted past Chess at the few lighted windows on the receding Kentish hills. "How far out do you have to go?"

"You'll tell me," said Chess. "Quicksilver, I reckon your quarry was."

There had been no fortuitous ave out of which Chichuwee might forcibly milk and boil Lizzie's ghost, but Swinburne had brought him one of her handkerchiefs, and so the old bird man had used it as a "plumb line" to facilitate a session of automatic writing by means of a pencil on a felt-footed disk. Her ghost had seemed to volunteer a response, with weak squiggles that only occasionally formed words, but Chichuwee had said that if the responder was indeed Lizzie's ghost, it was already remote—out of the river and into the sink of the sea. The only chance of meaningful contact was for Swinburne to try calling her from a boat out of sight of land.

"Yes," Swinburne said now, shivering, "she didn't linger."

He didn't tell Chess that the reason Lizzie's *ghost* had not sat dormant in the river might be because her *identity* had powerfully repelled it by being negatively charged—even diabolically charged.

Her ghost, it seemed to Swinburne, might be her fugitive inno-cence.

"Out of sight of land," he added.

Chess nodded. "They're always that," he said. "Why don't you go below? You're no use up here, and we can fetch you when we're in the Ghost Roads."

Swinburne eyed the little square hatch cover in the deck with dis-taste, but a gust of even colder wind blew tears out of his eyes and he nodded and began groping his way aft.

THE BELOWDECKS SPACE WAS only dimly illuminated by a fire visible through vents in a small cooking stove, but Swinburne could see that the height of the place was no more than four feet, from the plank floor to the plank ceiling, and about eight feet long and perhaps seven feet across at its widest point, though it narrowed to nothing up at the bow end. In this confined space, Chess and his companions had crammed a surprising amount of stuff—a railed crockery shelf, a square teakettle fitted in a square niche, bunks, and bundles of canvas and rope. Soon the inside of Swinburne's nose had warmed enough for him to grimace at the smells of fish and sweat and tar, and he pulled out Baudelaire to have at least the mental perfume of the decadent Frenchman's verse.

But after a few minutes of trying to recline with the book held up to a beam of orange light from the stove, Swinburne found himself sliding forward and then rolling up against one of the bunks, where he clung as the boat rolled the other way, and he guessed that they had sailed out past the barrier of the seawall. Hastily he pulled a flask from the breast pocket of his overcoat and gulped some brandy to stave off seasickness, and he anxiously watched the stove and the piles of tarred rope, ready to bolt up onto the deck if the vessel's pitching should spill burning coals onto the rope. Regretfully he stopped trying to read *Métamorpho-*

ses du vampire, shut the volume of Baudelaire, and tucked it back into his pocket.

He thought of Lizzie, and the night she had bitten him on the wrist as they had been drunkenly playing cat-and-mouse on the drawing room carpet while Gabriel had been working down the hall in his studio. Swinburne had a moment earlier presumed to call her by the pet name Gabriel used for her, Guggums, and after the answering bite she had said, in an oddly harsh voice, *Call me Gogmagog.* Swinburne had laughed delightedly and tried to bite her in return, but she had got up and hurried out of the room; and when he had gone looking for her, he had found her with Gabriel in the studio, and she had claimed to have been there for the last half hour.

Probably she had been! Probably the Lizzie who had bitten him was a mimicking apparition, an inhuman impostor, like the couple in Gabriel's drawing who confronted the originals of themselves in a forest.

After perhaps half an hour, the rolling abated a bit and one of the old men lifted back the hatch cover and called down the hole, "It's time."

Swinburne was glad to crawl across to the hatch and stand up with his head out in the fresh air—and then he quailed and sagged, for the wind was icy and shot with spray. He ducked back into the low space and found the boots and scarf that Chess had mentioned, and when he had got them on, he took a deep breath and then crawled back to the hatch and climbed out onto the rocking wet deck.

A couple of flaring kerosene torches mounted at the bow and stern threw a white glare over the dark water, and the nearer waves glittered as they rolled past, like living, diamond-dusted obsidian.

Chess was braced up by the bow, and Swinburne staggered forward against the force of the wind to join him, both to see better ahead and to be nearer to the flame.

Chess was holding the unstoppered bottle of holy water, and Swinburne could see that half of its contents were gone.

Swinburne's face was already numb with cold, but the chill shivered through his belly too when he looked ahead and saw . . . white figures standing out there over the waves in the night.

They moved bonelessly like splashes of milk in oil, and the holes that were their eyes and mouths appeared and disappeared as randomly as spots of moonlight on pavement below windblown trees; their arms waved above their shapeless heads.

And over the wind in the rigging he could hear their voices, a shaking cacophony like wind chimes. Men and women, and children, their frail cries rang away across the infinite dark face of the sea in weird atonal harmony.

Swinburne clung dizzily to the bow gunwale. Flying sea spray stung his eyes.

Then one voice out there was clear: "Hadji!" it called. "Save me with your blood!" Swinburne saw the figure now, only a dozen yards away and clearer than the rest. And even out here, even without an organic throat to propel it, the voice was one Swinburne recognized.

Chess leaned toward Swinburne. "You need to throw some of your blood into the sea," the old man said, speaking loudly to be heard over the ghost chorus and the wind. "The bird man told you that, right?"

"No," said Swinburne, his gloved hands gripping the slick gunwale. He shook his head.

"Well, it needn't be gallons—just a few drops will do." With a sharp click Chess opened a clasp knife and pressed the grip into Swinburne's palm. "Finger's fine. That's your fugitive, is it?"

Tears were blowing back along Swinburne's cheeks, mingling with the sea spray.

"No," he said.

Hadji had been Swinburne's childhood nickname. This was the ghost of his grandfather, who had died two years ago; Swinburne had written about him, *"the two maddest things in the north country were his horse and himself"*—old Sir John Swinburne had been a free-thinking follower of Voltaire who was once sent to prison for insulting the Prince Regent, and young Algernon had loved and admired him.

"Hadji!" came the cry again across the water, distinct over the wailing of the other ghosts. "Some of your living blood!"

"You have to answer," said Chess, leaning in close to be heard, "or he'll hang about and drown out any others." He grinned. "Huh. Drown out."

"It's my *grandfather*," said Swinburne, near sobbing. "I can't bear it that he's dead—out here."

Chess laughed harshly. "My grandfather is dead too, and out here. At least yours doesn't have to work a Purgatorial fishing boat."

That made Swinburne look directly at the old man beside him, and then he hunched around to look aft at the two figures standing halfway back along the deck, black silhouettes backlit by the stern torch.

Swinburne suddenly felt cold all through, colder than the windborne spray. Very aware of the multitude of ghosts and the vast night sea around them, he turned back to face Chess. "Am I," he quavered, "dead myself?"

"I think you hope to die," said Chess, shouting into Swinburne's ear, "but haven't the industry to kill yourself in a straightforward fashion." He laughed. "No, lad, you're not dead—nor am I. But it seems we both have grandfathers wanting such care as dead men can receive."

With his gloved right hand he pulled back the bunched left sleeves of his coverall, coat, and sweater, and then quickly tucked it all back into the glove gauntlet, but not before Swinburne had glimpsed a raw cut on the man's wrist.

Swinburne squinted ahead at the curling wisp that was his own grandfather's ghost. "But this isn't *them*." He pounded one fist on the gunwale. "I mean—*is* it?"

Chess said loudly, "They break up, when they die. The core goes away, but the shell sometimes stays. And even the shell is part of what they were." He nodded out over the bow. "And there's your grandfather's."

"No," said Swinburne. And then he shouted, "No!" at the white figure curling in the darkness.

"What for me?" piped his grandfather's ghost.

"Nothing from me," said Swinburne into his clenched hands on the gunwale; he had spoken almost too quietly for even Chess to hear him over the thrashing wind, but the ghost sprang to fading mist.

Swinburne raised his head, glaring into the infinite night.

"Lizzie!" he called now. "Lizzie Siddal!"

The ghosts all just stood out there, like a million bleached banners of a long-ago defeated army.

"Lizzie!" he called again.

And another ghost came into sharper focus where his grandfather's had been, and this one managed to look vaguely feminine in its shifting outlines.

"Algy, who are your friends?" it said, and its voice was like notes violined out of glass and sharp edges of bone.

Swinburne's spray-stung eyes strained with the effort of getting her into focus. "Sailors," he shouted. "Lizzie, I—"

"The dead leading the blind," said her ghost. "Algy, it's always cold here."

"I've come to take you back," Swinburne called, cupping his hands around his mouth.

"Back! How?"

Swinburne's teeth stung as he took a deep breath. "Marry me! I love you! With Gabriel it was just 'till death did you part,' and that's—done. Marry me and live in me, in this body, this warm body. 'One flesh.'" He was still holding Chess's opened knife, and now he stabbed his finger right through the leather glove and shook drops of blood out into the wind. "With this blood I thee wed!"

But the white figure was now smaller and less distinct. "I'm naked," came its fainter voice. "You mustn't look at me."

"Clothe yourself in me! I love you! We can—travel, read, eat, drink, together!"

"I don't have that anymore."

"Have it all again, in me! Marry me! Here's a ship's captain, we can be together, a hermaphrodite—"

"No," came her voice; then, much louder, *"No."* And she was gone. The other ghosts, filling the night apparently to the invisible horizon, crowded closer, their arms waving like a moonlit kelp forest on the sea floor.

Swinburne gaped at the space where Lizzie's ghost had been.

Chess pushed away from the bow. "Shouldn't have spilled your blood till she agreed to take it," he said before striding back along the rocking deck.

The old man shouted to his two dead crewmen, and they shambled to the tiller and rigging, and in moments the boat was heeling around in the wind.

Ghost limbs flailed at the taut shrouds and were whisked into vanishing fragments, and for a few tense moments as Swinburne clung to the bow their voices were a buzzing, clattering racket in his freezing ears.

"Don't listen to them!" shouted Chess from behind him.

But Swinburne couldn't ignore their voices, the things they were saying: "Here, where the world is quiet; / Here, where all trouble seems / Dead winds' and spent waves' riot / In doubtful dreams of dreams . . ." These were lines he had written himself, and so they were convincing. "Even the weariest river / Winds somewhere safe to sea . . ."

He had already got one knee up on the gunwale when Chess tugged him back to sprawl painfully on the deck.

"Not your style," Chess called to him.

Then the boat had come around and was surging northwest before the wind, and the ghost multitude quickly receded into the remote blackness.

Swinburne got wearily to his feet and gripped the rail, lowering his head and taking deep breaths of the cold sea air.

"You'll be among 'em soon enough," said Chess, not unkindly. "Why don't you get in out of the wind now."

Swinburne climbed back down to the belowdecks cabin, stunned and despairing, for he had thought his main challenge would be finding Lizzie's ghost—it had not occurred to him that she might refuse his proposal.

WHEN THE BOAT'S PITCHING fell to a gentle rise and fall, he knew they had passed the Sheerness breakwater, and he pulled himself back up onto the deck. The kerosene torches had been extinguished, and the old lantern was again glowing on the mast.

The lights on the Kentish hills were bright yellow dots in the night. Out in the cold air again, Swinburne was shivering violently, and he had to ask Chess, who shambled up to him, to repeat something he had just said.

"It don't work with fishing-boat captains," the old man said more loudly.

"Wh-what doesn't?"

"Shipboard marriages." He shook his head. "But did you truly expect me to marry you to a ghost?"

"Oh, what d-does it matter now?"

Chess grinned, without cheer. "Just so you know in future—they couldn't say 'I do.' There's no *I*, and they haven't the wherewithal to choose to *do* anything."

"She chose to reject me!"

"That wasn't a choice, lad—that was an empty gun saying *click*."

"She chose to reject me," said Swinburne again, and Chess shook his head and shambled back to rejoin his laboring dead ancestors.

After a few minutes, the mariners let the sail go slack and one of them leaned on the tiller, and Swinburne saw the pier only moments before Chess threw a line over a bollard on it and began pulling the bow in.

And the figure standing at the foot of the pier wasn't visible until a match flared in the darkness and lit what must have been the end of a cigar.

Chess and his ancestors finished mooring the boat and tying up the lowered sail, and then Chess plodded wearily across the deck to the mast and extinguished the lantern; the darkness was total. A minute later Swinburne heard the hatch cover clatter down.

His business here seemed to be ended.

Swinburne shrugged and stepped up onto the pier.

"And how do you do, sir?" he called toward the tiny orange-glowing coal of the cigar.

"Stupidest question I've ever heard," came the gruff answer.

Swinburne clenched his teeth and made himself step forward, but the cigar coal bobbed in quick retreat.

"Stay back, you fool!" came the unseen man's voice. "Don't you know anything? I can survive their notice, but I doubt you could."

Swinburne forced his voice to be steady. "Whose notice?"

"Not at night, under an open sky. Noon tomorrow—in the Whispering Gallery in the dome of St. Paul's. Stand at the southernmost point, by the stairs. Don't fail to be there, if you hope to save your life or your soul."

Then the cigar coal fell to the ground and went out, probably under a heel. After Swinburne had called hello a few times, he slowly but resolutely began walking forward, but his measured trudging took him all the way up to the road without hearing a sound from the man who had spoken to him; and he exhaled and relaxed and began trudging back toward Sheerness to get a room at the hotel for the remainder of the night.

ST. PAUL'S CATHEDRAL WAS a particularly daunting white splendor in the cold noonday sun. It stood blocking out most of the blue sky on a wide railed square at the crest of Ludgate Hill, the highest point in the

City, and though he couldn't see the dome from the foot of the broad marble stairs out front, the two widely separated towers and the two lofty rows of paired columns between them made Swinburne feel as insignificant as the limitless dark ocean had done last night. The bottom third of the enormous building, the hundred-foot extent from the projecting entablature between the two galleries of columns down to the pavement, seemed a slightly darker shade of white, as if the sea had once tried to engulf the cathedral and then impotently receded.

And I'm out of my depth, he thought as he began reluctantly tapping up the steps. He was wearing a hat and gloves, not because of the cold but because direct sunlight had begun lately to irritate his skin—at least this distasteful place offered welcome shade.

It was of course a church, a Christian church, and mentally he recited lines from a poem he'd written: *Thou hast conquered, O pale Galilean; the world has grown grey from thy breath; We have drunken of things Lethean, and fed on the fullness of death.*

Certainly Swinburne didn't seem to be conquering by pursuing the pagan sorts of supernaturalism. They were real enough—as proved by the two ghosts he had spoken to out at sea last night!—but the world had indeed grown gray, grayer than he had guessed when he had written the poem; and he was afraid that he would never be able to drink of Lethe's river: to forget his love for Lizzie . . . and her refusal of him.

The broad interior of the cathedral, with its columns and the arches of its ceiling peaking impossibly far overhead, made him feel like a rodent; no service was going on at the moment, fortunately, and the isolated figures praying in the pews were all facing away from him. Who, he wondered as he scuttled through slanting beams of rainbow-colored light from the south-facing stained-glass windows, is this man who wants to talk to me? And why does he?

Far overhead, the interior of the great dome ballooned up in what must have been eight huge triangular concave panels with vague dark murals painted on them, but Swinburne slanted off to the right across the marble floor, to the stairs, before he would have to walk under its ornate high immensity; and the tall white-and-gold altar was thankfully still farther away down the long central aisle.

The corkscrew staircase was comfortably narrow and dim; it was warmer than the vast nave had been and smelled reassuringly of tallow and old book paper. He took off his hat to keep from bumping it against the low ceiling. After about a hundred ascending steps, he reached a gallery with a library at one end of it, but the Whispering Gallery proved to be higher up, so he returned to the stairs and kept climbing.

After puffing his way up an even greater number of stone stairs than before, he stepped out into the highest gallery inside the cathedral, a circular catwalk high above the nave, at the very base of the incurving dome.

A ring of tall windows in the dome above him let in bright daylight, and above them were the huge murals he had glimpsed the bottoms of from the nave floor below. He stepped out to the railing and looked down—a hundred feet directly below, the white-and-black checkerboard pattern of the floor was interrupted by a wide compass-rose mosaic.

The enormous Gothic geometry of it all, the slanting insubstantial buttresses of sunlight, and the sheer volume of empty space above and below him, were dizzying, and it was several moments before he remembered that he was supposed to meet someone right here—at the south rim of the dome, by the stairs.

He pulled out his watch and squinted at it: noon exactly. Three or four other people stood at other points around the gallery's circumference, peering up at the murals, but none of them was paying any evident attention to him.

The view below chilled his belly, and he stepped back to lean against the rounded wall below the windows.

And at his ear came a whisper: "Poet"—he glanced around quickly, but no one was within a dozen yards of him—"stay where you are."

Of course, he thought nervously, the *Whispering* Gallery! The interior of the dome must carry sounds right around the whole stone ring.

"What?" he said softly.

"Speak against the stone," came the disembodied whisper again.

Swinburne obediently pressed his cheek against the cold stone wall.

"What do you have to tell me?" he muttered.

"You're in love with a ghost." The disembodied sentence seemed to carry an implicit *you fool* at the end of it. "You shouldn't need me to tell you this, and if you've got a brain in your head you understood it last night, but—have no further contact with the thing. I'd say 'with her,' but—as you probably noticed—it's not really a 'her' anymore. Go meet a real flesh-and-blood girl, and fall in love with *her*."

Swinburne was frowning. Could this man somehow represent the Church, or the government? Was there some old law about necromancy still on the books? He peered at the other people standing at intervals around the gallery, trying to guess which of them might be the one speaking to him. "You—" he began. "This is absurd. A ghost? You're obviously drunk—"

"One of us probably is," came the whisper, "but it's not me. Chichuwee told me all about your conversation with him, and I know a couple of things that the bird man doesn't."

Swinburne could feel his face blushing against the cold stone, and he blinked out across the dome—a beam of sunlight from one of the windows had moved onto him, and he shuffled sideways to be out of the sun's glare. There was a tall, white-bearded old man standing on the opposite side of the railed ring, a hundred feet away across the empty air of the dome—surely that was the furtive speaker. "This is none of your—"

"It is of mine, boy," came the eerily far-traveling whisper, and the tall old man at the northernmost point of the gallery hunched his shoulders as the voice reached Swinburne's ears. "If it weren't for a sin of mine, the embodiment of which was broken but now grows again behind my jugular vein—if not for that—you could go sailing out to talk to your dead girl every night; but you're not the only one who loves her now, and your rival is inclined toward tumultuous jealousy and will surely kill you."

"Rival? Who, Gabriel? He doesn't—"

"No," and this time it was spoken: "you fool. I don't know who Gabriel is, nor who you are, and it doesn't matter. I only know the rival. Hah! Ask Chichuwee about the Nephilim, though I expect the answer will cost you many more birds than your previous consultation did. There's a creature, call it a goddess, an archaic goddess, who loves your ghost-girl, and who will kill any mortals who love her too, or who she loved, back when she still could. Fortunately for you, this—this *goddess* is wounded and blinded right now, for another day or so, and is not aware of your ill-advised expedition last night. *Don't repeat it.*"

Swinburne shuffled sideways again to stay out of the sunbeam. He was trying to be amused by this grotesque conversation. "Her husband, Gabriel—*he* loved her, and she loved *him*. Is this goddess of yours going to kill him?"

"Unless he has joined a god's family too. And I *don't* need yet *another* member of that sort of family to deal with, so heed me. This—why are you moving?"

"Moving?"

"Along the wall."

Swinburne shrugged. "Staying out of the sunlight. What is this family—"

"Step back into it." The old man on the far side of the dome was clearly staring at him now. "Yes, you've seen me. Now humor me—step back into the sunbeam—or I'll drag you outside without a hat."

Swinburne was sweating, and he glanced sideways at the sunlit patch of wall.

He took a deep breath and let it out. "I'd truly rather not."

"Bloody hell. Does it hurt, sting?"

Swinburne shrugged, then reluctantly nodded.

"And have you lately begun to . . . write poetry?"

"I've always written poetry, I—"

A hundred feet away across the dome, the old man waved impatiently. "Damn you," came the whisper along the wall, "has it suddenly become *very good*? Better than you had imagined you could write?"

Swinburne's mouth fell open. "Yes," was all he could say.

"Step into the light. It won't hurt your sorry hide today, trust me."

This stranger knew so much about him that Swinburne, dazed, did as he was told: he shuffled sideways into the shaft of sunlight—and it was simply warm, not astringent.

"Well, through glass," he muttered, mistrustful of the apparent relief, "and holy glass, at that—"

"Try it again when you're outside. She *bit* you, didn't she? Before she died?"

Swinburne rocked his head against the stone wall, feeling the mild sun on his face. "Yes."

For a few moments there was no skating whisper along the wall, and the only sounds were the windy echoes of random footsteps and coughs from the nave below.

At last the stranger's soft voice came again. "I had hoped your dilemma was simpler. It's her poisonous attention on you, in you, that reacted to sunlight . . . but her attention right now is many times decimated and concentrated only on her wounded self. You have at least one more day, I think, before she'll be expanded enough to have regard for you again. You must leave England within twenty-four hours. She won't sense you on the other side of the Channel, the wide, cold salt water."

Swinburne was looking at his own right hand in the sunlight, savoring the simple warmth of it, and for a moment he let himself imagine starting over again, in France, say, with no history, free of—

"Would I still be able to write poetry?" he asked suddenly.

"Not like you've been writing recently, no. Not like Byron and Shelley and Keats, who shared the affliction you're now free to shed. But—like Tennyson or Ashbless, probably."

Swinburne relaxed and smiled, very relieved that this decision had turned out to be so easy; and he stepped back out of the sunlight, toward the doorway to the stairs. The old man on the other side of the round gallery looked fit enough, but if he chose to give chase it was unlikely that he'd be able to catch him.

Swinburne went down the curling stairway like a dancer spinning and tapping through a very fast allegro sequence.

I will never, he thought, go near the English Channel again.

CHAPTER ELEVEN

You will not be cold there;
You will not wish to see your face in a mirror;
There will be no heaviness,
Since you will not be able to lift a finger.
There will be company, but they will not heed you;
Yours will be a journey of only two paces
Into view of the stars again; but you will not make it.

—*Walter de la Mare, "De Profundis"*

For six days Lizzie's body had lain in an open coffin in the upstairs parlor at 14 Chatham Place, and though Gabriel had spent nearly every waking hour in the room with her, watching her face by candle-light because the curtains were drawn across the river-facing windows, he had been sleeping on a cot in William's room at the Albany Street house.

Now the downstairs front door at Chatham Place was open, and the black-draped laurel wreath that had hung there for six days was taken down so that the pallbearers wouldn't snag against it when it came time to carry the coffin out. The hearse had not arrived yet, but over the course of the last couple of hours a dozen black-clad friends and family members had solemnly stepped inside and climbed the stairs to the now-crowded sitting room. The flaring gas jets were supplemented with candles on the mantel and on two high, cleared bookshelves.

The coffin rested on a long table against the curtained windows. On a credenza against the door-side wall were several platters of sliced ham and pickles and a huge glass bowl of rum punch, and the crowd of guests was kept moving by people sidling up to the credenza to refill plates and cups. Many of the mourners took the little funeral cakes, disks of sponge cake wrapped in white paper and sealed in black wax with a skull imprint, but these they mostly pocketed as remembrances.

Christina, wearing one of the black bombazine dresses she'd worn for a year after her father's death, was sitting beside Maria on the sofa that faced the coffin and the curtained windows, and both of them were watching Gabriel warily. He was standing behind the coffin; Swinburne stood beside him, nervously fingering his gingery mustache, but Gabriel only stared down at Lizzie's smooth white face.

He had been incredulous a week ago when his sisters had told him where Christina believed the diabolical little statue was located, and then for several hours he had adamantly opposed the plan Maria had devised from new study in the Reading Room at the British Museum—but he had finally relented, and he had even helped his sisters cut out the mattress and lining of the coffin in order to attach to the wooden floor the hammock-like array of etched and stained downward-facing mirrors.

Christina was relieved now to see that the white cambric mattress and silk linings showed no signs of their tampering, at least with Lizzie's pale and oddly undeteriorated body now occupying the coffin. The veil Maria had constructed lay beside Lizzie's head, with a few locks of her red hair draped over it to keep any mourners from getting too close a look at it.

❧❀❧❀❧

"WHAT THE NEW TESTAMENT calls 'unclean spirits,'" Maria had explained to Gabriel and Christina six nights ago, "the old Jewish mystics called *dybbuks,* though originally the word was more a verb than a noun. The identity of one of these spirits is not confined to its body but is a standing spherical pattern of radiation, like Faraday's description of electric fields."

Christina had needed to have that explained to her, though Gabriel had claimed to know all about it.

Maria had gone on, "It's a pattern that fills space, and matter is only a—like a cloud, to it. A mirror can cripple one of these spirits by reflecting part of its wave-form back on itself, so that the waves interfere with each other—they break the coherent patterns of its identity, causing arbitrary patches of awareness and oblivion, clear sight and blindness, presence and absence."

"But," Gabriel had objected, "if matter is just a cloud to them, why should a *mirror* be distinct?"

"It's distinct if their attention is called to fix on it," Maria had told him. "If one of these spirits incorporates a mirror into its particular attention, the reflection occurs. To be sure Uncle John fixes on the mirrors we use, they must be etched, and the incised grooves filled with blood that he recognizes and—and desires—and that he therefore will focus on."

Gabriel had been drinking brandy and pacing around the table in his studio, to which Lizzie's body had been carried. Delivery of the coffin had been promised for the next day.

"Where do we place this mirror—"

"Array of mirrors," said Maria, "for maximum diffraction."

"—This *array* of mirrors?"

"Gabriel, we must place it directly over the statue, which is the kernel of Uncle John's identity; and that's in Papa's throat, in his coffin. We must line the bottom of poor Lizzie's coffin with these mirrors, facing downward, and then she must be buried directly on top of Papa."

To Christina's surprise, Gabriel had not objected to this. He had nodded moodily and said, "It would be a real acknowledgment, finally, that she is—was—a member of our family."

Both Christina and Maria had stirred, but neither of them spoke; it was true that the rest of the Rossetti family had not ever warmed to Gabriel's melancholy bride.

Without discussing it, all three of them had known that the blood in the mirror grooves must be Christina's. And both sisters had insisted, over Gabriel's initial protests, that smaller etched and inward-facing mirrors must be sewn onto Lizzie's veil too, just in case poor Lizzie had after all not managed to escape the Nephilim's domination.

The blood on Lizzie's mirrors, they all finally agreed, must be Gabriel's.

THE SMELLS OF HAM and pickle and candle wax in the stuffy, crowded room were beginning to nauseate Christina, and she stood up, intending to go downstairs and stand in the street for a few minutes, when she saw Gabriel straighten from beside the coffin and frown at something behind her.

She turned to scan the crowd, and a moment later she gasped when she saw Adelaide and her veterinarian companion sidling over to the trays of food.

Christina stepped up beside Gabriel and whispered, "You and I both made them part of our family." He started around the coffin toward the uninvited newcomers, but Christina closed her hand around his black crepe armband. "And because of you and me, their daughter is menaced by what took Lizzie."

Gabriel exhaled and gave her a smoldering glance, then nodded.

Swinburne was leaning in dizzily behind Gabriel's shoulder.

"Who *are* they?" he asked. Christina exhaled through her nose to repel the fumes of rum on Swinburne's breath. "I must say," Swinburne went on, "women look fetching when they're in mourning."

"Oh, never mind, Algy," snapped Gabriel. "They're not important." He stared into the coffin again. "Nobody is, anymore."

Swinburne frowned thoughtfully and stepped back, though his eyes followed Christina.

She turned toward the door, consciously put on a smile that should appear at once sad, surprised, and welcoming; and when she felt she'd got it right, she began threading her way through the guests toward Adelaide and Mr. Crawford.

"WE'RE FRIENDS OF MISS Christina," said Crawford for the third time in two minutes. "No, we didn't know Mrs. Rossetti." He was sweating in his black frock coat.

McKee had read about Lizzie Rossetti's death and impending funeral and had insisted that the two of them attend; Crawford had reluctantly agreed when she promised that this would be their last visit to Highgate Cemetery.

They had made visits to the cemetery on four of the last six days— McKee had gone alone on the days when Crawford's practice took precedence—and twice they had even climbed the wall, separately, to search the grounds by night; and they had not caught one glimpse of anyone who might have been their daughter, Johanna.

Crawford now looked at McKee, who had her arm linked through his to prevent them being separated in the press of mourners, and he reflected that she looked a good deal more tired and discouraged than she had when she had come to his surgery at dawn eight days ago, even though at that time she had believed Johanna was dead.

He supposed he looked tired too—he'd been staying up late to do accounts that ordinarily would be done in the afternoons. It would be good for both of them when this last cemetery excursion was done, and the two of them would be able to go their separate ways—though probably McKee would spend the rest of her life monitoring the marble-studded lawns at Highgate Cemetery.

Just this funeral to get through, he thought—and then he realized that many of the starkly gas-lit faces he could see around him also seemed to reflect an imperfectly concealed relief. Apparently Gabriel's friends believed the marriage had been in some ways an ill-advised one.

Through a gap in the milling mourners he caught a momentary glimpse of Lizzie Rossetti's still profile in the coffin, and though she looked nothing like Adelaide McKee, she brought his thoughts back to McKee; one day McKee too would be dead. Though it was obviously true, the thought troubled him with something like a premonition of guilt. Crawford and McKee had not talked very much during the past week's expeditions, but they had quickly established an unconsidered partnership, seldom having to discuss who paid for cabs or coffee or spoke first to a cemetery guard or policeman, always understanding from a nod or frown or gesture what was proposed to be done next.

His thought about Gabriel was echoing in his head—an ill-advised marriage.

And across the room he now saw the piping-voiced little bald gentleman they had met at Christina Rossetti's house last Monday—Crawley or something, his name was.

McKee had noticed him too. "Christina's suitor, Cayley," she whispered, "who disapproves of her work with the lower orders."

Crawford nodded, remembering. Cayley seemed to be registering disapproval today too, blinking across at one of the guests whose coppery red hair could admittedly use cutting, or at least brushing.

From the stairs beyond the doorway at his back Crawford heard someone say, "The hearse is here." The phrase was repeated in muted tones through the crowded room, and people began bolting the remaining punch in their cups and crouching to set plates down against the walls.

"Pigs," whispered McKee, and Crawford shook her arm reprovingly.

"Well, they *are*," she whispered.

"Artists," he said quietly. "Poets." He picked up one of the paper-wrapped funeral cakes from the tray by the door, blinked at the skull imprint in the black sealing wax, and tucked the thing into his pocket.

An old man moved aside from in front of them, and Crawford found himself looking straight into Christina Rossetti's wide brown eyes. Her face looked both paler and younger by the gaslight, framed by her pulled-back brown hair and the high black neckline of her dress.

"Adelaide!" she said softly. "Mr. Crawford! It was good of both of you to come. I'm terribly sorry I wasn't able to—Gabriel and I weren't able to go with you, last week." She looked at McKee. "And I'm very sorry to perceive that you haven't found good news." She glanced back toward Maria and Gabriel, and then whispered, "But we hope to end, today, the peril that we discussed at the zoo."

"End it?" said McKee. "How?"

The little Cayley fellow had sidled closer and appeared to be trying to hear.

"I—" said Christina, "I'll tell you after it has been implemented. The arrow is in flight, there's nothing to be done but wait—for an hour or two."

The people around them were shuffling toward the door, rocking from side to side the way people always did at solemn events, and Christina took McKee's elbow in her left hand and Crawford's in her right and led them forward.

"You came by cab?" she said. "I'm to be in the coach ahead of the hearse, but I'll get you places in one of the mourning coaches."

MARIA WAS STANDING BESIDE Gabriel now.

"It's time to close the coffin," she told him softly, and she leaned in and pushed Lizzie's hair aside to lift the veil, which was heavy with the little inward-facing mirrors she had sewn onto the inner side of the lace. She carefully draped it over Lizzie's calm face, making sure that it was even and wouldn't be dislodged, and turned away with tears in her eyes.

Swinburne and William had taken hold of the coffin lid and had begun to swing it up, but Gabriel stopped them with a raised hand.

"I—I need to leave something of myself with her," he said. His voice was unsteady. "Wait a moment."

He blundered through the mourners and hurried down the hall to the bedroom, and very shortly he had returned carrying a battered octavo-sized notebook.

"All my poems," Gabriel said hoarsely. "I send them with her." He laid the notebook on Lizzie's cold crossed hands and then bent over and rested his head on it.

Swinburne opened his mouth and closed it, blinking at the notebook in the coffin, and then said, "No, Gabriel, that's just rude—she wouldn't want you to sacrifice your poetry."

William had been frowning, but now he said, "It's for you to decide, Gabriel."

Gabriel's face was expressionless, but tears were coursing down his cheeks into his goatee. "My poetry henceforth is for her alone. Close it."

Swinburne exhaled and spread his hands, but he and William nodded and solemnly closed the coffin.

THE HEARSE IN THE street out front was a black carriage with glass sides, and black ostrich feathers waved above the gold trim along the edges of the polished roof. The gold was dull under the gray morning sky. Four black horses were harnessed to it, blowing steam from their nostrils, and in addition to the coachman there were half a dozen attendants and two traditional "mutes," all of them apparently provided by the undertaker and all wearing black silk hatbands and gloves; Crawford reflected that the funeral must have cost Gabriel a fair packet.

The four mourning coaches were designated by black velvet cloths roped over their roofs, and blankets of the same material on the pairs of horses.

Christina led Crawford and McKee down the pavement to the last of the four mourning coaches, behind which stood several cabs and carriages. Christina glanced back, but none of the attendants had followed them, and so with an impatient sigh, she herself stepped up to take hold of the silver handle and pull the door open.

She hopped back down, and, before turning away and returning to her family, she said, breathlessly, "Today I think we will free the world of my uncle."

Crawford and McKee exchanged a wide-eyed glance, and then he helped her up into the coach and followed her in and took the rearward-facing seat.

He took his hat from the seat beside him and set it on his lap when another couple climbed in, and again he had to explain that he and McKee were friends of Christina's but had never met the deceased. The newcomers shook their heads, probably wondering why such comparative strangers should merit seats in one of the mourning coaches, but contented themselves with frowning and staring out the windows. McKee caught Crawford's eye and bobbed one eyebrow.

From where he sat, Crawford couldn't see the pallbearers carry out the coffin and slide it into the hearse, but the line of vehicles eventually began moving and traced a long rattling curve out of the Chatham Place square and proceeded north between the stately old office buildings along Bridge Street.

The procession rolled along at a steady pace onward up Farrington Road, for many of the wagons and omnibuses and cabs gave right of way to the line of black-draped vehicles; and in less than an hour they had crossed the North London Road and were among country roads bordered by leafless trees, and the funeral carriages spread farther apart as the horses were urged into a fast trot. At bends in the road, Crawford could see the attendants who had been walking alongside the hearse now perched on top of it, clutching their hats among the fluttering black ostrich feathers.

The procession slowed and closed up again as the horses pulled the carriages up Highgate Hill, and when the road leveled out, the yard in front of the Highgate Cemetery arches was close by on the right.

McKee and Crawford let the other couple disembark first, and when they had followed them down the coach step and onto the packed sand, McKee led Crawford away from the press of carriages and horses and mourners rearranging their coats and hats.

"Christina aims to do something consequential, here, today," McKee said. "You ever have any dealings with pickpockets?"

Crawford shook his head, looking around at the brick tower and the gates and the lawns beyond, which had become disappointingly familiar sights to him over the past week.

"Well," said McKee, "if your attention is being called to one place, you're often well advised to look in all other directions instead."

Gabriel and five other men were carrying the coffin in through the gates, and Crawford took McKee's arm and started forward across the crowded yard. Under the overcast sky, nobody cast any shadows.

THE CEMETERY CHAPEL WAS drafty, and the gray daylight muted the colors of the tall stained-glass windows. The men among the mourners had removed their hats, but everyone kept their coats. The walls were dark stone, and the ceiling was lost in the shadows of massive crossbeams.

The coffin, draped in a white cloth now, rested on a platform at the front of the central aisle, and Crawford could see the backs of Gabriel's and Christina's heads up in the front pew, along with others who were probably relatives.

The priest standing in front of the shadowed altar had been speaking for several minutes without Crawford being able to make out his words, but now he said more loudly, "'I am the resurrection and the life,' saith the Lord, 'he that believeth in me, though he were dead, yet shall he live: and whosoever liveth and believeth in me shall never die.'"

"Bad news for that Lizzie girl," whispered McKee.

"He means 'believeth in God,'" Crawford whispered back, "not—their uncle."

"I hope she caught that distinction."

Crawford nudged her to be quiet, for the priest had stepped down from the railed-off altar and around the coffin and begun walking slowly toward the doors, and Gabriel and the five other pallbearers—one of whom, Crawford noticed, was the fellow with coppery red hair sticking out in all directions—had stood up and taken hold of the coffin handles and begun shuffling down the aisle behind him.

The family members in the front pew stepped out one by one and filed along after it, their footsteps on the stone floor echoing in the arches of the high ceiling, but Christina Rossetti stepped out of the line and into the pew where Crawford and McKee stood.

She had bumped Crawford so that he would make room for her in the pew, and now gave him an awkward smile. He noticed that in spite of the chilly draft, her forehead was misted with perspiration.

"Distract me," she whispered.

An old woman who might have been Christina's mother gave her a wondering frown, but kept moving after the coffin toward the doors.

Crawford nodded. "Uh, puree of veal is the best remedy for general cat malaise," he told Christina quietly. "Chicken or beef, though the cats might relish them, are of no avail."

McKee had heard Christina's whisper and reached into her bag and lifted out three of the little paper-wrapped funeral cakes and began juggling them—to the evident surprised irritation of the few mourners who were still filing past the pew.

Crawford, his face reddening, grabbed her arm to stop her making a spectacle of herself, and though McKee managed to catch one of the cakes and Crawford snatched uselessly at another, two fell down under the padded kneeler at their feet.

Crawford and McKee both bent to retrieve them and knocked their heads together; McKee's bonnet fell down over her face and she sat down, whispering curses as she shoved it back into place.

Crawford sat down too. He had managed to pick up one of the cakes, and he scowled at it while he rubbed his forehead. The wax seal had cracked, and the imprinted skull was split—the smaller piece came off in his palm.

"Here's Death's jawbone," he told Christina, and the ringing in his ears made him speak more loudly than he meant to.

Someone lagging behind the tail end of the mourners' procession was suddenly leaning over him.

"To whom are you referring, sir?" came a harsh whisper.

Crawford blinked up at the speaker and was not very surprised to recognize Trelawny. The old man had hung back from the rest of the crowd and seemed to be more observer than mourner.

Crawford mutely held out the fragment of black wax. "This," he croaked.

"Ah!" said Trelawny scornfully. "You clowns again! Diamonds, you do yourself no service associating with these idiots."

Christina's lips were pressed together, and she nodded solemnly. "But, Samson, can *you* juggle?" she asked him, crouching to retrieve the third cake and taking the others from McKee and Crawford and holding them all out toward Trelawny.

The old man looked past Christina's shoulder, and apparently saw that the funeral party had all exited the chapel; and then he tossed one of the cakes in the air and followed it with the other two, and in a moment he had all three whirling in a crisscross pattern in front of his face.

When he had done it for enough seconds to demonstrate that he could, he let one hand drop to his side, caught all three cakes in the other, and handed them back to Christina.

"Anybody can do three," he said. "I can do five."

Christina stepped past him into the aisle. "Will you all be so kind as to accompany me to the committal?" She was smiling, but her face was pale. "You are all wonderfully diverting."

Trelawny scowled and rocked on his heels for a moment, then shrugged and took her arm and started for the rear of the chapel. He sniffed the air. "It's you he's paying such intense attention to, isn't it?"

Crawford and McKee shuffled along behind them, listening.

"Yes," said Christina in a strained voice. "It was this way at my father's funeral too—I should have known it would happen again, when I'm—once more within a stone's throw of where the statue which is his core is buried."

"A stone's throw," said Trelawny hollowly, shaking his white-maned head. "And you know where it's buried? I've been here several times, during this past week." He jerked a thumb back at McKee and Crawford. "Saw Rahab and Medicus here once, though I made sure they didn't see me."

"But I can ignore his . . . wordless song," Christina went on, "while I have you three to tell me things like . . . what cures cat malaise."

"Veal," said Trelawny firmly.

"Just as I said," put in Crawford.

The gray daylight outside seemed bright after the dimness of the chapel, but the air was colder, and Crawford shivered and squinted after the funeral procession. The line of mourners had crossed a gravel-paved yard and was mounting a short stone stairway between high walls with tall green cypress trees beyond.

Christina hurried after them, her boots crunching in the windy silence, and Trelawny and Crawford and McKee lengthened their strides to catch up.

At the top of the steps the funeral party was shuffling and bobbing down a lane between trees and patchy lawns to the left, and Christina stepped after them—but McKee halted and caught Crawford's upper arm in a tight grip.

He glanced at her and noticed her wide-eyed stare—she was looking to the right, away from the funeral procession, and he nervously
followed her gaze.

There was a small figure standing in deep shadow between a vine-
draped oak and a marble monument with a stone dog on it.

It appeared to be a thin little girl standing there, and Crawford felt
his scalp tighten and the backs of his hands tingle before he consciously
realized who it might be.

McKee had released Crawford's arm and was hurrying across the
gravel path toward the shadowy figure; Crawford looked back—Trelawny had paused, and met Crawford's eye and waved him on impatiently before turning away and following Christina.

Crawford ran after McKee and skidded to a halt when she paused
on the verge of the grass.

"Johanna?" called McKee hoarsely, half extending her hands.

It was indeed a girl, Crawford could see now, and she stepped back
out of the shadows into the gray daylight—she wore a long-sleeved
black shift but her feet were just wrapped in bundled rags; the limp
brim of a floppy hat framed and shadowed her face, and her hair was a
weedy tangle over enormous dark eyes.

"I'm—your mother," said McKee, her voice breaking.

Crawford took a breath. "And I'm your father," he said.

"We want to take you home," McKee said.

The girl blinked at them in evident confusion, and then she spun
and began sprinting away across the hilly grass between the tall tombstones.

McKee hiked up her skirt and went running after her, and Crawford was right behind her.

The girl was shorter than many of the monuments along the lane,
and while McKee ran straight after her, Crawford slanted out to the
right and ran along the path, hoping to see the girl as she darted between
the tall gray tombs and obelisks.

He was sure he was running faster than she was, but after a dozen paces he let himself clop and scuff to a halt.

"She disappeared," he called to McKee, who was running more slowly on the damp grass.

McKee shook her head and kept running. When she had got even with Crawford, though, she stopped, panting and almost sobbing.

"She's close by," she gasped. "We must search among the graves."

What do we do if we catch her? wondered Crawford; but he nodded and began striding through the grass between the gravestones.

He quickly saw that there were only a few corners in the immediate area where even a very small person could hide, and within a minute he and McKee had walked around all the nearby blocks and columns of marble, and peered up into the bare tree branches, and were standing face-to-face.

"She's alive," panted McKee. "She can't have vanished."

Crawford remembered the way the doglike creature that Trelawny had called Miss B. had disappeared in Regent's Park last Tuesday, and he strode around the nearby stones peering more carefully at the damp grass; and at the foot of a chest-high granite tomb set against a low hill he noticed a patch of newly flattened grass blades.

He walked over to look at it more closely. The crushed area, he saw, extended right to the wall of the tomb—and some grass blades appeared to be lying *under* it.

The tomb wall was divided into nine coffered squares, each about a foot and a half across, and the streak of flattened grass was centered on the middle square of the bottom row.

He crouched beside it. "I think," he began, and he pushed at the stone square. It slid inward.

McKee was beside him then, and she pushed it in as far as she could without lying down; and then she pulled her hat off and lay down prone on the damp grass and pushed the block inward until her shoulder was against the stone wall of the tomb. When she pulled her arm out, she was holding the hat the child had been wearing.

"I can fit through here," McKee said, and she stretched her arms through the hole and began to pull herself forward.

"I should go first!" exclaimed Crawford, but already McKee's shoulders had disappeared inside the tomb; and the toes of her boots were tearing at the grass to push her farther in; and he bared his teeth and snapped his fingers impatiently until her boots disappeared into the narrow square of darkness.

And then he had tossed his hat and coat aside and was crouching to lie flat on the grass himself, and sliding his hands forward into the hole.

As the top of his head scraped under the low second-row square, he tried to spread his arms. To his left there was some empty space, and he could feel the block they had pushed inward, but to his right and above him the passageway was no wider than the hole he'd crawled in through; and when he had slithered in a yard farther, his groping hands discovered that the open space on the left closed up too. He was glad that he had left his coat behind; even so, his shirt was scraping the stone walls on both sides, and he had to keep his right shoulder lifted a bit so that his rib cage was diagonal in the square tunnel, since there was no room for him to lie flat. Very quickly he had left behind the gray daylight.

He could hear McKee pushing herself along ahead of him, and from beyond her puffed a cold, clay-scented draft.

He could feel that his feet were inside now. The surface under him felt like dirt-gritty stone, and then it was just flat stone, textured with what felt like chisel grooves.

Crawford was panting, and the noise of it was batted back at him by the very close stone surfaces, and it occurred to him that he could not touch his face: even if he raised his arm to the top of the square tunnel and ground his elbow into the corner, there wasn't room for him to swing his forearm backward.

Instantly the breath stopped in his throat and his palms slapped the floor and began pushing him backward while he tried to tug himself along with the skidding toes of his boots. His shirt was snagging against the walls and bunching up around his neck.

Then he was breathing again, in rapid gasps, but over the noise of that and his thunderous heartbeat he heard McKee call softly from the darkness ahead, "Crawford, what is it?"

And he could hear in her voice the tightness of nearly unbearable strain, of savage panic savagely suppressed.

Clearly she was experiencing everything that he was, and she was not clawing her way back out. She was ahead of him in this tunnel, and that was horrible, but all he could do about it was to be there too, with her.

He forced himself to exhale all the air from his lungs; then he flexed his invisible fingers and inhaled. He realized that his crumpled shirt was sodden with sweat.

"Nothing," he said. "I—thought I felt a spider."

After a moment he heard her cough out two tense syllables of a laugh. And then she was moving again, and he resumed pulling himself along after her, suppressing all thoughts.

CHAPTER TWELVE

What be her cards, you ask? Even these:—
The heart, that doth but crave
More, having fed; the diamond,
Skill'd to make base seem brave;
The club, for smiting in the dark;
The spade, to dig a grave.

—*Dante Gabriel Rossetti, "The Card-Dealer"*

A DOZEN OF THE mourners had come all the way to the grave in the familiar clearing among the elm trees, which Christina thought had grown taller since her father's funeral here eight years ago. She took a step closer to the deep rectangular hole cut in the grassy sod and looked across it at the faces—there was Gabriel, his face a sagging blankness, and William, and Maria with a handkerchief to her eyes, and their mother and aunt, and twitchy Swinburne who had not removed his hat, and the priest—and that white-bearded man was Edward Trelawny!—and, hanging back with their caps in their hands, the four gravediggers—but where had Adelaide and Mr. Crawford got to?

She looked down into the hole, but she wasn't standing close enough to see the top of her father's coffin, if indeed it was now exposed; but perhaps the gravediggers had left a layer of soil to lie between her father's coffin and this new one.

She had asked one of them about the condition of her father's grave before they had dug the fresh hole, and she had been disturbed to hear the man's offhand remark that there had been a mole hole in the grass over it, and that their shovels had ruptured segments of the hole all the way down.

But there was no way Christina could ask them to clear all the dirt away from her father's coffin to see if there was a hole in it.

The pile of earth they had dug out—for the second time in eight years—was a mound under a green tarpaulin off to her left, though a token shovelful of dark loam had been left on the brown grass beside the grave.

The priest was shaking holy water onto Lizzie's coffin now, the drops beading up on the varnished lid like raindrops, and he was reading something from the Bible in a frail voice that the breeze snatched away.

Lizzie's coffin lay now on a black-velvet-draped bier on the grass to the right of the group of mourners. It would have cost Gabriel quite a bit—not just the two-inch-thick polished oak and the brass handles and plaque, but, as William had whispered to her, the sacrificial offering inside it of all of Gabriel's poems!

Christina reflected with a shiver that she could never sacrifice her own poetry that way. It would be like burning an old lover's letters—destroying something that was not entirely hers to dispose of.

The thought of her poetry brought on another dizzy, fiddling wave of her uncle's attention, so strong that she almost expected to see him among the mourners, staring intently at her with the eyes of the portrait on the wall at home; but she knew he was down in that hole, inside her father's coffin, in fact inside her father's dead throat.

If only the damned priest could hurry, and at last . . . *at last let the gravediggers fill in the hole,* she thought quickly, steering her mind away from a thought she must not let her uncle perceive.

She frowned and shut her eyes and tried to pray, though she was even more afraid of God's attention than of John Polidori's.

EVENTUALLY, "A WELL," CAME McKee's voice from the darkness ahead. "I think."

Crawford kept crawling forward until his fingertips brushed the soles of her boots in the pitch blackness.

"Don't crowd me," she said. "I can feel rungs down in it, like the one by St. Clement's. Damn, I should have come in feet first."

She was hesitating, and Crawford almost said, *Let me go first,* before he realized how useless that thought was; then she said softly, perhaps speaking to herself, "I think we're closest to St. Mary-le-Bow in Cheapside. 'I do not know, says the great bell at Bow.'" Then, louder, she said, *"Aedis te deum nosco."*

Her boots moved forward, out of reach, and he heard the fabric of her dress sliding against stone.

"What are you going to do?" Crawford asked hoarsely.

"I'm going to grab hold of one of the rungs below me, and then—do a somersault, I suppose, and try to hang on through it."

Crawford tried to picture what she was describing, and he couldn't see how she could maintain her grip through such a move.

"Are there," he asked desperately, "rungs *above* you?"

"Good thought."

He heard her dress rustling and tearing, and her shoes knocked and scuffed in front of his face. He reached out and lightly touched the soles of them, and he realized that she had managed to roll over onto her back in the tight tunnel.

She shifted farther ahead, and then exclaimed, "Yes! Solid! Thank

God one of us is thinking—I believe I would have killed myself going down headfirst."

Crawford nodded in agreement, though there was no way she could see it. Sweat rolled down into his eyes.

He heard her shift forward in stages, and then it was just her heels skidding on stone and he heard her panting outside the narrow tunnel; after a few moments he heard her boots clunking on iron—they ascended a few rungs, and then descended, echoing in some bigger space.

"I'm below you now," came her voice. "Roll over and slide out."

Crawford was bigger around than she was, but he managed to get onto his side and push his way forward until his head and arms were projecting out of the tunnel, though there was still no light at all.

The wet-clay draft was now palpably coming from below him, chilling his wet shirt, and the noise of his breathing echoed away in a big volume of air. He could hear McKee's boots scraping on metal some yards below him, and beyond that he now heard a low, many-toned humming—and he remembered McKee's description of the *vox cloacarum*, the sound caused by pressure differences in the infinite old sewers. This seemed different.

He groped upward with one hand and found a metal rod—he tugged it, and it didn't give, so he pulled himself farther out and was able to roll more and get his other hand on it too.

He pulled himself farther out into the black abyss and had to push with his heels to get his shins out past the top edge of the tunnel, but at last he was able to set his feet on the bottom edge of it, and then up onto the rungs.

Then he was following McKee in her audibly slow descent, past the tunnel mouth and farther down into the well.

After climbing down a few more rungs, he said, "That wasn't 'oranges and lemons.'"

"It was Latin for 'I know thee as the god of the temple,'" she said. "Now hush."

Crawford was too sore and tired to do more than twitch at the first touch of the insect wings, and after the surprise of the first flutter at his cheek, he ignored their feather touches on his face and hands. The work of moving one hand and one foot, and then the other hand and the other foot, and the rhythmic chuff of his breath against the stone wall in front of his ever-flexing knuckles, became nearly automatic, and he tried to imagine the long-lost people who must have built this well. Into his mind swam images of Roman soldiers battling men who fought naked with crude black-iron swords.

"Again there's a drop," came McKee's voice from below him, jarring him out of the insistent daydreams. "I can't see a thing below, but— Johanna did it, so we can."

Crawford's first thought was that if he heard McKee fall a long way he could climb up the ladder and make his way back through the tunnel to the open air—but he couldn't permit that.

"I've," he said, "got a new watch. Let me drop it and we can listen and see how long it takes to hit something."

"A capital notion, my dear," she said, and he heard a shiver of exhaustion and relief in her voice. "I owe you a lot of time."

He pulled his watch out of his waistcoat pocket and fumbled one-handed at the little bar on the end of the chain; it was tucked through a waistcoat buttonhole, and when he finally poked it free, he lost his grip on the watch.

"There it goes," he said hastily.

He waited several seconds, but heard nothing.

His belly was suddenly icy and tingling at the thought of a vast drop below them, and he gripped the rung he was holding on to tightly and tried to flatten himself against the wall.

"Climb . . . back . . . up," he said distinctly through clenched teeth.

McKee's quavering voice said, "But—she must have come this way—"

And then another voice, a little girl's, spoke hesitantly from not far below them: "I caught it before it could fly away. And you must fall too."

Crawford didn't like the sound of *must fall*, but he said to McKee, "I'll climb down and drop as soon as I hear you land and step aside."

THE FOUR BURLY GRAVEDIGGERS in their rough corduroy trousers and jackets had slung a pair of ropes under the gleaming black coffin, and now they came forward out of the tree shadows and lifted it off the bier and plodded across the grass toward Christina, with the coffin swinging between them. She stepped back hastily, and two of them moved to each side of the grave and then began lowering the coffin into the hole.

The mourners shuffled closer, with the white-haired old priest leading the way; Christina wondered what the old cleric would do if he knew what was in the grave. And Gabriel looked ready, Christina thought with sudden agonized sympathy, to jump into the grave himself. And this is all my fault, she thought; and Papa's too, and Papa's too, for bringing the hellish thing back from Italy and then giving it to me.

The ropes went slack, and two of the gravediggers rapidly drew them up and coiled them, and then all four stepped back.

Christina's face went icy cold—for her uncle's attention was still a quivering shadow on her mind; desperately she steered her thoughts toward her father's old headstone and away from the panicky realization that her uncle's identity was *not* fragmented now that Lizzie's doctored coffin sat on top of her father's.

The priest shook more holy water down into the grave and said, "'We therefore commit her body to the ground; earth to earth, ashes to ashes, dust to dust; in the sure and certain hope of the Resurrection to eternal life.'"

Christina made the sign of the cross, though she wasn't Catholic. He is paying such exclusive attention to me, she thought, because I'm still physically close to his petrified body. The terrible attention will wane as I drive away.

And she knew that Polidori had caught that thought and ruefully agreed with it; though his intrusive identity seemed to promise a more lasting intimacy someday soon.

Gabriel stepped forward and crouched beside the shovelful of dirt beside the grave, and he picked up a handful and scattered it gently into the grave.

CRAWFORD HAD HEARD MCKEE splash into mud when she dropped from the last rung, and so he was not surprised when his boots plunged into viscous muck; and he had landed with bent knees and managed to stay upright.

The humming he had heard earlier was louder now and sounded even less organic.

"Johanna!" called McKee. "Where are you?"

Crawford jumped as a chorus of harsh voices, all speaking in unison, echoed in reply, "She is here with me. Come in." The voices seemed to reverberate from another chamber than the space in which Crawford and McKee stood.

Crawford didn't move now, and from the silence that followed the echoes of the voices, he knew McKee didn't either; then he heard a rustle of clothing and a faint metallic scrape, and his nostrils caught the pungent smell of garlic. Hastily he dug his own little bottle out of his waistcoat pocket, though he didn't unscrew its lid yet.

He heard her step forward in the mud to his left, in the direction the voices had seemed to come from; and, though his face was icy with sweat and his knees were shaking so badly that he feared he might fall down, Crawford made himself lift one foot and swing it ahead and then put it down in the unseen mud and set his weight on it, and then lift the other. His free hand was extended out in front of himself, and when he heard McKee slap some surface, he found no obstacle, though through his boot toe he felt a rounded shelf to step up onto.

Her whisper came to him from a yard away to his left: "A sort of bent pillar, here."

"An opening here," he muttered. "And a step."

Her hand touched his shoulder, then slid down to his hand and squeezed it. "Thank you for staying," she whispered. "You are— Oh, hell. Thank you."

He could think of no answer, and only squeezed her hand in the moment before she drew it away.

With his boot he could feel the edge of a hole in the curved surface of the step, and, carefully sliding his leading foot around it to move ahead, Crawford felt a close concave wall in front of him with an opening in it; he reached up and down to trace the shape of the opening—it was tall and narrow, and the top third curved to the right so that he would have to go through sideways, leaning forward. Whatever this structure was, it appeared to have no straight lines or corners.

"Hole in the floor," he told McKee softly. "Opening in the wall directly ahead."

He could still see nothing, but he strongly sensed sentient presences on the far side of the curved slit in the stone wall.

He managed to whisper, "I'm stepping through."

There was no reply beyond her fast breathing, so he gritted his teeth and slid through the narrow, bent gap and found himself standing on a smooth, slanted floor. The air was warmer on this side of the partition, and smelled of incense and machine oil.

McKee scraped through behind him, and her shoulder bumped his.

At that moment, glaringly bright yellow flames sprang up overhead all around them—Crawford yelled in surprise and leaped back, throwing one arm across his eyes, but the slick floor sloped up steeply behind him; his heels skidded and he found himself sitting down and sliding forward to where he'd been standing a moment before.

He stood up again, slowly, holding his arms out for balance. McKee had dropped to a tense crouch. Blinking and squinting, he could now see that they were in the narrower end of a large, roughly egg-shaped chamber, as if they had entered a barn-sized bubble in solid tan marble; torches blazed at intervals high up on the incurving walls.

A dozen vaguely man-shaped figures that seemed to be made of shifting mud swayed on a lower level in the middle of the chamber—the humming seemed to emanate from irregular sputtering holes in the fronts of their heads—but Crawford's attention was helplessly fixed on the man who stood on a wide rise beyond them. They were of human height, but the man towered above them, and Crawford's first impression was that the man was very far away, miles away, and stood as high as a mountain.

Then Crawford saw that the man held in his arms the little girl they had seen running away among the gravestones, and this restored the perspective—the man and the girl were no more than forty feet away—though Crawford's eyes ached with the effort of trying to keep the man in focus.

The man's outlines and colors flickered, as though he were a magic lantern projection, but at the same time he radiated so aggressive an impression of physical volume that his body seemed to possess mass beyond its boundaries, as if it occupied more space than ordinary dimensions permitted—what quality was this that transcended volume, as volume transcended mere area? It took Crawford a moment to note the mundane details—dark curly hair, a mustache, an indistinct black coat, and eyes like glittering black glass.

The mud figures below him all suddenly spoke clearly, in unison: "My name has been John Polidori," and Crawford knew that the man beyond them was speaking through them.

"You are the fleshly origins of this child," the voices went on, "and she is ready now to abandon the cords of merely human flesh."

McKee took a step forward on the concave ivory floor. "No," she said in a loud but level voice, raising her little bottle of crushed garlic, "she is not."

Crawford desperately wished she hadn't advanced, but he made himself shuffle forward to stand beside her. The bright torchlight was still making him squint, and he couldn't stare directly at Polidori—but in his peripheral vision he could see the little girl swinging his watch on its chain.

McKee threw the opened bottle toward Polidori—and several of the mud figures instantly splashed upward in a single solid sheet; the bottle and its spilled contents cratered into the mud surface, which then collapsed back to the pit in the floor.

CHRISTINA NOTICED THAT SWINBURNE kept looking back toward the grave as the funeral party trudged away toward the stairs that led down toward the yard and the chapel and the waiting coaches. Does he think we left someone behind? she wondered.

When the group had descended the stairs from the lawns to the crushed-stone yard, Swinburne exhaled and shoved his hands into his coat pockets and looked around at the mourners—and then his eyes widened and he stepped back toward the rear of the group.

Christina looked in the direction Swinburne had been facing and saw that Trelawny was staring after him.

Trelawny caught her gaze and fell into step beside her. The white-bearded old man's back was straight and his shoulders were almost militarily squared—in something like defiance, Christina thought.

"Who is the young poet?" he asked.

Christina glanced back after Swinburne. "He *is* a poet, actually! Algernon Swinburne."

"One of your damned crowd? I should have expected it."

"He's a friend," said Christina, "an especially good friend to Gabriel and Lizzie."

"I daresay."

"Thank you for coming," she remembered to say.

"You mentioned, Diamonds, that you know where that statue is—"

"I don't want to think about—I don't want to think," she said desperately. " 'The world is a tragedy to those that think,' " she recited at random, " 'a comedy to those that feel.' "

She had reversed Walpole's aphorism, but Trelawny nodded, conceding the point. "Even from here I can feel his attention on you still, like heat from a fire. I won't question you now." He frowned for a moment, then said, "I once bought a Negro slave, in Charleston, in America, it must be thirty years ago now—shall I tell you about that?"

"Oh, yes, please," said Christina, exhaling as if she'd been holding her breath. "As long as it's not . . . relevant."

"No, not relevant to anything this side of the Atlantic. They're fighting a war to free the slaves over there now—well, I did my part back in, let's see, in '34, by buying this fellow and immediately freeing him . . ."

As he rambled on, Christina listened hungrily to each distracting detail, though she noted every step that took her farther away from the grave and the thing in her father's throat. Soon, she thought, soon, our uncle's terrible attention will fall off me like a snagged cape.

THE BLACKLY SHIMMERING FIGURE of Polidori still stood holding the little girl at the far side of the chamber.

"Garlic," said the remaining mud figures, and then they made a rackety snuffling sound. "Sulfur, that is, and an agent that interferes with us binding ourselves to the defining spiral threads of your fabric."

McKee had straightened up from her throw and stood beside Crawford, panting. Crawford gripped his own bottle of crushed garlic in his pocket and waited tensely for Polidori to go on, but for several seconds none of the figures in the chamber moved, and the only sound was an occasional pop from one of the torches stuck into holes high up in the domed ceiling. Polidori seemed to have stopped paying attention to the two intruders, and the little girl in his flickering arms was swinging

Crawford's watch and quietly reciting something in a nursery-rhyme cadence.

Crawford's gaze darted around the chamber, and he noticed a wavy seam across the top of the dome, and the term that occurred to him was *coronal suture*. He blinked sweat from his eyes and looked at the low curling ridge to McKee's left, and he thought, *ethnoid bone* and *cribriform plate*. We entered through the right superior orbital fissure, and we are standing on the frontal bone.

On the far side of the chamber, Polidori was standing on the central ridge of the occipital bone. The mud things were standing down in the concavities of the temporal bone.

Crawford was suddenly shivering as if he were very cold, though he was able to think, objectively, We are inside a giant's skull.

And as soon as he thought it, the light went dim and the air was moving and very cold and smelled of rust and wet stone; the floor under his feet had changed in an instant, and he skipped to keep his balance on what was now flat stone. He could hear water splashing and echoing.

His eyes were still dazzled by the vanished torchlight, and he took hold of McKee's hand and peered ahead. The only light was a dim gray glow, possibly daylight reflecting down a shaft, from a gap in the arched stone ceiling.

They were standing on a projection of cracked old masonry, a stone ramp that was broken off jaggedly a yard in front of their boots, and below it rushed a shadowed stream about twenty feet across.

The tall darkly glowing figure on the far side, which at first Crawford mistook for a streak of residual retinal glare since it almost appeared to shift when he moved his eyes, must be Polidori.

Now Crawford could see that Polidori was standing on, or was projected onto, a similar broken ramp on that side; clearly there had once been a bridge across this stream. Crawford couldn't see Johanna, but he heard her ongoing soft recitation mingle with the rattle of water against stone.

Polidori spoke in a deep and oily voice, and Johanna's little-girl voice spoke too, matching his, syllable for syllable; Crawford was horrified to feel his own tongue and throat twitch, as if Polidori's will were partly eclipsing his own too, even way over here on this side of the stream.

"The child and her organic father are strangers to each other," said the voices of Polidori and Johanna, "but her mother loves her. The mother must be snuffed out."

Johanna's voice alone said, "Will you unravel her?" in a tone of mild curiosity.

"No, child," answered Polidori's not-quite-human voice, "that would leave a ghost unquiet in the river. I will crush her identity to nothing."

McKee called hoarsely, "I do love you, Johanna!"

Crawford pulled his own bottle of garlic out of his pocket—there were apparently no mud men here to block his throw, and his free hand darted toward the screw-on lid—

—but Polidori had raised his arm, and the air solidified around Crawford's hands and violently twisted the bottle away; he heard it splash into the stream.

"My garlic," he whispered bleakly to McKee. "He reached across somehow before I could open it."

McKee just exhaled.

"I'd like to have her ghost to keep with me," said Johanna.

"You shall have the man's ghost, if you like. I will simply kill him."

"Unravel him?"

Polidori raised one hand.

Crawford grabbed McKee's arm and took a quick step backward, but he was unable to pull her after him; he peered back to see what had caught her.

A black halo encircled McKee's head, a ring so much darker than the surrounding gloom that it seemed to glow. Her face was in deeper shadow than it should have been, and he realized that her head was in a translucent globe that only looked like a ring because he was seeing the apparent boundary curve end-on.

He stopped trying to pull her. Crawford reached for McKee's face—and he was able to push his hand into the dark globe against resistance, though tugging at her jaw didn't move her head at all. He felt her rapid panicky breath on his hand in the moment before he drew it back—and then he took a deep breath and simply thrust his own head in beside hers.

The globe visibly expanded to enclose his head too, and he couldn't hear or see anything, and his body had gone completely numb—he didn't even know if he was still standing.

He was aware of two minds existing in a nonspatial proximity to his, one female and one male; the male one was in some sense vastly more prominent, and had begun exerting inexorable pressure on the female one, but—

Crawford's mind spasmodically conjured up a string of images to fill the intolerable sensory vacuum and visualize what was happening: he imagined a walnut in a lever-operated nutcracker shaped like a squirrel with a gaping mouth; a hairy hand picking up one drinking glass and then fumbling it because it was actually two glasses, one nested in the other; a machinist stepping back from a workbench to wiggle one of the two handles of a pair of pliers so that the slip-joint would allow a wider spread of the jaws, for a grip bigger than had originally seemed necessary.

And then the imagined readjusted pliers were brought to bear and closed in and something began to go wrong with his mind. Memories intruded forcefully into his narrowed attention, broken and jammed together, like roof beams crashing into a bedroom under an unsustainable weight: the image of his son Girard replaced a dog that Crawford was cutting open for surgery; and he saw the heads of his parents on crows flying over the London Bridge; and his wife Veronica's face instead of his own staring at him from a mirror, and then the mirror sprang forward and shattered against his forehead and Veronica's mind was leaking into his.

Her memories were brutal—a hot haze of drunkenness veiled a dim view of naked men with the heads of bulls and birds of prey, and a wailing baby that was carried away by animated skeletons, and fingers tense on the wet grip of a knife—

And his flickering awareness grasped that these were not a distortion of *Veronica's* memories, but of *McKee's*—

Adelaide! he thought.

The psychic pressure increased, and he caught one last image from her smothered mind—it was of McKee in a white wedding dress in a church, and Crawford was standing beside her on the altar.

And then his mind was too compressed to sustain consciousness.

CHAPTER THIRTEEN

Now, sweet daughter, but one more sight,
And you may lie soft and sleep to-night.
We know in the vale what perils be:
Now look once more in the glass . . .

—*Dante Gabriel Rossetti, "Rose Mary"*

A T FIRST CHRISTINA thought the sense of constriction signaled the onset of a headache or some distress in her stomach, and she shifted on the leather carriage seat and looked away from Cayley to face the window and take deep breaths of the cold fresh air. The carriage had passed under the stone arch of Highgate Cemetery's entrance and rocked in a left turn onto the road, and she dreaded the shaking of the increased speed that was sure to follow.

But the uncomfortable tightness was somewhere else, not in her—somewhere in the oppressive and unceasing attention of her uncle.

"Are you well, my dear?" asked Cayley, leaning forward solicitously.

Polidori's disembodied attention was all to do with squeezing and crushing something, and Christina had to breathe deliberately just to convince herself that she could. She held up her hand to put off answering Cayley.

And then it was gone. She had apparently moved at last out of the sphere of Polidori's ground-state attention, and she felt all at once lighter and younger. The increasing headwind sluicing through the open window as the horses quickened their pace was pleasantly cooling on her damp forehead.

"Yes, Charles," she said, her voice lively with surprised relief, "I'm fine."

Deeply and gladly she inhaled the cold air, and she stretched her fingers on her lap, feeling as though she had at last shed a pair of gloves that she'd worn for decades.

His attention was always on me to some extent, she thought, during these seventeen years, and it's finally completely gone.

I'm alone on my own.

LIKE A TAUT ROPE suddenly cut, the stretched awareness of the thing that was largely John Polidori snapped back—and then reflexively reached out again to reestablish the broken connection; and its attention fixed on what seemed to be its goal but was instead only streaks of familiar blood in grooves cut into a cluster of mirrors . . .

And the wave-form that was the Polidori thing's identity was reflected back onto itself and instantly fragmented into a turbulence of nullifying contradictions and meaningless emphases.

A BOOMING CRASH OF collapsing masonry and the thudding of tons of dirt jarred Crawford, and he rolled over painfully on a wet floor, blinking at shadowed stone walls and coughing grit out of his throat. He could feel hot blood running from his nose and clotting in his mustache and beard, and he peered around him in the darkness, assuming that he was in a building that had partially collapsed.

He knew vaguely that there were a number of ages he might be, but he had no idea which of them might include this experience, whatever it was.

He could hear water rushing in a roofed channel very close by, and now he could dimly see that someone was lying on the stone floor near him—a woman. Had she been injured in the collapse? Had he? He tried to stop coughing and think.

Memories prickled in his consciousness, opening one clear area after another. He was older than he would have guessed, and he was wearing the torn ruins of a linen shirt and creased woolen trousers—he had been at a funeral!—and the dim radiance filtering down the shaft overhead was probably the light of a far-off overcast sky; the woman lying beside him was . . . was the mother of his daughter!

Then with a mental expansion that felt like his ears popping, he remembered it all, and he quickly rolled over to peer across the rushing stream; but through a haze of dust he saw that the stone platform and bridge-end that had been on that far side were gone now, buried under a new slope of jagged rock and freshly turned earth.

Johanna had been standing over there, with the Polidori thing.

He tilted his head back to stare up at the hole in the arched ceiling over the stream; the ceiling was high, and the light that touched the stone edges of the hole was very faint. He turned to look behind him, in the direction from which they'd come, but could see nothing.

He reached across and shook the woman's shoulder. "Adelaide!" he whispered.

Her shoulder was yanked away and he heard her scramble into a crouch, suddenly panting.

"I've got a knife," she gasped. "Come near me and I'll kill you."

"Adelaide, listen to me." He got to his feet and reached toward her—then snatched his hand back and heard the blade whistle through the air where it had been.

"Keep back!" she said. "I'll kill you and that Carpace bitch, both. Tell her—"

"Adelaide," he interrupted, "Carpace is dead. I killed her. I'm John Crawford."

She hesitated. "Killed her? What place is this? Strike a light."

"I can't. We're underground, under Highgate Cemetery." And our daughter is dead, he thought.

"Highgate—do you work at the Magdalen Penitentiary?"

"No, you've been out of there for . . . two years, I think you said."

"What year is this?"

"1862. And we have to—"

"Ach, so old, all at once? And who are you?"

"John," he said, "Crawford. I—"

"John!" For several seconds she didn't move, and then her head whipped around to stare at the spot across the stream where the other stone platform had been.

And she wailed and fell to her knees when she saw the new slope of churned earth and rubble over there.

"*Johanna!*" she screamed; and then she screamed it again, making Crawford wince, but the third time her voice broke into sobbing.

After a few seconds, she caught her breath and choked, "What happened?"

"I don't know!" He too was staring at the tumbled stone and dirt across the stream. "I—I believe I slowed him down, in his attack on you, when I interposed my head in his psychic vise—and then he began to crush us both—but I lost consciousness and revived only a moment before you did."

"This is Sister Christina's stroke," said McKee softly. "It was her stroke that stopped him from crushing our minds, and crushed him instead—and my daughter."

Our daughter, thought Crawford.

"There's nothing more we can do," he said. "We need to get *out* of here, back up to daylight."

Slowly, panting as if she'd been running, McKee straightened and peered around in the darkness. To the right, the ledge they were on slanted uphill for at least some distance before it was lost in shadows, and he took her elbow.

She shook it off. "I saw into your head, when he was crushing us— you must have seen into mine."

"I think so." He remembered now the image of a wedding, but only said, "Just—distorted fragments."

"That's—all?"

"Yes. We've—"

"You're sure?"

"Yes!" He spread his fingers and then clenched his fists and repeated, "We've got to get *out* of here!" He reached out and fumbled for her hand, but she snatched it away.

"Don't touch me," she said.

"Wha—why?"

"Why do you think?" She was still panting. "We tried to save Johanna, and we failed, she died. I failed, which is shameful, and you failed, which is shameful."

"For God's sake, Adelaide," he said, starting forward along the ledge and then pausing, "what more could we have done? Damn me, how is it that we did as much as we did?"

McKee stared again for several moments at the jagged slope on the other side of the stream. Then, "Let me lead the way," she said quietly, stepping around him, "and please don't speak unless you perceive some danger along our course."

THEY GROPED THEIR WAY through pitch-blackness, in silence except for the scuff and stumble of their boots on stone and in mud, and when they came to cross-tunnels, or broad areas that seemed spacious judged by the echoes of their breathing, McKee shuffled around until she had found the uphill direction, and they followed that—though several times it crested out and led them farther down. Twice Crawford saw hints of reflected firelight far away down what must have been side corridors, and at one point, when he and McKee were edging along a narrow ledge over a pit, he heard monotonous singing or chanting far below. They clambered blindly over heaped stones that sometimes felt as if they'd been shaped by tools, and made their way up out of waist-deep pools by climbing ancient stone stairs, and edged around boulders made of rusted-together pieces of metal—Crawford's fingers traced corroded spoons and sword hilts and coins of unguessable age all stuck together like clusters of barnacles.

After at least an hour, he and McKee found themselves walking along a concave floor that was straight and smooth but very slippery—the smell was now very bad, like full chamberpots and rotten eggs—and Crawford heard McKee patting a wall.

"This is modern brick," she whispered. "The Northern High Level Sewer between Hampstead and Stoke Newington, it must be. There'll be a ladder."

And there was, though to find it they had to climb over two chest-high brick walls that McKee called diversion dams. The ladder rang faintly when McKee's groping hand collided with it.

Crawford gingerly patted his way around McKee and then preceded her up the new iron ladder, and when his head bumped a metal grating, he felt along the bars of it until he was touching the latch, and he managed to climb a few rungs back down as he lowered it on its hinges with one hand.

Above that was a square of solid iron, but it was hinged too, and he trusted the new ladder not to break under his boots when he braced his shoulders under the manhole cover and forced it upward. It squeaked up—he braced his hands in dazzling gray daylight on the steel rim embedded in the street pavement, and pushed—and then the cover fell away behind him with a loud clang that echoed between close housefronts.

He didn't hear hooves or wheels bearing down on him, so before looking around, he scrambled out of the shaft and reached down for McKee's hand. And when they had both got to their feet on the crushed stone of the street surface, and he had swung the iron cover back into place, and he and McKee had stumbled to a curb, he saw through narrowed eyes that they were in front of a pastry shop window.

"Would you like a cup of tea?" he croaked. "I've got some money."

Then he flinched at a woman's harsh voice from behind them. "Breaking into cellars, then, were you?"

Crawford turned toward the voice. In the gray but blinding daylight, an enormous woman in an apron was striding across the street toward them.

"You're the ones made off with my pig, eh?" she went on loudly.

"No, no," called Crawford hoarsely, "street collapsed in Highgate— women and children swept into the sewers—"

"Come along," muttered McKee, grabbing his arm and pulling him into a trot.

"Get help!" yelled Crawford for verisimilitude over his shoulder. "Ropes, ladders!"

He had at least succeeded in baffling the woman, who had stopped and was looking uneasily at the manhole cover.

McKee had yanked Crawford around a corner and the two of them were now walking, as briskly as they could in their clinging wet clothes, against a bone-chilling headwind that made his eyes water. She had let go of his arm.

"Tea!" she said scornfully. "We look like we crawled out of a cesspool!"

Crawford looked at her as she strode along, then glanced down at himself.

It was true. Her dress and his shirt and trousers were slimed with what he hoped was just black mud, though in truth both of them smelled pretty horrible. His beard was stiff with dried blood, and McKee's dark hair looked like a plundered bird's nest.

They had been walking south down the middle of a rutted dirt road between old overhanging Tudor houses, stared at with disfavor but with no active interference by a couple of cart drivers who passed them, but now McKee stopped, hugging herself and shivering.

She faced Crawford and spoke clearly. "Our daughter is dead—and thank God she will at least stay dead, with the resurrecting devil killed too." She took a deep breath and let it out. "I'm leaving London. There's nothing I can hope for in this city." She squinted at him, as if to fix his face in her memory. "This village is Lower Clapton—I know it well, I've often caught birds near here. Kingsland Road is that way," she said, waving to the east, "and if you walk south along it for two or three miles, you'll get to the river at London Bridge. I suggest you jump right in."

"Can I—" he began; then he shook himself and just said, "I wish you would stay."

"It would only remind me of lost and impossible things. Everything you and I had in common is gone." She turned and began striding away in the direction opposite to the way she had directed him.

"Adelaide!" he called after her, but she didn't alter her pace.

When Polidori had vanished, Crawford had felt his mind popping by degrees back out to its former extent, like a half-crushed hat being poked back into shape; now one last dent seemed to spring back out, though it felt as if he'd been living with this one for years.

"Adelaide," he yelled desperately, "marry me!"

She hunched in her ragged and fouled clothes, as if someone had thrown a stone at her, but kept walking—and through one last dissolving thread of the compaction that Polidori's attack had imposed on their minds, he caught a final thought from her: *So we can have more children?*

Implicit in the thought were the names *Johanna* and *Girard*.

That froze him in place for a moment; then he was stumbling after her in his sopping trousers, ignoring the horrified cries of a crowd of children leaping out of his way.

McKee had rounded the corner of an old three-story whitewashed public house, and when he came skidding around it after her, she had disappeared.

A narrow lane or alley lay between the pub and a stable on the far side, and he hurried to it, but she was not visible between the old structures and there were no apparent doors or gates she could have gone through. A mongrel dog lying on the path lifted its head mistrustfully.

He walked back to the pub entrance, but as soon as he had pushed open the heavy wooden door and stepped into the blessedly warm lamplit interior, several men in shiny corduroy jackets blocked his way.

"Smell too bad, you do," said one of them, extending an arm to keep Crawford back.

"Don't want us to bust you up, now, do you?" asked the other cheerfully. "Just shove off then, there's a good boy."

Crawford stepped back and stared at them while he caught his breath.

"I'm a friend of hers," he said at last. "You must have noticed that she was as . . . soiled as I am."

"Soiled women! Not in here, mate. And it's up to her who her friends are."

Crawford looked from one of the two amiably implacable faces to the other. McKee had said she caught birds near here, knew this village—doubtless she was known at this pub and had hastily told these friends of hers to keep him out.

Other men were visible now behind these two.

Crawford opened his mouth and yelled, "Adelaide!" as loudly as he could—and a moment later he was lying on his side in the road, clutching his abdomen and trying to get breath into his stunned lungs, and gradually realizing that one of the men had punched him very hard in the stomach.

He rolled over and saw the man grimacing and rubbing his knuckles on his sleeve.

Two men behind him in the doorway were now holding empty beer bottles by the necks.

Crawford waved and shook his head and slowly got back up on his feet, able now to take short, wheezing gasps.

The men in the doorway watched impassively as he struggled to catch his breath.

"I'm—leaving," he finally managed to say. "Tell her—I love her."

Their expressions didn't change.

He turned away and began slowly plodding toward Kingsland Road, aching and limping and shivering in the cold.

CHAPTER FOURTEEN

June 1862

Thank God who spared me what I feared!
Once more I gird myself to run.
Thy promise stands, Thou Faithful One.
Horror of darkness disappeared
At length: once more I see the sun . . .

—*Christina Rossetti,*
"For a Mercy Received," January 1863

GREEN LEAVES THREW waving shadows on the glass of the window overlooking Albany Street, and through the open front door swept a warm breeze carrying the scent of robinia blossoms.

Through the hall doorway Christina heard William shout, "This desk won't fit through the door, nor fit back into the house. I think we're going to have to break it into pieces."

Christina laid down her pen and stood up, stretching.

"Leave it," she called. "Gabriel can rub grease on it when he comes, and we can all push on it."

William's irritable call came back, "It's not like a pig stuck in a fence, 'Stina, it's—oh—well, you wouldn't be joking about it if you—" He paused. "I think you'll have to go down the steps," he said, speaking out into the street, "and come up from the kitchen—or climb over this thing."

Christina heard a squeak and a hollow dragging sound, and then steps in the hall, and Maria appeared in the hall doorway in a black linen dress, not looking as if she had just moved heavy furniture, as apparently she had.

Seeing Christina's raised eyebrows, Maria shrugged and said, "It only needed a lift and a twist." She looked around the parlor, with its bookshelves and upholstered chairs and framed pictures leaning out from the walls. "The Cheyne Walk house is a good deal roomier than this."

"It's lovely," Christina agreed, her face blank.

Maria stared at her for a moment, then both of them laughed.

"He'll have Swinburne living there," said Maria. "I can't quite see Swinburne and Mama playing whist together on winter evenings."

"And the household finances will be a shambles."

Christina's book, *Goblin Market and Other Poems,* had been published two months ago, but though it had got enthusiastic reviews in journals like the *Athenaeum* and the *Saturday Review,* and its three-thousand-copy first printing was reported to be selling well, she had no confidence that she would reap any substantial profit from it, and she was watchful of the family's expenditures. Gabriel often bragged about making two thousand pounds a year with his paintings, but Christina and her sister and mother and aunt were all still living almost entirely on William's income.

"He'll be disappointed," said Maria.

"Not really. He'll have his noisy friends, and it would impede him to have women relatives about who rise before noon."

Maria asked quietly, "How long do you think *William* will live there?"

"A month. Then he'll be back here, at least half the time. He can't be falling asleep at his office."

"Still," said Maria with a shiver, "I'm glad Gabriel has moved out of the Chatham Place house."

"Well, yes." Christina glanced at the waving green branches beyond the window to drive away memories of the winter—Lizzie's death, poor Adelaide searching for her child, the waking vision of Mouth Boy in Regent's Park, the alarming Trelawny.

The gambit Maria had come up with from her obscure studies had clearly worked—she and Gabriel had lost their sensitivity to sunlight, and Christina had even gone bathing in the ocean a few weeks ago! And she no longer dreamed of Polidori, in his own handsome form nor as the hideous Mouth Boy.

She had not written much poetry since the publication of *Goblin Market*—since Lizzie's funeral, really—but at least she had not found herself writing any more of "Folio Q" either.

After seventeen harrowing years, John Polidori was no longer a part of her life, and she wanted no reminders of that darkly exciting passage. On the wall was still the portrait of Polidori—her mother's brother, after all—but she never looked at that section of the wall.

But now she heard a familiar voice from out in the street: "William! Are you moving?"

"Stay," said Christina to Maria.

"That poor man," sighed Maria.

Christina stepped into the hall and walked to the street door. The desk was now out on the pavement, and William and John Crawford stood on either side of it.

"Hello, John!" called Christina, to save William the embarrassment of coming inside to ask if she was at home. "Do come in."

John Crawford climbed the steps and followed Christina into the parlor, holding his hat. His hair and beard, Christina noted, showed streaks of gray that hadn't been there five months ago, and his face seemed leaner.

"You remember my sister, Maria," said Christina. "Can I get you some tea?"

"Miss Maria," said Crawford, nodding. From his salutation he apparently thought Maria was younger than Christina. "No, thank you, I was just passing by your street—"

As so often, thought Christina.

"—and I thought I'd stop and ask if you might have heard anything of Miss McKee."

"Not a word, I'm afraid. But as I've said, I'll certainly—"

"I'm sorry, I know you've promised to let me know at once. It's just that I worry . . ."

On his first visit after Lizzie's funeral, Crawford had told Christina that the girl Johanna had died, and he had mentioned it again at least twice; Christina was weary of pity, and hoped he would not bring it up again.

"We really will let you know," said Maria from the couch. Though unlikely to have any romantic attachments herself, or because of that, she had enormous sympathy for star-crossed lovers.

"But," added Christina with an apologetic smile, "you must trust me to apprise you of any word of her as soon as I learn anything. These visits, so far out of your way—"

"Yes, you're right," said Crawford. He smiled at her, deepening the lines in his cheeks. "We were allies for a while, weren't we?"

"In a campaign that succeeded," agreed Christina. "A campaign that is over," she added, perhaps a bit more forcefully than she meant to. "My uncle—the devil that wore my uncle—is dispersed in the grave."

"And we part ways," he agreed, stepping toward the hall. "'One watching for the mere bright day's delight, one longing for the night.'"

It was a couplet from *Goblin Market*. He nodded and walked out of the house, and Maria got up to watch him out the window.

"The poor man!" exclaimed Maria again.

"His troubles now are his own," said Christina. "The troubles we shared with him are ended." She walked over to stand by Maria and watched Crawford's black-clad figure striding away north toward Albert Road.

"Ended," she repeated firmly.

BOOK II

Good Enough in
the Daytime

October 1869

CHAPTER ONE

Love that is dead and buried, yesterday
Out of his grave rose up before my face,
No recognition in his look, no trace
Of memory in his eyes dust-dimmed and grey.

—*Christina Rossetti, "Love Lies Bleeding"*

THE COPPERY LEAVES of the elms within the walls of Highgate Cemetery hung motionless in the still autumn air, but the yellow grass in the shadow of one north-facing gravestone was shifting. The grass blades, which had been flattened by rain earlier in the day, now stood up like a porcupine's quills, and quivered.

Several minutes later a white point poked up from a hole in the middle of the patch of upright grass blades and rose to a height of a foot before expanding out in a makeshift parasol of muddy white silk. The shaft of the parasol was a long splinter of oak, polished on one side, and the bottom end of it was gripped by a tiny gray hand.

With a series of peristaltic ripplings, a wrinkled gray newt-like fig-ure ejected itself up and out onto the wet grass, and it huddled under the canopy of dirty silk as its snake-like lower half separated into two legs.

In the long fingers of its free hand it carried a tiny fragment of broken mirror.

Its ribs flexed in and out for several minutes under its gray skin while its tiny black eyes swiveled around, scanning the clearing under the elms. Then it got its legs under itself and stood up; and the parasol wobbled over it as it took high steps to a rose bush a few yards away.

In a hollow under the rose bush, hidden from the view of any person more than three feet tall, was a substantial pile of tiny mirror pieces, and the gray creature laid this last one down and then hunched away to the roots of the nearest tree, and its spidery fingers began scrabbling in the damp dirt for beetles; when it found one, it stuffed the wiggling thing into its mouth and began chewing eagerly and immediately commenced digging for another.

CHRISTINA ROSSETTI WAS STARING absently at one of the ukiyo-e prints that William had hung on the grasscloth-lined walls of the drawing room. The wood-block print, rendered in several colors by incomprehensibly patient Japanese artisans, was a view of a mountain that seemed to be floating in the white sky, and Christina was frowning, for there was something ominous in the idea of a mountain freed from the surface of the earth.

She looked away from it finally and laid down her pen in order to refill her glass from the sherry decanter. Her new physician, Doctor Jenner, had advised her to sleep late, eat plenty of carrageen seaweed jelly, and drink what seemed to Christina to be extravagant amounts of sherry.

Her ailment or ailments were obscure, their only symptoms being a constant cough and listlessness. Certainly this malaise was preferable to the anemia and angina pectoris and nightmares from which she had suffered prior to Lizzie's funeral seven years ago. Sometimes Christina suspected that her present lack of energy and alertness, and Gabriel's failing eyesight and insomnia, were consequences of being deprived of some supernatural sustenance their uncle had been providing . . . before they choked him with the mirrors at the funeral.

She sighed and got slowly to her feet, taking the glass with her to the French doors; they opened onto the first-floor balcony, and she blinked through the panes at the Ionic columns of St. Pancras Church across Upper Woburn Place, and at the red-and-gold trees in Euston Square off to the left. Evening had fallen, and only the topmost spires and chimney pots were still touched with a rosy glow.

Her brother Gabriel had found a house to rent in Cheyne Walk down in Chelsea, but two years ago the rest of the family had moved from Albany Street a few streets west of here to this house on Euston Square.

She opened the window door and stepped out onto the roofed balcony. The breeze was chilly through her flannel nightgown, and smelled of smoke from a hundred chimneys.

Of course they were still living on William's salary from the Inland Revenue office, which only this year had risen to eight hundred pounds. Three years ago the banking and broking firm Overend Gurney had failed, and in the ensuing financial crisis and recession, many other firms had collapsed too—there had been panic and even bread riots— but William's government position had insulated the Rossettis from anxiety.

None of the other siblings could help appreciably. Gabriel squandered his money. Maria was teaching Italian and had written a textbook, and Christina earned royalties on the British and American editions of *Goblin Market,* but together the sisters added less than two hundred pounds to the household income in a year. And Maria was forty-two and Christina was nearly thirty-nine now, and neither was likely to marry.

The leaves on the curbside chestnut trees were still green, and between the boughs she saw shiny carriages and hansom cabs whirring along Upper Woburn Place. Their neighbors here were respectable stockbrokers and lawyers, but Christina missed the old house on Albany Street, where most of the family had lived for thirteen years.

She had written poetry there, for a time.

She shook her head impatiently and took a sip of the sherry. What was she thinking—she still wrote poetry!

—At a more labored pace, and without the psychic spark she had felt while writing verses before 1862.

Some of the poems that she had written since then had been published by Macmillan three years ago, in a volume titled _The Prince's Progress and Other Poems_ . . . and the _Saturday Review_ had noted "a good many tame and rather slovenly verses" and "a dull, pointless cadence" in it. In the _Athenaeum,_ a reviewer had said, "We do not see the conflict of the heart, but the sequel of that conflict," and had lamented that the tone of the poems was that of a dirge.

Christina drained the glass of sweet wine and clanked it down on the rail so hard that the stem snapped off.

My _life_ has a dull, pointless cadence, she thought furiously; I am _in_ the sequel of that conflict, and a dirge is the appropriate tone!

She still regularly wrote prose pieces—mostly religious short stories now, for the _Churchman's Shilling Magazine_—but she couldn't pretend that they had the sprightly warmth of the work she had done before 1862.

Well, so be it. If her inspired poetry depended on the attentions of a devil, she was incalculably better off without it.

She turned back toward the drawing room, glancing at her hand to see if she had cut herself. There was no blood, but her thumb and forefinger were stained with ink. What had she been writing, while staring idly at the Japanese mountain?

A notebook lay open on the table beside her chair, and she laid down the broken pieces of the glass and picked it up.

And when she read the first lines that she had written on the open page, she knew what it was—more of "Folio Q."

Her face was suddenly hot. She repressed a quick smile but reached out with her mind to see if the remembered psychic attention was again there—and she sensed only vacancy, a yawning silence.

If his personal attention *had* been turned on her once again, after these seven years of absence, she wouldn't have needed the evidence of the renewed story in the notebook; she would immediately have felt it in her mind like tingling in a newly unconstricted limb.

Seven years ago she had speculated to Gabriel and Maria that her uncle—ghost or vampire or whatever he was—was not deliberately writing through Christina's hand at those times when she had found herself writing "Folio Q," that Uncle John might not even have been aware that she had been physically transcribing his story.

Eagerly she scanned the lines, but though they were in the familiar handwriting of her uncle's spirit, they were disjointed and rambling:

. . . there need not be . . . wisdom or even memory . . . shall I not one day remember thy bower, one day when all days are one day to me? You have been mine before—how long ago I may not know: but just when at that swallow's soar, your neck turned so, some veil did fall . . .

So he was somehow up again, now, awake again, but the fullness of the old connection had not been restored.

She reached out again with her mind, but she could not sense him.

Evidently the mirror confusion they had imposed on him seven years ago, though it had not lasted forever as she and Maria had hoped, had at least severed the link that had connected her with her uncle since that night when, at the age of fourteen, she had rubbed her blood on the tiny statue.

If that were so, she could still go out in the sunlight without being burned . . . but by the same token she would still suffer from her current distracted listlessness . . . and she would still not be able to write the sort of poetry she had written before Lizzie's funeral.

But perhaps Uncle John was simply coming back slowly, to his old attentive extent! Christina would have to go out into the sunlight to see if it once again stung.

And she urgently needed to speak with Maria and Gabriel. Maria was off teaching, but Gabriel would probably be at his house in Chelsea.

Christina hastily scribbled a note to Maria, then hurried to her bedroom to change into street clothes.

THE BAY WINDOWS OF the first-floor drawing room at Tudor House on Cheyne Walk faced the river and the shoreline elms and, farther off, the webby silhouettes of ships moored at the timber docks on the far side of the darkening water, but Gabriel Rossetti was looking impatiently toward the doorway in the southern end of the long room, beyond the big dining table and next to the cabinet full of Dutch china and Oriental curiosities.

He had just lit the gas jets, and now he laid the matchbox on the mantel of the marble fireplace. The burnt wood smell lingered in his nostrils.

"Yes?" he called again. "Dunn, is that you? Algy?"

He heard the scuff and rattle repeated in the corridor—and then two figures moved into the room.

The first was a small, thin boy draped in one of the black velvet curtains from the drawing room and carrying a ludicrous parasol made of sticks and dirty rags—on his feet he wore two cigar boxes that knocked and scraped on the wooden floor. Gabriel's instant surprised anger chilled to horror when he looked more closely at the intruder's face—the boy's skin was gray and stretched so tightly over the teeth and cheekbones that the open mouth seemed to be simply the result of it splitting, and the eyelids looked inadequate to cover his blank black eyes.

But the second figure froze the breath in his throat—it was a tall, red-haired woman in a visibly damp white dress, and after seven years Gabriel recognized her face more by the hundreds of pictures he had done of it than by actual recollection—the face was that of his dead wife, Lizzie.

She was breathing audibly, and the floor creaked under her bare feet.

"Lizzie!" he burst out. He had tried, on a number of occasions since her death, to contact her in séances, but the spirits who had answered his questions had never really seemed to be her. Suddenly and terribly he missed her, missed the cheerful innocence that had first drawn him to her.

"Stay," he went on dizzily, trying to ignore the hideous child beside her. "Don't leave me again—"

The two figures interrupted him, speaking in unison; the child's voice was a harsh quacking and the woman's a metallic whine: "Call me Gogmagog."

Gabriel flinched and stepped back, and he could feel his heart thudding rapidly in his chest. Now he could see the alien and almost inorganic alertness in the woman's eyes, and he noted the slackness of the face.

"You're the one—" he whispered; "I *shot* you, in the park—you *can't have* my wife—"

The two figures took a step forward, and the fabric of the woman's dress tore rottenly at the knee.

"We have both loved her," they said again in their grating voices, "my husband and I. She has two true parents, a rarity." The woman's head inclined toward her small companion, and they went on, "My husband is free again now, but wounded—you need to renew your lapsed vows to him."

Gabriel's pistol was in his bedroom, dusty and neglected; he crouched to pick up a black iron poker from beside the fireplace, and he straightened and held it up like a fencing foil. "Cold iron," he said, his voice shrilled by fear. "Come near me, *either* of you, and I'll—I'll bash you." He squinted at the boy. "Are *you* her—husband?"

The little gray figure's mouth opened wider, further exposing the prominent white teeth, and when he spoke now, the woman didn't join him. "No—I am promised to someone else," he said in his flat monotone. He waved a sticklike arm at the woman beside him. "Her husband is your uncle, who today I finally roused from his long sleep, which cost him much."

The mirrors, Gabriel thought, the mirrors we put into Lizzie's coffin. This awful child must have somehow removed them.

The walls of the parlor and entry hall downstairs were hung with dozens of mirrors—how had these two creatures got past them, if Maria and Christina were right about the properties of mirrors?

But the mirrors had apparently worked in the grave, at least for seven years. Gabriel now snatched up a silver platter from the table, scattering the letters and envelopes that had lain on it.

He held it up with the polished top side toward the two intruders.

"Look," Gabriel cried, "look at your reflections!"

From behind the platter came their jarring, imperturbable voices: "Renew your vows. Invite him in."

The sudden crash of shattering glass made Gabriel jump and drop the platter, which hit the floor with a ringing clang. He had scrambled back with his arm thrown up across his face, but his visitors were gone—apparently they had dived through the south bay window, for most of the panes were gone but no glass lay on the floor or the carpet.

Whimpering, he rushed forward through the suddenly cold air, but he ran toward the door to the hall and didn't look at the window; and in the doorway he collided with a figure who was hurrying in. A glimpse of copper hair made Gabriel think that it was the vampire in Lizzie's body again, and he grabbed for its throat—

But his hand closed on a stiff collar and tie and the lapel of a jacket; and, peering through tears, Gabriel saw that it was the much shorter and thinner figure of Swinburne.

"Gabriel!" Swinburne exclaimed, pushing his hand aside. "What on earth?"

"Algy," gasped Gabriel, "Algy, I—"

Swinburne was peering past him into the drawing room, angling his oversized head to see down the length of it.

"Did they jump out the *window?*" he asked incredulously.

"Yes, Algy, they—!"

"Why?" Swinburne stared at Gabriel wide-eyed. "Gabriel, it was Lizzie! Alive!"

He ran past Gabriel to the window and leaned out through the ragged gap in the panes, his curly red hair blowing around his face.

"There's no one visible below," he said; then, *"Christina!"* he yelled out into the evening air. "Did you see anyone fall?" He leaned out as far as he could without touching the broken glass on the bottom edges. *"Fall,"* he repeated. "Oh, never mind, wait, we'll be down in a moment!"

Gabriel made himself step up beside Swinburne at the window. He waved vaguely down at the figure of Christina, who had closed the street gate behind her and was hurrying toward the house, and then he cautiously inclined his own head out into the chilly breeze, but Swinburne was right—there were no figures on the narrow patch of grass or on the walk.

"Algy," he said, "you were downstairs—did you invite them in?"

"Of course I did, it was Lizzie!—and some sick child. Come on!"

Gabriel stepped back from the window. "A *dead* child, Algy, and Lizzie was dead too. *Is* dead. That wasn't her."

"Of course it was her, she knew me! We've got to go downstairs; they're probably hurt—"

Gabriel gripped his shoulder and shook him. "Algy, damn it, it was not her! It was a ghost, a demon in her form—do you think *I* wouldn't *know?*"

"A *demon?*" Swinburne had raised his hands and now dropped them. He exhaled and brushed his windblown hair out of his face and squinted at Gabriel. "But it was not her ghost. I—that's not how ghosts look, and her ghost—wouldn't be *here*." He looked out across the Cheyne Walk pavement to the dark river. "But she did know me," he added quietly, almost to himself.

He looked back at Gabriel, and his eyes were bright. "A *demon*, you say?" And he actually laughed. "An archaic goddess, perhaps!"

Gabriel shook his head unhappily. "You don't know anything about it, Algy."

"Good God!" came a voice from the hallway door, sounding flat with no resonance from the missing window. Gabriel looked up to see his young assistant, Henry Dunn, gaping at the wide new gap in the windowpanes. "What happened?"

"I leaned on the glass," said Swinburne.

Dunn stared expressionlessly at Swinburne for a moment, his mouth open, then said to Gabriel, "Your sister is here. Christina."

And in fact Christina now hurried into the room right behind Dunn. She glanced from Gabriel to Swinburne through narrowed eyes, not even looking at the window.

"Algy," she said, breathing hard as if she had run up the stairs, if not all the way from Euston Square, "I need to talk to my brother privately, if you would excuse us."

Swinburne nodded and bobbed to the door. "It was a goddess!" he called before disappearing down the hall.

Dunn crossed to the remains of the window and pulled the curtains closed; they rippled, but they were heavy enough to keep out the river-scented breeze and the indistinct roar of the city. Then he nodded too and stepped back out of the room and closed the door.

"I saw two clouds of smoke," Christina said, "—distinct, not dissipating in the air, like—splashes of ink in oil!—they burst out through your window and churned away over the river! Darker than the night! Our uncle John—"

"Is awake again; I know," said Gabriel, pulling two chairs out from the table and slumping into one of them. "My visitors told me. My inky visitors. God."

"It wasn't him, himself, then," said Christina. "Thank God for that." She sat down in the other chair and took his hand. "Who were they?"

"One was a boy, like a starved corpse galvanized. The other—" He had run out of air, and had to take a deep breath to go on. "The other was—Lizzie. Or your Celtic queen, the one who died in A.D. 60, *animating* my Lizzie."

"Lizzie? But she was blocked with mirrors too! Did they all *dissolve?*"

Gabriel rocked his head back and stared at the rings of gaslight on the high ceiling. "Corrode, tarnish, I don't know." He put a hand over his eyes, but his voice was still steady when he said, "My poor Lizzie! This thing said that what's left of my wife has two true parents, meaning our uncle and this Boadicea creature."

"And . . . the other one, the boy?"

"God knows who the boy is, or was. They said I need to renew my lapsed vows." He gave his sister a bleak smile. "They said Uncle John is wounded—by your mirrors apparently, while they still worked." He leaned forward to see the clock over the mantel, then glanced moodily at the waving curtains. "William is due soon for dinner. I suppose we'll eat in the breakfast room, rather than in here."

"That room has several mirrors," Christina agreed. "And I left a note for Maria, saying to join me here."

"All four suits together, Diamonds, to play this hand."

Christina shook her head and pursed her lips. "I can't imagine what William will think of all this. But we've got to try to warn him."

"He's big on science. We'll tell him that it's all to do with magnetism."

WILLIAM STOPPED AT THE Euston Street house to refill his tobacco pouch—Gabriel's guests always smoked up the tobacco he left in a box on the mantelpiece at Tudor House—and so he and Maria arrived there together in the cab William had hired.

William only spent a night or two a week in his room at Tudor House, because, unlike Gabriel, he generally had to arise at eight in the morning to be at his office at the Board of Inland Revenue in Somerset House by ten. He was forty years old and had worked there since the age of fifteen, and he was now the assistant secretary in the Excise Section.

His real allegiance was to art and poetry, but he had no particular skills in them himself—he had written a translation of Dante's *Inferno*, but Macmillan had rejected it twelve years ago and reconsidered eight years later only because William's mother contributed fifty pounds toward the expense of its publication—and he tried to be content with being a financial and emotional support to his sister and brother as they pursued their areas of genius. He was currently devoting a lot of his free time to editing a collection of Shelley's poetry, a project that had brought him into contact with Shelley's oldest-surviving and most controversial friend, an old pirate named Trelawny.

Neither he nor Maria noticed the broken first-floor window as they stepped from the cab through the streetlamp radiance to Gabriel's iron gate, but Christina met them on the walkway and hurried them inside, glancing nervously at the dark sky.

She led them upstairs to the studio, where they found Gabriel staring at his painting *Beata Beatrix,* a portrait of his dead wife, Lizzie, as Dante's Beatrice. The painting, still unfinished seven years after it was begun, portrayed Lizzie in three-quarter profile with her eyes shut, as a dove dropped a poppy into her limp hands; behind her stood the indistinct figures of a man in black and a woman in red, who Gabriel said were intended to represent Dante and Love.

William had always thought it was a morbid picture—the Dante and Love figures looked sinister in their shadowy blurriness, and he thought it was in doubtful taste to show a poppy being given to a woman who had died of an overdose of laudanum, which was a potent mix of opium and grain alcohol.

William stepped carefully around the many half-finished paintings that lay on the floor to the fireplace, but the tobacco box was once again empty. Grumbling, he fished his old briar pipe and tobacco pouch from his coat pocket.

Christina had pulled Maria down beside her onto the sofa. Behind them was a small window blocked with the dead leaves of one of the trees in the back garden.

Gabriel was tugging at his goatee and scowling as he paced the floor between the pictures, and when William had finally drawn up one of the easy chairs, and raised his eyebrows quizzically as he struck a match to his pipe, Gabriel said, "Lizzie was just here. *Lizzie.* Christina saw . . . saw her exit, right through one of the drawing room windows. She then apparently *flew away.*"

"Oh no," moaned Maria, clasping Christina's hand. "The mirrors . . . ?"

"Mirrors?" asked William, keeping his voice merely level.

"It's magnetism!" blurted Christina, and then blushed.

Gabriel curtly explained to William that the three of them had surreptitiously lined the bottom of Lizzie's coffin with downward-facing mirrors stained with Christina's blood; the ghost of their suicide uncle was apparently in the coffin directly below Lizzie's, in their father's coffin—and Gabriel claimed that the "corporeal kernel" of their uncle's ghost, or possibly vampiric devil, was a tiny statue lodged in their father's throat.

William cleared his own throat and shifted in his chair. "Did—did you say," he asked, "in Papa's *throat?*"

"Yes," said Gabriel levelly.

"I see."

For a moment no one spoke, and William just puffed on his pipe, and the tarry smell of latakia tobacco drove away the big room's usual scent of linseed oil. He considered asking how they believed they knew this, but the thought of the occult explanation that would surely follow wearied him in advance.

Then he thought of all the mirrors that were hung throughout the house—so many that a visitor saw more of himself than of his companions.

"But why mirrors?" William persisted.

Gabriel explained that if one of these creatures—*one* of them? thought William—could be induced to fix its attention on a mirror, its identity would be reflected back on itself, causing its identity to fragment.

"Any order in its field would arguably be lost in interference fringes," conceded William, nodding. He looked at Christina. "This is what your 'Folio Q' was about, I think?"

"Yes, but not specifically enough," she said. "Maria repeated some of Papa's studies to discover it." She squinted miserably at William. "I know you don't believe any of this—"

"That's not *quite* true," he said carefully, "any longer. I frankly admit I'm dubious of this story, but ever since the night when—on the night I'm sure you remember, when you did some automatic writing in my presence in the old house on Albany Street, I've been investigating spiritualism." He glanced at Gabriel.

"It's true," Gabriel said. "We've held séances in this house."

"Oh, William, Gabriel, no!" exclaimed Maria. "Consulting the dead!"

William smiled and leaned back. "It's science, Maria! Possibly magnetism, as Christina said. I've been to a good twenty séances, here and elsewhere, and now I'm at least willing to concede the possibility that there is some sort of life after death."

"You should have been here ten minutes ago," growled Gabriel. "You'd have conceded it and then some. Algy saw her too, saw Lizzie."

"And I've been writing more of 'Folio Q,'" said Christina mournfully. "Our uncle is clearly active, though the writing seemed distracted; there were no clear statements." She spread her hands. "The mirrors have somehow stopped working."

"Lizzie—" said Gabriel, "the Lizzie thing—said that he's wounded now, at least."

Christina shuddered and said, "I wonder if the statue is even still in Papa's grave? I remember the gravediggers at Lizzie's funeral pointing out what they called a 'mole hole' that went all the way down."

"Wait a moment," said William. "This statue—is it that little black one that Papa kept on a shelf in his bedroom?"

"Yes," said Gabriel.

William remembered the childhood nightmares that had always stopped when their father put the statue in a glass of salt water. "I begin," he said cautiously, "to find this marginally plausible. Why is it in Papa's *throat*?"

"He choked on it," said Christina.

William opened his mouth to ask how that had occurred, but Gabriel was already speaking.

"If it is still there," said Gabriel, "we need to exhume it and destroy it once and for all."

"Impossible, surely," said William, "for a dozen reasons! For one, you can't . . . cut open our father's throat! And in any case, you couldn't do it on the sly—there are night watchmen."

Gabriel held up a hand and then stepped to the fireplace, where he lifted a brandy decanter and poured a couple of inches of liquor into a used coffee cup. He drank it off in two quick gulps, then said, quietly, "As to your first objection, William, I think the presence of that thing in Papa's throat defiles his final rest."

The sisters nodded, Maria grudgingly.

Gabriel gave his siblings a defiant look. "And as to the second—I've been in correspondence with Henry Bruce. Do you remember him?"

William tamped the smoldering tobacco in his pipe and frowned.

"Involved in your commission to paint the altarpiece in the cathedral at Cardiff?"

"That's the man. He was member of Parliament for Merthyr Tydfil at the time. He's now the Home Secretary." Gabriel took a deep breath. "I have lately concluded that Millais and Burne-Jones outstrip me in the execution of art."

"Nonsense," said William, and Christina echoed him.

"That's kind of you to say, but, begging your pardon, even though my eyesight is failing, I can see that much. And so I've decided to establish my name in poetry instead—or as well, at least." His face when he looked around was tensely expressionless. "Milton wrote *Paradise Lost* after he was blind."

William raised his eyebrows inquiringly.

"Well," said Gabriel, "don't you see? I want to stand now on my poetry, but my best poems are—"

"Oh, Gabriel!" burst out Christina. "Not the notebook you laid in her coffin!"

"That was a sacrifice," Gabriel nearly shouted, "and for seven years I've endured the sacrifice!" More quietly he went on, "This is, must be, kept a secret, for all our sakes—if it should somehow become known that I did it, and you hear of it, you must react as you would if this conversation never took place. That is, dismiss it, deny it. I implore your thoroughness in this, for all our sakes. But the Home Secretary has officially granted me permission to exhume Lizzie."

"Granted *you* permission?" said Maria. "But you're not the owner of the grave—Mama is."

"That was an obstacle," said Gabriel, nodding, "but I prevailed with the argument that it was the grave of my wife."

"Was it," said Christina slowly, "only your poems that you hoped to retrieve?"

She seemed to brace herself as she asked the question, as though it might provoke Gabriel, but Gabriel just gave his sister a haggard smile.

"If my purpose had been to free our uncle from the mirrors and revive my strangled Muse—*our* strangled Muse!—I would have abandoned the plan tonight, when we learned that he is in fact somehow free of them now. I don't want the—the consequences of his help anymore, but I would like to have the work I did in the days when I *had* his help."

"Muse?" said William. "Help?"

Gabriel bobbed his head and waved toward Christina.

She pursed her lips and shifted on the sofa. "These things are vampires, and—and when they've established a connection with you, one of the results is often that you write . . . a better sort of poetry than you could do unaided."

William shivered. *A better sort of poetry than you could do unaided.*

"Gabriel and I haven't written first-rate poetry since Lizzie's funeral," Christina added.

"And they sustain the lives of their human . . . partners," grumbled Gabriel. "I don't think Christina would be an invalid now if we had not strangled him at Lizzie's funeral—and I don't think I would be losing my eyesight."

William found that he was suddenly eager to believe this story, and he tried to revive his habitual skepticism. He turned to Gabriel. "What are the consequences that you *don't* want?"

"These vampires," said Gabriel, "love the humans whom they initiate into their family—"

"Initiate with their teeth," said Christina quietly.

"—and," Gabriel went on, "they are toweringly jealous of anyone whom each new family member has previously loved. They—kill any such, unless those have been initiated into the family themselves."

"But . . . will your eyesight recover now—now that our uncle is . . . somehow awake again?"

"No," said Christina and Gabriel together. Christina went on: "Our connections with him were evidently broken when we shut him down at the funeral, and so the people we love are still safe—as long as we continue to resist him." She turned an anxious look on Gabriel. "How did Lizzie get into the house tonight? I gather you didn't invite her."

"No, Algy did. Her and this starved dead boy." To William and Maria he said, "Lizzie was accompanied by what must have been the ghost of a boy, though he—seemed unusually solid, for a ghost. I don't know who he was."

William stood up, still trembling. "It will be one thing to legally exhume Lizzie," he said, "and retrieve your poems. But it will be quite another to dig further, and break open our father's coffin, and then actually cut open his throat! We should establish first whether or not that statue is still there. Our uncle's recent activities may be the result of this statue's having lately . . . dug its way out?"

"What sort of dowsing rod would you use?" asked Gabriel.

William smiled. "We should hold another séance here, with Diamonds and Clubs joining Hearts and Spades, for a full deck."

"I will not participate in any such thing!" exclaimed Maria.

"You can watch," said William, suppressing impatience, "and in proximity pray more effectively for our souls."

Christina didn't look any happier about the idea. "But who—what spirit would we ask to speak to?"

"Uncle John himself, I would think," said William. "Or, failing that, Lizzie—she was lying right over him; it's likely she would know."

"It's time we went in to dinner," said Gabriel. "It's to be in the green breakfast room tonight, and Algy is probably getting impatient." More quietly he went on, "Let's hold the séance soon—on a night when Algy isn't here."

IN THE SHADOWS OF the hall, Swinburne stepped back from the doorway and hurried to his room so that he could pretend to have been asleep when someone came to summon him.

CHAPTER TWO

We shall know what the darkness discovers,
If the grave-pit be shallow or deep;
And our fathers of old, and our lovers,
We shall know if they sleep not or sleep.

—*Algernon Swinburne, "Dolores"*

A THIRD OF A mile north of Tudor House stood Pelham Crescent, a semicircular row of splendid white houses designed thirty years earlier by Elias Basevi, who had also been the architect of Belgrave Square. Separated from one another by iron railings like rows of upright black spears, each house's doorway was up three steps from the pavement and framed by square pillars that supported a first-floor balcony. The gentlemen who entered or alighted from glossy carriages at the curb wore tall silk hats or the newer round creations of William Bowler, and their starched linen collars and cuffs were bright spots against well-tailored black overcoats.

From Number 7 on this February evening, though, emerged a contrary figure in a brown sack coat with an open-collared shirt and no hat;

his white beard was untrimmed and his glance up and down the street was arrogant. Edward Trelawny waved his cane, and a hansom cab obediently slanted in to a rocking halt in front of him.

"New Cut Market," he called to the driver, flipping a half-crown coin toward the man's perch behind and above the cab.

The driver turned the coin carefully in the dim radiance of a streetlamp, but it evidently appeared genuine, for he tucked it into a pocket and nodded.

Trelawny snorted and stepped up into the cab.

As the long reins snapped over the roof and the cab surged forward, Trelawny sat stiffly upright, scornful of the padded seat back, but inwardly he was uneasy, and he was cautiously reassured by the angular bulk of the pistol tucked behind his belt buckle.

He had not seen anything of the terrible Miss B. for seven years now, not since two days after that Rossetti woman's funeral. At that funeral he had learned the identity of the woman previously known to him only as "Diamonds," and he had called on her at noon the next day.

She had received him in the parlor of a modest house in Albany Street, with her fat sister sitting beside her on the sofa while he sat in a chair on the other side of a table on which rested an array of tea and biscuits, which he had ignored.

"MY CONDOLENCES, ON YOUR loss," he had said formally.

"Thank you," said Christina Rossetti.

"You mentioned, Diamonds," he said, "that you know where that statue is buried."

The sister—Maria—turned a startled look on Christina, but Christina stared evenly at Trelawny and said, "It doesn't matter now. We have strangled it."

"You did indeed," he acknowledged with a respectful nod. "Last night I visited an acquaintance south of the river, a woman who was afflicted by your uncle—"

At that point Maria burst out, "How does this man know these things?"

"Mr. Trelawny is an ally," said Christina, and she smiled. "At least as much of an ally as we can hope for. Do go on."

"This acquaintance of mine," said Trelawny, "was distraught. For some months she has been receiving your uncle in rooms above her dolly shop in New Street, and hers is the only such shop without a crucible glowing away in a back room for melting down stolen silver, since your uncle doesn't approve of metals. She was on the roof last night, weeping, and her fingers were all chewed bloody in desperate hope of calling him back." Trelawny spread his hands. "That *would* have drawn him, if he'd been conscious anywhere in the British Isles! But she remains bereaved, and her old illnesses, which he had held back, are on her again."

No one spoke as he pulled a cigar from his coat pocket, though he frowned and put it away again when he saw Maria wince. Finally he said, "You don't want to tell me where the statue is buried."

"No," admitted Christina.

"If you are *certain* that you have somehow killed your uncle, then it doesn't matter. Without him, his spouse—my patron, whom you saw Monday last in Regent's Park and whom your brother shot—"

"Gabriel *shot* someone?" exclaimed Maria. "With that gun of his? 'Stina, you didn't *tell* me?"

Christina waved her hand impatiently. "She wasn't human," she said, "or not very much so. She seemed more to be a dog—a dog wearing clothes, that is. And when Gabriel shot her, she burrowed into the ground like a sand crab."

Trelawny laughed at the expression of baffled dismay on Maria's face.

"If, as I say, you are *certain* that you've killed him, then I don't *need* to know where he's buried, since his poor maligned spouse—you really didn't see her at her best—cannot accomplish their purpose alone. But I would like—"

"What is—was—their purpose?" asked Christina.

"My patron," said Trelawny, "would like to do again what she did in A.D. 60."

"You will explain all this to me," said Maria stiffly to Christina, "with diagrams, directly after this conversation."

"Yes, Maria, I'm sorry!" To Trelawny she said, "But what did she do in A.D. 60? Besides die? Oh! She burned London."

"It burned," agreed Trelawny, "but first she shook it to pieces."

"You mean Boadicea," said Maria. "She was, or is, one of these things like our uncle, I presume."

Trelawny bowed in his chair. "I see it's only Gabriel who is witless among your family."

"You haven't met," began Christina; "—oh, never mind."

"He's not *dead*," said Maria quickly, as if in spite of herself, "our uncle. Just . . . perpetually disrupted, shattered—cross-eyed!"

"How were they intending to destroy London?" asked Christina, apparently as much to change the subject as from curiosity. "It's a much bigger city these days!"

"The same way she did before," said Trelawny. "She and her daughters had been consecrated to the old British goddess known as Andraste and Magna Mater and Gogmagog, and then one of her daughters was raped by a Roman who was consecrated to a similar goddess in the Alps—the effect requires parents from two continents—and with certain rituals the birth of the resultant child was made to flex the continents, physically, like bending a sheet of glass."

"An earthquake," said Maria.

"That's it," said Trelawny. "And she would like to be that sort of catastrophic 'grandmother' again—to have one of her forcibly adopted family of the British goddess beget a—beget what you might call a

'child'—by a victim of the European devil that animates your uncle."
He shrugged. "Snap the continental whip again."

"'Consecrated to,'" said Maria fastidiously, "means 'bitten by,' I gather."

"To put it vulgarly," agreed Trelawny.

"Are *you* . . . consecrated to her?" asked Maria.

"No—not that way, at least, not as *consummated* as that. Shelley was, but he was born into it, poor old fellow; and Byron was, but he had no self-control. I did invite her into my house twelve years ago, but I was able to protect myself and my family from her. I'm in a privileged position—I'm the precious Rosetta stone between the two species, the bridge, as long as I've got this half statue growing in my throat—"

Maria looked helplessly at Christina, who rocked her head and waved reassuringly.

"—but because I invited her in, she sticks to me like my shadow. I'd like to free myself, and even more so the world, from Miss B. Therefore—"

"'Miss B.!'" exclaimed Maria with a smile. "That's genteel."

"Fewer syllables to say. *Therefore,* I would like to know how you managed to 'disrupt and shatter' your uncle."

"So that you may do it with Miss B.," said Christina, "who is—you said—your patron."

"Soon to be my former patron, if you'll tell me how."

"But, as you say, you would still be the bridge, the Rosetta stone."

"That's right, and the simplest thing to do would be to have the statue cut out of my throat, you mean?—and then the overlap between the species will be gone, and the vampires will all be 'melted into air, into thin air.'"

He picked up his cup of tea and drained it; it was lukewarm, and he wished they had served plain cold water instead. "The man who previously served as the Rosetta stone, the *overlap* between our species, a centuries-old Austrian, had his ambassador-statue cut out of him in 1822. He died of it."

"Are you particularly afraid to die?" asked Maria; she was so earnest that he felt obliged to answer the question seriously.

"I've risked my life a hundred times," he told her, "sometimes frivolously. But I'm convinced that this life, this mortal coil, is all there is. 'Our little life is rounded with a sleep,' and there's no Heaven or Hell afterward. I'm seventy years old, and with luck my purse of years is nearly emptied, but while I don't mind laying my remaining days down on a decent wager, I don't want to simply toss them away."

Maria nodded sympathetically and said, "Or even *spend* them, on saving the lives of strangers?"

Trelawny took a deep breath and repressed an irritable reply. After a few seconds, he said, "You're devout, aren't you? Some species of Christian, I imagine?"

She smiled faintly. "Yes."

"I would say that was a mark against your intelligence, but since you're both nice girls, I won't say it. But you assume a sequel to this life, one in which noble sacrifices are rewarded, or at least noted. I'm convinced that no note is taken at all, and that, as far as any one of us is concerned, the universe comes to an end at the moment of his death."

He smiled. "But if you'll tell me how you got your uncle cross-eyed, I can do it to Miss B., and then I don't think there will be any active vampires left in England."

"But don't their victims who die become vampires, in turn?" asked Christina. "There must by now be a number of those about."

Trelawny exhaled through clenched teeth. Could these women not answer a plain question?

"My suspicion," he said carefully, "is that your uncle and Miss B. have *sustained* any such; without that sustenance, any second-generation vampires will probably just fall down belatedly dead, like marionettes with the strings cut. Your uncle's are now presumably laid to rest—I'd like to do the same for my patron's."

"Probably," said Christina. "Presumably."

"Your suspicion," added Maria.

Trelawny smiled coldly and got to his feet. "I apologize for wasting your afternoon, ladies. Perhaps your brother would be good enough to shoot her with his silver bullets again, from time to time."

"Mirrors," said Maria quickly.

Christina sighed. "Do sit down, Mr. Trelawny."

Trelawny resumed his seat and leaned forward, raising his white eyebrows.

"My sister appears to have faith in you," Christina said. She blew a stray strand of hair out of her face. "I trust you'll use this information as you say, and not to help your . . . *patron* protect herself!"

"I will use it as I say."

"Very well." Christina bit a fingernail, then spoke in a rush: "These creatures won't ordinarily fix their attention on a mirror, because it would reflect their identities back on themselves, you see, and that's like—apparently it's like randomly rearranging a complicated first-person sentence, so that the verbs and adjectives and nouns are all in the wrong places, and it's all just contradictory gibberish."

"They can no longer utter themselves," put in Maria, "as it were."

"But," Christina went on, "if you scratch lines in the glass and rub some of your blood into the lines, the creature *will* focus on it, out of its love and concern for you." She blinked several times rapidly and looked away, and Trelawny realized that she had to some extent loved her uncle too.

Maria took up the slack. "Then keep that mirror in position—I'd advise putting her and the mirror in a box together, and hiding the box in a secret place. It needn't be a big box, probably—she's likely to diminish in substance a good deal."

THAT WAS SEVEN YEARS ago, Trelawny thought as the hansom cab rattled south through the lamplit streets of Chelsea toward Battersea

Bridge, and I'm seventy-seven years old now. And I did not succeed in catching Miss B. in a mirror—though I did manage to drive her away from me. That has been a relief, I do steadfastly insist.

DIRECTLY AFTER LEAVING THE Rossetti sisters' house in Albany Street on that February afternoon in 1862, he had bought a three-foot-tall framed mirror and scratched the glass and rubbed blood from a cut finger onto it, and then he had set it in the chair he usually occupied, and himself sat down cross-legged behind it with a pipe and a book of Shelley's poems to wait for twilight and Miss B.

It was a nostalgic and half-melancholy vigil. Miss B. had loved him, in spite of his evasions and derelictions and their unconsummated pairing, and in the twelve years since the night when he had found her in the ravine outside King's Norton she had shown him marvels that had astonished even *him,* who had fended off vampires in Italy and questioned ghosts with Lord Byron in Athens and ridden with devils in the gorge below Mount Parnassus!

Trelawny put down the pipe and the book and leaned back against the chair legs, staring into the fire in the grate.

She had shown him visions of the earth as it had been before the sunlight changed, before the air was poisoned by the harsh, flammable element exhaled by the spreading greenness—when the creatures later called Nephilim or fallen angels had filled the red skies with their yet-unwithered wings and shaken the young mountains with their glad choruses . . .

And on moonless nights she had taken him out in a boat on the western sea, where the luminous curtains of the aurora borealis were reminiscent mirages of the walls of long-perished palaces . . .

And she had offered him immortality, of a much more tangible sort than what the Rossetti girls looked forward to in their Christian faith . . . but it would have required that he renew it periodically.

Trelawny shuddered behind the chair at the thought of that bloody, predatory renewal. He shook his head. In his arrogant youth he might have been able to extend his life by taking the lives of others, but he certainly could not do it now.

There was the rap of a boot on the hall floor—

And then he heard Miss B. fling open the chamber door and step heavily into the room, and he huddled motionless behind the chair. Look at the mirror, he thought; look at my blood. In spite of the fire, the air was suddenly so cold that he could see his breath.

"I see through it to you," came her voice, heavy as gold. "I see through you."

The floor jumped under Trelawny and the curtains swayed across the rocking walls, and as he clutched at the carpet he heard pictures and books hitting the floor, and gritty plaster dust sifted down onto his gray head and he heard a loud clank behind him, which must have been the mirror falling forward out of the chair and landing face-down on the heaving floor.

"You are the translation bridge between our kinds," said her voice. "I must not kill you. I withdraw from you."

And then his ears had popped and the window had burst inward with a crash, and a powerful draft had knocked the chair over and flung papers out into the hallway—and she was gone.

AND SHE DID WITHDRAW, he thought now as his cab rattled over Battersea Bridge. Looking out through the side window, over the forward-rushing rim of the left wheel, he watched distant boats silently interrupting the moon's glitter on the water. Seven years it's been, now, since I've laid eyes on Miss B., though she's presumably still active, somewhere, with somebody. Well, that poet, for one—Swinburne.

On the south side of the bridge, the cab angled northeast through Kennington to the Lambeth Road; and when they arrived at Waterloo

Bridge Road, the glow in the sky and the increasing roar of a hundred raised voices let Trelawny know that they were on the threshold of the New Cut. Soon the cab halted, blocked by dozens of milling pedestrians.

He climbed down from the cab and stood for a moment in the middle of the crowded, noisy street; behind him the rows of houses were lost in darkness in spite of the dim yellow rectangles of windows, for ahead of him the street was spangled with dazzling constellations of red and white and yellow light; gas jets fluttered over butcher shops, the pearly glare of gas lamps eclipsed the ruddy radiance of grease lamps, and candles and dips stood everywhere, in glass chimneys at the doorways of shops and stuck into vegetables on the high-piled carts of costermongers. The night breeze was from the east, funneling down the churning street, and it carried a pungent mix of smells: curry, candle wax, fish, perfume . . .

Booths crowded both sides of the street, and in the space of six yards Trelawny could have bought bootlaces, tin saucepans, or a smoked codfish nearly as tall as himself; and he threaded his way between gentlemen in silk hats, tradesmen in caps and leather aprons, and headless dummies wearing embroidered waistcoats and Norfolk jackets. From all sides rang the din of vendors announcing their wares: "Hot chestnuts!" and "What do you say to these cabbages?" and "Three a penny, don't pass it up!" and "*Here's* your bloaters!" as if Trelawny had misplaced the disreputable fish in question and had been looking all over the city for them.

As he stepped around some pedestrians and was jostled by others, he kept one hand on his belt buckle, directly over the pistol tucked into his trousers; he wasn't risking some pickpocket making off with it.

Above all the flares and banners on the south side of the street stood the theater he remembered as the Coburg, now known as the Royal Vic, the Corinthian capitals of its four tall pilasters underlit by the lights below, and behind the high scalloped cornice he could just see the brick structure that had been built to hold the stage's famous crystal curtain, which could not be rolled or folded but had to be raised all of a piece.

Trelawny didn't believe he'd been followed, but he made for a gin shop he knew of on the east side of the theater.

The door was already ajar, spilling a streak of yellow gaslight across the stained pavement, and though in pushing it farther open he nearly knocked down a burly fellow standing just inside, Trelawny's fierce gaze made the fellow merely touch his cap and shuffle backward. Trelawny nodded by way of token apology and stepped inside.

Just by the smell, Trelawny could tell that the place had apparently converted from gin to rum since he had last visited—the warm sweet reek of it nearly overpowered the tobacco smoke that hung in layers under the low wooden ceiling, and a big cask rested on a shelf behind the bar with a sign on it that read CHOLERA MIXTURE! He recalled reading that a doctor had recently advised rum as a preventive for that disease, and apparently all the men and women in this narrow gas-lit room were busily attending to their health—though the place still served drinks in pewter mugs, which were reputed to get a person drunk faster than ceramic or glass vessels did.

The white-haired landlady who sat behind the bar took a blackened clay pipe out of her mouth when she saw him.

"Trelawny, you villain," she said, "don't you trust me?"

He recalled that he had loaned her money at one time.

"Keep it," he said curtly. "I just want to pay my respects to Oatie."

"I remember that!" she exclaimed, giggling toothlessly. "It's been a while since anyone gave the poor old soul a thought. I think the door's locked—here. You can leave the key in the lock; I'll send a boy after you to fetch it back."

Trelawny grinned and caught the tossed key, then strode toward the back of the place. Oatie Granwell had been a scissors-and-knife sharpener who had died in 1836, and after his wake had been held in the back room of this place, people had for years continued to use "paying respects to Oatie" as an excuse to leave by the back.

When Trelawny unlocked the door at the far end of the room and swung it open, he saw that the entire rear chamber was gone—he was standing in a dark alley by the loading bay doors of the Royal Vic. Quickly he sprinted across the pebbled pavement to a remembered set of stairs, and when he had climbed them to the narrow unlit first-floor balcony, he was relieved to see that the old beam still spanned the ten-foot gap between this balcony's railing and the roof of a bakery next door. He hopped nimbly up onto the rail, and then stepped carefully across, disdaining to hold his arms out for balance.

And on the bakery roof he was pleased to find that he remembered the path between the skylights; even in daylight they were hard to discern, being as black with soot as the rest of the roof surface, and he knew from experience that an unaware pursuer would inevitably put a foot through one black pane or another.

From the coping on the far side of the roof he leaped across a four-foot gap to the next building, a boardinghouse, and a couple of groggy drinkers sitting by the stairway shed looked up at his booming arrival on the roof, but they made no objection as he stepped over them and clattered away down the interior stairs.

When he stepped out through the south door of the place, he was in New Street, and the only light now was the faint glow behind him in the foggy sky over New Cut; by memory more than sight he found the recessed doorway of Number 12 on the far side of the street, and he groped his way up the dark stairs within.

At the top of the stairs he paused on the landing, straining his eyes to see in the near-total blackness.

This morning in his house in Pelham Crescent he had glanced at the mantelpiece and noticed that the ace of spades had fallen over inside the glass dome he thought of as his Byron bell jar.

In 1824, in Greece, Trelawny had clipped a lock of hair from Lord Byron's corpse, and after the Rossetti woman's funeral in 1862, he had glued a strand of the hair to the playing card so that the card was held nearly upright, and then he had set a lit candle beside it and sealed the glass dome over it all. The candle had soon used up all the vital air in the confined space and gone out, leaving the card and Byron's hair in an atmosphere similar to the primeval Earth's.

And at some time during the last day or so—he did glance at the bell jar pretty regularly!—the strand of Byron's hair had contracted, pulling the card over onto its face.

Byron had been bitten by Doctor Polidori in 1822, in Italy. Trelawny reckoned that the hair was a link to Polidori, a tripwire . . . and it seemed that the Rossettis' uncle had recently tripped it, in spite of the assurances of Christina and Maria that their uncle had been banished for good. Inefficient women!

If Polidori was up and active again, then Polidori and Miss B., wherever she was these days, could resume their seven-year-interrupted effort to bring another earthquake to London. And it would be partly Trelawny's fault, he having invited Miss B. back into the world.

On the other hand, it could be that human hair just naturally shrank over the years. He had to make sure.

Long ago he had told the Rossetti sisters about the woman who lived in this house, over the dolly shop.

If she was still alive, if she still lived here, she would surely be approached by Polidori, if in fact he was resurrected.

By touch he established where the corners of the landing were. He was directly in front of her door.

He took a deep breath and knocked.

"Go away," came a woman's languorous voice from within.

Trelawny smiled in the darkness. "You've invited worse things in, Gretchen."

"My God, Trelawny? You must be a hundred years old. Go away, I've got company."

Trelawny tried the doorknob—it turned, but the door rattled against an interior bolt.

"Let me in, Gretchen," he said.

"Write me a letter," came her muffled reply.

Trelawny stepped back and drew the revolver from under his waistcoat, then lifted a boot and kicked the door near the knob. Wood cracked and the door flew inward and banged against some article of furniture.

Trelawny's nostrils flared at a mingled scent of roses and clay as he took two quick steps across the wooden floor inside, spinning to scan the whole room over the sight bead at the end of the gun's barrel.

By the dim glow of a red-shaded lamp he saw two figures reclining on a sofa by an open window on the street side of the long room. One was a woman in a filmy gown, and the other—Trelawny felt his heart begin thumping in his chest—was a pale man with curly hair and blood gleaming on his lips and chin under a disordered mustache.

The man wore a tight-fitting black coat and trousers, ragged at the hems and torn at the elbows and knees, but it was difficult in the faint light to be sure how big or far away he was. Trelawny was careful not to look into the man's eyes.

Trelawny swung the barrel to point at the man's chest, but the woman had stood up and blocked the shot.

"Will you kill me, Edward?" she asked, nearly laughing.

"Yes," he said. "It'll go through you to him." But he couldn't clearly see the figure of the man now, and Trelawny knew he had lost what he sometimes called the elephant of surprise. He blinked away sudden sweat.

The man behind the standing woman seemed to flail long arms, as if trying to stand up, or fly. "Who is it?" he said in a shrill voice like a drill bit twisting in green wood. "I see steel. I smell silver."

The pistol grip was suddenly very hot in Trelawny's right palm; but he held it more tightly and aimed it at a point below the woman's ribs that seemed to cover the broadest part of what might be the man's chest—

But in the moment when he pulled the trigger, the barrel was jerked upward, and the gun fired into the ceiling.

Momentarily deafened by the confined explosion and blinded by the lateral flares from the gap between the barrel and the cylinder, Trelawny leaped back into the doorway; he managed to juggle the hot gun in his nearly sprained hand and not drop it, but his retinas were hopelessly dazzled by the after-glare.

Over the ringing in his ears he heard the man's creaking voice cry, "It is the bridge man!"

Trelawny swung the gun barrel toward the voice, but a clatter at the window and the rippling, receding flutter of wind in cloth told him he was too late—the creature had flown away out the window, having probably abandoned its vulnerable human form even before the gun had gone off.

Trelawny had been holding his breath and now exhaled, feeling every day of his seventy-seven years, and he realized that he had been strongly hoping that it had been some natural effect that had knocked over the card in the Byron bell jar.

The woman had moved up between Trelawny and the lamp, and he could see well enough to make out her slim form against the glow. He almost thought he could see the lines of her bones through her translucent pink flesh. She shook her head angrily, then stepped past him into the hall.

"Nothing, nothing!" she shouted. "Back to your holes, idiots!"

She shoved Trelawny aside as she came back in, and he had no trouble hearing her slam the door.

"Why didn't he kill you?" she demanded furiously.

"He doesn't dare," said Trelawny, still blinking toward the window. He walked around the couch to it and leaned out over the sill, looking first up into the night sky and then down among the shadows of the street, but he saw no motion at all, and all he could hear over the ringing in his ears was the muted crowd noise from the New Cut Market a street away.

He pulled the window closed and latched it, then turned back toward the room.

Gretchen was sitting at a table near the lamp, and she pointed at a chair on the other side. Trelawny crossed the room and cautiously lowered himself into the chair, still holding the pistol in his burned hand but pointing it now at the floor. He peered at her and saw fresh blood gleaming on her bare throat. In the red light the blood looked black.

"Damn you, Edward," she said, touching the blood and looking at her finger. "He might not be back now for a week, and he *needs* me now."

Trelawny laid the gun down on the table at last. "Do you have cold water?"

Gretchen scowled at him, but she got up and lifted a basin from a table near the bed and shuffled back to set it heavily in front of him. It was half full of rocking water, and he gratefully sank his hand into its coolness.

"That lad must be new," he remarked, wincing as he flexed his fingers. "He looked like a black chicken."

She was clearly affronted. "Lad? A chicken? There hasn't been time for any to die and come back. That was my very own—" She waved her hand.

"That was Polidori *himself*?"

"He's been broken for seven years. He's only just back—and he's ill."

Trelawny touched his neck and nodded toward her. "But you're helping to restore him to his old stature."

"I do what I can for him," she agreed, nodding. "*He* loves me."

Trelawny drummed the fingers of his free hand on the table. He sighed. "No use offering you garlic, or the pistol."

"Give me the pistol and I'll shoot *you* with it." She stretched sleepily. "What do you mean, he doesn't dare kill you?"

"You heard him say it. I'm the bridge man." He touched his neck again. "If this flesh dies, the bridge between our two species dies. So he wouldn't thank you for shooting me."

Her eyes were half shut, and she cocked an eyebrow. "Really. Edward John Trelawny is the mixer."

"The catalyst." He smiled wearily and got to his feet. "I'm it."

"Well then, you take good care of yourself, Edward," she said, "and I think a visit every seven years is too frequent for our acquaintance—I'd be grateful if you'd simply forget the way to this house."

"Gladly." Trelawny picked up the pistol, and it had cooled enough for him to gingerly tuck it back into his trousers.

He opened the door, walked out to the landing, and began descending the stairs. I won't be able to do anything with Polidori, he thought, at least not here—but I might have another go at Miss B.—I believe I know a close friend of hers.

CHAPTER THREE

One moment thus. Another, and her face
Seemed further off than the last line of sea,
So that I thought, if now she were to speak
I could not hear her.

—*Dante Gabriel Rossetti, "A Last Confession"*

T HE LOG IN the fireplace collapsed in a swirl of sparks at the same
moment that the knock sounded at the door, and John Crawford
wasn't sure he hadn't imagined it, in the same way that he sometimes
imagined voices in the splashing sound of a tub filling, or footsteps in
the clatter of leaves blowing across empty pavements.

But he put down his glass and stood up unsteadily and weaved his
way to the hallway and the street door.

He pulled his dressing gown more tightly across his shoulders
before unlatching the door and pulling it open, and he winced when
the chilly night air swept inside—but there was no one on the doorstep.

He pushed his lanky hair out of his eyes and peered up and down
the street, but he could make out no distinct figures in the close-pressing
shadows of Wych Street.

He was about to close the door again when he looked down and saw a rounded metal disk on the top step, and he bent carefully to pick it up.

It was a gold watch, and it was warm.

The watch had been holding down a scrap of paper, and he managed to slap his palm onto it before it could blow away; holding the watch and the paper, he straightened and stepped back into the house and closed the door.

He shuffled back to his chair and picked up his reading glasses from the table beside it—and his chest went cold when he fitted them on and looked more closely at the watch.

It was his own watch, one that he had lost. He pried up the back cover and looked at the engraving on the inside of the cover: *John Crawford, 7 Wych Street, February 12, 1862.*

But, he thought, I smashed this watch against a wall in the sewers seven years ago, to repel the ghosts of my wife and son! He looked hopefully back toward the entry hall—could *they* have put it together again somehow, and brought it back? Were they even now outside, waiting?

But no—I bought another watch a few days later, and had this engraving done in it. Yes, that was February of '62. What became of it?

As if it were a belated effect of the cold air he had inhaled at the door, memory blew the alcohol fumes and maudlin fantasies out of his mind.

He had dropped it in the tunnels below Highgate Cemetery to gauge the depth of the well he and Adelaide McKee had climbed down.

And he remembered a little girl's voice calling from the darkness below them: *I caught it before it could fly away. And you must fall too.*

It had been McKee's daughter—his daughter—Johanna; and later he had seen her cradled in the inhuman arms of John Polidori, swinging this watch by its chain.

He laid the watch down on the table and quickly spread the scrap of paper out flat beside it.

Scrawled on it, in awkwardly penciled letters, were the words *HELP ME JOHANNA*.

Crawford's face was suddenly cold.

Perhaps she had *not* died in that cave-in.

But—the last time he had seen Johanna, she had been with the Rossettis' monstrous uncle, Polidori; and pretty clearly she had been bitten by him. Christina Rossetti's trick that day, whatever it had been, had apparently killed Polidori, but would it have freed Johanna?

All the warnings his parents had given him, and which Adelaide McKee had reinforced, about carelessly inviting entities into his house, flooded back into his mind now. He should run upstairs and fetch his neglected old garlic jar—he was pretty sure he knew where it was—and smear the stuff around the door and window frames, and then go to bed with the obliterating whisky bottle.

But he had run away from Girard, nine years ago . . . and Johanna had written "help me."

Sweat dripped onto the note.

How long had it been since he had taken the watch and note inside and shut the door? Would she leave? He took a deep breath and let it out, and then he strode quickly back to the front door and pulled it open, and he had scuffed down the steps to the pavement before noticing that he was wearing his slippers.

But he peered up and down the street, puffing steam in the cold air and straining to see into the shadows below the overhanging upper floors of the old houses.

"Johanna?" he called.

There was no reply, and he couldn't see anything in the deep shadows all around.

The cold breeze corkscrewing down the narrow street got up his pants legs and into his collar, and he was about to run back inside for at least a coat and boots, when at last he saw movement on the far side of the street, in the recessed doorway of a house to his left.

He forced his eyes to focus—it was a small person, he could see that much—and then the figure stepped forward, and by the light that slanted down from the Strand he saw that it was a young person with long hair trailing from under a hat.

"Johanna!" he called again, starting forward across the crushed gravel of the street, but she stepped back into the shadows and he lost sight of her.

"Damn it," Crawford muttered, shivering. "Come in," he said loudly. "I'll help you!"

"Shut up!" yelled someone from a window overhead.

Oh, for—"I'll leave the door unlocked!" Crawford called, and then hurried back into the house.

He even left the door an inch ajar as he hurried up the stairs to find boots and a coat and a scarf, in case he might have to go out to talk to her—but when he got back downstairs, carrying his outdoor gear, the front door was shut, and he heard the couch creak in the parlor.

He froze in the hall. What *had* he just invited into his house— thoughtlessly *invited into his house?*

Trembling, remembering the creatures he had seen on Waterloo Bridge and at Carpace's salon and under Highgate Cemetery, he laid the coat and boots on the floor and then peeked fearfully around the doorway jamb into the parlor.

But the young girl sitting on the couch did not seem to be any sort of vampire. Her face, framed by a slouch hat and disordered locks of brown hair and the pushed-up collar of an oversized wool coat, was pink with the evening's chill, and her bright blue eyes held only cautious curiosity. One of his distressed cats, a Manx with only one eye, was sitting on her lap, audibly purring.

"I'm pure human," she said in a light voice. "But you *shouldn't* ask things in so quick. But—I'm glad you did tonight."

"You're . . . Johanna."

"You look older, your beard is gray. Yes, I'm Johanna. I do too, I'm

sure—people say I'm probably fourteen now." She yawned. "You said
that time that you're my father."

She really did seem to be fully and only human. He let his legs and
shoulders relax. "Yes. And your mother said you were born in March of
'56, so you're . . ."

"*Thirteen.*" She shrugged, then looked directly at him. "Is my
mother still alive?"

"She was when I last saw her," he said. "That was on that day we
saw you." He felt his face reddening. "You, uh, didn't die when that tunnel collapsed."

"No," she agreed. "I crawled up a side tunnel before it all fell in."

"I'm sorry—we assumed—"

She shrugged again, apparently with no resentment.

After a few moments of silence in which his breathing and heartbeat
slowed to their normal paces, he sighed and asked, "Are you hungry?"

She nodded solemnly.

There were no servants in the house; Mrs. Middleditch had died
peacefully in her attic room three years ago, and since then Crawford
had got by with a maidservant and a charwoman, both of whom came
in three times a week.

"You can bring the cat into the dining room," he said, pushing open
the door on the far side of the room from the curtained windows. He
looked back—the cat had jumped away, and the girl paused to pick up
the watch and thrust it inside her coat.

In the narrow dining room, he turned up the gas jets and waved her
toward a chair at the table, but she came tapping after him in her narrow boots to the stairs that led down to the kitchen and scullery.

He paused at the stairway door. "I'll bring some things up."

"I'll come along down." She reached into her voluminous coat
and pulled up the grip of a knife, then slid it back, apparently into a
concealed sheath. "Cold iron," she said. "And I've got garlic too. I don't
smell any of that in this house."

"It's been seven years since I've needed it," he told her. Then, after looking directly into her eyes, he laughed in surprise and added, "*I'm—how did you put it?—pure human!*"

She peered at his face, then nodded. "I suppose you are."

"Wouldn't you rather wait up here?"

"No."

"Very well. You can bring those things along if you like, but I'd advise leaving your coat and hat up here."

She nodded and shrugged out of the coat—under it she was wearing shiny brown corduroy trousers and at least two plaid flannel shirts—and threw it and her hat into a corner. The sheathed knife was on a leather strap around her neck, and she tucked it into the shirts.

He led the way down the stairs, each step of which was more damp than the one above it.

The steamy kitchen was a tiny dark room with three soot-blackened windows just under the low, beamed ceiling, and when Crawford struck a match to the kerosene lamp over the stove, he winced at the look and smell of the place.

The boiler over the stove gurgled like a colicky cow's stomach. Shirts and stockings, still visibly damp two days after washing, hung from a clotheshorse attached to one of the ceiling beams, and he had to duck around them to step to the larder. He tried to carry the lamp so that his small guest would not see through the doorway on the left, into the scullery, where he saw dirty dishes still piled in the sink over the wet stone floor.

But she seemed unconcerned by the squalor. "Ham!" she said. "And onions! And cheese! Have you got mustard?"

"Back upstairs."

"We can do without. Better we talk underground."

"The last time we talked, it was underground."

Johanna had reached up to the larder shelf and hoisted down the platter of ham, and she carried it carefully to the narrow servants' table by the oven and clanked it down.

"Dirt's an extra roof," she said, going back for the cheese. "Hides him from the sun, hides us from him."

Crawford frowned. "'Hides'? But he's dead . . . surely." He found a knife in the scullery and wiped it on his shirt, then tugged an onion free from a braid of them and joined her at the table. He set the lamp down beside the platter.

"I thought so too," she said. Her tone was light, but she had pulled her knife out to cut the ham, and he saw the blade shaking. "But he—visited me!—this evening."

"Good God!"

She darted a glance at him and might have briefly attempted a smile. "He's thin now, his clothes are black paper, and he smells like mud. He's got to start over, and he wanted to bite me again, get me in his boat again. I ran away from him." She twitched the knife blade. "I already had this, but I got some garlic quick."

Belatedly it occurred to him to wonder how she had been living during these past years. "Stay here. You're safe here."

"Here! He's on to you too. He fancied your mother but got jilted by her, he said—my grandmother!—in the long ago, in Italy. And he can always find *me*." Her voice broke at last as she added, "He says by his reckoning I'm his d-daughter."

"You're *my* daughter," Crawford said, with more feeling than he had anticipated. "And I'll protect you from him."

"However much you can. But thanks." She sniffed and scowled and brushed her sleeve across her eyes, and then went on almost briskly, "Was your mother's name Josephine?"

"Yes. How did you—?"

"He used to call me that, sometimes. How did you see him, that day under the cemetery?"

Crawford blinked. "See him?"

"*Where* did it look like you saw him? In the old tower full of rolled-up books? On the glass seashore? In the big skull? In the hanging boat? Among the giant wheels?"

"The skull," said Crawford. "You were there—you didn't see the interior of an enormous skull?"

"I only saw a dark tunnel and an underground river with a broken bridge over it. The skull means he's worried. Was. With good reason, as it turned out." She had cut several ragged pieces of ham free of the bone, and now wiped the knife on her sleeve and sat down in one of the two wooden chairs.

"I don't," she said quietly, "want him to get me again. You killed him then, and he stayed dead for seven years. Can you do it again?"

"It wasn't me that did it then." Crawford crouched to draw two mugs of beer from the cask by the coal scuttle, and he set them on the table and then sat down and began slicing the onion. The smells of ham and beer and onions made him realize that he was hungry, and he wondered where there might be clean plates. "But I know the woman who did it. We can tell her it needs doing again."

"I hope she's still alive."

Crawford wrapped a strip of ham around a lump of cheese and some rings of onion and took a bite of it. It tasted wonderful.

"She is," he said as he chewed. "She's a poet, and she's been publishing things steadily." He wondered if Christina Rossetti would still remember him, and he was embarrassed to think that she might.

"A poet?" said his daughter. "I hope her poems haven't suddenly got better."

Crawford remembered Trelawny saying, that day in the cage in Regent's Park, that writing good poetry was "one of their gifts."

"She gets bad reviews," he said hopefully.

On the black brick wall above the doorway to the stairs, a bell rang, loud in the narrow kitchen; both Crawford and the girl jumped.

He had installed an electric doorbell a few years ago. "I believe that means there's someone at the front door," he said.

"Stay down here! You locked the door?"

"Yes."

Crawford had half stood up, and now he sank back into the chair and picked up his beer mug in a trembling hand.

The bell rang again.

He took a long swallow of the lukewarm beer and set the mug down—but a moment later he whispered a curse and stood up. He lifted his chair and carefully walked across the flagstones to the street-side wall, and he set the chair down slowly below one of the ceiling-abutting windows and stepped up onto it.

The window glass was black, and he could see nothing outside.

The bell rang a third time, and then faintly, through the glass in front of his face more than from down the kitchen stairway behind him, he heard the door knocker rapping.

He glanced back at Johanna; she had stood up and was pressing a finger to her lips.

The rapping sounded again, louder, and after thirty seconds he heard boots descending the housefront steps.

The boots clinked against the stone.

The breath stopped in his throat and he glanced over his shoulder at the stairway and calculated how long it would take him to rush up the stairs and down the hall to the front door—too long, perhaps.

So he hopped to the floor, dived to the table and snatched up his beer mug and flung it as hard as he could at the high narrow window.

Even as the broken glass was clattering across the bricks of the area outside and the steamy kitchen air was roiled by the sudden chilly draft, he was on the chair again and calling through the broken pane,

"Adelaide!"

The clinking footsteps halted, then rang down the iron stairs from street level to the bricks of the area, and a moment later Adelaide McKee's remembered face was peering in at him, dimly lit by the lamp on the stove behind him. She must have been practically lying down on the pavement out there.

"John!" she said breathlessly. "Open the damned door and stop breaking your windows!"

She looked past him then, and her eyes widened in astonishment. She tried to speak, then just bit her lip and gave him an urgently questioning look.

"Yes," he said, "it's our daughter."

Crawford looked over his shoulder at Johanna, who was standing by the stairs with her knife drawn.

"Johanna," he said, "it's your mother! She's fully and only human—aren't you, Adelaide?—run upstairs and open the door!"

He turned back to face McKee, and he thrust one hand through the broken window to clutch at her gloved fingers.

"You can't open your door yourself?" she said, squeezing his hand. Tears glinted on her cheek in the lamplight.

"I—" It hadn't occurred to him. "I don't want to let you out of my sight."

The cold night air clearly carried the snap of the door bolt retracting, and McKee glanced upward.

She released his hand and got to her feet, and now he could see only her boots, with the familiar metal pattens strapped to the soles. He heard her say, "I can't stay long."

FIFTEEN SECONDS LATER JOHANNA and McKee were seated at the table, and Crawford was dragging up the cask of beer to sit on.

By Crawford's calculation, McKee was thirty-four now, but she looked as young as Johanna as she gazed wide-eyed at her daughter's face by the now-flickering glare of the lamp.

"You—" McKee said to her, "we—we thought you were killed—I never should have—"

Johanna nodded. She seemed only interested, not upset. "*He* got killed, that day. It was a good day. But now he's alive again."

"You know?" McKee turned to Crawford. "That's why I came here tonight, to tell you, warn you. The songbirds are in a state. Chichuwee says all the ghosts are jabbering about it and fleeing straight to the river and out to sea. Sister Christina's trick has worn off, or broken, and he'll know us, you and me."

She looked back at Johanna. "And you. How long have you been living here? How did you know he's back up?"

Johanna gave her an uncomfortable smile. "If I'm living here, it's only been for about half an hour—Mr. Crawford's name and address were in his watch." She pulled the watch out of one of her shirt pockets and laid it on the table. "And I've known that *he's* back for . . . about two hours. He came straight to me, but I got away from him, dove into a mountain of shoes and he couldn't follow me among the million old footprints. He's lost all his suppliers, and he can't see very well."

McKee turned a blank gaze from one of them to the other. Then to Johanna she said, "You've had the watch all this time?—seven years!—and you only came to your father *tonight?*"

"I couldn't read, for a long time. And up to now everything's been good enough."

"What have you—" McKee waved a hand. "Where have you been *living?*"

Johanna puffed her cheeks and blew out a breath. "Lately in a room off Petticoat Lane, by the Old Clothes Exchange; I sometimes pick up porter work, baling up leather trousers and wigs for Ireland, and old rugs for Holland . . . I've been sharing a room with two women, and when I can't make my share of the nine-pence week's rent, I sometimes bring home some rug pieces for the floor, so when we drop something it doesn't go straight through the cracks to the donkey stable below. But before that . . . a rooftop shed against a chimney, for a while, right after *he* went away; I was a beggar then, without even deciding to be . . . then on a boat by Southwark Bridge, working for the Mud Lark man . . . I lived with a coster family for a couple of years, I think, selling apples on the streets."

"You live here now," said Crawford firmly. After a second or two, he made himself look at McKee. "Our daughter is not dead." His voice was steady. "Do you remember what I said—the last thing I said to you—in that village, Lower Clapton?"

McKee sat back in her chair, and after glancing around at the narrow kitchen, she looked squarely at him.

From her ragged handbag Crawford heard the mutter of a songbird.

"I'm—where do I start?" she said in a flat voice. "After that day under Highgate Cemetery, I went back to Sudbury, since I'd no longer be bringing a devil's murderous attention with me. But it turned out my parents were dead by that time, and I thought Johanna was too. I came back to London."

But not to me, thought Crawford. With a chilly, sinking feeling in his stomach he remembered her saying, a few minutes ago, *I can't stay long.*

"What," he began, but his voice was hoarse. He cleared his throat. "What does he do?"

McKee's stare was defiant. "He's a dealer in metal spoons."

Johanna caught Crawford's eye and then glanced meaningfully at McKee's brown coat and faded blue dress, and he gathered that the garments didn't look top class in the girl's professional appraisal.

Crawford met McKee's gaze and nodded gently. "You said there was nothing for you to hope for, anymore, in London."

"Nor anywhere else, I discovered." She shrugged. "And I knew the ins and outs of London already."

Crawford remembered her despair, at their last meeting, and he suspected that she had taken up with this spoons seller out of that despair, out of that self-disgust.

He sighed, emptying his lungs. "How long can you stay?"

"I don't—not long, he gets jealous, and I don't want him spending any money on—but Johanna!" She threw Crawford an uncharacteristically helpless look. "Can she live here?"

"We'll need garlic and mirrors aplenty," said Johanna. "And soon."

"Yes, of course she can stay here," said Crawford.

McKee nodded. "Does that watch work?" she asked Johanna.

"No. And it's been in the river a few times."

McKee glanced at Crawford and then away, and he remembered her saying, *I owe you a lot of time.* A debt to be written off, he thought.

"God knows what time it is," she said, and got to her feet. She looked yearningly at Johanna and said, "I'll be back soon."

"Tomorrow?" said Johanna with some eagerness. "Morning?"

McKee smiled. "Yes. I promise."

"Bring some mirrors and garlic, and some of your old man's spoons, if they're silver. I'm not going to dare sleep a wink tonight, with just these." She patted her shirt and pants pocket, indicating the knife and, presumably, some garlic.

McKee nodded, tight-lipped. "He sleeps late. I'll tell him he sold the spoons and spent the money on rum," she said. She glanced again at the inert watch. "Unless he's already done that by now."

"Never mind," said Crawford hastily, "I've got crowns and shillings—plenty of silver."

"I knew somebody did," said McKee. She took a cloth-wrapped bundle from her handbag and set it on the table; from inside it Crawford heard a muffled cheeping. "Take that now. A goldfinch—if he really yipes, duck and get your garlic ready." She started to say something more, but exhaled and turned away. Finally she said, "I'll see you tomorrow."

Then she was gone, tapping rapidly up the stairs. A few moments later Crawford and Johanna heard the front door close, and, through the broken window, McKee's metallic footsteps receding.

Johanna was swinging her feet under her chair. "The last thing you said to her, before, was asking her to marry you?"

Crawford stared at her and managed to smile. "Yes."

"That's a man's coat she's got on, much mended, and the boots don't match." She rolled some cheese and onion in a piece of ham as Crawford had done and bit off half of it.

Crawford got up, found another mug, and filled it with beer. As he sat down, he said, "I can show you to your room after we're done with this . . . supper. I've got probably half a dozen mirrors around the house, and you can have them."

She nodded, chewing. "And," she said finally, "after he bites you, he'll know about the mirrors and not look at them. No, we neither of us should sleep tonight, especially with a window broken. Fetch the mirrors down here and we can make a wall of 'em. And bring your shillings! We've got knives, and—" she added as she dug a jar out of her trouser pocket, "here's garlic."

"Stay down here all night?"

"Why not? It's partly underground." She grinned. "We can tell stories till dawn. What happened to your cats? I saw another one in the hall, and it only had three legs."

He stared at her for several seconds, then shrugged. "I'm a—an animal doctor," he said. "When I find hurt cats, I bring them home and take care of them." He took a sip of beer and then began cutting up more ham and onion. "I've got a blind one too, and she knows every corner of the rooms and furniture; she can run from one end of the house to the other and not bump into anything."

Johanna nodded. "She should have married you. My mother should have."

"Not the cat," Crawford agreed. The thought of his poor cats had reminded him of something. "Uh . . . have you been—by any chance— baptized?—since we saw you last?"

Johanna had taken another bite of the rolled ham, and she nodded as she chewed. "The Mud Lark man has all the Larks baptized before they can scout for him."

Crawford wondered who this Mud Lark man might be, and what sort of scouting he had his young charges do; but there was all night in which to ask.

"Good, good." He got to his feet. "I'll fetch the mirrors and silver—don't eat all this before I get back."

CHAPTER FOUR

꙳ ꙳ ◈ ꙳ ꙳

Ah, not as they, but as the souls that were
Slain in the old time, having found her fair;
Who, sleeping with her lips upon their eyes,
Heard sudden serpents hiss across her hair.

—*Algernon Swinburne, "Laus Veneris"*

IN HIS DRAWING room in Upper Brook Street, Algernon Swinburne stood staring out through the open windows at the still-dark houses in the stale night. He had come home hours ago, but he was still dressed in the flannel trousers, white shirt, and woolen sweater that he had worn on his latest visit to the Verbena Lodge in Circus Road, when the evening had been fresh and full of anticipation.

Ordinarily he would have indulged himself now in the opportunity for mild pain by sitting and leaning back in a chair, but this evening's drunken excesses at Verbena Lodge had left him slightly—only slightly, and certainly only temporarily—disgusted with the formal pretenses he engaged in there. None of the whippings and spankings that went on ever caused any actual injury, or even any real hurt.

He turned his back on the window. By the light of two gas jets on the far wall, for the fire had gone out while he'd been gone and he hadn't the energy to fetch more coal, he surveyed the room's ornate furnishings—the rosewood chairs, the imported Herter Brothers sofa, the gold-stamped book spines vertical and horizontal on the shelves— finally noting, hung on the walls above the bookshelves, the token whips and birch rods; and even, for the bravura of it, a pair of crossed rapiers over the mantelpiece.

Sad evidences, those were, of his gallingly restrained inclinations, which were unlikely to be really indulged while he still lived.

He sighed. The only satisfactory thing about it all, he thought—as he faced the window again and peered out at the dark patch that was Grosvenor Square and listened to the whir of a distant cab out in the night—is that my vigilant Miss B. cannot mistake the activities at the Verbena Lodge for anything having to do with love.

Girls in staged schoolrooms being struck with birch rods on their behinds by women pretending to be strict governesses—other girls taking money to spank patrons like Swinburne who took the roles of boys needing punishment—none of it would engage Miss B.'s inhuman attention, rouse in her that response which was comparable to homi- cidal jealousy in humans, and the spankings Swinburne received were far too mild for her to perceive them as attacks on him. The girls at the lodge were safe. Swinburne certainly didn't love any of them, nor did they love him.

He hadn't loved any woman since Lizzie, and she—her ghost, at any rate—had refused his offer to let her inhabit his living body. Since her refusal he had surrendered himself to the strenuous and enervating affection of Miss B., and, on the side, the largely symbolic Sadean activi- ties at the Verbena Lodge.

He didn't dare love anybody, nor even seem to. He had loved his sister Edith, and she had died only a year after he had committed him- self to Miss B., and immediately afterward he had persuaded his parents to take an extended Continental tour; since then he had avoided them, and so they were still alive. And when Gabriel Rossetti had arranged for Swinburne to take a mistress in the conventional way, the woman died less than a year later, in spite of precautions Swinburne had thought would be adequate; he hadn't loved her—she had complained that "spanking was no help" in making love—but even his unsatisfactory behavior with her had effectively mimicked it, to the woman's fatal misfortune.

Miss B. will have no rivals, Swinburne thought now as he stepped to the sideboard and poured one last inch of brandy into a snifter—though he knew that it was a mistake to attribute human motivations to her kind. She was more like a sun that ignited a reciprocally fueled solar fire in him, while simply incinerating any lesser planets that presumed to orbit him. *Then felt I like some watcher of the tombs,* he thought, paraphrasing Keats, *when a new planet swims into my ken.*

Mentally he recited a verse of his own: *Though the many lights dwindle to one light, / There is help if the heavens has one.*

Do I love that one light, he wondered, do I love *her?* I'm *awed,* by the ancient alien majesty of her kind, certainly; baffled by the nonhuman mathematics of her logic—but I certainly do love her gift: my gift is single, my verses . . .

He set down his glass, the brandy untasted, and shivered in the draft from the open window.

His first book, *Atalanta in Calydon,* had been published in 1865, three years after Lizzie's funeral—and the long verse play, a vivid retelling of the pagan Atalanta myth from Apollodorus and Homer, had won praise from the *Edinburgh Review* and the *Saturday Review.*

His next collection of verse, though, *Poems and Ballads,* which had been published the following year, was savaged by the critics; and their denunciations of the vicious sensuality of the poems was so widespread and harsh that an obscenity indictment from the attorney general seemed likely, and the publisher withdrew the book only a month after its publication. But a bolder publisher picked it up before the year's end, and by then the book had found passionate admirers among the young men at Oxford and Cambridge, and a few critics hesitantly began to concede that Swinburne's poems, for all their pagan and even anti-Christian excesses, held a power not seen in English literature since Shelley and Byron and Keats.

Naturally, thought Swinburne now. I share the same species of Muse that those poets had. The attentions of the antediluvian stony tribe kill those we love and make us suffer in sunlight, but, in a side effect that they may not even be aware of, awaken language in us, make of it a living beast that can be harnessed and ridden.

Christina had it, for a while, though in recent years she writes religious stories instead of her old clear-eyed poems about death, and ghosts in the sea, and seductive goblins.

But she might have it again now—now that her uncle has apparently been freed from the disruptive mirrors that she put into Lizzie's coffin.

Swinburne recalled the conversation he had overheard at Tudor House six or seven hours ago, which had sent him hurrying to the Verbena Lodge so that his thoughts might not dwell too much on it and draw Miss B.'s attention: Christina's uncle's living and conscious identity was concentrated in a little statue stuck in her dead father's throat!—and the identity had been somehow scrambled and made impotent seven years ago, but was awake again now—though wounded.

Something to remember.

He looked up suddenly—he had clearly heard the street door downstairs, which he knew he had locked, open and then close.

TRELAWNY HAD WALKED NORTH from Pelham Crescent to Upper Brook Street, skirting the shadowed expanse of Hyde Park where Shelley's first wife had been drowned in the Serpentine, and peering around

from under the brim of his old hat at the dark houses that stood on either
side like closely ranked tombstones, the dimly seen windows and balconies making hieroglyphic epitaphs. Here and there a light shone like
a firefly in some room, and he wondered if lone, fevered poets labored
in those rooms over unmerited verses. The costermongers would be
assembling by the river now, with their carts of fish and vegetables
agleam in the dockside lamplight, but none of them would have begun
to venture north yet. There was no one abroad to see his quickly striding figure, and in any case the paper-wrapped parcel he carried looked
like a plain shoe box.

Lights were on in an upstairs room in Swinburne's house, and the
windows were open; but the young poet had been at his filthy Verbena
Lodge until after midnight, and he had probably forgotten the lights
and the window and was soddenly asleep by now.

Trelawny tapped nimbly up the steps to the front door, and on the
lamplit stage of the threshold he flourished his lock pick as confidently
as if it had been the key. A moment's one-handed twisting of it had the
bolt retracted, and the old man opened the door and stepped inside,
closing it behind him. The hall was dark, but he could make out the
shape of the carpeted stairs, and he took them silently, two at a time.

At the top of the stairs he paused to strip the paper from the box he
had prepared, and he swung back the hinged lid, taking care to make
no noise—but when he stepped into the brightly lit drawing room, he
saw Swinburne standing, fully dressed, by the fireplace; and he had evidently heard Trelawny's entry, for he was even holding a sword.

The young poet raised it in a fair en garde. "Get out of this house at
once," he said in his shrill voice, "or I'll kill you."

Trelawny grinned. "Or whip me, eh? Unless that's just for the girls
at the Verbena Lodge."

Swinburne looked disconcerted and lowered the blade an inch. His
thatch of orange hair made his head look like an unhealthy overgrown
flower on a frail stalk.

He peered more closely at Trelawny. "I know you."

"Of course you do. We've been to church together, you and I."

Swinburne frowned, started to say something, then just muttered, "You call the salons churches?"

"I mean the time we met in the Whispering Gallery at St. Paul's."

"Oh!" He lowered the blade a few more inches. "But—what are you doing here? You advised me then to—quit England, sever my connection with . . ."

"Which I perceive you haven't done."

Swinburne's left hand flew to his throat and pulled up his collar.

"No, lad, I've only observed the marks in your verse—and they're more plain there than any punctures in your scrawny neck."

Swinburne colored. "Did she . . . *send* you here?" The young man seemed frightened.

"No. And are you jealous? Don't be—I don't write poetry; my relationship with her has never been"—he paused to touch his own throat—"consummated."

Swinburne stepped away from the fireplace and sat down in a chair by the open window. The sword, still in his hand, had dragged a furrow in the nap of the carpet. "What do you want then? Go away."

"I had hoped to take what I want while you slept; if you'd only been drunk enough, it might not even have wakened you." Trelawny shrugged. "I want just a bit of your blood. A few drops, merely."

Swinburne's scanty orange eyebrows were halfway up his high forehead. "No! Get out of here."

Trelawny rocked back and forth on his heels. "Allowing for difficulty," he said, "I obtained detailed statements from two of the girls at your lodge. Many would find the accounts shocking and disgusting, but I think most would find them—well, shocking and disgusting, yes, but laughable too. And pitiable. There are houses that would publish these things. Your own publisher, Hotten, would probably do it—he'd extend you the courtesy of changing the names, but everyone would know who the subject is."

After a few heartbeats, "You'd see to that, I suppose," said Swinburne sourly.

Trelawny shrugged.

Swinburne shook his head as if to clear it. "Blood? What do you want my blood for?"

"To kill flies, to scare children, to keep Christians away from my door, what do you care? Just a couple of drops, no more than what you'd lose if you try to shave this morning."

Swinburne made a fist of his free hand to hide its shaking.

"Blood," he said, as if to remind himself of the subject at hand. "And you'll give me these *statements* you got from the girls? In exchange? And not get more?"

"That's it."

Swinburne sat back, brooding. "*She* might not like it. My blood is hers."

"You know I'm an ally of hers. She could hardly blame you."

"If she blames a person for a thing, there's no help in him being justified."

Trelawny exhaled. "Damn it, little man, if Shelley'd been as lily-livered as you are, he'd never have . . . just go and shave the lint off your chin and then look the other way while I steal the towel afterward!"

Swinburne shook his head. "Go home. This is insane."

"Humor an old lunatic."

"What do you want it *for?*"

"Ahhh . . ." Trelawny tried to think of something plausible. "Well, if you must know, rejuvenation." He tried to look mildly shamefaced. "I've reason to believe that a few drops of your sort of blood, in brandy in an amethyst cup, might restore me to—"

"*Semi*-decrepitude."

Cheeky bugger, thought Trelawny. "If you like."

"You're as bad as the supplicants under London Bridge."

Trelawny just stared at him from under his bushy white eyebrows. The mix of vampire-tainted blood with brandy in an amethyst cup was indeed a drink sought after by certain perverse folk, and Trelawny had heard of a sort of club called the Galatea under London Bridge, where such people gathered.

Swinburne shifted in his chair. "You'll leave immediately afterward?"

"I'll be away down the street before you've heard the door close."

Swinburne stared at him, then shrugged and got to his feet, the sword still trailing from his right hand—and then his nervous gaze fell on the box Trelawny still carried.

"What's that?"

"A box. For cigars. If you have any, I'll put them in it."

But Swinburne's eyes were suddenly wide. "That lid!—is a *mirror*, on the inside!" He stepped back hastily and raised the rapier again as the gaslight threw his shadow across the whips hung on the walls. "Get out! I know what mirrors can do to her sort—you'll not deprive me of my poetry! Get out, I say!"

Trelawny set the box on the mantel, then spread his hands placatingly and stepped forward, but Swinburne wasn't letting the old man get near him—Swinburne's sword snapped forward, and Trelawny yanked his right hand back just in time to avoid losing a finger.

The old man sighed and shuffled backward to the fireplace, and he reached up to pull the other rapier free of its hook. He suppressed a wince as his scorched palm closed firmly on the grip.

"I'm sorry you know it," he said, exhaling.

Swinburne laughed in surprise. "You'd fight me? I'm not yet near forty, and you must be twice that—and you should know that I've studied fencing."

"I must be a fool," Trelawny agreed. *And I'm only seventy-seven,* he thought. He raised the sword, holding the grip as he would hold a hammer.

Swinburne relaxed again into the en garde position, and his disengage and thrust at Trelawny's wrist was contained and fast.

Trelawny parried it with a deliberately clumsy swat that rang the blades, and he retreated a step, his rear heel knocking on the hearth bricks; he didn't want the young man to experience any mortal alarm that might call up Miss B. prematurely.

"Hah!" exclaimed Swinburne. "You fence like a man trying to hang wallpaper!"

That was in fact the impression Trelawny wanted to give. Blisters on his palm were broken now, and the sword grip was wet.

"I'll cut you," said Swinburne, and he licked his lips. "It'll hurt."

If she senses his mood now, Trelawny thought sourly as he tightened his hand on the slick leather grip, she'll simply imagine he's gone back to the sport at the Verbena Lodge.

Swinburne lunged, driving his point toward Trelawny's shoulder, and at the last moment spun the point around the old man's bell-guard and jabbed for the elbow; but in the same instant Trelawny fell backward, folding his arm across his chest, and sat down heavily on the hearth, rapping his tailbone against the bricks and rattling the fire screen.

Swinburne paused over him and giggled breathlessly. "Now I *know* that all your exploits in your books were lies! Pirates, sea battles, Arab brides!"

He eyed Trelawny's raised knee and dropped his point toward it.

And Trelawny straightened his leg forcefully, kicking Swinburne's forward ankle out from under him; as the young man fell on him, Trelawny parried his blade aside and with his free hand punched the young poet very hard on the shelf of his descending jaw.

Swinburne tumbled into his arms, unconscious.

Very quickly, for Miss B. would have sensed that blow, Trelawny pushed Swinburne's limp form off him—the little poet hardly weighed more than a child—and stood up to snatch the box from the mantel.

The poet had rolled over on the carpet and was now face-down, and Trelawny crouched beside him and flipped him onto his back, and with a fingertip collected a smear of blood from Swinburne's lip—and he had no sooner smeared it around the grooves in the box's mirrored interior than his panting breath became a visible plume of steam.

The room was suddenly very cold, and books and papers flew in a whirlwind as a loud, fracturing buzz rattled the few pictures that weren't tumbling off the walls.

Trelawny spun toward the window and flinched as he held the open box up in front of himself.

Boadicea of the Iceni had arrived from out of the night.

Iridescent gleams played over the scaled serpent's body as it swung heavily in the vibrating air, its wings a blurred gale of rainbow colors; vertically slitted eyes like poisonous golden apples swiveled back and forth in the room's brightness.

Trelawny could feel the freezing chill of her gaze as it swept past him—and then his hands were numbed as she focused on the box.

And the serpent shape rippled and seemed to implode, and the floor shook as it fell and crashed to the carpet. Trelawny kept the box aimed at the bending, darkening shape. Streamers of heavy black smoke blew away from her and out the open window.

The eyes had shrunk to black stones, but they could not look away from the mirrors that were etched now with Swinburne's beloved blood.

Boadicea was a spasming black fetus now, waving stiffening limbs on the carpet as more of the thick black smoke burst out of her and spun away; Trelawny was able to scuff closer on his knees, and he could still feel the electric shiver of her attention in the box in his aching hands.

At last, with a loud crack, she lay still on the frosted carpet, a black statue no more than two inches long—and he lowered the box onto her and gingerly tilted it to scoop her inside as he swung the lid shut.

For nearly a minute he didn't move, but just knelt there, gasping as the night breeze from the open window warmed the room. Thick black soot stained the floor and wall and windowsill.

Carefully he lifted the box an inch, and it was not particularly heavy—and he allowed his muscles to relax a little; her mass was nearly all gone, presumably carried away in the billows of leaden smoke. This trick had indeed drastically diminished her.

At last he got shakily to his feet and swung the latch on the box's exterior, shutting her in. He tucked it under his coat and gripped it against his ribs with his elbow.

Swinburne, sprawled on the carpet over by the fireplace, had begun to snore. Trelawny retrieved both rapiers and hung them back up on their hooks; the scattered papers and books he left where they lay, and after taking a deep breath and letting it out in a long, shivering exhalation, he turned and walked out of the room, pulling the door closed behind him.

CHAPTER FIVE

Our little baby fell asleep
And will not wake again
For days and days, and weeks and weeks,
But then he'll wake again,
And come with his own pretty look,
And kiss Mamma again.

—*Christina Rossetti*, Sing-Song,
A Nursery Rhyme Book

JOHANNA HAD BEEN living in the house on Wych Street for three days, sleeping in Mrs. Middleditch's old room—apparently more in the closet than on the bed, according to the maid, and always with McKee's bright-eyed goldfinch close at hand—and haphazardly assisting Crawford in the surgery, when Christina Rossetti finally responded to Crawford's note.

When Christina arrived at one P.M., Johanna had only ten minutes earlier returned from the latest of her so-far daily "shoreline sorties," which took her to the river for conferences, or it might have been fights, with the newest crop of Mud Larks; when she had returned from the first such expedition with a black eye and scraped knees and mud stains on her new clothes, Crawford had told her not to go there again, but she had insisted that she needed to—the Mud Larks were all prepubescent children who had had dealings with the Nephilim, and they were hired by the old Mud Lark man to recognize and follow people who "had a whiff of the Neff about them" and report any such to the old man. "There's a lot of stirring about among the Neffies," Johanna had told Crawford as he'd dabbed some Lugol's iodine on her knees—he gathered that the term referred to people who were currently or had once been infected by a vampire or were perceptibly soliciting it—"I'm too old now to mix with the Larks anymore, but they're all real aware of *him* being out again, picking up his old sources. I need to—we need me to—keep track of him as much as can be done."

Adelaide McKee had stopped in for brief visits every afternoon, and yesterday she had viewed Johanna's black eye with rueful fatalism. "Those Mud Larks are mostly a damaged lot," was all she had said. "Always see a way out and have your knife handy."

Johanna had nodded. "I know," she said, "I was one myself for a while," making McKee and Crawford both wince.

Yesterday afternoon Crawford had taken Johanna with him to Allen's riding school in Bryanston Square. Mr. Allen hired out his horses as much as he used them for lessons, and even in the off-season he charged five or six guineas rent a month, and so he was anxious to keep them healthy; hardly a week went by without Crawford getting a summons from him. Yesterday Crawford had shown Johanna how to press her ear to the left side of the horse's chest, just forward of the seventh rib, and use his new watch to count the heartbeats; she had used some mnemonic system she'd learned for estimating the number of loose shoes in different-sized shipping crates to memorize the proper pulse rate for different breeds and ages of the horses.

Now she was kneeling on a stool by the marble counter, kneading linseed oil into a mix of bran, mashed turnips, and lard—the concoction was to be sent to Mr. Allen's for a horse suffering from strangles, inflammation of a gland behind the jaw. The goldfinch's cage was on a shelf by the windows.

It was not a day when Crawford had servants in, so when he heard the door chime, he leaned a mop against the wall and hurried through the dining room and down the hall to the street door and pulled it open.

Standing on the gravel pavement in the midday sun, Christina Rossetti looked older than the intervening seven years could justify; her hair was the same shade of brown as before, and her face and throat were still smooth, but some spirit or liveliness seemed to have been taken out of her.

Crawford touched his own gray beard. "Miss Rossetti," he said quietly, "thank you for coming. Let me take your hat and coat. We're in the back, in the surgery."

Christina stepped up over the threshold, and Crawford saw her glance at all the mirrors that were now hung in the entry.

"And your house reeks of garlic," she noted in an approving tone. She took off her coat and handed it and her bonnet to him. "You wrote that Adelaide is with you?"

"Not exactly." Crawford hung the things on hooks between mirrors. "Not at the moment," he added, leading the way. "I'm with our daughter, Johanna."

Christina Rossetti shuffled after him through the dining room into the white-tiled surgery, and she blinked around, in the gray light from the windows, at beakers and books and mortars and pestles and the rows of glass-stoppered Winchester bottles full of variously colored liquids like extract of belladonna, sugar of lead, and spirits of turpentine. She wrinkled her nose at the cacophony of smells, not least of which was the acid odor from the mop bucket, and then stared uneasily at a big print hung on the far wall, an etching of a horse exhibiting thirty numbered equine maladies all at once.

Johanna looked up and raised her lard-caked hands. "Hello!" she said brightly, wiggling her fingers. "Have you had lunch?"

"This is our daughter, Johanna," said Crawford nervously. "Uh, careful, the floor's wet. I was mopping."

"You—" began Christina; then she gasped and said to Johanna, "You were following me yesterday!"

"Oh!" exclaimed Johanna. "Yes! You had on a brown coat and bonnet. The girl I was with—"

Christina looked ill. "Ragged leather trousers with braces? That was a girl?"

Johanna nodded and resumed kneading the poultice. "I hear she cuts her face with cold iron whenever she gets frightened. Nancy doesn't talk at all, but she's a wonder for sniffing out Neffies. She could smell your history on you, and she wanted to see if you'd got bit again." Johanna looked up and smiled. "Lucky for you she decided you haven't been!"

"No," agreed Christina, blinking bewilderedly at the girl. "I haven't been."

"Uh," said Crawford, "speaking of such things, I wrote to you—because—"

The doorbell rang again.

"Excuse me," he said, and hurried back to the front door and pulled it open.

McKee stood there in the dress she apparently always wore.

"He's passed out drunk," she said evenly. "I can stay for an hour." She stepped past him into the house. "Johanna's in the surgery?"

"With Christina Rossetti. She—"

"She finally responds to her correspondence! And I'm sure her brother was lying."

Crawford nodded as he led her through to the back of the house. He and McKee had found the Rossetti house in Euston Square, and Christina's brother William had told them on several visits that his sister was not at home.

McKee sniffed and spat when she stepped into the surgery. "Always smells in here like somebody tried hard to burn something that doesn't really burn."

"Ah," said Crawford, "Miss Rossetti, Miss—Mrs.—" He waved vaguely. "You know each other."

"Adelaide!" said Christina with a warm smile, "it's wonderful to see you again! I'm sorry I was too ill to receive you on Sunday and yesterday!"

McKee nodded, half smiling. "You're here now," she allowed.

"Miss or Mrs.?" said Christina, raising her eyebrows.

McKee frowned and opened her mouth to reply—but at that moment the caged bird cheeped several times, and a banging crash sounded from the front of the house, and then heavy boots were clumping in the hall.

Christina sprang nimbly to the doorway and leaned against the wall beside it, one hand in her handbag; Johanna snatched her knife out of the sheath inside her shirt, swearing softly as she gripped it in her greasy right hand; Crawford sprang toward the cabinet where the scalpels were kept and slipped on the wet floor and sat down hard; and McKee, shaking her head, crossed her arms and stood in the middle of the tile floor.

She was looking through the doorway into the dining room, and she said, "Tom, what the *hell* are you doing?"

"Don't speak to me, whore!" yelled a big unshaven man who now reeled into the room. "Where is he?"

His face was red under a shapeless hat, and the old black coat he wore was stretched across massive shoulders, and in his gnarled fist he gripped a foot-long iron rod. He blinked blearily at the people in the room, and his watery gaze fixed on Crawford, who had hurriedly got back on his feet.

"Hah!" the man said to him. "You don't even buy her clothes! *I* do!"

"Tom," said McKee loudly, "go back home. You know I buy my own—"

Tom turned toward her and raised the iron bar—

And a short, sharp explosion concussed the air of the little room, and everyone flinched.

Crawford, still clutching a scalpel with a ludicrous inch-long blade, straightened and blinked around. His ears were ringing, and the reek of burned gunpowder now eclipsed the room's ordinary smells.

Tom had stepped back, half lowering the iron rod, his face blank; Johanna had ducked under the counter; and McKee was staring at Christina, who was holding a smoking revolver in both hands.

Crawford's gaze swept over Tom, but he saw no blood, and then Johanna, peeking up from under the counter, pointed behind him. Crawford turned and saw a ragged hole in the plaster of the wall.

McKee stepped forward and wrenched the bar out of Tom's hand. "Well done, Sister Christina!" she called, without taking her eyes off him.

Abruptly a second gunshot shook the room, and this time Crawford cringed at the shrill twang of a ricochet and saw the pistol spin across the tile floor. Johanna darted out and snatched it up and pointed it at Tom, who now had his eyes clenched shut. The goldfinch was fluttering wildly in its cage.

Johanna briefly caught Crawford's eye and nodded toward the cabinets in the dining-room side wall, where another hole had been punched through the white-painted wood of one of the doors.

Christina had evidently dropped the gun, and it had gone off when it hit the floor—and the bullet must have missed her by only a yard or so.

Her face was white, but after looking around at everyone, she managed an awkward laugh. "I'd dig those out," she quavered. "They're silver."

"You get out of here," said Johanna, straightening up but keeping the gun barrel leveled at Tom. "Never come back."

"Johanna," said McKee, "he's your—"

"Stepfather?" said the girl calmly. "I'll step on *him*."

This disrespect seemed to snap Tom out of his daze.

"Give me that," he growled, stepping forward.

Johanna cocked the hammer with her thumb and smiled at him, and Crawford wondered if the child might have killed someone before.

"Bullet holes in the walls," Johanna said, "respectable people menaced in their own home by a drunk vagrant, a little girl kills the man—you think I'd do any time?—even be arraigned?"

"Vagrant!" Tom sputtered. "Drunk!" But he had retreated to the doorway.

"Go home, Tom," said McKee. "Nothing immoral is going on here. I'll be along in an hour."

Tom was breathing hard, and he wiped a grimy hand across his mouth. "Your front rooms stink of garlic," he said gruffly, "and you got mirrors everywhere—and I know the uses of silver! There's people who go the other way, drink out of purple glasses under London Bridge—I can bring your troubles to you, wait and see if I can't."

Then he had spun and was clumping quickly through the dining room to the hall.

McKee caught Johanna as the girl began to hurry after him. "Let him go, child."

The front door banged loudly.

"We need to kill him!" Johanna protested, as McKee grabbed the gun with her thumb under the hammer and pulled it out of the girl's hand.

"Johanna, he's my husband!"

"Do you have any sherry?" Christina asked Crawford.

Crawford nodded and stepped past McKee, who was holding on to the gun. A moment later he was back from the dining room with a decanter in one hand and a small glass in the other.

"You won't drop it again?" McKee was saying to Christina as she handed the gun back to her.

"No," Christina said sheepishly, tucking it back into her handbag. "I hope I didn't sprain my hand shooting it! I only carry it in case I should run into something like what Gabriel shot, that day in Regent's Park."

"The eighteen-hundred-year-old British queen," said Johanna, still scowling toward the front of the house, "who looked like a dog."

Christina stared in evident surprise at the girl.

Crawford mussed Johanna's hair and told her, "You did very well there."

"Not as well as Nancy would have," said the girl darkly. "I think he broke our front door."

Christina took the glass of sherry after Crawford had poured it and handed it to her, and she gulped it and held it out again.

"That was—" she began, as Crawford refilled it. "Uh," she went on, "the child lives here, I gather? With her father?"

"That was my husband, yes," said McKee with a defiant look. "And yes, Johanna lives here, for now."

"Only one glass?" said Johanna. "I could use a bracer myself."

McKee looked down at her in alarm and said, "Never mind, I think we could all use some tea. In the parlor, if my husband has verifiably left the premises."

"I CAN NAIL IT shut," Crawford said as they sat down in the parlor, "and we can come and go by the back door until I get a carpenter in."

The garlic smell was, as Tom had noted, very strong in the room.

"I'll pay for it," said McKee.

"You didn't do it," said Crawford.

Johanna put in, "Let him sell a lot of *spoons* to pay for it." One of the three-legged cats pulled itself up onto the couch beside her and she began petting it.

Crawford cleared his throat. "We imagine," he said to Christina, "that you know your uncle is up again. Whatever it was you did at the cemetery worked for these seven years, but—"

Christina's hand had flown to her mouth. "Has he . . . molested you people? His connections were all broken then, I'd have hoped—"

"Yes," said McKee. "He seems specifically to want our daughter."

"I'm so sorry! We've got, my siblings and I, a plan to stop him finally, kill him. We hope to—"

"How?" asked Johanna.

"When?" added McKee.

"Well—soon. Gabriel is getting permission to . . . to go to where he is, where his physical form is . . . " Her voice trailed off.

"And it's a statue, the physical form, you said," recalled Crawford. "Small enough for a fourteen-year-old girl to put under her pillow and sleep on."

"And you rubbed blood on it," added McKee.

"I'm glad *you're* my father," Johanna remarked, "not that old *shit wagon*."

"Damn it, Johanna," McKee burst out, "that old shit wagon is my husband!"

"Common law," said Johanna.

Christina was frowning and had closed her eyes.

Crawford started to speak, but he feared that his voice might catch if he spoke, so he just reached across the table to pat Johanna's hand.

Johanna noticed Christina's evident disapproval. "At least I know better than to wake up devils," she said, "and *I'm* only *thirteen*."

Christina opened her eyes and nodded. "A valid point, my dear."

"Where *is* the statue," asked McKee, "that you need to get permission to go there? A vault in a museum?"

Christina looked distressed. "I can't—it's not my secret to reveal—"

"It's in a grave in Highgate Cemetery," said Johanna casually. "He dreamed about it a lot when I was with him."

Christina turned to face the girl. "Do you know if it's still there, in the grave? We fear that his recent activity might be the result of the statue having dug its way out."

Johanna shook her head. "Do I still look bitten? I haven't been *with* him since that day you killed him." Then she shivered and clasped her hands. "But the *statue* doesn't have to be out of the grave for *him* to be out."

"That's true," conceded Christina.

"It's in her coffin?" asked Crawford. "Lizzie's? Or was, at least? You buried it that day?"

"No," blurted Christina, "it's in my father's coffin—in his throat, to be precise!" She pulled a handkerchief from her sleeve and patted her forehead. "We buried Lizzie right on top of him and put mirrors in her coffin to reflect him back on himself."

"Then it *must* have unburied itself," said McKee, "or else somebody dug it up." She shook her head. "No use you getting permission to open the grave—and was that your whole plan?"

Christina took a breath. "Yes," she said, exhaling.

"Damn. I was hoping you could do the 1862 thing again. I wonder if we could flee to America."

"We offered you passage to America ten years ago," said Christina, "as an indentured domestic, and you can still do that." She looked at Crawford. "And they might need veterinarians."

"And their child?" asked Johanna.

"I'm—not sure," Christina admitted.

"Tom would never agree to go," said McKee hopelessly.

For several seconds no one spoke. And, thought Crawford, in any case they probably have as many spoon sellers in America as they need.

He cleared his throat and said to McKee, "I wouldn't go without you, not again."

"That's the boy!" said Johanna.

"We, my family and I," said Christina hurriedly, "are going to find out, try to, tonight, whether in fact the statue is still in the grave."

McKee raised her eyebrows. "Find out how?"

"We're going to try to talk to Lizzie." She shrugged and rolled her eyes upward. "We're going to hold a séance."

THE BAY WINDOW HAD been repaired since the devils had crashed through it four evenings ago, but the side panels were now unlatched and swung open to the cool night air. A bell at the nearby Church of St. Luke tolled eight P.M., giving punctuation to the fainter bells of boats on the river.

Gabriel and his assistant had carried a smaller table into the dining room and pushed the long table to the side. A pad of drawing paper and a handful of pencils had been laid out on the smaller table.

The gas jets had been turned off, and a candle on the table, and half a dozen more on the mantel, made the long room seem churchlike and much bigger.

Maria sat at the far end of the room, expressionless but nevertheless radiating disapproval, and Christina sighed and got up from beside her to cross to the table.

"Where have you sent Algy tonight?" she asked Gabriel.

He sat down beside William and waved his sister to the third chair. "He's off at . . . some club he belongs to. He probably won't be coming back here."

"Just as well," said William. "He wouldn't be serious."

Christina suppressed a smile as she sat down. Who would have thought that the skeptical William would be so earnest about fishing in the supernatural? But of course he considered it science.

"How do we do it?" she asked, ignoring a sigh from the far end of the room.

"I've written the alphabet," said Gabriel, "on the top sheet of paper. One of us asks a question aloud and then touches each letter in turn— the table will rap, or perhaps tilt, when the right letter is touched. If the question can be answered yes or no, one rap means yes, two means uncertain, and three means no. Five is a request to use the alphabet again."

"They're not always . . . precise," warned William. "Even the brightest of them has trouble spelling, sometimes."

"Do they lose their intelligence, when they die?" Christina asked, remembering her father's fishlike ghost in the river.

"I think it's more that they don't clearly see the paper," William replied, "and . . . well, and they do seem to lose some power of concentration." He smiled. "So we have to concentrate especially hard." Formally and more loudly, he said, "Is any spirit present?"

Several seconds ticked past.

Then a knock shook the table, and Christina shivered and glanced at her brothers, but they were both frowning intently at the paper.

"Spell your surname," said William, and he began touching the penciled letters slowly, one by one.

As he touched the letters, four spaced knocks shook the wood under Christina's hands.

"*E-R-O-S*," said Gabriel. "Eros? Hardly helpful."

William said, "Is *E* the initial of your Christian name?"

A single rap.

"Is R the initial of your surname?"

Another rap. Gabriel's face gleamed with sweat in the candlelight.

William said, "Are you Lizzie, my brother's wife?"

Gabriel's "Yes" overlapped the single knock.

"Do you know I love you?" asked Gabriel, his voice a controlled monotone.

Ten seconds passed with no knock.

William cleared his throat. "Do you—"

"Give her time!" interrupted Gabriel.

Another ten seconds passed, and Gabriel looked away and fluttered his hand.

William said, "Do you know if the statue of our uncle is still in our father's grave?"

Three knocks sounded, then, after a pause, two more. *No,* thought Christina. *Not sure.*

Abruptly there were five knocks in a row. Christina jumped.

William obediently reached out to touch the alphabet letters again; and he touched *S-T-O-P-T-H-I-S.* Then, after a pause, *G-O-D-B-Y.*

"Lizzie," said William, "are you still with us?"

Three sharper knocks shook the wood. *No.*

"Are you a different spirit?"

A single rap. *Yes.*

God help us, thought Christina, who is this?

"Do *you* know if the statue is still in our father's grave?"

A single knock sounded in reply.

"*Is* it?" blurted Christina. "Still there?"

Again a single knock.

"This might be anyone," William cautioned softly. More loudly, he went on, "Can you tell us your name?"

Three raps. *No.*

"Do you *have* a name?"

Three more raps.

William looked up at his brother and sister and shook his head in evident bafflement.

A thought occurred to Christina. "Can you spell?" she asked.

Three more knocks sounded in reply.

William shrugged. "I don't know how much we can learn from this spirit, with just *yes* and *no* and *maybe*."

It's not Uncle John, thought Christina—he can write whole stories. "Can you draw," she asked, "if one of us holds the pencil?"

A single knock sounded in reply. *Yes.*

"Christina," called Maria from the other end of the room, "don't give it your hand!"

But Christina had already picked up the pencil, and Gabriel tore the top sheet of paper off the pad.

"Draw yourself," said Christina.

Her hand dropped the pencil and then picked it up again, holding it now as if it were a lever; and then it lunged toward the pad and quickly outlined two crude figures, one tall with circles for breasts and a rank of lines for long hair, the other figure shorter and stick-thin. Then four lines and a zigzag made a broken window behind them.

It's Lizzie again, thought Christina; no, Boadicea—but her hand drew a circle around the head of the smaller figure.

"Damn me," whispered Gabriel, "it's that starved child-ghost!"

"How do you know," asked William, "that the statue is still in our father's grave?"

Christina's hand was beginning to ache from its awkward grip of the pencil, which now again moved jerkily, outlining a horizontal rectangle and, inside it, a quick back-and-forth squiggle that seemed to be a recumbent body—and between the round head-loop and the oval of the chest it ground a black dot into the paper.

"That's our father's coffin!" whispered Gabriel. "And that dot is in his throat."

"But how do you *know*?" persisted William. "Who are *you*?"

Christina winced as her hand now drew another rectangle directly above the first one.

"I wish he could hold a pencil properly!" she gasped.

More slowly, the pencil outlined another supine body in profile, inside this second rectangle. Peering past her own hand, Christina saw a curve indicating a bosom and another curve, bigger . . . pregnancy? A coffin directly over our father's . . . that must be meant to represent Lizzie's body.

Her hand drew a little spidery asterisk inside the pregnancy curve, then circled the asterisk shape and drew a line from it to the circle it had drawn around the head of the stick-thin figure in the first drawing.

Gabriel gave a choked gasp and pushed himself back from the table. "Merciful God!" he whispered. "It's my child; it's the child Lizzie was carrying when she died!"

William leaned back quickly, half raising a hand, and Christina knew that her own face must be as stiff with horror as his was.

But her hand would not release the pencil, and she could not pull it away from the paper.

The pencil lifted and returned to the figure of the pregnant woman—and though the point was getting blunted, it drew a curve from the spidery fetus to the bottom line of the coffin, and there it drew a series of Xs along that line; then the point made a line straight up, right out of the coffin rectangle and off the top of the paper.

Perhaps because it was her own hand making the picture, Christina understood it. "It broke the mirrors," she said softly, "and carried the pieces away to the surface."

"He," said Gabriel in a hollow tone. "Not it."

A hand on Christina's shoulder made her jump, but it was just Maria, who had at some point walked up behind her.

And now Christina's hand sprang open, dropping the pencil, and she pulled it back and massaged it with her left hand.

"Destroy that drawing," said Maria, and her voice was oddly low in pitch, and getting lower: "and . . . the . . . pencil . . ."

Sudden gray light dazzled Christina, and her chair shifted as if in an earthquake; she grabbed for the table but fell forward and her outstretched hands slapped against a horizontal plank, and she wasn't in the chair at all but sitting on a similar plank; and when she squinted quickly around herself she saw gunwale rails and rope rigging, and realized dazedly that she was sitting alone in a boat.

And the boat was swaying from side to side, but with the keel swinging most widely, as if the boat were a pendulum. She gasped and leaned back, gripping the thwart she was sitting on, and the cold wind that fluttered her hair smelled of steamy smoke, like a fire doused with water.

She looked upward to see what moored the top of the mast, but saw only gray sky above it.

Then she wasn't alone. "It won't fall," said a heavy voice from in front of her.

She gasped and lowered her head and was not entirely surprised to see the young man sitting now on the thwart across from her. The deep eyes and curly dark hair and mustache were of course familiar from the portrait that had hung on the wall of every house she'd lived in. But he was hunched over and deathly pale.

For one flickering moment the figure was the squat, eyeless form of Mouth Boy, and then it was John Polidori again.

Christina could hear her pulse throbbing in her temples.

"You crave two things," he said. "Your poetry and me. And we are one thing. You have found my attention again, but not yet my help again. You must let me help you. And therefore you must help me."

Three lines of one of her poems occurred to her: *There's blood between us, love, my love, / There's father's blood, there's brother's blood, / And blood's a bar I cannot pass.*

And though she had only thought the lines, he gave her a stiff smile that did nothing to change the humorless cast of his eyes.

"You use my gift to say me no," came his voice, and she noticed that the sound of it lagged behind the motion of his lips, as if he were far away.

"I am a jealous god," he went on, "and I offer you the same. Will *you* be jealous if I take . . . your sister, Maria?"

"Maria," Christina said hoarsely, gripping the thwart under her, "is consecrated to your adversary."

Polidori opened his mouth, and now he quoted four lines of a poem of Gabriel's:

Of the same lump (as it is said)
For honour and dishonour made,
Two sister vessels. Here is one.
It makes a goblin of the sun.

"Help me," he said. "I have always loved you best. Maria is not who I want."

Christina's heartbeat had slowed, since the impossible boat did appear to be securely moored somehow, and she ventured a glance out over the gunwale—in the middle distance, winged things with bodies like octopi and jellyfish flapped heavily through the humid air, and dimly in the remoter grayness she could just make out tall mountains or towers.

Maria would recoil from any whiff of this, she thought. And I will at least turn away.

"No," she said, blinking back tears. "I can live without me—I mean, without you."

"What you can do without me," he said sadly, "is die. Talk to me—you know how."

And then she was sitting at the table in Gabriel's dimly lit dining room again, panting hard and clutching the seat of her chair and wincing at Maria's tight grip on her shoulder. She glanced around wildly, but the pinpoint radiances of the few candles in the room were not enough for her dazzled eyes to see anything.

"Maria, let go!" she gasped, and Maria's hand was gone. "Gabriel, William, are you here?"

From across the table came a croaked "Yes" that might have been either of them. "Yes," came a second assent, this one recognizably Gabriel's breathless voice.

"Ach!" coughed Maria from behind Christina's chair. "Why did I touch you? Our terrible uncle! I must wash my hand."

"Gabriel," said Christina, "light, for God's sake."

One of the figures on the other side of the table blundered to its feet, and she heard the rattle of a matchbox.

"I," said William, "saw none of you there."

A match flared, and then Gabriel had lit a gas jet on the wall and turned the valve all the way open. Christina squinted in the relative glare as the cabinets and wallpaper of the familiar room became visible again. She looked over her shoulder and saw Maria scowling.

"Where were you?" Gabriel asked.

"A room," said William, rubbing his eyes, "in a tower, I think. It was full of scrolls, poetry, and I could read them all. And I knew—" He stopped and shook his head. "And I can't remember *any* of the verses now—and they were all beautiful."

Like Coleridge unable to remember the unwritten bulk of *Kubla Khan,* thought Christina—and suddenly she was sure that, in William's vision, he himself had been the author of the vanished verses. Recalling his real-world attempts at poetry, Christina winced now in pity.

"I was on a beach made of glass," said Gabriel. He shuffled carefully to the next gas jet and struck another match. "There was an ocean, and it was made of water, but the waves . . . walked, toward me." He shivered visibly, and had to strike another match.

William dropped his hands and blinked at Christina.

She hesitantly described her own vision but found that she had finished without having mentioned their uncle's presence in it.

"Into my head," came Maria's voice from behind Christina, "against my will!—he projected a view of the interior of a—a *skull,* an enormous skull. I seemed to be standing inside it. And he was there, and he said filthy things to me."

"What did he say?" asked William, but Maria just shook her head.

Christina wondered if their uncle had been in all their visions, and only Maria was innocent enough to mention it.

And she wondered if he had said, to each of them, *Talk to me—you know how.*

Maria was still staring at her hand, which had been gripping Christina's shoulder when the visions began. "All the perfumes of Arabia will not sweeten this little hand," Maria said, perhaps to herself.

"You shouldn't have touched me during it," said Christina crossly. Then she shook her head and said, "I'm sorry, Maria! You're always getting into trouble trying to help me."

William cleared his throat. "This . . . statue," he said, "is evidently still in our father's grave. We need to—you say we need to—get it."

"And destroy it," added Maria.

Now Gabriel strode to the windows and pulled them closed, and Christina saw him peer fearfully outside as he latched them.

And she wondered if his son was out there—how had he described him? *A boy, like a starved corpse galvanized.*

JOHANNA SNAPPED AWAKE WHEN the air was suddenly cold and metallic in her nose and the light brightened beyond her closed eyelids, and her hand was on the old leather grip of her knife in the same moment that she opened her eyes.

And she flinched back in the bed, but it wasn't a bed—she was on a curved, hard ivory slope that was broken at the top edge, and though two figures stood forty feet away on the opposite side of the bumpy ivory bowl, her gaze was helplessly caught by what was moving outside and above the broken-edged rim.

What seemed to be a tower as tall as a mountain stood in the yellow sky—but it was just perceptibly broader in the middle, and she knew it was a wheel viewed from directly in front. It was too far away for its motion to be immediately visible, but she knew that it was rushing in her direction at horrifying speed.

Knowing what she would see, she nevertheless looked up to left and right, and saw sky-scraping wheels in those directions too; and, looking straight up, she saw the miles-high rim of another above the cracked edge of this wide ivory cup.

She had been here before, and she remembered that the wheels never did actually arrive or roll past—that in fact it became difficult, if you watched them, to know in which direction any one of them was turning, though they were palpably spinning at mind-withering speeds—and that soon it would be possible to make out eyes like stars along their rims.

She shivered and drew her knife, panting. It had been a long time since she had felt at home in this place.

Her gaze snapped back down then, for one of the figures on the other side of the bowl had begun to move.

She had never seen it before; it was a skeletal boy in an overcoat of something like dead leaves, and his eyes and white teeth protruded from the gray skin stretched tightly over his skull.

He was hopping toward her over the bumps and hollows of the skull bottom, and Johanna quickly got up in a crouch and held her knife ready.

The boy paused, his eyes gleaming at her above his wide, helpless grin.

"Josephine, my daughter," came Polidori's leaden voice from behind the insectlike figure.

Johanna decided not to correct him again about her name. She breathed rapidly and kept her eye on the swaying mummified boy.

"This is your betrothed," Polidori went on, "consecrated to Boadicea as you are consecrated to me. Together you will have an offspring that will fulfill her purpose, break the land."

Without looking away from the terrible lean face that was now only a few yards from her, Johanna was peripherally aware that the remote eyes were glaring in the wheels; and then she did glance up quickly, for the sky had gone darker.

And she was viewing a city from all directions at once, no part farther or nearer than any other part, and she could trace the old buried rivers and tunnels and pipes and the towers and bridges and the decorative brass plates around doorknobs.

And then the wheels were visibly turning—and the city was moored to them and began to tear apart. The buried rivers opened to take the towers, and gravity pulled in a hundred directions.

And the boy was upon her. At the first impact of his bony knees and shoulders she lashed out convulsively with her knife, and a cold exhalation like the burst of gas from a rupturing deepwater fish was in her nostrils; then one knobby fist had bounced off the socket of her left eye, and a moment later the boy was rolling away down the ivory slope.

She blinked away tears and looked past the figure flailing in the central depression now, straight at Polidori.

He seemed somehow less distinct than he had when she had been a child and he had been her lord—she could see the eyes and the mustache, but his outline seemed to churn in her vision like an afterimage of glare.

"You will be glad to bear his child," Polidori said, "after you invite me back." Suddenly he was closer. "Invite me back."

She flipped the knife and caught it by the tip, then drew it back and flung it toward the boiling center of him.

And her bed crashed to the floor in darkness, and Johanna was cursing shrilly as she scrambled out of it and wrenched open the bedroom door.

By the time she had scuffed barefoot down the stairs to the landing there was a light under her father's door, and he opened it just in time for her to leap into his arms, nearly making him drop the newly lit candle.

"He's found me," she gasped into the shoulder of his nightshirt. "And he's got—"

She couldn't describe the skeletal boy right now, and just clung to her father. He patted her back and started carefully toward the stairs, for he knew she'd want to spend the rest of the night in the cellar.

CHAPTER SIX

To-day, while it is called to-day,
Kneel, wrestle, knock, do violence, pray;
To-day is short, to-morrow night:
Why will you die? why will you die?

—*Christina Rossetti, "The Convent Threshold"*

WITH INADVERTENT IRONY, the window of his office at the Board of Inland Revenue gave William Rossetti a close-up view of the triangular pediments over the second-floor western windows of King's College. If he stood up from his desk and moved around to the left side of it, he would be able to see, off to the right, a slice of the brown Thames and a warehouse or two on the south shore; but when he was sitting at the desk and reviewing his daily lot of orders and petitions, he was confronted by the school he had attended, negligently, from the ages of eight to fifteen. And he was forty now.

This morning the sight was somehow especially maddening. Last night he had, albeit in what had apparently been a hallucination, unrolled a scroll and read verses as sublime as any his brother or sister had written, and they were in his own handwriting! And there were dozens of scrolls, and he had known that all of them contained poetry he was destined to write—

But the—the *librarian* had come in before he could look at any more. And William had recognized the intruder from the picture his mother always kept on the parlor wall, wherever they lived.

A confident atheist, William dismissed belief in Heaven and Hell as archaic superstitions, but at a number of séances he had seen evidence that personalities did survive physical death—though the spirits who could be contacted that way always seemed to have become imbecilic, scarcely able to comprehend questions or frame answers—like Lizzie, last night, simply trying to spell out her own name!

But Polidori had offered William a different sort of survival, a virtual immortality, one in which he might seal his own identity and intellect against erosion, albeit at the cost of . . . well, at an abominable cost.

William pushed away the document he had been reading—a petition requesting a Civil Service pension for the widow of a deceased Excise officer—and closed his eyes to better remember the vision.

The attraction of his uncle's offer did not lie primarily in survival of death.

What might be written on those other scrolls? What unimaginable, radiant odes, sonnets, ballads?

Gabriel and Christina, and Swinburne too, accepted William as an equal in education and appreciation of literature and art, but he was always aware of a dimension the three of them shared, lived in, that he could not enter. Their verses would be read and admired for centuries, while his translations of Dante and his edition of Shelley's works would surely be superseded long before he even retired from the Board of Inland Revenue.

He had not moved very far from that school outside his office window.

His hand had been twitching, and looking down he saw to his alarm that he had scrawled words across the widow's petition. He must make another copy, get her solicitor to sign it—

Then he read what he had written:

not as thyself alone,
But as the meaning of all things that are;
A breathless wonder, shadowing forth afar
Some heavenly solstice, hushed and halcyon

He felt the hairs on his arms standing up, and he blinked away tears; these were lines from the scroll he had read in the vision last night, and he could almost remember the next line . . . something, and then *furthest fires oracular . . .*

It was gone.

His uncle—for it *was* his uncle too—had asked for help, and said, *Talk to me—you know how.*

"Uncle John," he whispered, "are you there?" and he reached out to touch an *A* in the petition, and then a *B*—

And then all at once the air on his face and hands was hot, and he was standing and stumbling forward to keep his balance in deep dry sand, squinting against a glaring sun.

He gasped in surprise and felt the hot dry air parching his lungs.

After a moment of dazed incomprehension, he clapped his hands just to hear the sound of it and feel the faint sting; and he experienced both sensations. This was as evidently real a place as his office had been a moment before.

Before him stretched an infinity of serrated dunes under the empty blue sky, and the silence was profound; no slightest breeze flicked the ridges of sand. He slid his shoes through the mounded grains to get a full-circle view—

And he gasped again. Half a mile behind him a black stone cathedral stood up as tall as St. Paul's, taller, with nothing behind or around it except more empty miles of tan dunes.

Its pillars and arches and remote dome were rounded by centuries or millennia of erosion—and then he saw that the thing wasn't a building at all, but a vast weathered statue: towering legs, buttresses that might have been wings, and a promontory head with no features remaining.

Eyeless, it nevertheless seemed to stare with antediluvian defiance at the sun and the wasteland.

Into William's head came Shelley's lines: *Round the decay / Of that colossal wreck, boundless and bare / The lone and level sands stretch far away.*

He was shivering, but at the same time his tie and waistcoat and woolen trousers were smothering him.

He tore loose his tie and collar, but the sense of heavy oppression only intensified, and he realized that all of this, the sun and the heat and the desert, were being projected onto him by a watchful identity in the stone colossus; and the colossus itself was a projection of that identity.

A thought appeared forcefully in his mind, and he translated it into words: *Help me.* There was a task to be done, and of it William got only a blurred impression of blood smeared across black stone, but on the far side of it were the poems that had been written on the scrolls he had seen last night.

He tried to concentrate on that required task, to open it to articulate elaboration; and he was able to find words to convey it: *The blood of my*—something like onetime hosts; strayed children, adopted ones; canceled clients?—*is redundant, just . . . repetition*—*reiteration! of myself. I am*—again there was a cluster of applicable words: broken, ill-defined, illogically phrased—*and*—*I cannot, impossible to, restore myself as I need to be restored.*

William was shown two images: of a man and a tiny black statue, and also a series of images in between: seen left to right, the images showed the man shrinking and darkening, but viewed right to left they traced the expansion of the statue into the man.

Another thought: *I need to be fully restored. Fully.*

That had been conveyed clearly!

I need to be—and William intuitively provided the word *quickened—fully, but with blood infested by,* no, more like *animated by the other of my kind, the one who is not me, spouse in relation to me, the west of my east.*

The view of the desert and the colossus wavered, as if they were now just figures painted on a tapestry in a breeze. William thought he glimpsed the rectangle of his office window through them.

The intrusive identity was fading, but it raised a last thought that William phrased as, *Soon, while her blood in her children still lives, circulates, reddens and fades and reddens again.*

And then William was just sitting at his desk in the Excise Section wing of Somerset House, blinking out at the windows of King's College.

His tie and collar were loosened, and he pushed his chair back to look at his shoes; a shaking of sand grains clung to the laces, but even as he watched, they evaporated to nothing.

He snatched up the widow's petition—but the lines of verse on it had disappeared, and he couldn't now remember what they had been.

His hands were shaking as he refastened his collar and knotted his tie, and he patted his hair and beard in case they had got disarranged in the hallucinated desert. But there were tears in his eyes.

I can't have it yet, he thought. Our uncle needs to be quickened fully, freed from his long petrification; and for that he needs the blood of a . . . client, a child, a *host* of this other creature of his kind—the creature that is something like his spouse, referred to with a clear flavor of "she." Perhaps there were only two of these creatures. And for some reason her vital renewal of her hosts' blood seemed likely to cease soon.

He would, he thought almost ferally, ask Christina what she knew about that.

UNDER THE GRAY OCTOBER sky, the river was the color of steel, and the light breeze carried a smell of distant fires. Crawford and McKee and Johanna had walked out onto the broad stone pier of the old York water gate and paused just short of the steps that led down to an empty half-walled shed and a ramp that disappeared into the water; Crawford could make out a few of the paving stones that continued sloping away under the water's surface, and he wondered how far out into the river the ramp extended. A hundred yards beyond, the tall black smokestack of a steam launch moved jauntily past, but other boats and the south shore were vague angularities in the mist.

It had been Johanna's idea to venture down here before noon, and as Crawford looked back at the pillars of the old water gate, he reflected sourly that if McKee had proposed it, he would probably have refused.

Johanna's left eye was swollen nearly shut; her second black eye in four days! And this morning they had found her knife stuck in the wall over her bed.

Crawford glanced down at her again, and touched her shoulder; she squinted up, but he just smiled and shook his head and let his hand fall away.

To the right of the pillars he could see the ranked phalanxes of chimneys along the roof of the elegant Adelphi block of flats, and the many rows of windows shone only with repetitions of the cloudy sky. Waterloo Bridge was farther off in that direction, its arches dim in the fog.

McKee followed his gaze. "That's where we first met," she said quietly, "about at the second arch."

Johanna had been watching the visible extent of George Street beyond the pillars behind them, but now she looked up.

"When he saved your life?" she asked.

"Yes," said McKee.

"And I was *conceived*," Johanna added. Clearly she had been told the word sometime and remembered it.

McKee gave Crawford an accusing look, and he shrugged helplessly.

"I know about such things," Johanna assured her. "I was nearly married to a coster boy last year."

"Good heavens," said Crawford.

"I didn't fancy him," said Johanna, shrugging, "so I ran away."

This was straying far too close to the events of her vision last night; clearly McKee thought so too, for she put her arm protectively around Johanna and started to say something, then just shook her head.

McKee had come to Crawford's house early this morning, with a carpenter to make an estimate for fixing the door, and at first she had assumed that her daughter's black eye was again the work of one of the Mud Larks; and when she had heard the full story of the attack by Polidori, and what Polidori had proposed, she had forbidden all further talk of it for now.

Crawford knew that even before the events of last night, McKee had hated not living with her daughter—apparently she didn't believe her common-law husband could be trusted with the girl—but she clearly couldn't bear it now.

McKee had mentioned, on the walk down to the river this morning, that Tom had not come home last night after his spectacular rage in Crawford's surgery yesterday. It was hard to tell what she felt about that.

From not too far away, Crawford now heard high piping voices taking turns reciting something in a nursery-rhyme cadence—he was able to make out the words *When the sky began to roar*—

Abruptly the goldfinch in Johanna's bag cheeped, and half a dozen seagulls that had been standing at the edge of the pier spread their long gray-and-white wings and flapped away into the sky.

"Larks coming," said Johanna tensely. "I know some of 'em, a bit."

Crawford looked back up the street, between the gate pillars; and he glimpsed a couple of children dart from one side of George Street to the other, and then a third child scampered back the other way. They were all ragged little scarecrows, with lean, blackened limbs flexing in tattered clothes. They seemed to move as rapidly as spiders.

Crawford was suddenly afraid that they might stressfully remind Johanna of the skeletal boy in her vision. He glanced at her out of the corner of his eye, but she was already shaking her head reassuringly at him.

"These are alive," she told him.

"They shouldn't hurt us," said McKee. "We're not infected."

"I *was*," said Johanna, "and I'm sure you two still carry the smell of Neffy attention." She touched the knife hilt under her coat. "And the Larks are crazy. I was."

Now three of the wild children scuffed barefoot out onto the flagstones of the pier, their knees bent and their scrawny arms held out from their sides; their faces held no expression. Crawford shivered, remembering the morning he and McKee had eluded a previous generation of these children seven years ago.

And then he shivered violently enough to click his teeth together, and his chest suddenly felt cold and empty—for he remembered thinking then that his lost daughter would be the same age as those eerie children; and now, for the first time, it had occurred to him that she might very well have *been* one of them.

Johanna was scanning the dirty, vacuous faces. "Where's Nancy?" she called.

A boy came out from behind the pillars and joined the first three in the gray daylight. He mumbled something.

"Down, sick or dead," muttered Johanna to her parents. "This boy hasn't got many words."

More loudly, she said, "You see that we're clean. Take us to the old man. The *old man*, right?"

Her brown hair was blowing around her face, and Crawford was struck by the contrast between her evident health—even with the black eye—and the wasted faces of the Mud Larks. She gave Crawford an uncertain grin. "I think they know I was one of them once. They knew it yesterday, at least."

The boy said something that sounded to Crawford like a chicken gobbling.

"I'm as clean as you are," Johanna said scornfully; and Crawford suppressed a reflexive nervous smile at the apparent inappropriateness of the remark. Johanna waved a hand around her head. "Are you already too old to see?"

The boy shrugged and stepped back, and another one of the children took an egg-shaped clay ball out of a pocket and blew into it.

It produced a prolonged low note that seemed to vibrate in Crawford's abdomen, and he realized that he had heard this same sound on many mornings and assumed it was some sort of maritime signal.

OVER A SCANTY BREAKFAST this morning—in the surgery, since the carpenter was making too much noise for comfortable talk anywhere else—Johanna had told her parents that the Mud Larks between Hungerford and Blackfriars Bridges, unlike their brethren farther up or down-river, didn't make much of their living by grubbing in the Thames mud at low tide for tools and brass nails dropped overboard by shipfitters. These local ones ventured out into the mud mainly to bag the awkward fishes and river worms that had become inhabited by recently deceased ghosts, which they passed along to the old man who provided them in return with food and a boat to sleep in. "And we used to—well, they still do—range inland before dawn as far as Covent Garden, to watch for the glow of bitten people and follow them to where they lived. The old man would pay silver for an address like that."

And she had pointed out, in a matter-of-fact tone Crawford found unnerving, that if the old man could be induced to provide one of those addresses today, the three of them might be able to "ambush the vampire with silver bullets when he next visits that place."

McKee had paced Crawford's surgery, chewing a piece of toast and glancing at the holes made by silver bullets in his wall and cabinet, and finally said, "We have to try it. We've clearly got no real way of *eluding* Sister Christina's damned uncle."

THE CHILD ON THE old stone pier blew into the clay egg again, and once more the penetrating low note rolled away up through the city streets and out across the river.

McKee was frowning at the ragged clothes and soot-stained faces of the Larks. "I gather this old man isn't much concerned with the welfare of his young employees!"

Johanna peered up at her. "You take one in sometime and try to civilize him! We—they're all stepped on by the vampires and lucky to have got away. We wouldn't look at a bath, we ate like dogs, and new clothes wouldn't have stayed new long in the river mud." She shifted on the pavement, peering up the street. "I was lucky to find that costermonger family that needed help, after I got too old to see the way the Larks do. I was a young wreck—afraid to bathe, always hiding food in odd places around the house, hardly able to speak English. The costers had a lot of patience—gave me a bit of refinement."

Crawford looked out over the rippling water, not wanting to meet McKee's eyes.

And so he saw the canoe slanting in toward the water gate a moment before its keel scraped against the ancient ramp, and with a chill that tightened his scalp he recognized the old man who hopped out of the narrow craft and waded in hip boots up to the steps, holding a mooring rope.

"The luckless Medicus and Rahab," said Trelawny with piratical cheer as he crouched to tie the rope around a rusted cleat. He stood up and stretched. He was hatless this morning, his white hair and beard all blown outward into spikes, and his collar was open. "And," he began, glancing at Johanna—but the derisive smile unkinked from his scarred lips. "Ah," he said, squinting and frowning intently now, and he snapped his fingers; "Johanna!" He stared at her. "I'm glad to see you well, girl, except for that aubergine eye." He jerked a thumb toward Crawford and McKee. "You're with these two? You could do better."

"And worse," said Johanna cautiously.

"*You're* the, the Mud Lark man?" asked Crawford.

"I serve that purpose," the old man said.

"Samson," said McKee, and it took Crawford a baffled moment to remember the name Trelawny had given them on that day in Regent's Park—*My spiritual hair has almost completely grown back, I believe*—"we need to get the address of one of the Polidori vampire's currently living subjects."

Trelawny sighed. "Who are you looking for? My Larks only monitor—"

"*Any* subject," McKee interrupted. "We simply want to know an address he's likely to arrive at—a place he's been invited into."

The old man nodded. "You want to cripple him down, as Mr. Hearts did to Miss B. that day with his silver bullets. That's a *prohibitive* lot of risk to take, my dear, just to buy a few days of his absence."

McKee nodded. "Nevertheless."

Trelawny looked away up the river, then back at her. "Well, I—" He blew out a breath, and the laugh that followed was rueful. "I'm afraid I wrecked any chance of an ambush at the only address I knew of, as it happens. Five days ago I tried that myself, but I wasn't able to get a clear shot, and he fled. He won't go back there, and his—his *subject,* poor old creature, has certainly moved by now."

"You," said Crawford cautiously, "weren't able to get a clear shot."

The old man scowled at him. "You weren't there! You think you could have done better? My eye is still better than—"

He shook his head, then crouched beside Johanna and patted her arm.

"It does me good to see you so healthy these days, child. But who gave you the black eye then? Not one of these two, I hope for their sakes! And what business have you got with them?"

"These are my parents."

"Ah!" he said, straightening up. "Yes, it was mentioned that they had a daughter."

"And I got the black eye—" she began, but McKee shushed her.

"He needs to know it," Johanna insisted. "The Polidori vampire came to me in a vision last night . . ." Her voice trailed off.

Trelawny seemed to notice the cluster of Mud Larks by the pillars, and he dismissed them with an angry wave. When they scattered, he pointed at Johanna. "You were *one* of his, weren't you, before he went into eclipse? I suppose he wants you back again."

"Yes," she said, "but for a purpose—" And though her voice quavered and she clutched her parents' hands tightly, she described the vision, and Polidori's presentation of what he described as her betrothed husband, and the destruction that their anticipated offspring would accomplish.

Trelawny's face went blank and came to look much older as she spoke, and when she had finished, he stepped back and turned toward the river.

"I wonder what went wrong with Diamonds's damned mirrors," he said quietly. Then he added, "I should have put three or four rounds through old Gretchen right away."

McKee caught Crawford's eye and shrugged with one eyebrow.

Trelawny looked at Crawford. "I *might* . . . have been a bit out of breath. I had to do some running and jumping to get to where he was, you see." He scowled again. "I doubt *you* could even have kept up with me."

"I'm sure you're right," Crawford agreed helplessly.

For several seconds the four of them stood there in the wind at the end of the ancient pier. From away up the street Crawford could hear the whickering drone of a hurdy-gurdy playing some Scottish-sounding melody.

"We thought—" began McKee.

"You did not," snapped Trelawny. "Let *me* think."

Johanna started to pick her nose, and McKee pulled her hand away.

"I know about this scheme to wreck London," Trelawny remarked absently. McKee opened her mouth to ask something, but Crawford waved at her not to interrupt. Trelawny went on, "Miss B. did it once before, successfully—she's out of the picture right now, but it seems that she had a—a child, so to speak, somehow . . ." His eyes widened. "Was Elizabeth Rossetti pregnant when she died?"

"I don't know," said Crawford.

"I'll lay you pounds to pinfeathers she was. Such a child would be . . . well, I have no idea what it would be. But it wouldn't be a subject of Miss B. *or* Polidori. Undead but never bitten! Knock either or both of them down and you wouldn't stop *it*." He bared his teeth and shook his head quickly, as if to dispel nausea. "And this thing wants to— *marry!*—have this offspring by!—*Johanna?*"

It seemed to be a rhetorical question. For another several moments the four figures stood silently on the pier.

"You should take her to America," said Trelawny. "My daughter Zella and her husband moved there ten years ago, at my insistence and expense, and so my grandchildren are safe. The vampire things generally can't cross that much salt water, unless you carry them along with you— as I did in '33, necessitating my near-fatal swim across the Niagara River to get free of it." He was chewing on a knuckle and frowning at Johanna. "Even France might be far enough. The Channel is a lot of water."

"We might do that," said McKee, surprising Crawford. "But is there anything . . . quicker? Something we could do today, tomorrow?"

This time Trelawny was silent for so long that Crawford wondered if the man had forgotten the question.

"There's a certain crazy trick," he said at last. "Have you ever heard of the translator men in St. Giles?"

McKee grimaced. "Devil worshippers, I've heard."

"Not good Christians, certainly—not their clients, at any rate. But the trouble is that Miss Diamonds *is* a good Christian, and you'd need her cooperation—hell, you'd need her *presence* there. She *should* do it—she's got amends to make, like us all—but it'd be wrong to tie her up and take her there by force." He paused and then nodded. "Yes, that would be wrong."

"Devil worshippers?" ventured Crawford.

"They make shoes to hide you from God," said Johanna solemnly.

"That's right, my dear," said Trelawny. "And their clients pay a lot too, silly fools, to hide from somebody who's not even there in the first place. But . . . if there *were* someone there, their trick might work." He squinted at Johanna. "And *you're* in a position where there *is* someone there to hide from."

Crawford was frowning. "If you don't believe God exists," he began—Trelawny glowered but didn't contradict him, so he went on—"then why do you have the Mud Larks baptized?"

Trelawny visibly restrained himself from throwing an angry glance at Johanna.

"Pascal's wager," he snapped. "Dunking them and saying the words is no trouble or expense, and if there *should* be a God, the Larks are thus benefited. If not, I'm nothing out of pocket. If baptisms cost a penny a shot, I wouldn't bother."

"I presume you've been baptized yourself, then," Crawford went on.

Trelawny spat. "I won't unmake who I am. If I thought there were more than a negligible chance of such a being existing, I'd get a pair of translator shoes myself."

"How do they work?" asked McKee. "These shoes."

"They don't, Miss Rahab—they can't, as I just now said. But what they *aim* to do is deflect—refract, reflect!—the special mutual awareness between redeemer and redeemed. Hah! To make the shoes, they use consecrated wine from a Catholic Church—what they believe is the blood of their Redeemer. I don't believe people have a Redeemer . . . but Polidori surely has one, and with luck you can talk her into contributing some of her blood for a special pair of shoes—the blood she rubbed on him years ago to quicken him. With that blood fixed in your daughter's shoes, your daughter will seem to his special sight to be just a stray reflection of the actual living Miss Diamonds."

Crawford tried to imagine talking Christina Rossetti into cooperating in this. "Wouldn't *your* blood work?" he asked. "You're the—what did you say?—the Rosetta stone between the species?"

"Impersonally, at a distance—like the tidal effects of the sun compared to those of the moon. Miss Diamonds is Polidori's immediate redeemer, by her personal blood."

"You think, then," said McKee dubiously, "that this has a chance of actually working?"

Trelawny pursed his scarred lips. "I'd be very surprised if it did. But I wouldn't be . . . *astonished.*" He turned and began striding away from the river, toward the close pillars and the pavement of George Street.

Crawford raised a hand, intending to call him back, then just let his hand fall.

"So much for our ambush idea," he said.

McKee shrugged. "We could do what Trelawny's daughter did. Sail to America. Or France—Trelawny said that might do. The Magdalen Penitentiary might still front me money for passage, if I undertake to work it off as a domestic servant."

"I could buy three tickets," said Crawford, squinting thoughtfully. "To France, at least. And we'd want some money for food and lodging. I might need to convert some things to cash."

"In the meantime," said Johanna glumly, "there's the blood shoes."

"One way or another," said McKee, "we need to talk to Sister Christina again." She started to walk away in the direction Trelawny had taken, but Crawford caught her arm.

"If passage to America should be possible—or to France, I can certainly afford that—for the three of us here, you'd do it?" Suddenly he despised his own circumlocution, and he said directly, "Would you come with me, and leave Tom?" His heart was beating rapidly.

"Yes," said McKee in a level tone, "if that would save Johanna."

Crawford nodded. "Are you married to this Tom fellow?"

McKee raised her chin. "Common law."

"Will you marry me? Properly?"

For several seconds, McKee didn't speak. Crawford could peripherally see Johanna staring intently at them, but he didn't take his gaze from McKee's.

She looked away. "That would probably be necessary, for us to get travel documents with our child."

Johanna exhaled audibly through her teeth.

"What I mean is," persisted Crawford, "do you *want* to marry me?"

McKee looked at him almost angrily. "Do *you* want to marry *me?*"

"Yes," said Crawford. "As I have for seven years." He was still holding her elbow.

She rolled her eyes. "*Yes,* if you've got to have it said straight out. I still think you saw that in my head, then, in that tunnel."

Johanna clapped her hands. "Oh, well done, you two."

Crawford couldn't take a deep breath, and just nodded. He took Johanna's hand in one of his, and McKee's in the other, and started walking back up the pier toward the pillars and the Strand beyond. McKee was looking only straight ahead, but she was holding his hand tightly.

"Where does Johanna sleep?" she asked finally. "At your house."

"It's been Mrs. Middleditch's old room, on the second floor," said Crawford. "You didn't meet her, though, did you? But last night we both wound up in the basement, and I think I'm going to set up two beds down there, for now."

"Could you set up a third bed? Over on Johanna's side of the stove?"

"Easiest thing in the world," said Crawford.

CHAPTER SEVEN

Listen, listen! Everywhere
A low voice is calling me,
And a step is on the stair,
And one comes ye do not see,
Listen, listen! Evermore
A dim hand knocks at the door.

Hear me; he is come again;
My own dearest is come back.
Bring him in from the cold rain . . .

—*Christina Rossetti,*
"Death's Chill Between"

IT WASN'T ONE of Gabriel's raucous dinners, with jokes and impromptu limericks flying back and forth under the two dozen candles in the Flemish brass chandelier—it was just family and Charles Cayley, whom William had invited mainly to discuss the handling of some ambiguous verbs in translating Dante—but Christina had excused herself after the soup and retired to one of the downstairs sitting rooms to lie down on the sofa under the big, ornately framed mirror.

She glanced at the clock on the mantelpiece—ten o'clock, and though Maria would be getting tired, the men would probably go on talking until after midnight.

Of course it would not have occurred to poor William, lost in his merely voyeuristic concerns with literature, that Christina might find it awkward to sit down at dinner with Cayley, whose proposal of marriage she had refused three years ago.

He had been so earnest, that day in the parlor at the Albany Street house, and so disconcerted when she had gently told him that she couldn't marry him!

She had been thirty-five years old then, and Cayley was surely the last suitor she would ever have—and she had always been very fond of him, and he virtually worshipped her. He had even managed to overlook what she knew he thought of as an element of coarseness in her, excusing it as an inevitable result of her charitable work among the prostitutes.

And her diabolical uncle had been, as far as she then knew, laid to permanent rest four years earlier—so there was no reason to fear having children . . . and she would have loved to have children.

Ultimately she had simply not considered it fair to Cayley, to marry him when she—

When she—

Go ahead, she thought now as she looked up at the mirror in Gabriel's sitting room, admit it.

When she loved another.

But she was a good enough Christian to suppress and starve that love, and to pray that the object of it might somehow one day be saved from Hell.

She had convinced herself that she was glad, when they had laid Lizzie's poisoning coffin over him; and she had convinced herself that she was horrified, five days ago, when it became clear that he had evaded the mirrors and risen from that grave.

She closed her eyes now, and tears spilled down her cheeks. Assume an attitude long enough, she told herself, and it will become your real one. But if only I had been permitted by circumstances to have a child! Even a niece or nephew—but her siblings were not likely now to have children either.

But, she thought, a child of my own—!

A soft thump on the Sarabend carpet made her open her eyes, and then she simply stared, disoriented.

This wasn't another vision, for she was still in Gabriel's sitting room—but a little boy was standing only a few feet away from her now, wrapped in one of Gabriel's purple Utrecht velvet curtains.

Then she blinked and looked at him more closely—and sat up, alarmed and guilty, for he had clearly been long neglected—he appeared in fact to be near death from starvation: his wide bright eyes sat deep in the round sockets of his skull, and his mouth and nostrils looked like torn spots in a thin sheet of overstretched leather. In fact, if it hadn't been for the lively attention in his eyes, she would have believed he was dead.

Her face and hands stung with a sensation that wasn't tingling only because it was steady, and she was vaguely aware that her heart was pounding rapidly.

But—this must be the boy Gabriel described, she thought. His undead son, born from Lizzie's dead body in the grave.

She didn't even move, except to tilt her head back, when he sprang nimbly onto the back of the couch and, reaching up with his long gray tree-branch arms, draped the curtain over the corners of the big mirror; his arms seemed to stretch out even thinner, like taffy. Now he was wearing only a breechcloth made from one of Gabriel's towels; his knees were the widest parts of his bone-thin gray legs, and his ribs stood out like ridges in eroded wood. The still air was rank with a smell of clay and loam.

Christina pushed back her suddenly damp hair with both trembling hands and tried to think. Gabriel had described the boy as dead, but perhaps he wasn't, quite.

Then she noticed a flapping cut in the gray skin below his left ribs.

"Let me—" she burst out instinctively, "let me get you to a doctor!"

He looked as if he would have blinked at her, if his eyes were able to close, and she pointed a trembling finger at his side.

"I don't bleed," he said. His voice was a harsh quacking.

Perhaps the wound wasn't as bad as it looked; certainly there was no sign of blood. "Then let me—at least—get you some—" she stammered, "something to eat."

"You can't sustain me now."

"But you—what's your name?"

"I haven't got a name. I told you that when I drew you the pictures."

Her right hand twitched, involuntarily. That's right, she told herself—this is the thing we contacted last night, the thing that had no name and couldn't spell. But he can't be alive at all, if we contacted him at a séance!

Don't make it angry, she thought cautiously as the perspiration beaded at her hairline. It doesn't seem to be intelligent.

"What can I," she began, and then the breath stopped in her throat.

A woman had stepped hesitantly into the room, groping as if blind, and Christina recognized her first by the long auburn hair that tumbled over her pale face and down her shoulders.

Christina sagged on the couch, as unable to move as if this were a nightmare.

"Lizzie," she was able to whisper.

"No," said the woman hoarsely. "Her spirit left this form long ago. And the one I have shared it with is gone now too—she is shrunken and hardened and stopped in a box of mirrors. I'm alone here." Lizzie's body tossed its head, throwing the lank hair back, and her heavy-lidded eyes were fixed on Christina. "I need you, my dear. *Your* mirrors broke *me,* and I'm not reassembled properly. I love you as I always have—give me your blood, and then you can do what is needed to restore me."

"You're," said Christina softly, "you're John, my uncle John, returned to me . . ."

For a moment the form of Lizzie Siddal wavered, and in the instant before it snapped back into focus, Christina glimpsed the remembered man's face, the mustache and the lips and the melancholy eyes.

"All borrowed images," came Lizzie's scratchy voice, "but this woman's image is less effort to maintain, to reflect light in, since my partner wore it so recently." The visible body inhaled deeply, lifting the appearance of Lizzie's bosom under the rotted black cloth of the dress. "Last night you refused me," the voice went on, "but we weren't alone. Do not refuse me now, when I need you so desperately."

Christina glanced at the skeletal gray boy.

"He," came Lizzie's voice, and her face was actually smiling, "does not compromise 'alone.'"

Algernon invited these two into this house, Christina thought. They have power here. Still, John doesn't seem willing to simply force me.

"What," she said carefully, "is needed to restore you?"

"Something like cross-pollenization," said Polidori through the appearance of Lizzie's mouth. "Something like sexual recombining of strengths."

Christina's heart was hammering in her chest, and she couldn't speak.

"I need you to get the stone figure that is my physical self," Lizzie's voice went on, "and rub on it the blood of one of my partner's subjects."

"Your partner?" said Christina. My blood was good enough once, she thought, and then she smothered the thought. "That's . . . Boadicea?"

"Yes, to the extent that I am Polidori. She is *not me,* and the blood of a subject of hers, charged with her essence, will convey her different-ness to me. It will fill these present fissures in me with her unrelated vitality. I will be healed."

"And soonly," grated the nameless gray boy.

"Soonly," agreed the Lizzie figure, swaying with evident weariness. "Blood is made in bones, and every particle of it only lives a hundred days before it dies. My partner is in no position to renew any of it now, and she was stopped five days ago, and the blood of her subjects was not newly imprinted with her essence even then."

He's talking as if it's already agreed that I'll let him have me now, Christina thought. Can I leap up and run out of here? To where?

No, she thought as her heart pounded and her breath came rapid and shallow, I'm not certain I can even get to my feet, and he or the boy would catch me in any case. There's nothing I can do, nothing I can do.

She heard steps in the hall, and the bony gray boy darted to the far side of the couch and huddled himself below the arm of it.

"Whoever comes," said the Lizzie apparition, "make them go, or we will kill them."

Who is it? thought Christina. Whoever it is is only delaying the inevitable.

And it was Charles Cayley who shambled awkwardly into the room, some book in his hands, his bald head gleaming in the light of the one gas jet over the mirror.

"Oh!" he said, blinking at Christina on the couch and the figure of Lizzie standing on the rug. "I don't mean to intrude. I was just . . ."

Christina stared at him, wondering if she dared wait out another of his interminable pauses. After several seconds, she said, "If you'll excuse us, Charles, we're having a confidential discussion."

"Ah!" he said, bobbing his head and waving the book he carried. His face was red. "Certainly, excuse me, I—"

"I'll say good-bye before we leave," Christina interjected.

Still bobbing his head and mumbling polite inanities, Cayley turned and shambled out of the room. Christina recalled Gabriel's judgment of him: *The man's an idiot.*

The hideous gray skull face of the boy—Gabriel's undead son— poked up from behind the arm of the couch.

"Soonly," he said again in his flat voice.

"You love me still," said the Lizzie thing, clearly smiling now, and for a few moments the figure was once more John Polidori, as darkly handsome as he had been in 1845, when she had been fourteen.

"That," quavered Christina, "doesn't settle the issue." She made the sign of the cross, and the figure reverted to the appearance of Lizzie Siddal, who glanced at the gray boy for a moment before returning its attention to Christina.

"You sinned with me once," it said. "God will not forgive that—give yourself to me, and never die, evade His judgment."

"I think," whispered Christina, though she was far from sure of it, "He will."

"But I'm dying, your mirrors have broken me—will you condemn me to everlasting Hell, when you could heal me?" For a moment the face was Polidori's again, and the eyes glittered with tears.

No, John, she thought, never!

But she found that she simply could not say it; instead, though it felt like a treacherous lie and it turned her stomach to say it, she answered, "He will forgive you too, whatever you are."

"I can simply take you," came its voice, sounding more crystalline than organic now.

The boy behind the couch shifted his feet, staring at her with his wide eyes.

"Possibly you can," Christina whispered.

The figure of Lizzie glided toward the couch as Christina stared breathlessly up into its alien eyes—she seemed to be tilting forward, falling—

And then she grimaced involuntarily at a sudden, powerful reek of crushed garlic.

The face of Lizzie Siddal was just an array of curved planes and two glittering spots as it turned to Christina's left.

Christina looked in that direction and saw Charles Cayley standing again in the doorway; his hands were trembling, but were now gleaming wet and bristling with yellow shreds.

The gray boy scampered to the river-side window—Cayley jumped in huge astonishment at his sudden appearance but held his ground—and the long gray fingers unlatched it, and when the boy had pushed it open, he and the Lizzie figure broke up into pieces like images viewed through a rotating kaleidoscope, and the pieces turned black and spun churning out through the open window.

Christina exhaled and found that she was sobbing silently.

Cayley stepped to the window and with shaking hands pulled it closed and latched it again.

"Charles," Christina was able to say gaspingly, "I believe—you just saved my soul. I—should be grateful." She took a deep breath, and then said, "How did you know to get garlic?"

Cayley blinked at her in evident bewilderment. "Well, she's dead, isn't she? I was at her funeral, you recall." He smiled hesitantly, though his face was even paler than usual. "I couldn't see you in peril and not try to save you."

She almost said, *I should have married you, Charles.* But with her uncle John up again, she didn't dare love anyone.

And, she thought, the original obstacle, God help me, probably *still* applies.

Gabriel's harsh voice broke the moment: "What was Algy doing in the hall?" he asked, then frowned at Cayley's hands. "What on earth—" He sniffed. "Is that garlic?" He glanced quickly at the closed window, and then at his sister. "What's been going on here?"

"Lizzie," she answered weakly, rubbing her eyes. "And that boy. Charles knew how to chase them away."

"Really!" Gabriel looked at Cayley more closely. "That was good, Charles. I—that was good, thank you."

Cayley began stammering out some reply, and Christina interrupted, "I think you could wash your hands now, Charles."

Cayley nodded and hurried out of the room.

"Algy was in the hall?" said Christina. "I didn't know." She stretched and thought she could stand up now.

"Eavesdropping. William and Maria are ready to go home." Gabriel seemed distracted. "Was anything important said here?"

Christina laughed weakly. "Oh, you know, just social pleasantries! Yes, some things were said. He wants—"

"Who, that boy?"

"No, it was Uncle John, in Lizzie's form."

She told him what Polidori had said about rubbing on his little statue the blood of one of Boadicea's victims. "He didn't know that you plan—we plan—to do exactly what he wants—at least to the extent of digging up the statue."

Gabriel shuddered visibly. "We won't do what he wants—no blood at all must get on the thing. Did Swinburne hear any of this? But you didn't know he was there."

He was snapping his fingers nervously. "It's tomorrow night that Lizzie is to be exhumed. Charles Howell has arranged it with the Black-friars Funeral Company. I'm supposed to wait at Howell's house in Ful-ham while the exhumation goes on—Howell is to retrieve the poetry notebook and bring it to me there. But I've arranged with the funeral company to attend as a third gravedigger, hanging back as if to mind the carriage, and after Charles has left with the poetry notebook, I'll bribe the other two to step away while I attend to Papa's coffin. I'll have a hammer and chisel—it shouldn't take long."

"And a knife," said Christina. For Papa's throat, she thought.

"Er, yes. And then—I think we ought to destroy the statue as soon as possible . . . ?"

Christina stood up, staring at the window. "I suppose so." Then she shook herself and caught Gabriel's arm. "*Yes*," she said, "the moment you've got hold of it."

CHAPTER EIGHT

It is that then we have her with us here,
As when she wrung her hair out in my dream
To-night, till all the darkness reeked of it.
Her hair is always wet, for she has kept
Its tresses wrapped about her side for years . . .

—*Dante Gabriel Rossetti, "A Last Confession"*

I USED TO HATE sunlight," remarked Johanna as she and Crawford and McKee hurried across Tottenham Court Road at the junction of Oxford Street on Thursday, dodging the horses pulling cabs and carriages. Now she had taken off her bonnet and shaken back her hair to let the afternoon sun shine on her face. "Now it's like strong beer."

Crawford gave McKee a worried glance. Johanna had had a glass of Mieux stout with her steak-and-ale pie, and he was hoping she wasn't fated to be a drunkard—especially since they had decided to flee to France. Crawford had the idea that the French drank wine all day long.

Yesterday he had approached another London veterinary surgeon to negotiate selling his practice to the man, and they had agreed on a deal that involved the man taking over Crawford's office and caring for the cats, and this morning Crawford had gone to Barclay's Bank to arrange for a draft of all his savings and operating capital to be transferable to a bank in Paris.

Last night the three of them had slept in the basement, in shifts, with mirrors, silver, garlic, and iron knives ready to hand, and he was anxious to get to Newhaven, where British tourists commonly took a boat across the English Channel to Dieppe.

But this errand was important.

"A church, around here?" he asked now as they stepped up the curb in front of a long five-story building that narrowed Tottenham Court Road. He wasn't aware of any church very close by here—the only vaguely communal institution he knew of locally was the Oxford Music Hall under the big clock that projected out over the pavement traffic ahead.

But McKee turned to the right before they got that far, into the narrow lane that was Bozier's Court, known as Boozer's Alley because of the public house on the corner.

"Yes," McKee said, sounding defensive, "a church. Both of you behave yourselves now, we need a big favor from the priest."

Crawford and Johanna exchanged a mystified look but followed McKee. In the narrow court the rattle and clop of the traffic behind them was muted, and their own footsteps echoed back at them from the close brick walls.

McKee led them to a pair of tall wooden doors under a pointed arch in the tall street-side building, and before pulling one of them open, she dug a couple of lacy handkerchiefs out of her handbag and tied one over her head and gave the other to Johanna.

"And you take off your hat," she told Crawford.

When they had stepped into the cool dimness and pulled the door closed behind them, Crawford could at first see only the high mottled-gray disk of a stained-glass window in the far wall of the narrow, high-ceilinged room; then after a few moments he saw ranks of glass-dimmed candle flames, and finally he was able to make out rows of pews and an altar at the far end. The cool air carried the scents of old wood and incense. A few huddled figures sat in the pews, and a tall man in a robe was striding down the side aisle on the right.

"Confessions?" the man said in a quiet but carrying voice. "Thursdays aren't generally—why it's Adelaide!" The priest was close enough now for Crawford to see the man's thin, deeply lined face. "I'm sorry— you just looked like a particularly sinful trio."

Johanna nodded solemnly. "*Are* we here for Confession?" she asked McKee.

"No," said McKee. "We need a pretty substantial favor." She pointed at Crawford and herself. "He and I want to get married. Uh, Father Cyprian, this is John Crawford, and this is our daughter, Johanna."

The priest nodded sympathetically. "One does tend to keep putting these things off, doesn't one? But that's not so substantial—we do weddings with some frequency here."

"But we want to be married soon—tomorrow or Saturday. There's no time for banns to be posted."

Father Cyprian raised his eyebrows. "Why the haste?" He glanced at Johanna, as if to note that the child was already, long since, born out of wedlock.

Then he crouched beside her. "Who's been pounding on you, child? Not one of these two, I hope?"

"It happened in a dream," Johanna told him.

"Oh?" The priest stood up and turned to McKee. "Why the haste?" he asked again.

"We may," McKee began, then paused and looked up at the beams in the ceiling. "We may all three of us be dead soon, or worse, and—"

"*And* we love each other," said Crawford sturdily, "and we want our daughter to have my name."

The priest nodded. "Let's start with 'or worse,'" he said. "What's worse?"

"Do you remember," McKee asked him, "why I originally came to *this* church, after I got out of the Magdalen Penitentiary?"

Father Cyprian frowned. "Sister Christina sent you, as I recall, yes. Yes." He squinted at the old tiles of the floor. "There's apparently been some turbulence among the local devils just in this last week—one up, the other down. Your troubles have something to do with that?"

"The newly up one has particular designs on Johanna here," said McKee.

Johanna nodded and touched her throat. "I used to be one of his. Not all the way to death and resurrection, but . . . *his.*"

"And he wants her back," said McKee. "Her more than the others, it seems. We plan to cross the Channel to France in the next couple of days, and travel and lodging and financial arrangements will apparently be easier if we can show that we're legally married."

"It'd be nice to have the lines," said Johanna, using the coster term for a marriage certificate.

Father Cyprian nodded thoughtfully, then looked up at McKee. "John here says he loves you. Do you love him?"

"I—wouldn't marry just for expediency."

"But," said the priest, "travel plans and legal protocols are what you advanced as your reasons."

Johanna and Crawford were both looking at McKee.

"Yes, I love him," she said, exhaling. "I have for seven years."

"For seven years?" said the priest. "Unfair to that spoons man, in that case, even on a common-law basis . . . with no 'lines.' Terry?"

"Tom. Yes, I suppose it was." McKee leaned against one of the pews and rubbed her forehead. "I should apologize to him, before we go."

"I wouldn't," said Father Cyprian. "He's been in here once or twice, looking for you." This visibly surprised and dismayed McKee. The priest went on, "I would let sleeping mad dogs lie. And I trust," he added, looking Crawford up and down, "that you've chosen a different sort of man this time."

"She has, she has," said Johanna.

Crawford didn't look at her but squeezed her hand.

The priest turned toward the pews that filed away toward the altar. "Christabel!" he called softly.

An old woman halfway up the aisle looked around, then laboriously got to her feet when the priest beckoned and began shuffling toward the back of the church.

"Tomorrow," said the priest quietly to McKee.

When old Christabel had made her way back to where they stood, Father Cyprian asked her, "Christabel, did you hear it these last three Sundays when I announced the banns for John Crawford and Adelaide McKee?"

"Of course I did," the old woman wheezed. "I hear everything you say."

"Do you recall the names?"

"A Crawford, it was, and our dear Adelaide." She touched McKee's shoulder. "Haven't seen you here this past week or two, my dear. You've not been ill, I trust?"

"No," said McKee, smiling. "Just . . . distracted."

"And is this Mr. Crawford?" Getting a nod, the old woman said to him, "Be good to our girl, Mr. Crawford. It's time somebody did."

"I will," said Crawford hoarsely.

Christabel nodded and turned around and began shambling back toward her pew.

Father Cyprian looked after her. "Sister Christina has sent us a lot of parishioners," he said. Then, to McKee, "Ten in the morning? Not a lot of people in here on a Friday at that hour. Bring fourteen shillings— two are for the banns, I'm afraid, but the receipt is necessary for the certificate."

McKee smiled. "I'll send out invitations at once."

"And I," the priest said, "have to make some corrections in the banns list."

He shook Crawford's hand and then strode away back toward the altar and the door to the sacristy, and McKee led Crawford and Johanna back out into Bozier's Court.

THAT NIGHT AN ODDLY warm October breeze shook the bare branches of the oaks and elms in Highgate Cemetery. The fire the gravediggers had kindled next to the grave made a spot of glaring orange light in the moonlit landscape of headstones and waving groves. Far overhead, ragged clouds surged across the spotted face of the moon.

Gabriel had been leaning against a tomb thirty feet away, where he could watch the gravediggers plunge and lever their spades in the loam while the cloaked figure of Charles Howell stood by the fire and stared into the deepening hole; but when one of the men eventually climbed out of the grave and fetched a couple of ropes, Gabriel stepped closer, and when the two gravediggers had hauled the dirt-caked coffin up out of the hole and swung it heavily onto the firelit grass, he edged around behind a thickly vine-hung elm to view the proceedings more closely.

He was viewing the coffin from the foot now, from a distance of only a couple of yards, and so when the men pried up the lid and laid it aside, he found himself looking directly at Lizzie's face by the fire's illumination.

Howell and the gravediggers were momentarily motionless, staring into the coffin, and Gabriel stepped hesitantly forward, out of the shadows, and peered.

Lizzie's face was pale but apparently undecayed, framed in masses of red hair that gleamed in the firelight—much more hair than when he had closed the coffin in the Chatham Place flat seven years ago!

Belatedly it occurred to him that the mirror-veil Maria had made was no longer over Lizzie's face.

Gabriel could see the poetry notebook. He had laid it in on top of her hands at her funeral, but Lizzie's smooth white fingers were curled around the edges of it now, and—he blinked rapidly and stared—her fingernails seemed to have grown too, in the grave, and now indented or even pierced the binding.

Lizzie's body was fresh and undecayed, but the notebook was now stained and warped.

Gabriel choked and blinked back tears, glad that her eyes were closed. He retreated back into the shadows behind the elm tree. The warm wind in the trees seemed to be full of whispering voices.

His view was blocked then as Howell at last leaned in and worked with both hands; Gabriel heard popping and scratching, and whispered curses from Howell, and then the man had straightened up, panting, holding Gabriel's ragged notebook. Howell curtly said something to the gravediggers, dug some banknotes out of his waistcoat pocket— the twenty-two pounds with which Gabriel had provided him—and handed it to them and then strode away quickly through the sparse red-lit grass toward the lane and the stairs. Gabriel stepped back as he passed, deeper into the shadows.

The two gravediggers were refastening the lid onto Lizzie's coffin when Gabriel heard Howell's carriage snap and clatter into motion, and he stepped forward into the firelight.

One of the gravediggers looked up at him from under a battered tweed cap. "You weren't along to help, I reckon."

"No," Gabriel agreed. "I came along to pay you to take a rest now, down in your carriage." He dug six gold sovereigns from the pocket of his Inverness cape and gave three to each man. "I'll call you when the rest period is finished."

The men blinked in surprise, and then one of them said, "Take your time, guv'nor!" and they ambled away across the grass toward the stairs.

Gabriel waited until he heard their steps on the gravel lane below the stairs, then crossed to the open grave and stared down into it as he pulled on a pair of gloves.

In the deep shadows he could see a few patches of wood showing under the scuffed dirt, and he sighed and sat down on the edge with his feet swinging in the hole.

I can drop down, he thought, and avoid putting my feet through Papa's coffin, but can I get out again? Will I have to call those two back to help me?

Oh well, I've paid them enough to provide that service too.

He pushed off and landed with a thump, his boots straddling the long mound that was his father's coffin. Quickly he reversed his feet and then crouched, tugging the hammer and chisel from his belt.

He set the chisel blade crossways to the grain of the wood and swung the hammer. There was enough dirt still on the coffin to mask the shape of it, and he hoped he was not about to see his father's feet.

The clang of steel on steel seemed awfully loud, but he supposed the noise was muffled somewhat by the walls of dirt; and after a dozen blows he was able to drop the tools and reach down to pull up a splintered section of still-glossy oak. He wrinkled his nose at a smell like toasted cheese made with a very old, metallic-tasting blue cheese.

He tore the section of wood away, and then by the reflected light of the fire on the grass above he was staring down at his father's collapsed and withered face, black as coal.

His only emotion was intense anxiety to get this over with, and he supposed that he would feel guilt and horror later, at his leisure.

Gabriel pulled the penknife out of his pocket and opened the long blade, but when he pushed his father's cold chin back, the whole neck simply broke, like a roll of frail glass sheets. He brushed thin black shards off his gloves. His hands were visibly shaking now.

He tapped the base of his father's throat with the back end of the knife, and it clinked, steel on black glass.

Whispering shrilly and not even listening to what he was saying, prayers or curses or the multiplication table, he put the knife away and picked up the hammer again—and then he rapped his father's throat smartly with the head of it.

The glassy flesh shattered inward in a thousand pieces, and he picked among them, tossing them aside—and, deeper than he would have thought, he felt the rounded head of the little statue; he gripped it and pulled, and with a creaking and snapping and a shower of glassy throat fragments, the thing was free, and he was holding the little statue he had last seen on the high shelf in his father's bedroom, back in the old house on Charlotte Street.

And there was a faint pressure in his mind, a flavor of greeting and promise.

Suddenly he was moving with feverish haste—he shoved the statue into his pocket and wedged the broken piece of wood back over the hole in the coffin and his father's now crookedly uptilted face, and then he had gripped the grassy edge of the hole and pulled himself up and swung a leg up onto the surface, and a moment later he was lying on his back on the grass, panting so hard that he was blowing spit onto his goatee.

He rolled up onto his hands and knees. The gravediggers had taken their spades away with them, so with his hands he shoved piles of dirt down into the hole until he supposed any evidence of tampering must be concealed—he wasn't going to actually look, for he could imagine the broken piece of wood knocked aside now and his father's black face peering blindly up at him—and he got wearily to his feet.

All at once immensely tired and longing for his distant bed, he trudged to the lane and the steps down to the yard, where the gravediggers straightened up and knocked the coals out of their clay pipes and began trudging back up the steps with their shovels.

Now I've got to get to Howell's house, Gabriel thought as he hurried to the rented Victoria carriage he had left tied up on the far side of the chapel, and convince him that I've been there all along—and if he's there ahead of me, as is likely, I'll claim I had to take a ride in the fresh air.

But I've violated my wife's grave, and my father's, and probably broken my dead father's head right off. It will, he thought as he anticipated the self-loathing sure to come soon, take a powerful lot of fresh air to put some distance between me and the memory of this.

CHAPTER NINE

I heard the blood between her fingers hiss;
So that I sat up in my bed and screamed
Once and again; and once to once, she laughed.
Look that you turn not now,—she's at your back . . .

—*Dante Gabriel Rossetti, "A Last Confession"*

O H! I COULD *never* have done that," said Christina with a breathless laugh. "But luckily there's no need now."

She leaned back in the forward seat of the hackney coach and smiled
warmly at Crawford and Johanna and McKee, who were sitting on the
opposite seat. Smells of cologne and damp wool filled the coach.

The traffic was not too badly congested on this rainy Friday morning, and the coach was rattling at a steady pace across the puddled intersection that was Oxford Circus, and Crawford, seated between Johanna
and the right-side window, could see through the veils of rain down
Regent Street past Jay's Mourning Warehouse to the round, pillared
façade of the Argyll Rooms.

Oxford Circus still looked more or less the way John Nash had designed it in the '20s, and, what with Christina's unexpected good news, Crawford let himself indulge in a reassuring sense of continuity.

We don't have to go to France after all, he thought; I don't have to sell my practice. Adelaide and Johanna and I *will* still be here a year from now. Ten years from now. Not eating frogs in France somewhere, thank God. Perhaps one day we'll be going this way to attend Johanna's wedding, and these awnings and rooftop windows and ranks of chimney pots will mostly still be here.

"Gabriel woke William last night and told him that he had found it," Christina went on, "and by now I'm sure he has destroyed it."

McKee smiled at her with her eyes nearly closed. "I got the impression he sleeps late."

"Well," allowed Christina, "soon he will have destroyed it, if he didn't last night. He has all manner of hammers at his house, and he's only two steps from the river. In any case, we don't have to think about using my *blood* to make a pair of magical *shoes!*"

Crawford thought sourly that she might, now that it was apparently unnecessary, at least pretend that she would have gone to the trouble, if called on. *She* should *do it*, Trelawny had said two days ago; *she's got amends to make, like us all.*

"I need to know that he's done it," said Johanna quietly. "And how he destroyed it."

Christina sobered. "Of course, child—I'll inform you all directly I know it's done. He intends to pound it to powder and sift it widely into the river; it's my uncle's physical body, so that should certainly . . . unmake him."

She seemed distracted then, and Crawford had to repeat his next question: "What's become of the other one, the one Trelawny travels with?" The priest had said, *one up, the other down.*

"I believe she's gone too, now," said Christina. "My uncle appeared to me two nights ago, and he said that she was—how did he put it— 'shrunken and hardened and stopped in a box of mirrors.' The way *he* was, for seven years, apparently." She shook her head. "Queen Boadicea of the Iceni, shrunk to a pebble and locked in a box! I think it must have been Trelawny who managed to do it at last—Maria and I told him long ago how we stifled our uncle."

The coach had passed the Oxford Music Hall—Crawford noted that the time on the clock was ten minutes to ten—and now swerved in to stop in front of the pub at the corner of Bozier's Court.

Crawford levered open the coach door and stepped down to the pavement while opening an umbrella, and Johanna, in a new cambric dress and pink velveteen coat, hopped out right behind him; he reached a gloved hand up to help McKee down, and she too was wearing a new dress: blue silk with a hip-length cape. He remembered the enormous crinoline dress she had been wearing on the night they first met, and he was glad such things were apparently no longer in style—he would probably have had to hire a second coach.

Under a woolen overcoat he was wearing the formal frock coat he had bought seven years ago to replace the one he had lost in Highgate Cemetery. All three of them would have preferred to wear more ordinary clothing—McKee had said this church favored informality—but Christina Rossetti had insisted on buying the new clothes for McKee and Johanna.

Christina herself was clad in a woolen coat and plain brown muslin dress, as resolutely unfashionable as ever. Crawford took her hand as she carefully lowered one foot and then the other onto the wet pavement.

Once inside the church, they shed their damp hats and boots and overcoats in the vestibule and shuffled forward down the center aisle toward where Father Cyprian stood below the altar in the gray light from the stained-glass window above and behind him.

The only other person in the church on this rainy morning was old Christabel, who nodded and smiled when Crawford glanced at her. He waved uncertainly.

"The certificate is made out and the parish marriage-record book is ready to be signed," said the priest, "so there's no use delaying." To Crawford he said, "Do you have a ring?"

"Yes." In his waistcoat pocket he had brought along his mother's wedding ring; he hoped it would fit McKee.

"Let's—" began the priest, but he was interrupted by the squeak of the front door.

Crawford looked back and was somehow not very surprised to see the lean, white-bearded figure of Edward Trelawny in the doorway. The old man glanced around the dim interior and had begun to step back outside when he visibly recognized the people in the aisle.

He grinned and came in, pulling the door closed behind him, and when he had walked up to stand between Crawford and McKee he said, "Any of you know why a dead boy with a parasol should be anxious to get in here? I followed him up from Seven Dials."

Johanna jumped, her eyes suddenly wide, and she exclaimed to Christina, "What if killing your uncle doesn't kill the dead boy?"

"Clearly Gabriel hasn't done it yet," said Christina, though she was frowning.

"Ah!" said Trelawny. "This would be the phantasm who intends to marry you?"

Father Cyprian's eyebrows were halfway up to his hairline.

Johanna was very pale, and Crawford took a firm hold of her upper arm.

"Where is he now?" she asked.

"I showed him a pistol and he climbed away fast like a monkey up the side of this building. His arms stretch like gray rubber, don't they?"

Christina's lips were sucked in and her eyes were almost as wide as Johanna's, but she nodded jerkily. "Yes," she whispered, "they do."

"You all here for last rites?" asked Trelawny.

"A wedding," said Christina in a reproving tone.

"I'm marrying Medicus," said McKee.

"You could do worse, I suppose." He looked around the nearly empty church. "Who's to give away the bride?"

"Nobody," said McKee. "Ghosts."

"I'd be happy to do it."

Crawford and McKee both stared at the dark-faced, white-bearded old man with his permanently sneering scarred lips, and then they looked at each other.

"I suppose I have no substantial objection," said Crawford.

"I'd be pleased, thank you," said McKee.

"And," said Father Cyprian, "if any *dead boy* should try to interfere in the ceremony, you can show him your pistol again."

"I do that once," said Trelawny cheerfully. "Next time I blow his grinning head off."

"Don't miss," said Johanna.

"Miss!" said Trelawny, almost spitting. "Girl, I—"

"Dearly beloved!" interrupted the priest loudly; and then he went on in a conversational tone, "we are gathered together here in the sight of God, and"—with a wave toward Christabel—"in the face of this congregation, to join together this man and this woman in holy matrimony."

Crawford stood up straighter and smoothed his damp hair and beard.

ALGERNON SWINBURNE HAD SEARCHED the whole of Tudor House, as well as he could—he had looked inside all the lacquered Japanese and Indian brass boxes that seemed to occupy every shelf, and peered behind all the stacked canvases, and stirred the salt and sugar jars with a knife. He had gone through every item in the drawers of the Elizabethan Spanish oak armoire in which Gabriel had once, as a joke, hidden a prized Nankin dish of Howell's. But the statue the Rossetti siblings had talked about was not to be found. He wondered fretfully how big it might be—not too big to clog an old man's throat, according to their story.

Gabriel must have it in his bedroom.

Swinburne glanced nervously toward the stairs. Gabriel suffered from insomnia, but in the mornings he did seem to be newly awake—blinking, distracted, grumpy. Perhaps he did all his actual sleeping in the few hours just before he got up, which was generally about noon.

I've got to risk it, Swinburne thought as he started up the stairs. If he awakens while I'm in his room, I'll think of some excuse for being there.

It had been a full week since horrible old Trelawny had knocked Swinburne unconscious after their hasty sword fight, and Swinburne had had no contact with Miss B. since then. He was sure the ghastly old man had succeeded in capturing her in his mirrored box—and so Swinburne needed a new patron. For these last seven days, no verses at all had sprung into his mind, and it was like being color-blind, or . . . or insomniac. And there were physical effects too—during these last several days, his forehead seemed always to be damp with sweat, and his vision seemed blurred, and his hands shook no matter how much brandy he drank.

At the top of the stairs he took off his shoes and tiptoed in his stocking feet to Gabriel's bedroom door, where he very slowly turned the knob; he lifted the door against the hinges as he swung it open.

The air was stuffy and stale. The windows that overlooked the back garden were heavily curtained, and the only light was a gray radiance through a closed window in the opposite wall. Swinburne could make out the vast mantelpiece, with its ivory-and-ebony crucifix, facing the mirror on a chest of drawers on the other side of the room and, between them on the broad figured carpet, the enormous old four-post bedstead.

Gabriel's balding head could be dimly seen above the blankets, and he was breathing audibly enough for Swinburne to be confident that he was in fact asleep. Swinburne stole forward silently, peering about for Gabriel's trousers or cloak so that he could rifle the pockets.

FATHER CYPRIAN LOOKED UP from his Book of Common Prayer and said, in a stern voice that echoed among the beams of the high ceiling, "I require and charge you both, as ye will answer at the dreadful day of judgment when the secrets of all hearts shall be disclosed, that if either of you know any impediment, why ye may not be lawfully joined together in matrimony, ye do now confess it."

Crawford couldn't remember if his wedding to Veronica twenty-five years ago had included this order; possibly Father Cyprian had added it specially after having dispensed with the three-week announcement of the banns.

Crawford hoped Trelawny wouldn't do anything irresponsible; but the old man made no sound.

After what Crawford thought was a rudely prolonged pause, the priest went on, "John, wilt thou have this woman to thy wedded wife, to live together after God's ordinance in the holy estate of matrimony? Wilt thou love her, comfort her, honor, and keep her in sickness and in health; and, forsaking all others, keep thee only unto her, so long as ye both shall live?"

"I will," said Crawford strongly.

The priest turned to McKee. "Adelaide, wilt thou have this man to thy wedded husband, to live together after God's ordinance in the holy estate of matrimony? Wilt thou obey him, and serve him, love, honor, and keep him in sickness and in health; and, forsaking all others, keep thee only unto him, so long as ye both shall live?"

Crawford was reassured to hear happy firmness in McKee's voice when she answered, "I will."

The priest smiled. "And," he went on, "who giveth this woman to be married to this man?"

Peripherally, Crawford saw Trelawny take McKee's arm and step forward.

"Take her from the hand of an unrepentant sinner," Trelawny whispered to Crawford.

The priest cocked an eyebrow at the old man, and Crawford restrained himself from rolling his eyes. Shut *up*, he thought intensely.

It occurred to him that Trelawny's statement was just reflexive bravado at finding himself on this rainy morning participating in a ritual in a Christian church; but he had mentioned sending his daughter and grandchildren to America, and seven years ago, in the cassowary cage at the London Zoo, he had said, *I've been* making amends *for things I did in Greece, in Euboea and on Mount Parnassus, forty years ago.*

And he baptized all the Mud Larks.

I don't believe, thought Crawford, that you're as unrepentant as you'd like us all to suppose, old man.

SWINBURNE FINALLY SAW GABRIEL'S trousers crumpled in the shadows by the foot of the bed—but as he began to crouch and reach for them, he saw the glass of water on the bedside table.

Something like a short black cigar was sunk in it.

He straightened very slowly, willing his knees not to pop, and took another long step forward and reached out with two fingers. The water was cold and faintly caustic, but he pinched the top of the thing—it did appear to be made of stone—and lifted it out of the glass.

And immediately he knew he had found the described statue, for he felt an alien eagerness and desperation in his mind.

Drops of water fell from it back into the glass with a sound like lightly plucked violin strings, and Swinburne closed his fist around the thing.

As carefully as he had made his way into the room, Swinburne began retracing his steps across the carpet. Now that he had hold of the thing, he was sweating with fear that Gabriel might awaken and take it away from him; but he was able to slide out through the doorway silently, and he turned and hurried down the stairs.

⋆⟡⊙⟡⋆

CRAWFORD TOOK HIS MOTHER'S ring out of his waistcoat pocket and slid it onto the fourth finger of McKee's left hand, and then, prompted by the priest, he said, "With this ring I thee wed, and with all my worldly goods I thee endow: in the name of the Father, and of the Son, and of the Holy Ghost. Amen."

Trelawny yawned audibly, but when Crawford glanced at him, the old man looked away, as if interested in the framed stations of the cross paintings mounted high on the wall.

The priest was intoning some long prayer involving Isaac and Rebecca now, but Crawford was remembering Christina Rossetti saying that Trelawny had apparently "stopped in a box of mirrors" the woman he had met by moonlight in the Roman ruins of Watling Street years ago, and whom he had traveled with ever since.

Were the words of the wedding affecting him? Perhaps the love of those creatures for their victims, Crawford thought, is not always entirely unrequited.

The priest finished the prayer with "through Jesus Christ our Lord," and Crawford said "Amen" along with McKee and the priest and Christina in a pew behind them.

Father Cyprian now took Crawford's right hand and put McKee's right hand into it; she laced her warm fingers through his.

"Those whom God hath joined together," said Father Cyprian, "let no man put asunder. Forasmuch as John and Adelaide have consented together in holy wedlock, and have witnessed the same before God and this company, and thereto have given and pledged their troth, each to the other, and have declared the same by giving and receiving a ring, and by joining of hands; I pronounce that they be man and wife together, in the name of the Father, and of the Son, and of the Holy Ghost. Amen."

Crawford, McKee, Johanna, and Christina all echoed, "Amen."

"That's it," said Father Cyprian, closing his book with a snap. "Since this is a somewhat rushed ceremony, I put the parish record book and the marriage certificate in the first pew."

Crawford and McKee both signed the book, and Trelawny and Christina signed as witnesses, and when Crawford tucked the folded certificate into his waistcoat pocket, he remembered to give the priest fourteen shillings.

"Thank you," said Father Cyprian, smiling crookedly. "Bless yourselves with holy water on the way out," he advised, stepping back. "It might discourage your dead boy."

Trelawny snorted. "I'll bless *him,* with a silver bullet." He turned to the others. "Where do you go from here?"

"Well," said Christina a bit stiffly, "*I'm* going to go to my brother's house, to make sure the statue is destroyed. Thank you, uh, Reverend!" she added, speaking past him.

The four of them had begun walking down the aisle toward the doors, but Trelawny stopped and caught Christina's shoulder. "You people *got* it? The Polidori?"

"Yes," said Christina, frowning as she glanced at his hand. "My brother retrieved it last night. And—"

"And you want to *make sure* it's destroyed? It might not be?"

"Well, he . . . as Adelaide noted, my brother does sleep late . . ."

Trelawny started for the doors again, moving faster now but still clutching Christina's shoulder.

"Where is it?" he barked as they stepped into the puddled vestibule. "Now?"

Everyone except Trelawny was snatching up coats and hats and umbrellas.

"At—at my brother's house. Really, Mr. Trelawny, I must ask you to—"

Trelawny pushed one of the doors open and pulled Christina out into the cold alley air, with Crawford and McKee and Johanna following, tugging at hats and coat sleeves.

"Are there other people at that house?"

Stray drops of rain were finding their way down between the close-set buildings, and Christina blinked and tried to open her umbrella. "My brother William slept there last night—and Algernon Swinburne may be there, he often is—"

"Swinburne!" The name was an obscenity when Trelawny spat it out. "Does *he* know about this, about the statue?" Trelawny was marching them up the cobbles of Bozier's Court toward the gray daylight of Oxford Street.

"No, I—" Christina hesitated. "Yes, I think he may. He was eavesdropping—"

"We're all going to that house right now," Trelawny pronounced, stepping right out into the street with Christina stumbling along beside him. She still hadn't got her umbrella open, and the rain was coming down harder than before.

Trelawny flagged a passing clarence cab by practically blocking its way, and though the driver was making some protest about being engaged to pick up some other party, Trelawny released Christina to hop up beside the man and give him some money and say something to him, and the driver grimaced unhappily but nodded.

Trelawny glanced down, his eyes blazing above his white beard. "Where is your brother's house?"

"16 Ch-Cheyne Walk, in Chelsea!"

Trelawny relayed the address to the driver, then sprang down to the pavement, yelling, "In, in!"

Johanna was the first one to scramble into the cab, and she seemed to share Trelawny's sense of urgency—she reached out to grab her father's hand and tug on it until he was sitting beside her. Trelawny was the last to step up into the cab, pushing McKee and Christina ahead of him.

The cab surged ahead as he pulled the door closed and sat down next to Crawford. Already the interior of the cab was steamy, and Trelawny smelled of cigar smoke.

"Swinburne!" Trelawny exclaimed again. "He *needs* it, needs your damned uncle—he's been without a vampire patron for a week."

"Swinburne?" exclaimed Christina. "He's one of—the victim of one of these—"

"You've read his poetry," said Trelawny bitterly.

"I should have known," she whispered.

"Assuredly you should have, if in fact you didn't."

Christina was apparently too distracted to take offense. "He was one of . . . Boadicea's?"

"Of course. And I caught her just as you said, shortly before dawn last Saturday, poor old girl."

"He wants," said Christina, trying now to collapse her partly opened umbrella, "my uncle wants someone to rub the blood of one of Boadicea's victims onto his statue. Our mirror trick, though it didn't keep him down forever, did evidently damage him—and now he needs blood vivified by another of his kind—I—didn't catch why."

"She infects the victim with her blueprint," said Trelawny with a shrug. "I suppose the victim's blood could impose her blueprint on your uncle's fractured self—let him re-knit, like a shattered bone, according to its directions."

Johanna leaned out from beside Crawford. "I'll kill myself," she remarked, "before I'll let him have me again."

"You shame me," Christina said to her softly.

For several seconds no one spoke, as the cab rattled down Charing Cross Road toward the Strand.

"Congratulations, incidentally," said Trelawny to Crawford, reaching over to shake his hand.

"For what?" asked Crawford absently, shaking the old man's hand as he stared at his daughter.

"You just got married," put in McKee with a dry smile.

"Oh! Oh, yes, of course, thank you. I'm distracted by—"

Trelawny nodded and fished a flask from under his coat. "The pleasant times are always soon eclipsed." He unscrewed the cap and waved it around at the company.

Christina was the first to take it, and she took a solid gulp.

To Crawford's alarm, McKee declined it but passed it to Johanna; and when his daughter handed it to him, it felt only about a third full. It proved to contain neat brandy, and he was careful not to drink all that was left before handing the flask back to Trelawny, but the old man took only a token sip before recapping it.

For perhaps a couple of minutes they were silent in the rattling, rocking cab, and then Christina remarked, "He's not restored yet; I'd feel it if he were. Perhaps Gabriel hid it effectively."

Beside Crawford, Johanna nodded. "I'd feel it too, and I don't."

For the rest of the ten-minute ride, none of them spoke—they all simply stared out the rain-streaked windows at the passing dark buildings on the right and the leaden river on the left as the cab shook its way through Westminster and Pimlico.

At last the cab squeaked to a halt in front of a closely barred wrought-iron fence, beyond which stood a three-story red-brick house with projecting bay windows on the first and second floors.

Trelawny was first out of the cab, and he shouted at the driver to wait for them.

As the rest of them disembarked from the cab, Christina was saying something about going in first alone, but her four companions hustled her through the gate and across the walkway and up the five steps to the front porch.

"We need to settle it as soon as possible, Diamonds," said Trelawny, not unkindly, as he waved at the doorknob.

Christina lifted her handbag but tried the knob with her free hand, and the door proved to be unlocked.

"You all can wait in the west sitting room—" she began, but Trelawny had already started down the hall. He paused in front of the dining-room door, for stairs led away both to the right and to the left, and he waved from one to the other impatiently.

"You must wait," Christina said. "I'll go up and get him—"

Trelawny looked over her shoulder at Crawford. "You take the left and I'll take the right. Yell when you find his bedroom."

"To the right, to the right," said Christina desperately, "but let me lead!" She stepped around Trelawny and started up the circular staircase. "I can't have you all bursting into every room!"

Her companions were on her heels as she led them up past the windowed first-floor landing to the second, and then they followed her down another hall to a closed door.

Christina rapped on it. "Gabriel? It's Christina—"

Trelawny gripped her shoulders and moved her aside and opened the door. A moment later all five of them stood beside Gabriel's four-post bed, panting.

Gabriel was sitting up in the bed, blinking in evident astonishment. A small window beyond him let in the gray daylight.

"Trelawny," he muttered sleepily, "and—and the prostitute—"

Crawford exhaled sharply and started forward, but Trelawny threw an arm out sideways to block him. "No time," he snapped at Crawford, and to Rossetti he said, "The lady is this man's wife, you pig. *Where is the*—"

Crawford was staring angrily at the befuddled goateed face of Gabriel Rossetti, but he felt Christina shiver violently beside him; and in the same moment Johanna moaned and sat down on the carpet. The bird in McKee's handbag emitted a shrill squeak.

"We're—too late," gasped Christina. "Algy has blooded the statue."

At this Gabriel turned toward the table beside his bed, and he gave a wordless cry of dismay and snatched up a glass from it.

Water or gin splashed on his blankets as he held it up in front of his face.

"Is this empty, 'Stina?" he demanded. "I can't see."

"There's only water in it," she answered harshly. "Salt water, I suppose. Algy has—"

And then there were suddenly two new figures blocking the window on the far side of the bed, and Crawford snatched up Johanna and turned toward the door.

The door slammed shut before he could reach it. He shifted the girl in his arms and tried the knob, but it wouldn't turn and the door wouldn't shift at all, and he turned to face the two shapes.

The one closest to the window he had seen before: its head was a yard-wide flat disk with a mouthful of teeth that extended around the rim as far as he could see, and it had no eyes; the other was clearly the skeletal gray boy Johanna had described three nights ago—his temple and cheek were lit by the window at his back and were as hollowed as a skull's.

Gabriel roared in fright and rolled out of the bed onto Christina's feet, taking the blankets and the bedside table down with him; Christina lurched backward into Crawford, and salt water splashed across the carpet. Johanna scrambled out of Crawford's arms and looked around the room wildly.

The room shook, as if at the impact of Gabriel hitting the floor; Crawford hopped to keep his balance.

The flat-headed thing's mouth opened, all the leathery way across, and the remembered whispery voice said, "My daughter, I have brought your bridegroom to you. Consummation, now, at last—and then, soon, the offspring."

The dead boy made a hissing sound and flexed his long fingers in the gray light.

Crawford glanced at Johanna, who had retreated into the corner by the fireplace and was gripping a poker; her eyes were wide, and her lips were pulled back from her teeth. The floor still seemed to be swaying, and Crawford stumbled as he stepped in front of her and lifted a long fire iron.

But McKee had pulled a jar of minced garlic out of her handbag, and now twisted it open; the smell instantly filled the room.

"Sulfur," she said hoarsely, "and the agent that stops you binding to our spiral threads, you—shit wagon!"

The dead boy's fingers closed into knobby fists and he made a hooting sound, but the wide-mouthed creature flickered, in one moment seeming to be Gabriel's wife and in the next the mustached man Crawford had seen in the skull chamber under Highgate Cemetery seven years ago.

McKee whirled the jar in an arc, scattering wet yellow shreds across both figures; and immediately they lost all form, becoming churning black shapes; and a moment later the window exploded outward and they had funneled away through it.

Crawford rushed to the window and squinted against the rainy breeze. Two hunched figures in flapping black were hurrying away down the street below, both huddled under a ragged white parasol. Even as he watched, they diminished in size far more rapidly than their pace could justify, and then they seemed to merge with the river-side trees and disappear.

The floor was steady.

Crawford heard a clank behind him and turned to see that Johanna had dropped the poker. He dropped the fire iron he was holding, and then Johanna was in his arms.

"Were you going to *keep* it?" screamed Christina at her brother.

"I was—" Gabriel disentangled himself from the bedclothes and stood up. He was barefoot, wearing a long nightshirt, and he quickly picked up a pair of trousers from the floor, and then squinted around as if wondering where he might get dressed. "I was going to pulverize it today. I—"

Trelawny had found a pencil and an envelope, and he scribbled something and then shoved the envelope into Crawford's hand.

"Come sundown," said Trelawny, "he'll be back, stronger, and he'll block your garlic then. Here's where you can get the shoes for your daughter." He gave Christina a ferocious glare. "You must go with them. They'll explain why on the way."

Christina nodded wearily, her anger at Gabriel exhausted. "I know why. Yes, I—I must go with them."

To McKee, Trelawny barked, "You know the crossing sweeper who takes only a ha'penny?"

"Yes."

"Pass through the eye of his needle."

"Shoes?" said Gabriel, still holding his trousers and peering from the broken window to the empty glass on the carpet and back.

"Go back to bed," said Trelawny. He turned the knob, and the door opened readily now.

CHAPTER TEN

And when your veins were void and dead,
What ghosts unclean
Swarmed round the straitened barren bed
That hid Faustine?

—*Algernon Swinburne, "Faustine"*

THE CAB TOOK Crawford, McKee, Johanna, and Christina almost all the way back to the church, but McKee had the driver let them out a couple of streets east and south of it, at the stone circle in the center of Seven Dials.

"I don't believe I've ever been here," said Christina breathlessly as Crawford led them, running and pausing, through the ever-shifting maze of horses pulling carriages and wagons.

"I should hope not," said McKee, pulling Johanna up onto the Earl Street curb.

Crawford opened his umbrella and handed it to Johanna, who was yawning as if to pop her ears. "I can still feel his attention on me," she said.

Christina was panting. "So can I."

The overcast sky had a faintly brassy color from the haze of coal smoke, and the streets between the wedge-shaped buildings that ringed the circle were in deep shadow. Even in the rain the pavements were crowded—disreputable-looking young men in shapeless caps and old women in shawls slouched near at hand under the shop awnings, and men in overcoats hurried past under umbrellas. Johanna's pink velveteen coat and McKee's blue silk dress stood out in the drab crowd.

McKee stood up on her toes to look around among the bobbing hats and umbrellas all around them, and at last she said, "I see him," and started forward, still holding Johanna's hand.

Crawford followed behind Christina; she was taking short, scuffling steps, and he hoped their quest wouldn't involve too much walking.

Traffic in the next radius street was simply stopped, the drivers shouting and shaking their fists, and McKee led her group through the mud between the halted horses to the far side of it.

A crossing sweeper was busily establishing a path between a high-piled furniture wagon and a couple of hansom cabs, waving his broom at the drivers as much as using it to sweep the puddles aside, and a couple of timid-looking men in bowler hats tottered behind him across the wet gravel. At the far curb the old sweeper looked back, and he nodded when McKee waved her hat at him. A moment later he came scampering back between the wheels and hooves so nimbly that Crawford was startled to get a better look at him.

Under a floppy hat, the man's hair was sparse and white, and his face sagged in deep wrinkles—but his eyes were alert and merry.

He didn't seem to be at all winded. "A ha'penny to cross," he told McKee.

McKee tugged on Crawford's sleeve. "Give him a shilling," she said quietly, "and tell him you want it all back."

This felt like some kind of ritual, so Crawford did as she said; and the old man gave them all a reappraising look but nodded cheerfully and handed Crawford two sixpences in exchange for the shilling, a transaction that made the old man no profit at all.

"Like that, is it?" he said, and then without waiting for an answer he scuttled to the doorway of a nearby druggist's and left his old broom there and came back with another.

"A new broom sweeps clean," he said, and paused as if for a reply.

"Er," said Crawford, "but the old broom—"

"—Knows all the coroners," finished McKee.

Crawford had handed his umbrella to Johanna, and in their haste he had left his hat at Gabriel Rossetti's house; and now he wanted to spit out the coconut taste of macassar oil in the rainwater running down his face from his hair.

But before he could complain about the delay, McKee seized his hand and pushed Christina, and then they were all sprinting across the muddy gravel—glancing back to make sure Johanna was following, Crawford saw that the old man was right behind her, sweeping so furiously that muddy gravel as well as sprays of water flew to the sides. On the far side of the street McKee gathered the others up onto the curb.

"Till the rain stops, I reckon" the old man said, "and no more'n a hundred yards." He was not even panting as he touched his hat brim; and then he was hurrying back through the river of vehicles to where he had left his ordinary broom.

"It's about noon," said McKee, "and our footprints have been erased. Are you still with us, Sister?"

Christina had been leaning against a post-box, but now she took a deep breath and stepped away from it and took a fresh grip on the handle of her umbrella.

"I used to walk for miles," she said, "when I was a little girl." She tilted her head, as if listening. "And I don't feel his attention!"

Johanna held her hand out in the rain from under the gleaming umbrella. "I don't either, right now."

McKee nodded. "On to Dudley Street."

"I've heard of Dudley Street," Johanna said.

"It's good enough in the daytime," said McKee, starting forward, "though I'd have had us dress less grand."

Their way led them down a narrow side street where children and goats huddled in the shelter of eaves far overhead, and open doorways let out gruff voices and the smells of beer and dubious cooked meats, and then McKee guided them down a cross street to the left.

The houses on this street were all of blackened brick with haphazard ironwork over the windows, and a lone hansom cab moving down it was having to proceed slowly because of the multitude of shirtless boys kicking a ball around in the rain; they had marked out some intricate pattern on the street in white stones and seemed to be trying to kick the ball in a particular zigzag course across it.

Crawford noticed the recessed squares in the pavement only when he saw McKee crouch beside one, her blue silk dress trailing in the puddles, and wiggle a short pole that stood up from it.

After a moment a square of brown canvas was pulled aside from below, and Crawford saw that it had blocked a hole, and a squinting bearded face was now peering up out of it.

"We need translator shoes," McKee said, leaning forward to politely hold her umbrella over the hole. "The *hide* kind."

Crawford thought most shoes were made of hide, but the man seemed to comprehend a distinction.

"Farther up the street, under the shrouded cross," he said, jerking his head to the east, "for hiding shoes. And may God have mercy on you."

The bearded head withdrew down the hole, and the canvas cover was fumbled back into place and secured again from below.

Christina glanced up and down the unsavory street. "Perhaps this isn't a good idea after all," she said timidly.

"We're bringing *your* blood," said McKee, straightening up, "not God's. Come on."

But two of the boys who had been playing ball stepped in front of McKee now, and Crawford saw that they were older than the others—their cheeks were lined, and their chins were dark with whiskers.

"You two," said one of them, pointing at Christina and Johanna, "you got the smell of stony blood on you."

The other boy pulled what appeared to be a rough oval stone out of his pocket, and Crawford stepped in front of Johanna—but when the boy held it out on his palm, Crawford saw that it was some sort of oyster.

Rain was still thrashing down onto the puddled gravel of the street. The oyster opened, and a hollow voice clearly came out of it: "Some of your blood," it said.

The skin of Crawford's face seemed to tighten, and he found that he and his companions had all taken an involuntary step back.

"They've got a ghost in that oyster," said McKee. Crawford noticed that her knife was in her hand, and then he saw that Johanna had drawn her own blade from under the pink velveteen coat—but the two boys now pulled knives of their own from the backs of their waistbands.

"We heal fast when Mister Clammo gets fresh stony blood," said the boy with the oyster in his free hand.

Crawford braced himself to spring at the boys and try to block their blades with his gloved hands, but Christina Rossetti stepped forward—and pursed her lips and began to whistle.

Even in this tense crisis, the whistled melody jarred Crawford with its abrupt changes of key and its apparent distortions of some long-familiar tune . . .

No one moved as the shrill notes batted between the close black housefronts, and the only thought Crawford could hang on to was the bizarre idea that the very raindrops were halted in the air overhead.

And the oyster convulsed right out of its shell and fell with a tiny splash at the boy's feet. The rain came hammering down.

The boy crouched to pick up the limp white thing, while his companion stepped back uncertainly.

"Be damned," said the first boy. "It's dead!"

"Yes," agreed Christina with a cold smile. "And I know more stopping melodies. Shall I whistle another?"

The first boy let the white blob fall to the mud again, and then both of them were running away.

McKee and Johanna had tucked their knives away, and McKee was again leading the way forward.

"Where did you learn *that?*" she muttered over her shoulder.

Christina was stepping along at a more lively pace now. "From the girls at the Magdalen," she said breathlessly. "After your time, it may have been."

"Who . . . *wrote* that terrible music?"

"Nobody seemed to know." Christina shrugged. "Some mute, inglorious Merlin."

"That must be the shrouded cross," said Johanna, her hand pointing ahead from under her umbrella.

Crawford looked in that direction and saw what at first appeared to be a wet cloth kite hanging from an old iron bracket high up on a brick wall, and a moment later he realized that it was a large crucifix draped in clinging linen.

In the street at the foot of the old lightless house was another of the canvas-blocked holes.

Johanna tilted back her umbrella and looked through narrowed eyes at Christina. "You and I should flip a coin," she said. "Both of us need to hide from him."

Christina raised her shoulders in a shiver, and McKee said, "No, a reflection of Sister Christina *attached* to her wouldn't accomplish anything."

"But it was a generous thought," said Christina.

McKee crouched and again wiggled a post beside this canvas cover, and this time, since they were farther away from the street-ball game—ominous in memory now, with its arcane patterns—Crawford heard a bell clang somewhere below the canvas.

Grimy fingers poked up from under the canvas, and a moment later it had been pulled aside to reveal a lean, bone-pale face and magnified eyes blinking behind two pairs of spectacles, one jammed in front of the other.

"You be wantin' to hide from God?"

"*A* god," said McKee. "We brought our own Eucharist."

The face bobbed. "There's still a corkage fee."

The man tucked the cover aside and scuffed back down a ladder, out of sight.

Crawford shrugged out of his frock coat and laid it in the mud beside the square hole, then knelt on it and felt around with his boots for the top rung of the ladder; when he found it, he grinned reassuringly at Johanna and began climbing down; and as the gray daylight above was cut off, replaced by flickering lamplight from below, he was uncomfortably reminded of the tunnels under Highgate Cemetery.

The cellar floor was spongy wood planks that made sucking sounds when he stepped away from the ladder to give McKee room, and a mismatched couple of kerosene lamps on a low table threw a yellow glare across shelves of boots and shoes, all very well worn. Hammocks were hung on the other side of the chamber, and Crawford saw several wide-eyed children in them gaping at him. A dozen crude straw dolls, perhaps the work of the children, were hung at various heights from the uneven ceiling and jiggled in the windless stale air.

After McKee, Christina climbed carefully down the ladder, her handbag swinging, gasping as each boot found a new rung and then not feeling for the next until her other boot had been firmly planted beside it. When at last she stood on the yielding wooden floor, she sighed deeply and wrinkled her nose at the ammonia-and-curry smell of the cellar.

Johanna came hopping down last, holding Crawford's muddy coat.

All their clothes were dripping, but Crawford didn't see that it would matter here.

"I'm known as Beetroot," the man said cheerfully. "I don't want to know who you people are."

"We need a pair of shoes for the girl," Crawford said. He was watching the hanging dolls and found that he was nearly whispering. "And the, the *wine* to prime them with is"—he went on, gesturing at Christina—"in her veins."

"Oh? Oh!" The man frowned and took off both pairs of spectacles and then put them on again, reversed, and he waved the spread fingers of both hands rapidly in front of his face and peered at Christina and Johanna through the shaking fans of them. Finally he lowered his hands and said to Christina, "Which one did *you* redeem?"

"Which . . . one?" she asked weakly.

"There are only two sustaining originals, darling," Beetroot said.

Christina glanced at Crawford, who shrugged and nodded, and then she looked down at the soggy floor. Very quietly, she said, "The, uh, male one."

"Ah, the male one," said Beetroot, "the European one! Yes, I'll take a measure more of blood than ordinary, enough to make *three* pairs. No, *four* pairs, counting the pair for your girl." He rubbed his bony hands together. "I'll have my brats wear the others, to keep 'em from cooling off until I can sell them. People postpone hiding from *God,* or argue about my price for it, but I know three people who will pay quite a lot to hide from *him*." He grinned at Crawford. "The cost to you will be much less."

"No," said Crawford, "this woman isn't a—a cask for you to draw from! I've got money, I'll pay for the standard—"

"You haven't got as much as these fellows will pay, I assure you." The man's eyes rolled behind the doubled lenses.

Crawford opened his mouth to argue, but Christina shook her head at him and gripped Johanna's shoulder. "I owe it," she said.

Crawford sighed. "How much do I pay?"

"Since you're providing me with surplus product," said Beetroot judiciously, "make it one ha'penny—just enough so that you've committed yourself."

Crawford dug in his pocket and gave the man a ha'penny coin. Committed myself, he thought—to what, in whose record?

The man turned away and opened an incongruously polished wooden box on the table by the lamps and lifted out a little silver bowl, a short wooden stick, and a tool like a screwdriver with a small perpendicular flange half an inch from the pointed tip.

A fleam and a bloodstick and a bleeding bowl, thought Crawford, much like what I've got back home in my surgery!

"I thought you ordinarily worked with consecrated wine?" he asked suspiciously.

"True, lad, but I needs must mix it every time with the blood of a man born in the river, underwater." He had laid the tools down now and begun to roll up his ragged sleeve, and he held his right arm out toward Crawford. The inside of his elbow was hatched with white scar tissue. "Such as myself. Collision on the river in '25—my mother drowned, but they saved me." The man looked up at him and grinned. "Ordinarily I charge a good deal more than a ha'penny for this." He turned toward the hammocks and called, "Andrew! Come tap the fleam!"

Christina was staring wide-eyed at the blade of the fleam, and she wasn't reassured when a barefoot child came slapping up and picked up the instruments with grimy hands.

"Wait, I can do it," said Crawford hastily, "for you and the lady here. I've done phlebotomies on more horses than there are men in the moon."

"And I've had phlebotomies," said Christina faintly. Her eyes fixed on Crawford's. "Yes, I'd rather you did it."

Andrew immediately returned to his hammock, and Beetroot shrugged.

"Johanna," said Crawford, "can you hold the bowl?"

"Certainly," she said, picking it up. She seemed brightly interested in the whole procedure.

More to reassure Christina than from consideration of the man's health, Crawford lifted the glass chimney from one of the lamps and held the fleam blade in the flame until it was black; then he replaced the chimney and waved the blade in the air for a few moments to cool it off.

"Er . . . Adelaide," he said, "would you hold his elbow out?"

McKee gripped Beetroot's arm with both hands, presenting the inside of the elbow. The man was grinning, apparently at the unprecedented elaborateness of it all.

Crawford held the blade up, squinting at it. "You might not want to watch, Miss Christina."

"Squeamishness," she said, "is one thing I don't suffer from."

"Is there any liquor?" Crawford asked. "To clean the skin," he added when Beetroot gave him an impatient look.

"Oh. Bottle of gin under the table." The man laughed. "Clean the skin, is it!"

"Johanna, if you would. A splash on his elbow right over the vein, and then scrub it a bit with your handkerchief. And then hold the bowl under."

The girl did as he said, afterward absently tipping the bottle up for a mouthful before setting it on the table. The sharp juniper smell filled the cellar, and the straw figures hanging from the ceiling seemed to dance more vigorously in the still air.

Crawford tried to ignore the crude dolls. He laid the pointed tip of the fleam against the scarring over the man's median orbital vein, and then tapped the handle with the bloodstick—being careful to do it very lightly, for he was used to doing this on the neck of a horse, with a coat of coarse hair to get through.

Immediately a line of dark blood ran down and began puddling in the silver bowl Johanna held.

"Andrew!" called Beetroot. "Come watch as he does it to this woman. *This* is how you do it, not like you're driving a nail!" After several seconds, he unfastened a pin one-handed from his shirt and deftly poked it through the cut in his pale skin, and then folded his arm. "That's plenty."

Crawford took the bowl from Johanna and tilted it toward the lamplight—the blood in it was staying dark, not reddening in the air.

The man laughed, straightening his arm now and looping a length of thread around the pin in his elbow. "Trust a medical man to notice that! Always happens, with people born under the Thames—we're partly dead, drowned, always." He looked past Crawford at Christina. "And now the wine."

Christina stepped forward across the mushy boards but just gave Crawford a stare and didn't roll back her sleeve yet.

He nodded and wiped the fleam blade, then again lifted the lamp chimney and carefully turned the blade in the flame.

"Johanna," he said, "gin again, but just for the elbow this time, eh?"

Christina rolled up her sleeve and handed Johanna a fresh handkerchief, and Johanna poured gin on it and then swabbed Christina's elbow.

Crawford was aware of young Andrew standing beside him as he gently tapped the fleam against the soft skin of Christina's inner elbow, and he was glad to see that she didn't even wince as the blood flowed around her arm and dripped rapidly into the bowl Johanna was holding.

From the corner of his eye, Crawford saw that the straw dolls were hanging motionless now. "You've got the attention of all the children," said Beetroot, nodding.

When Crawford judged that several tablespoonfuls had run into the bowl, he reached for the handkerchief Johanna was holding, but the man caught Crawford's wrist.

"Not yet."

Christina just closed her eyes as more of her blood sluiced around her elbow and fell into the bowl.

After another thirty seconds, Crawford took the handkerchief from Johanna, and the man nodded reluctantly.

"I suppose that'll do." He pointed to another pin in his shirt, raising his eyebrows, but Christina shook her head and just wrapped the gin-soaked handkerchief around her elbow and then folded her arm to hold it tightly.

"Smooth work," she said to Crawford.

Beetroot took the bowl from Johanna. "Laces, now, laces!" he exclaimed, snatching up several lengths of string from the table and stirring them with his fingers into the mixed blood.

"Shoes, Andrew, shoes!"

The boy sprang to the shelves and tucked several pairs of shoes under his arm, then crouched beside Johanna and held them up one by one beside her right foot.

"These," he said, straightening up with a battered pair of high-topped black shoes.

Beetroot dredged one string out of the blood and handed the dripping thing to the boy. "You've got the left shoe, you're clockwise," he said.

And then the two of them were threading the strings through the lace-grommets of the shoes in a peculiar spiral pattern rather than the ordinary crisscross progression. Crawford saw that the man was stringing the right shoe counterclockwise. The dolls jiggled excitedly overhead.

At last Beetroot and Andrew tied careful knots in the middles of the spiral patterns.

"Here," Beetroot said, thrusting toward Johanna the shoe he had prepared as Andrew handed her the other. "These'll be a bit loose, since you're not to untie them, ever. Stuff 'em with rags to make 'em fit. Shoes!" he yelled to Andrew, fumbling in the blood for more strings. "You people can go," he said, his attention now on the next pair of shoes, and the two pairs after that.

"Put them on now," McKee told Johanna. "While we're still underground and it's still raining."

Beetroot looked up from stringing a fresh shoe and nodded.

Johanna's nostrils flared in distaste as she looked at the ugly old shoes and the bloody laces in them, but she handed them to McKee and then braced one hand against the wall to take off her boots.

Crawford picked up his muddy coat and dug out his handkerchief, and he gave it to Johanna to stuff into one of the shoes; then, after glancing around, he unbuttoned the collar from his shirt and handed it to her for the other one.

"Thanks," said Johanna as she fitted her stocking feet into the hiding shoes. She glanced around at her companions. "We all looked better at the wedding an hour ago, didn't we?"

"It's been a disheveling day," Crawford agreed, thrusting his arms through the sleeves of his soggy coat.

Johanna waved back at the room, though the jiggling of the hanging dolls seemed to be the only response.

"Let's get out of here," said Crawford, taking her arm and turning her toward the ladder.

He went first up the old wooden rungs, but the few people on the street, huddled in doorways against the rain, only glanced at him incuriously. He waved the rest of his party up, and in a few minutes McKee had led them to the more populated expanse of Earl Street, where she turned left, back toward Seven Dials.

Johanna was limping, but when Crawford gave her a concerned look, she told him, "I've worn worse, I'll get used to them." Then she grimaced up from under the umbrella. "But do I *sleep* in them?"

"I—don't know," he said.

Johanna shrugged and kept walking. "That boy Andrew didn't look well, did he?" she said after a few more paces. "I bet soon there'll be another straw doll."

Hurrying along beside them, Christina whispered something that might have been a phrase from a prayer.

The rain trailed to a stop just as they emerged into the irregular square at the junction of the seven streets, and a stray beam of sunlight flickered across the circle in the center, momentarily visible between wheels and horses' legs.

Christina had rolled her wet sleeve down again, and a stain of blood showed at her elbow, but she didn't seem to have any trouble walking, and they would be able to flag a cab here.

Then she halted and touched her throat and brushed her face as if she'd walked through a spiderweb. Crawford caught Johanna by the hand and asked, anxiously, "Miss Christina? Are you well?"

She managed an unhappy smile. "As well as I ever am. We seem to have reestablished our footsteps—his attention is *on* me again."

Crawford glanced quickly at Johanna, who tentatively spread her fingers and sniffed the air. "Not on me," she said softly. Then, more loudly, "He's not watching me!"

"Yes," said Crawford, starting forward again and peering around for a cab, "you sleep in them."

And it looks as if we're going to France tomorrow after all, he thought.

CHAPTER ELEVEN

'. . . I wander, knowing this
Only, that what I seek I cannot find;
And so I waste my time: for I am changed;
And to myself,' said she, 'have done much wrong
And to this helpless infant. I have slept
Weeping, and weeping have I waked; my tears
Have flowed as if my body were not such
As others are; and I could never die.'

*—William Wordsworth, "The Excursion," lines 804–811, as
copied by Christina Rossetti into her commonplace book, 1845*

WILLIAM AND MARIA were at Tudor House when Christina
arrived there at one thirty in the afternoon. Gabriel was sitting
at a small table by the bay window in the long drawing room upstairs,
cradling a moldy notebook in his hands and looking out over the river,
when young Henry Dunn showed her in, and William and Maria stood
in the far corner of the room, whispering.

"Good Lord!" exclaimed William, stepping around the long table.
"You're all wet and muddy! Did you fall somewhere?"

"I was saving a girl from our uncle," Christina said, "for a while, at least." She walked up to Gabriel and waved toward William and Maria. "Have you told them?"

He looked up at her blankly, but Maria said, "We know the statue is not yet destroyed—Gabriel has misplaced it here in the house somewhere." She was staring at Christina's dress. "I thought you were going to a wedding! Did you get in a fight?"

"I had to climb down a hole in a street in St. Giles, and"—pointing at her stained sleeve—"lose some blood."

Maria drew in a breath with a hiss, and Gabriel looked away.

"Algy didn't take it," he said. "I asked him." He idly flexed the old notebook in his hands, and bits of the cover flaked off in his lap.

"You've read his poetry," Christina said witheringly, echoing Trelawny.

Gabriel shrugged.

William cleared his throat. "We think Gabriel may have misremembered where he put it last night. I should have helped him hide it, after he woke me and told me he had retrieved it. But I just said, 'Good,' and went back to sleep."

Gabriel nodded. "I had a lot to drink before I finally went to bed. Understandable, I think, under the circumstances."

Christina's mouth was open in astonishment, and she said to him, "But you *saw* those two creatures this morning!—you saw them appear!—in your bedroom! And you must—"

"They've appeared in this house before," interrupted Gabriel irritably.

Christina looked out the window, and after a moment she pointed to a passing wagon. "And what is *that*?" she demanded.

Gabriel looked out the window. "What," he said, "trees, a street, a wagon . . ."

"What *kind* of wagon?"

Gabriel peered through his spectacles. "I don't know. A yellow wagon. Have you lost your wits?"

Maria had stepped up behind Christina and was peering over her shoulder. "Comer India Pale Ale," she said, giving Christina a mystified look.

Christina bent over to hug her brother and sighed. "Oh, I'm so glad your eyesight hasn't recovered!"

For a moment Gabriel's face clouded in real anger, and then he just laughed softly and pushed her away with one hand. He took a deep breath, then said, "You thought *I* blooded it? That wasn't what our uncle wanted—I was never one of Boadicea's victims."

And how can you be certain of that? wondered Christina; but she said, "It would nevertheless have constituted renewing your vows to him, I'm sure."

William was standing by Christina now. "We need to search the whole house, attic and basement too, and the garden," he said. "Gabriel might have hidden it anywhere, in his . . . distracted state last night. And Gabriel, you must try very hard to remember! Walk around the house with us! Christina, do you think you could sense the statue, if you were near it?"

Christina frowned and glanced at Gabriel.

He was staring out the window again. "Never mind, William," he said softly. "Christina is right. Algy has certainly taken it and rubbed his restorative blood on it." He took off his spectacles and rubbed his eyes. "The only thing my midnight escapade accomplished was to make our uncle stronger."

"And to recover your poetry," William pointed out, nodding at the moldy notebook in Gabriel's hands.

"Yes." Gabriel laid it down and wiped his hands on his waistcoat. "My poetry." Christina could smell the book's mildew.

Gabriel put his spectacles back on and stood up, and he gripped Maria's shoulders. "He almost took Christina by force on Wednesday night," he said. "The only thing that saved our sister was the timely intervention of Charles Cayley!"

"I know," said Maria, staring straight back at him, "of no way we can use to trap our uncle."

She turned and left the room.

Christina called after her, and crossed to the doorway to call again down the hall, but a moment later she stepped back into the room, shaking her head.

"Moony won't play," she sighed.

After a pause, "'No way we can *use*,'" echoed William, "Christian scruples of some sort?"

"Yes," said Gabriel, sitting down again. "And immovable."

"Can we . . . *get* it," said Christina, "from Algy? He'll have hidden it."

"We could torture him," said Gabriel with a shrug, "but he'd like that."

"Appeal to him?" suggested William. "In friendship?"

Gabriel shook his head. "Try appealing to a drunkard, in friendship. And this is vastly more compelling than drink."

"We must none of us marry, or have children," said Christina. "William, you and Maria have been safe up till now, you're apparently considered members of its family somehow—possibly because you grew up with the statue, you participated in its renaming of us all as card suits—a provisional protection at best, I think. You both need to begin taking precautions. Whenever—"

"Never marry?" protested William. "Never have children? Because a *ghost* would be jealous? I'm forty years old, I can't—"

"He's more than a ghost!" interrupted Christina. "You were there at the séance on Tuesday—and I think you saw him, and he even spoke to you, in your vision! I think he spoke to each of us."

William opened his mouth and then looked away, and in that instant Christina was sure that William had somehow met their uncle again, since the séance.

"You said he kills people we love," William went on stubbornly, still looking away. "Whom has he killed?"

"Well—he killed that veterinary surgeon's wife and sons . . ."

"He did?" William was looking at her now. "When was this? Killed them how?"

"Fifteen or twenty years ago," admitted Christina. "They were on a boat on the river . . ."

"I'll wager the coroner came to a different conclusion than 'killed by a ghost.'"

"Oh—your children will die, William, trust me! Gabriel, do séances have to be done at night?"

"Hmm?" He shook his head. "I don't know. They always seem to be."

"I can think of one ghost that might know how to unmake our uncle—your son. The dead boy. And ghosts don't seem to be able to lie."

"Oh God. He's not my son. No, damn it, he is my son—how did our poor father do this to us?" He got to his feet, looking much older than his forty-one years. "Not that we didn't cooperate." He held up one trembling hand. "Me too, 'Stina; I did it too."

"*I* haven't done it," said William, and Christina was unhappily sure that the statement had an unspoken *yet* at the end of it.

"Fetch your pencils and papers," said Christina. "If the creature can appear in your bedroom during the day, it can likely participate in a daytime séance."

THE CAB DRIVER WHO slanted his two-wheeled hansom cab in toward the curb when Trelawny waved at him didn't register any surprise or suspicion at being hailed by such a wild-haired and casually dressed figure in front of a Pelham Crescent house, and he didn't ask to see the money in advance, so Trelawny assumed that the man had dealt with him before.

"A tour of the river," he said as he climbed in. "Battersea Bridge first."

The morning's rain had stopped, and the arches and chimneys and business signs of the buildings along the Fulham Road flickered and dimmed with the intermittent returning sunlight.

He took out the box from under his coat and laid it on the seat beside him. "A last look 'round," he said to it, squinting against the bracing headwind. "You always preferred the night, but—can you hear me, even all broken up? The hell of it is, I know you still love me." He patted it with his wrinkled old hand. "We have had some times, these twelve years—haven't we?—since I found you in that ravine, and took you in."

This morning he had realized, with a chill, that he had not yet disposed of the box containing the petrified kernel of the Boadicea creature. And when this thought was quickly followed by a lately familiar breezy feeling that all was well and he should think of something else, he recognized the latter thought as . . . not his own.

Immediately he had pulled the mirror box out from under his bed, fetched a hammer from the downstairs kitchen, and on the fireplace hearth he had spilled the tiny statue out of the mirror box and quickly pounded it to tiny fragments. Then he had carefully swept up all the broken pieces, along with a good deal of the inadvertently shattered hearth bricks, and tipped them back into the mirror box.

And now he was going to sift a third of the debris into the river from Battersea Bridge, a third from Waterloo Bridge, and the last, down to the final shake of dust, from London Bridge.

The cab rattled on past Beaufort Street, which was the most direct way to the bridge; Trelawny glared up over his shoulder toward the driver, but the man had closed the communicating hatch. Then the vehicle went right past Park Walk too, and Trelawny reached out through the open side window and pounded on the outside of the cab.

"Idiot!" he yelled. "Turn south!"

The reins slithered through the bracket on the roof and the cab slowed, and at the same time a young man ran up alongside on the right and hopped up onto the step in front of the wheel, leaning in over Trelawny. He was smiling under disordered curly dark hair, and he was holding a wide-barreled old flintlock pistol aimed at Trelawny's side.

"Silver bullets," he said, with an accent Trelawny recognized as Italian. "Just sit tight for another minute."

From where he sat, Trelawny couldn't hope to knock the pistol aside, nor reach his own at all quickly.

The cab finally turned right, between the close buildings of Limerston Street, and then it was steered into the yard of the gray, narrow-windowed Chelsea Workhouse. The smell of bad meat and old oil was beginning to reassert itself over the acid scent of rain-washed pavement.

The mare had slowed to a walk, and the cab was rolling slowly toward a shadowed arch at the north end of the four-story building, where three men stood around a good-sized carriage with a couple of horses harnessed to it.

One of the men stepped out of the shadows and held up his hand—and even at a distance of a dozen yards Trelawny saw the black mark on the palm.

"You're Carbonari," he said to the man on the cab's step. "Don't interfere with me—in this box I've got the female vampire herself, petrified and shattered. I'm going to scatter her into the river."

"That was good work," said the man, smiling and cocking his head. "We'll toss your box in a dustbin for you."

"Dustbin? You idiot, did you understand what I said? It's the female vampire, the British one! Let me explain it to one of your dago friends who has more English."

"The vampires are about to be made *obsolete*," the man said, speaking the term with relish.

Trelawny guessed what the man must mean by "made obsolete," and he yawned and tensed himself for a grab at the gun barrel.

"Na-ah," the man said, hopping backward off the step to the cobblestones and raising his pistol to aim it at Trelawny's head. "We may not kill you if you play along, but we got no *reluctance* to deal with your corpse."

"*May* not kill me!" said Trelawny bitterly, relaxing back into the seat. "By cutting my throat!"

"Our man is a surgeon," called the young Carbonari, walking alongside the cab now and keeping the pistol raised. "He'll try to do no more cutting than's necessary to stop you being the bridge man."

Trelawny made himself breathe deeply and evenly. He touched his throat, feeling the bulge of the stone lump behind the pulse of his jugular. The thing had definitely grown, in these dozen years since he had invited Miss B. to come home with him.

And by trapping her a week ago, and breaking up her physical form, he had evidently lost her protective attention! Until a week ago the Carbonari would never have dared to threaten him with violence.

Trelawny forced himself to relax and think.

Perhaps this was the appropriate way for it all to end at last— Edward John Trelawny, onetime friend to Byron and Shelley, murdered by Carbonari agents in the yard of a London workhouse at the age of seventy-seven. He had long since made arrangements to be buried beside Shelley in the Protestant Cemetery in Rome. The goal of these Carbonari was to eradicate the vampire race and save London, just as his was—*could* he fight them?

He laughed silently and flexed his hands. Only to the death, he thought, and he rehearsed how he would draw his revolver and spring out of the cab on the left side, away from the men by the carriage.

The rattle of the cab was louder when it rocked in under the arch, and Trelawny quickly pushed the cab's leather flap aside and rolled out, dropping to his hands and knees as he drew his revolver and noting the men's legs and ankles as he brought the barrel up.

But one man simply dropped, with a spatter of red blood at his throat, and the others were now shouting and running; Trelawny got to his feet, cursing the pain in his knees that slowed him and set his heart to knocking.

The driver of his cab had drawn a revolver of his own, but he was pointing it away from Trelawny, at the other side of the cab. The pistol went off with a flare and a resounding crack, and then the man jumped down from the cab, landing awkwardly but limping away without a pause.

Two more pistol shots hammered the air under the arch, and somewhere on the other side of the horse a man screamed.

The mare was frantically shying away, backing the cab and grinding her flank against the brick wall, and Trelawny forced his sharply protesting knees to step back to avoid being knocked down and trampled. Through the slack reins he glimpsed men in some thrashing struggle, but his focus now was simply on the wedge of clear pavement between the wall and the jigging cab, and he grabbed the cab lamp with his free hand and pulled himself farther toward the rear of the cab, away from the stamping mare. He was panting and blinking sweat out of his eyes.

Then a squat figure had blocked the gray daylight in front of him, between the rear of the cab and the wall. Trelawny raised his shaking pistol and forced himself to focus on the lumpy silhouette, and he saw that it had no head, just a broad flat hat that rested right on its shoulders.

Trelawny recognized it—he had seen it in Rossetti's bedroom only a few hours ago—but in that instant the thing once again dissolved into oily smoke, and when the gun jumped and cracked in Trelawny's hand, it was too late. The pistol ball whacked into brick somewhere across the street.

Trelawny wasn't able to take a deep breath, and his vision was darkening; and he didn't resist when an arm caught him around the ribs and braced him up. He barely had the strength to lift the revolver and tuck it into his belt, and he let his unseen companion boost him up into the cab.

The long reins slid through the bracket on the roof and then were caught and drawn inside hand over hand, and the cab was rocking as the mare eagerly backed out of the shadowed arch into the bright yard.

After a few seconds of the cab rolling backward, the reins snapped and the mare snorted and stamped but began trotting obediently forward. Trelawny was rocked against the cab's right panel.

He rolled his throbbing head to look at the stranger who was now driving the cab from inside.

The teeth were bared in a permanent rictus grin in the skeletal gray face, and its wide eyes swiveled toward him and then back to the horse. The spidery gray hands on the reins were splashed with fresh blood.

The thing spoke then, and its voice was a flat squeak: "A spirit present? In a sense!" And it reached up with its left hand and knocked once against the cab's low ceiling. A few moments later it sighed, with a sound like sand spilling from a shovel.

It rolled its eyes toward Trelawny, and its involuntary grin widened. "Marry!" it said then in a voice like wood creaking. "Well, not the ceremony, but one part of 'marry,' yes!"

It reached up and knocked again.

GABRIEL HAD PULLED THE curtains across the brightening view of the river, and William had fetched the table while Christina assembled papers and pencils, and the first question they had asked when the three of them had sat down was, *Is there a spirit present?*

The table had shaken with a single knock—yes.

The next question had been, *Are you Gabriel's son, who wants to marry the horse-doctor's daughter?*

After a pause, there had again been a single knock.

"Our uncle," said Christina now, speaking into the air below the high ceiling, "was locked up for seven years. Do you know how we might banish him forever?"

THE GRAY BOY HAD guided the cab into an alley across Limerston Street, and then its nimble fingers had untied the strings on a canvas rain-flap that tumbled down to block the view of shadowed windows and doors ahead. The only light in the cab's narrow interior now was the dim reflection from the close brick walls visible through the windows on either side.

Trelawny made himself face his grotesque companion without flinching, though he allowed himself to press against the right panel. The creature had tucked a ragged parasol between its knees, and Trelawny noticed for the first time that it was wearing a big blanket wrapped around its shoulders like a toga, and a couple of little round holes in it seemed to be bullet holes, though there was no blood around them. The thing's breath, he noticed, was colder than the outside air and smelled of river mud.

The dead boy had picked up the mirror box in its left hand and was clutching it to itself, away from Trelawny.

"I do know a way," it said, and raised its right hand to the roof and rapped on it once.

THE TABLE SHOOK AT a single knock under Christina's fingertips.

"How?" she whispered.

The clock on the mantel ticked off a dozen seconds, and William cleared his throat.

"Remember it can't spell."

"Does it," asked Christina, "involve cutting Edward Trelawny's throat?"

"THEY KNOW ABOUT YOU," quacked the gray thing as it rapped the cab's roof once. It wiggled its bloody fingers. "Just as these dead men did."

"Those . . . dead men wanted to kill me."

"Fools," said the thing.

"They didn't want the box," Trelawny added, nodding toward the box in the thing's left hand.

"Fools," it said again.

Trelawny's heart was knocking hollowly in his chest, and he had to take a breath to speak again.

"You . . . *rescued* me from them?"

"I rescued her," the thing said, shaking the mirror box.

Trelawny's head ached. "Stop hitting the roof, will you?"

The dead boy shrugged his knobby shoulders under the blanket. "I can do it just as well with my teeth."

The thing wasn't looking at him, so Trelawny let his hand slip toward the flap of his coat that concealed the revolver.

"THAT'S A YES," SAID Gabriel. "I should have cut the old bastard's throat in Regent's Park."

"I wonder if that's what Maria won't tell us," said William. "She can't condone murder."

"Neither can we," said Christina.

"What do you call killing our uncle?" asked William.

"He's not human," said Christina desperately, "and he's died already, by his own hand."

"You," said Gabriel, speaking toward the ceiling, "had two human parents—"

THE DEAD BOY BESIDE Trelawny clicked its teeth together—three distinct times.

"I had at least *three* human parents," the thing said to Trelawny. "The first time, though, I was lost in a miscarriage."

"You look it," said Trelawny.

Then he snatched out the revolver, rammed it against the blanket over the dead boy's ribs, and pulled the trigger.

Even with the muzzle against the cloth, the detonation battered Trelawny's eardrums in the curtained cab interior.

❧❧❧❧❧

"NO?" SAID GABRIEL AFTER the latest three knocks, and the dawning relief was evident in his high-pitched voice. "Am I your father or not?"

The pause that followed this was so long that Gabriel had opened his mouth to speak again, when the table knocked once in reply. *Yes.*

"But Lizzie was your mother . . . ?"

Again there was the *Yes* reply.

"That's two! Both all too human!"

Christina was dizzy, and a high-pitched wail seemed to be keening in her head. "Was there ever," she said, speaking too loudly; she exhaled and went on, "a third parent?" Earlier? she thought.

The table banged once.

"Were you," she asked, "*reincarnated,* after that, as Lizzie and Gabriel's child?" She sat back and whispered, "Insistent to be born?"

She had half expected it, but the single rap made her jump.

TRELAWNY WAS COUGHING IN the haze of black-powder smoke as the dead boy's right hand reached across him and gripped the pistol, and its lengthening, twining fingers held the hammer down and prevented a second shot.

Blinking and gasping in the dimness, Trelawny could see that a fresh, smoking hole had been punched into the blanket over the boy's torso, but there was no drop of any blood, and the dead boy seemed unconcerned—the big white teeth had clicked again, four distinctly separated times, in the moments since Trelawny had fired the gun.

Trelawny tugged against the snaky fingers that enveloped his right hand, but the dead boy was strong.

"No, you don't leave here," the thing said, and Trelawny could hear air escaping from a hole in its ribs as it spoke, "until he congeals again and comes here, and takes you—your soul, with his teeth—from the *other* side of your neck, away from the stone."

I HAVE TO KNOW, thought Christina, though her forehead was already cold with perspiration. She looked at the dimly visible faces of her brothers, then looked away, toward the curtained windows. "Are you," she asked hoarsely, "the child I miscarried when I was fifteen?"

TRELAWNY WAS STARTLED WHEN, after a pause, the dead boy again clicked his teeth once. "That's it, my never-mother," it said. "I needed to be born, so my dead soul crawled among the sea worms on the dark river bottom until the other patron found me, and she found another womb for me."

His eel-like fingers tightened on Trelawny's right hand.

AFTER THE LAST KNOCK, Gabriel and William leaped up, for Christina had fainted and fallen out of her chair onto the carpet.

TRELAWNY SPREAD HIS CONFINED fingers to release the revolver, and the boy's fingers stretched out—each a full foot long now—and took the gun away from him.

"What," said Trelawny, "if I don't care to be bitten? She," he added, nodding toward the box the dead boy held, "never bit me."

"And look at her now! Your gratitude has near killed her. She was slow—you should have died and come back long ago. He will be here soon."

"I'm sure I'll be able to reason with him," said Trelawny with every appearance of relaxed confidence. Inwardly, though, he was bracing himself for a desperate move. Slowly enough not to seem threatening, he reached into his coat and drew out his pewter flask.

"I daresay you don't drink," he remarked to his cadaverous companion as he unscrewed the cap.

"What I drink is not in that container," the thing said.

It turned its bald granite-colored gourd of a head to the left as it tucked the revolver away beside the box on its side of the seat, and Trelawny gritted his teeth and reached into his side pocket for a box of matches.

In one motion he pulled out the box, slid it open, flipped out a match and struck it, and as it flared he whirled the flask in a circle, splashing warm brandy in every direction; he dropped the lit match and the flask as the cab's interior flared in a bright inferno.

The dead boy burst out in a loud wailing, thrashing on the seat and beating at the flaming blanket it wore, and Trelawny sprang forward; he swept the leather flap aside and put one boot on the low front partition and grabbed the reins, and then vaulted out onto the mare's back.

She lurched in surprise at the sudden weight, and then neighed shrilly and tugged forward, her flanks apparently stung by his flaming trousers. He fumbled his pocketknife free and leaned down to saw through the leather trace and the tug strap that held the shaft on the right side—the mare had helpfully drawn them out taut—and then switched hands and bent to do the same on the left side, and then the mare and her smoking rider were galloping down the alley, Trelawny desperately gripping the long, trailing reins right above their rings in the little harness saddle.

His hat and coat and beard flickered with hot blue flames, and as soon as the mare had rounded the next corner, he managed to rein her in and then slid off her back, and as she raced away in the direction of the King's Road, he found a broad puddle of icy mud to roll in.

CHAPTER TWELVE

Let all dead things lie dead; none such
Are soft to touch.

—*Algernon Swinburne, "Felise"*

THE AFTERGLOW OF sunset still shone pink on the steeple of St. Clement Dane's in the Strand, but Wych Street was in evening shadow. Lights shone in the windows of the pub on the corner, and Crawford had lit his porch lamp an hour ago.

Standing in the street, he reached up now to slide the latest box—scalpels, forceps, ropes, and muzzles—onto the back of the wagon stopped in front of his door, and then he leaned on the rear wheel to catch his breath.

This lot, which included a few good pieces of furniture, was going into storage, to be sent for when he had found a location for a veterinary surgery in France. His personal luggage was in a trunk in the parlor—Johanna didn't have anything to pack but a few clothes Crawford and Christina Rossetti had bought for her, and McKee had even less, and both of them kept their knives on their persons.

Johanna faced tomorrow's departure from England eagerly; her

impression of France was derived from a translation of Charles Per-
rault's fairy tales that she'd bought while she'd been a coster girl—and
she had been wearing the filthy translator shoes for six hours now, and
would have to sleep in them tonight, and she was volubly looking forward to taking them off on the dock at Dieppe and pitching them into
the sea.

Crawford was a bit disconcerted at his own readiness to abandon
the country of his birth; but his first wife and family were lost to him,
and he now realized that the city of London had for these last sixteen
years been a constant, enervating reminder of them. And he thanked
God that he had happened to wander out onto Waterloo Bridge, on that
February evening in 1862, and jumped into the river with McKee.

McKee, though, had been moody and quiet as she had made ham
and chutney sandwiches and then helped carry boxes down the stairs.
Crawford supposed that she was remembering whatever attractions her
renounced common-law husband had presumably once had.

Crawford fetched a cigar out of his pocket and cupped his hands
against the autumn breeze to strike a match to it. He stepped away
from the wagon and leaned against the area railing.

Tomorrow night they would be in France, at first among British
tourists in Dieppe and then, as soon as it was feasible, somewhere farther from the sea—ideally in some place where a British veterinary surgeon with a limited command of the French language might hope to
establish a practice.

Fast footsteps crunching on the street made him look up, and at
first his chest went cold to see the silhouette of a boy running toward
him; then the boy was closer to the porch lamp, and Crawford saw that
it was not the cadaverous figure he had briefly seen in Gabriel Rossetti's
bedroom this morning.

"Message for Johanna," the boy gasped. He wore a velvet skullcap,
and his hair was long in front and twisted into curls, and he appeared to
be about Johanna's age.

"I'm her father," said Crawford. "I can deliver it."

The boy shook his head. "She paid me to hear it herself."

Crawford was about to insist when Johanna came tapping down the stairs.

"Hullo, Ollie," she said. "Is he dead drunk somewhere, I hope?"

"Dead somewhere, is the fact," said Ollie. "Hanged hisself three nights ago, buried on Wednesday. Driven to the deed by grief, they say, being as his woman left him."

"Thanks, Ollie," Johanna said, and Ollie touched his cap and ran away back the way he'd come.

Johanna leaned on the railing beside Crawford. After a moment, she said, "I stole a shilling from you."

"You're welcome to my shillings," he said. His first reaction had been relief, but now he was wondering how McKee would react to the news.

"That was Ollie."

Crawford nodded and puffed on his cigar.

"I know him a bit from my coster time." She sighed. "I paid him the shilling to find out where that Tom fellow was—'spoon seller, common-law husband of Hail Mary McKee who does business mainly in Hare Street.'" She looked up at Crawford. "I wouldn't tell her till we're across the Channel."

He shook his head firmly. "No, I've got to tell her."

"She won't . . . change her mind about going, then, out of remorse, or something? Or get all weepy?"

Crawford sighed, blowing out a plume of smoke. "I suppose she might get weepy. Don't you, sometimes?"

"No. Not for years."

Crawford glanced up at the darkening sky. "We should be inside, even with your magical shoes."

"Filthy things," she said, pushing away from the railing and hurrying up the steps into the house.

Crawford followed more slowly, and he paused at the top of the steps to have a few more puffs of the cigar.

Perhaps he didn't have to tell her. How reliable was Ollie? An unfounded rumor . . .

Still, Crawford would have to tell her what Ollie had said. He sighed, pitched the cigar butt into the street, and went inside.

The parlor to his left was an empty room now, with pale rectangles on the walls where the pictures had hung, and most of the floor was bright clean wood, protected for years by the now-removed carpet. He could hear clatter in the dining room and pushed open the door.

Johanna had resumed wrapping glass jars in flannel scraps and packing them into a crate in the middle of the floor where the table had stood, and Crawford wondered if they would be unpacked again in his lifetime, or ever.

"Your mother?" he asked.

"Upstairs, I believe," said Johanna.

It was as if—in fact it was nearly literally the case that—his whole life was being disassembled from around and under him, and he had to let go of it and jump, as he had let go of the bottom-most rung in that well under Highgate Cemetery, with McKee and Johanna waiting below.

And they were with him now, and they were all he still had.

The whisky decanter sat on the floor near where Johanna was working, and he bent to pick it up and move it away from her, but he paused to take a mouthful from the neck of it.

He heard McKee's voice in the hallway now, and a man's voice.

Clearly he heard her say, "Oh, very well, come in then."

He exchanged one horrified glance with his daughter, and then he had dropped the decanter and both of them burst through the dining-room door into the parlor.

McKee was just stepping into the room, and right behind her, still in the hall shadows, came a tall, burly figure.

Not caring if he was wrong, hoping he was, Crawford took two running steps and launched himself at McKee—he had one second in which to see her startled face, with another face looming behind her with its mouth opening—and then Crawford had grabbed McKee around the waist and flung her back toward Johanna.

Crawford's momentum sent him plunging into the man behind McKee, and the man's arm whipped around Crawford's shoulders and yanked him into a tighter embrace—the man's coat was damp and smelled of clay—and then sharp teeth punctured Crawford's throat.

HIS VIEW OF HIS own house was odd—he could see the exterior and the hallway and the parlor all at once, and the figure of McKee was a wavy ribbon bending from the door around the interior corner and into the parlor. He could see himself too, a blurred streak from the dining room, and Johanna, whose streak extended to where the McKee ribbon met it.

The ribbon people—he knew the trails of their motions were threaded all through the City, if he cared to trace them backward—had detectable personalities, and he was one of them himself, but Crawford could feel an immensely bigger, older, fuller identity overshadowing him. It communicated simply by existing, and it promised him relief from the crushing disparity of their stations, and immortality, soon.

THEN SOUNDS CRASHED BACK on him as he hit the bare wooden floor with his knee and elbow, and the smell of garlic burned in his nose, and bright red drops of his blood were pattering onto the boards.

One of Johanna's awful old shoes was directly in front of his face, grinding backward as she straddled him and lunged. He rolled over onto his back and saw that she had plunged her knife to the hilt into Tom's throat. Yellow fragments of garlic were spattered across Tom's shirt and unshaven face, and in Johanna's left hand was an empty jar.

Tom's eyes were rolled back in his head, showing only whites, and he convulsively jerked backward, off the knife, and he turned and clumped into the hall and away down the front steps. He seemed shorter than he had a moment ago when he had loomed over McKee's shoulder.

Johanna ran after him and slammed the door, and as Crawford struggled up to a sitting position, he heard her shoot the bolt. He clasped a trembling hand to his throat and then lifted it away, and the palm was bright and shiny with fresh red blood—but the blood wasn't spurting. No vein or artery had been punctured.

McKee was crouched in front of him, her face white as sea foam. A moment later Johanna was beside her, her eyes wide.

"He—killed himself," Crawford gasped, "died, at least—" He waved at Johanna, who tersely told McKee what Ollie had said minutes earlier.

McKee wailed softly and pounded a fist on the floor. "And you took it, to save *me!*"

Crawford knew what he had to say, but for several seconds he simply couldn't do it.

"Go," he choked at last, "now. Take the wagon, sell what's on it, but—" To his agonized impatience, Johanna ran out of the room, but she was back in a moment with a towel, which she wrapped tightly around his neck.

"Don't go to Newhaven," he went on hoarsely, "or Dieppe. I know about those. Go by some other route, to some other country." His vision blurred, for tears were spilling down his cheeks. "If you ever see me again—God forbid—run. And have garlic and silver bullets ready."

"I invited him in!" said McKee. "Why in the name of—my *damnation* did I invite him *in?*"

"I should have told you immediately," Crawford said. "Go, both of you—Polidori can see through me, I'm sure of it. Adelaide, I love you. Johanna, I love you."

Johanna was sobbing, and she threw her arms around his neck, rubbing the towel painfully against his cut, but he caught her up in a fierce hug. "Don't get weepy," he whispered.

"You are," she choked.

He kissed her and pushed her back, and then McKee was hugging him, not sobbing but grinding her teeth and knotting her fingers in his hair.

"You're the best man I ever knew," she whispered, "or could ever hope to know."

"Likewise," was all he could think to say to her. "Go. Save our daughter. Don't look back."

"I—can't," said Johanna, shaking her head. "It's—too much, after everything."

"I love you both," Crawford said desperately. "Save the people I love, please."

McKee nodded and stood up and jerked Johanna to her feet. "We can do this for him," she told her daughter, and the two sets of footsteps, one dragging, receded down the hall as Crawford resolutely looked away.

After a few minutes he heard horses being harnessed to the wagon—and faintly heard McKee say "No" sharply—and then the wagon creaked and rumbled away toward the Strand.

His shoulders shook with nearly silent weeping as he struggled to stand up, and he looked with despair at the gleaming shards of the broken whisky decanter.

For what might have been several minutes he just leaned against the wall, breathing and pressing the towel to the throbbing wound in his neck.

Then motion to his left caught his eye, and he was not altogether surprised to see a chair in the previously empty street-side corner, nor to see that a man sat in it, holding out a glass.

"Drink up," the man said.

He was older now, appearing to be perhaps thirty, with a golden beard and broad shoulders, but Crawford recognized him.

"Girard," he said softly. Another chair stood now near the first, and Crawford wearily shambled over to it and sat down, accepting the glass of whisky with his free hand.

Crawford took a sip and then said, "Is it endurable?"

His son pursed his lips and rocked his head back and forth. "More endurable than being a plain ghost in the river, I think," he said, "though that does have the advantage of not lasting long. And I'm not much of myself anymore, in any case." He smiled, and Crawford remembered the smile. "You won't be either."

Crawford took a sip of the whisky and relaxed—and he wondered if he had truly relaxed in years, or ever. The wound in his throat didn't pain him now, and he let the towel fall away.

"I'm sorry I ran away from you, by the river," he said. "All those years ago."

Girard nodded judicially. "It would have been better for everyone if you had not," he agreed. "But you're at peace now."

"Is there . . . you're my son, still, in some ways . . . is there any way out?"

"Immediate high amputation has been known to prevent possession," said Girard, "but it's far too late for that, the seeds are all through your bloodstream by now—and in your case it would have involved cutting off your head." He laughed softly.

Crawford stared at him. "Your mother, and Richard—they're gone?"

"Down dead in the river beyond our reach, and certainly dissolved out in the sea long ago."

"Do you—can you—miss them?"

"No. You don't miss them either, do you?"

Crawford realized that in fact he did not. "If I hadn't run away from you," he said, looking curiously at the glass in his hand, "I'd never have met Adelaide. Johanna would not exist."

"Our patron would have got another girl. He will now, if he can't find this—this *Johanna*." Girard's nostrils flared as he pronounced the name.

"You hate her," Crawford noted. The glass in his hand was more transparent than it should have been, and it occurred to him that the taste of the whisky was more a memory of whisky than an immediate sensation.

The glass had no weight either. He opened his hand, and the glass dissolved in place, like a puff of smoke.

"You'll soon find better drink than whisky," said the figure in the other chair. It still had the appearance of a young man, but the likeness to Crawford's son had faded in a nondescript blandness. "When a son of mine, an extension of me, squanders his love on a mayfly, I hate the mayfly, and I would kill it. But she may yet become an extension of me." The figure smiled again, but it was no longer the smile Crawford remembered. "You can help us find her. She would be vulnerable to you—her emotions are stronger than her reason."

Crawford nodded. That was probably true.

He was aware of a springy lightness in his chest, a restlessness that had begun faintly to disperse the relaxation he'd been feeling moments ago. He wanted to be outdoors, in the streets, in the dark.

"Night is your time now," said the thing that was now simply Polidori, with the remembered dark hair and mustache and deep-set eyes. "You'll come to hate daylight. Your place by day will be among the tombs, and the regions under the tombs, but by night you will be a citizen of every place under the moon."

Crawford stood up, and when he looked around his chair was gone; and when he looked back, there was no chair or person in the corner.

He found that he was walking to the hall, and then that he was opening the door and descending to the street.

CHAPTER THIRTEEN

For he keeps the Lord's watch in the night against the
adversary.

For he counteracts the powers of darkness by his
electrical skin and glaring eyes . . .
For he can tread to all the measures upon the music.
For he can swim for life . . .

—Christopher Smart, *"For I Will Consider My Cat Jeoffry"*

THE FULL MOON was visible to Crawford's left, just clearing the
sawtooth rooftops and transfixed by the black spire of St. Clement's, but he walked the other way, into the shadows to Newcastle
Street, and then he dodged cabs and carriages across the lamplit Strand
to skirt the austere pillars and arches of Somerset House and turn left at
Wellington Street, which led out onto Waterloo Bridge.

Polidori's attention was as constant as a faint smell or a distant
noise, but Crawford was already able to ignore it most of the time.

It wasn't raining tonight, but when he had paid his ha'penny at the turnstile and walked out as far as the recessed stone seat above the third of the bridge's arches over the river, he stopped with such deliberateness that he roused himself from the acquiescent daze that had been almost pleasantly dispersing all connected thoughts.

It seemed to him that it had been raining, here, on some night long ago. Why had he come here tonight?

In his momentary alertness, he noted that he had come out without a coat, and his shirtsleeves were rippling in what must have been a chilling wind—but he felt nothing, warm or cold.

There were no lamps on the bridge, and by the slanting moonlight he could clearly see the dome of St. Paul's a mile away to the east.

He shivered as the nearly lost memory came back to him. It had been raining when he had walked out here fourteen years ago and seen Adelaide McKee for the first time—and a thing that must have been the Polidori demon had come rushing at them out of the sky, and Crawford had thrown McKee into the river and jumped in after her.

That had been the night on which Johanna was conceived.

He remembered now that Johanna and McKee were gone—*Don't go to Newhaven,* he had told them not an hour ago, *or Dieppe. I know about those. Go by some other route, to some other country. If you ever see me again—God forbid—run.*

And Polidori had said, *She would be vulnerable to you—her emotions are stronger than her reason.*

Fourteen years ago he had wondered why he had walked out onto the bridge, and he had speculated that his unexamined purpose might have been to jump off the bridge—to commit suicide.

In fact, he had wound up jumping off the bridge that night, though it had not been to kill himself.

But now he remembered what McKee had said to Gabriel Rossetti, in Regent's Park seven years ago, about Johanna: *If she does die . . . I want to see that she stays dead.*

The vampires' awareness, their power, didn't seem to work under the surface of the river. McKee had noted with approval that Crawford's instinctive reaction on the bridge that night had been to get them both into the river. At the time he had remembered his parents advising that course of action, though he couldn't remember anything about them now.

He walked past the remembered stone seat, slowly to the middle of the bridge. There was an inset seat here too, and he stepped up onto it.

The moon behind him was well clear of the skyline now, and the towers and chimneys of London were spread out in a vast receding mosaic of black and white on either hand, with the dark river moving wide between them.

Polidori's attention became more palpably intrusive, and it was increasing by the moment.

Crawford set one booted foot firmly on the broad rail, and then with the other he stepped right out beyond it, into empty air.

Without the sensation of air rushing past him, he seemed for a couple of long seconds to be floating in the sky.

Then he struck the surface feet first and plunged deep, and he could feel temperature again—the water was so shockingly cold that he expelled his breath in a muffled yell that blew a gout of bubbles past his face; and he had to summon up a flickering memory of Johanna and McKee to let himself keep on emptying his lungs, deliberately now, and holding his arms down at his sides.

They live if I do this, his mind shouted at his rigidly restrained reflexes. They live if I do this!

The silvery ripples of moonlight on the surface were quickly lost in darkness, and his ears seemed to be imploding with the pressure—the withering chill of the black water grew worse as he continued to sink, and irretrievable bubbles of air escaped from his lungs as hitching sobs—and finally his boots actually sank into mud, up to the ankles.

Knowing that he would soon begin involuntarily to struggle back up toward the distant surface in spite of his quaking determination, he forced the last tiny volumes of air out of his throat and mouth, and let himself sink toward a sitting position. He was shivering and clenching his teeth in a mouthful of salty river water.

In his head were ringing Trelawny's remembered words: *When I really thought I was drowning, I could feel the devil claws pulling out of me, reluctantly! I was as clean as a newborn babe . . .*

And Crawford felt something like a cold worm in his mind convulse and withdraw. He was all alone now in the dark and cold at the very bottom of the world.

By the time his spine overcame his brain and set his hands to flailing in the lightless water, his lungs were aching and heaving against his closed throat, and he had struggled only a few yards up from the bottom when his tugging lungs forced him to inhale, and then he was choking, his nose and throat full of water and his chest spasming uselessly.

THERE WAS NO LIGHT, but he could sense his own limp body drifting below him; and it seemed to him that the river floor was like the upthrust hands of a dense crowd, as a multitude of unseen fishes and worms hungrily groped and corkscrewed up toward him, toward his disembodied identity—but his identity was diminished and no longer able to feel any anxiety. The river was the world, flickering and agitated at its finite surface but eternally unchanging in the endless volume below.

Crawford directed his dimming consciousness downward, toward the approaching fins and tentacles.

But a shiver of something like a remembered melody or scent buoyed his awareness—and he sensed the approach of old companions who didn't quite forget, and a graciousness that was not wholly erased by death.

His eyes registered a dim phosphorescence, and his hands reached out—he was back in his body!—and he felt rippling fur against his palms.

Tails and arching backs moved in his vision, and paddling paws; and then in front of him hung the face of a cat—only one eye stared into his eyes, for where the cat's other eye should have been was an empty socket.

And he dazedly recognized the tufted cheeks and one crumpled ear—this was Raymond, one of his distressed cats who had died in his arms years ago.

Crawford was gratefully ready to expire in the ghost company of Raymond and all the other cats he had loved . . .

But Raymond poked his muzzle into Crawford's mouth, as he had often done when he was a kitten, and Crawford had to struggle not to push the animal away, for it felt as if the cat were sucking the remaining wisps of life out of him. But Crawford knew he was surely dying in any case, and he surrendered to his old friend.

Shifting forms gathered under Crawford's body, pushing him upward—when he groped below him, he felt tails, and velvet paws, and muscles under fur.

Now Raymond was exhaling, blowing lion's breath into Crawford's lungs, and inhaling, and exhaling again. The cat's breath drummed with a well-remembered purring, and Crawford could sense two paws against his chest alternately clenching and relaxing. And the backs of what must have been dozens of cats were pressing him upward through the shifting cold water.

When Crawford could see the moonlit ripples on the river surface above him, Raymond drew back and stared into his eyes for a long moment, and the one eye shone with unforgotten companionship and play, and then he and all the ghost cats swirled away below.

Crawford found that he was holding his breath, and he kicked and spread his arms out and down. Luckily he seemed to have lost one of his boots in the mud of the river bottom, for the remaining one was a heavy anchor on his foot; but he gave a last powerful kick and then his face was above the water, in the cold air, and he was treading water and coughing violently.

Within a minute he was able to inhale more air than he coughed out, and he held his breath and ducked his head under the surface, and unbuckled his remaining boot and let it sink away.

Raising his head, he found that his breath was still hitching and uneven—and he realized that he was weeping for the loss of gallant Raymond and all the other beloved small identities who had remembered him even after death, and saved him. Ancient Egyptians had believed that a cat's lives numbered nine—a trinity of trinities—and perhaps each of the cats who had loved him had saved one of theirs for him, saved its last breath.

He spread one hand flat on the surging dark water in a frail gesture of thanks and good-bye.

Finally, after one last racking series of coughs that dizzied him, he took a deep breath and shook his head to clear it and looked around him.

He couldn't see either shore, but he could see the descending north arches of the moonlit bridge. He forced himself to begin swimming as strongly as he could toward the north shore.

The mind-flattening attention of Polidori was gone, and he was desperate to find McKee and Johanna.

He could feel the weight of a handful of silver coins in his trouser pocket, but he didn't dig them out and let them sink—he would probably need it all to convince a cab driver to take a soaking wet passenger anywhere.

And there was only one destination he could think of.

CHRISTINA HAD BEEN HELPED to Gabriel's bedroom, and after changing out of her muddy clothes into one of Gabriel's voluminous nightshirts and downing a glass of brandy, she had fallen into a fitful sleep, and Gabriel and William had gone off to the studio.

When she awoke with a start an hour later, she hadn't known where she was—moonlight slanted in through the one tiny uncurtained window, and she had just been able to make out the crucifix on the far wall.

Did I fall asleep, she had wondered at first, in my room at the Magdalen Penitentiary? Not in such a grand bed . . .

Then with a sinking heart she had remembered where she was—and what she had learned at the séance—and she got out of bed and, barefoot, hurried downstairs to the dark kitchen. The stairs were carpeted, and the flagstones of the kitchen were warmed by the stove; and though the wind boomed outside the window overlooking the back garden, she was not at all chilly in the nightshirt over her chemise.

Without striking a match to the gas jet, she dipped a teacup full of water from a basin by the sink, and she found a saltcellar and salted the water heavily; and then she pulled down one of Gabriel's many hanging braids of garlic and crushed a dozen cloves of it with the flat of a knife and scraped up the pulp with a silver serving spoon.

She sat down at the cook's table in the darkness and gripped the spoon and the cup. She took a deep breath; the crushed garlic overpowered the usual smells of grease and coffee.

Finally she whispered, "Are you here?"

She waited several seconds—and then the table shook once under her elbows. One knock: *yes.*

"Is this—am I speaking to—the child I miscarried?"

Again the table jumped once.

Her voice was thick: "Come to me, child."

Abruptly the walls and ceiling and even the chair she was sitting on disappeared, and she sat down heavily in loose sand. A cold night wind instantly blew all the warm kitchen air out of the folds of her clothing.

She huddled in the sand, shivering and nearly whimpering but somehow still clutching the spoon and the cup; and after a few snatched breaths of the rushing air, she got her legs under herself and stood up, gripping the sand with her bare toes as she staggered in the leaching wind. Moonlit dunes stretched away under a sky more full of stars than any she'd ever seen, and there was not any compensating spark of light in the landscape.

"Mother," came a creaking voice from behind her.

She turned and then flinched at the sight of a towering black colossus starkly silhouetted by the star fields it eclipsed. It must have stood a good hundred yards away, but it dominated the view like a medieval cathedral. With its remote high shoulders and lowered head it might have been a primordial idol of a great bird, or a wolf, or a dragon; and Christina took a step backward in the sand, viscerally sure for a moment that the mountainous thing was tipping toward her.

But it stood motionless; and closer, much closer, only a dozen yards from her across the sand, was a figure she recognized.

The skeletal dead boy was naked now, and in the moonlight she could see several rents and holes in its taut hide.

"You," it said, "you and my bride, disappeared today, in the City. You came back into view, but she did not. Has not yet."

"William!" Christina screamed. "Gabriel! I'm in the kitchen, help me!"

But as soon as her words were flung away by the freezing wind across the limitless desert, she knew that she was somewhere fundamentally removed from Gabriel's kitchen, or Chelsea, or even the terrestrial world.

"Jesus help me," she moaned, hunching her shoulders against the cold.

"He knows nothing of this place," said the dead boy.

Christina bared her teeth as her hair flew wildly around her face. "Then let's bring Him here," she cried. The wind was at her back, and she flung the cupful of salted water straight at the boy's face.

The bony gray figure twisted away, making a sound like a bedsheet ripped in two.

"I baptize thee in the name of the Father, and of the Son, and of the Holy Ghost," she shouted after it. "God help you, child!"

Then she looked up—and her knees gave way and she sat down and began frantically pushing herself backward through the mounding sand, for, with a cavernous rumble that rolled away across the sterile land, the colossus moved, and she knew who it was.

A black head like a castle lifted against the moon, and storm cloud wings churned the wind as they unfolded and hid the horizon.

Christina had intended to throw the spoonful of garlic at Polidori, but it was ludicrously inadequate against this, the antediluvian thing that had for a mere billion human heartbeats worn her uncle's animate ghost.

She scooped up the crushed garlic and rubbed it over her face and throat, then sucked the spoon clean.

The night recoiled from her.

Into her head sprang a projected image of the water colliding with the face of the dead boy, and the boy shaking it off with impunity and staring back at her.

But that desperately advanced image blinked away. In actual fact, the skeletal gray figure was now convulsing in the sand; at one point its skull-like face was turned up toward the moon, and Christina saw black stains mottling the cheeks and covering the eyes.

She shivered and almost lost consciousness then as a wave of wordless rage scorched across the field of her thoughts and perceptions.

A black ripple like a blowing curtain to her left caught the fragments of her attention, and when she had somewhat mustered her thoughts again, she was able to recognize a sort of caricature of her uncle, its arms waving helplessly in the turbulent wind.

"Tell speak at the boy it no effect!" squawked the fluttering, nearly faceless figure. "Say him water only!"

"It *is* just water," screamed Christina. "It's baptism! I've saved his soul!"

The sketchy Polidori caricature wailed, "No soul!" and blew into scattering shreds—

And Christina slammed her hands against the kitchen table and slapped her feet against the tinglingly warm flagstones.

She was panting in the humid air of Gabriel's kitchen, clutching the edges of the table now as if to force it to stay, and her eyes darted around to gratefully take in the stove and the window and the hallway arch. The spoon and the cup were nowhere to be seen.

For nearly a minute she simply concentrated on breathing in and out, though the smell and taste of garlic was overpowering.

But that's right of course, she thought at last—a dead child has no soul in it to save. Still, the baptism clearly had some effect on his ghost. And it was all I could do.

She could still feel Polidori's rage in her head, muted down to the usual pressure of his attention, and it carried now a flavor of wrathful promise—dead children, disease, despair.

MCKEE HAD ROUSED FATHER Cyprian from his room by pounding on the rectory door, and eventually he had opened an upstairs window; and after she and Johanna had conveyed something of the urgency of their situation, he had come downstairs with a candle and unlocked the church and led them inside. There was only one window, high on the wall above the altar, and the moonlight through the stained glass shone with various brightnesses of gray. The pews below were in darkness except for the priest's bobbing candle and the candle in a red glass chimney burning beside the altar. The two banks of tiny votive candles that had been lit during the day had long since burned out.

McKee and Johanna sat down in the front pew, and the priest stood between it and the communion rail.

"Annulled?" he said finally. "Why? I don't think you've been married twelve hours yet."

"Because," said McKee in a tightly controlled voice, "my husband has—unmerciful God!—had the misfortune to fall prey—to the devils we mentioned yesterday." She inhaled and went on speaking. "My daughter—our daughter, and I, have to hide from him now, and I'm afraid the sacramental bond of marriage might be a thread he and his new master could follow."

Wind sighed against the stained-glass window, and the doors through which they'd entered, facing Bozier's Court, rattled on their hinges, making both McKee and Johanna jump.

The priest glanced toward the rear of the church and then looked again at McKee.

"The marriage has not been consummated?" he asked, and McKee turned her face away from the candle's dim amber glow.

"No," she said. "We've—been busy."

"An annulment would take time."

"We don't *have* time," said McKee, her voice cracking. "We've wasted more than an hour selling things in the New Cut Market, and we need to be on a boat bound *somewhere* tomorrow morning."

"I'm sorry, Adelaide—I could destroy the record and you could destroy the certificate, but—"

"That would only erase it in legal terms," said McKee, nodding hopelessly.

"An annulment," said Father Cyprian, "even a simple and uncontested one on the basis of non-consummation, would still have to come through the bishop." He spread his hands. "But it may be that the—the *spiritual* bond between you and him has not yet been forged."

"It's forged," said Johanna. "I'm the forgery." She sniffed. "The marriage *was* consummated—in advance, thirteen or fourteen years ago."

"That may be true," McKee whispered; and in the same moment, from the darkness at the back of the church, came Crawford's voice: "That's true."

McKee uttered a short scream and whirled around in the pew, her hand darting under her coat; Johanna scrambled to stand on the pew, facing backward; and the priest raised his voice:

"You have no power here."

"I have no p-power anywhere," said Crawford hoarsely, shambling forward. "Adelaide, Johanna—I've escaped him, the way Trelawny did in America, by drowning myself. Throw—" He was interrupted by a fit of harsh coughing, and his hands slapped one of the middle pew backs. "Throw garlic at me. Or roll your j-jar down here and I'll eat it." He gave a shaky laugh. "Wait till dawn and I'll—dance naked in direct sunlight."

Johanna took the candle from the priest and began walking down the aisle toward Crawford.

McKee shouted, "Johanna, don't!" She drew her knife and ran after her, but Johanna began running too, and the candle went out; and when McKee caught up with her daughter, the girl was already in Crawford's arms.

"Don't stab him!" yelled Johanna. "He's right! I'd know!"

"Get away from him," said McKee through clenched teeth.

"No! I say he's clean, and I was a Lark!"

"*Was.*" Holding her knife half extended for a stab, McKee reached out tensely with her free hand to pull Johanna out of the way; and she touched Crawford's sleeve. Then she let her fingers tap across his waistcoat.

"You're soaked," she said. "And shivering."

"I j-jumped into the river," he said. "Again. This time I went all the way to the bottom, and—and I very nearly died, but—ghosts found me and revived me."

"Ghosts did?" said McKee. "What ghosts?"

Crawford exhaled, and McKee got the impression that it was so that his voice wouldn't crack when he spoke. "Old friends," he said. "I—I look forward to seeing them again, when my time comes."

McKee didn't move for several seconds, then swore and tucked her knife back into its sheath.

"Father," she said, turning back toward the dimly visible altar, "never mind the annulment, but could we buy some dry clothes from you?"

⊱✦⊰

THE DOVER-TO-DUNKIRK STEAMSHIP WAS a 180-foot side-wheeler, and though its funnel was puffing black smoke into the blue morning sky and the pistons drummed under the deck, two sails on its foremast appeared to be doing most of the work. Beyond the white sails, the remote blue sky met the sea in every direction.

Crawford and McKee and Johanna were huddled with a dozen other passengers just aft of the big starboard wheel cowling. Crawford's cough had not abated, and he hugged himself inside the overcoat he had bought at a train stop in Maidstone.

"Sorry," he gasped after the latest coughing fit. "Thames water doesn't seem to be good for one's lungs."

"The cats," said Johanna, holding on to her hat in the breeze from behind, "probably gave you an extra life or two."

McKee just shook her head, staring out at the green waves of the English Channel. Crawford knew she was worried about his health, and the money that they were spending much more rapidly than planned, and the prospect of beginning life anew in a country whose inhabitants spoke a language she didn't know.

They were still an hour out of Dunkirk, and they had been told that the tide would be low there, and that the ship would not dock but land passengers in rowboats.

Crawford said to McKee, "What shall we have for *le petit déjeuner,* Madame Crawford?"

McKee had learned that much from him on the train. "Frogs," she said.

"Great bread and cheese," countered Crawford.

"And wine," put in Johanna.

"Will we ever come back?" burst out McKee. "Will we ever . . . see London again?"

Crawford leaned against the tall cowling, feeling the vibration of the big paddle wheel turning inside it.

"I think we had better hope not," he said.

BOOK III

Give Up the Ghost

March 1877

CHAPTER ONE

Did he lie? does he laugh? does he know it,
Now he lies out of reach, out of breath,
Thy prophet, thy preacher, thy poet,
Sin's child by incestuous death?

—*Algernon Swinburne, "Dolores"*

S NOW WHIRLED DOWN out of the gray sky, and the young woman who was crouched behind the big letters of the ENO'S FRUIT SALT sign high over Tudor Street pressed her back against the warm chimney bricks and began the song once again, singing loudly against the wind:

> *There was a man of double deed*
> *Sowed his garden full of seed.*
> *When the seed began to grow,*
> *'Twas like a garden full of snow . . .*

It occurred to her that she was in her own garden of snow up here, with rounded white drifts at various levels all around her, and icicles fringing roof edges and the projecting rims of cold chimneys.

The metal pattens on her boots were braced against the shingled roof of a tiny gable that poked out of the main slanting roof, and she wondered if anyone within might hear her; but the window would certainly be closed in this weather, and the little garret room probably wasn't heated—the chimney at her back wasn't radiating warmth from any hearth within a dozen vertical yards. She felt as if she were on the lowest-hanging skirt of some slow-moving airship, hidden by the snow and the fog from the earthbound city so far below.

She shivered and fished a flask from under her outermost coat and unscrewed the cap with trembling gloved fingers, then pulled the scarf down from her face and took a sip. The whisky was warm, and she exhaled a plume of aromatic steam before pulling the scarf back up.

She still couldn't hear a reply to her singing, and she hoped this unseasonably late winter weather had not diverted them from their usual early-March routine: go to the rooftops to watch for churning black clouds rushing over the skyline. She recalled seeing several of the things during her years as a Lark—sometimes the weirdly distinct little clouds were elongated perpendicular to the direction of travel, and waving at the ends like wings.

And in the moment before her recent singing was answered from another roof, she saw one—a rolling black shape nearly invisible in the snow-veiled distance to the northeast; it dipped and disappeared behind some paler building that blended into the uniform whiteness. *I'll have to mention it to them,* she thought, *when they get here.*

Only because she knew the song was she able to recognize the lyrics audible now from some nearby roof:

> *When the sky began to roar,*
> *'Twas like a lion at the door . . .*

She pulled down the scarf for another warming sip of the whisky and then screwed the cap back onto the flask and tucked it away.

She was twenty years old now, far removed from the deep perceptions and narrow lives of the Larks—even seven years ago she had had difficulties dealing with them. She wondered if she would even be able to convey the news of the black flier over Fleet Street.

She took a deep, whisky-fumy breath, and then sang,

> *When the door began to crack,*
> *'Twas like a stick across my back;*
> *When my back began to smart,*
> *'Twas like a penknife in my heart;*
> *When my heart began to bleed—*

She hesitated, for she could hear the muffled clatter of them scrambling across the far side of this roof, then sang the last line:

> *'Twas death and death and death indeed.*

Crouching on the roof now and squinting back up its slope, with one arm braced against the chimney, she saw three shapeless hats, then a fourth and a fifth, poke up from the roof crest above her against the marble sky. The lean faces under the floppy hat brims were in shadow.

"I need to see the old man," she called. "He sent for me."

"Bugger that," one of them growled. He or she was holding a long-bladed knife in one raggedly gloved fist.

"And I saw one of the black fliers just now," she went on. "It went down over Fleet Street, very near here. Did any of you sorry lot see it? He'll want to know about it."

The line of heads wobbled uncertainly, and another of them spoke up. "You got the Neffy smell on you."

"So do you, each of you. I used to *be* one of you, damn it. He sent for me, *call* him."

For several seconds the shadowed faces just peered down at her. Then regular clanking sounded from the far shoulder of the building;

at least one person of adult weight was ascending the iron ladder from
the adjoining rooftop. Could it be the old man already?

But she recognized the voice that called "Johanna!" and her eyes
widened in dismay.

The Larks had ducked away out of sight on the far side of the roof,
and Johanna scrambled up to the peak and glared down at where they
were crouched in the lee of an advertising sign overlooking Whitefriars
Street.

"Call the old man!" she said fiercely.

After a moment, one of the ragged Larks dug a clay egg out of a
pocket and blew the remembered low, mournful note; it rolled away
through the snowy air, seeming to shake the spinning snowflakes.

Johanna stared unhappily to her right, at a ridge between two
nearby chimneys in the direction opposite the gang of Larks, and
soon two bundled-up figures began to appear by labored degrees
from behind it, and Johanna recognized her mother's overcoat, and
then her father's cough. Her mother was forty-one now, and her father
fifty-three, and Johanna blinked rapidly to keep tears from spilling
down her cheeks and freezing on the scarf. They should both be sitting by the fire back in the rented house in Cherbourg, she thought
furiously.

Her father was holding her mother's hand as she stepped carefully down a snow-covered slope of shingles, the pattens on her boots
scraping up shavings of ice, and as he followed her McKee was facing
the Mud Larks across the flat section of roof that was hidden from the
streets below.

"Where is our daughter?" she demanded. "We heard her singing
with you."

"Up here," called Johanna through clenched teeth. She pounded a
gloved fist against the roof peak, loosening a little avalanche. "I told you
not to come after me! I *begged* you to stay home, in my note! I'm—an
adult now!"

"So are we," gasped her father, waving his arms to keep his balance on the squeaking icy roof. "And then some."

Johanna hiked herself up to sit astride the roof peak. "How did you . . . *find* me?" she called down to them.

"We followed the Larks," said her father, looking around the rooftop clearing in evident bewilderment.

"Why *now?*" wailed McKee, squinting up at Johanna. "Cherbourg was safe!"

The Lark blew the little whistle again, and the flat note stretched out over the rooftops.

"Safe for the last what, month?" retorted Johanna. "Just as Rouen was, or Amiens, or St. Brieuc, or—how long do you think it would have been before he found me in Cherbourg too?"

"But," McKee said, "with no preparation, in the winter—in the middle of the night!"

"And a dreadful day for a Channel crossing," said her father; he paused to cough, and then he went on, "We caught the first boat out of Le Havre, but you weren't on it. You must have found one right at the docks in Cherbourg." He coughed again. "What kind of springtime weather is this?"

Johanna sighed through her ice-crusted scarf, and was about to answer her mother, when a new voice intruded:

"I called her."

A lean figure in a black Inverness cape and a slouch hat stepped out from behind the tallest chimney, on the far side of the low square area below Johanna.

And she caught a hint of echo in her own head, a leftover of the mental connection that had conveyed his message to her in a dream two nights ago.

Her mother now had her back to Johanna, staring up at the newcomer.

"Are you—a ghost?" asked McKee.

The question seemed to irritate Trelawny—he swept his hat off and flung his head back, his white hair blowing around his dark face in the snow, and said in a booming voice, "I wish to God I were! It's a bad world that brings an old man out onto the roofs on a day like this. Back down to the streets, now—we're fools to talk under the bare sky, let alone all clustered together."

"I saw a flier two minutes ago," said Johanna. She waved a hand north. "It went to earth a street or two away northeast, probably in the Strand around St. Bride's or Ludgate Circus." In spite of everything, she smiled behind her scarf, pleased that she still remembered London geography after having been away for seven years.

"Fliers!" cried Trelawny. "So close! And such as you are on the roofs! Down, now. If we're not—"

"He called you?" interrupted McKee, though she was walking back toward the roof slope she had just descended, and the ladder on the far side. "How?"

"He can reach me in dreams," said Johanna, swinging a boot over the roof peak and sliding down to the surface her parents stood on, "just like the other can." She stepped across the icy tarred surface and stood worriedly beside her father. The bitter chill couldn't be good for his lungs.

Trelawny had skated down from his perch to join them, and now he raised his gloved hands. "Reach her from the opposite spiritual direction," he clarified. "These, you recall, are the hands that baptized her." He turned to the mute Larks on the other side of the flat roof and said, "Good. Resume your patrol."

"You *called* our daughter back to London?" said her father, who hadn't moved.

Trelawny's face was shadowed as he pulled his old hat back over his head. "I tried Chichuwee, day before yesterday," he said gruffly, "but he could provide no help."

"Help in what? Never mind, it doesn't matter—our daughter is leaving with us on the next boat back to France."

"You and Mother take it," said Johanna. She squeezed his hand through two layers of glove leather. "This is for me to do. You two will just get killed if you stay—wait for me in"—belated caution kept her from again saying the name of the city—"in the place we've been living."

"*What's* for you to do?" burst out McKee.

"*He,*" said Johanna, not wanting to pronounce the name *Polidori* out here either, "has got himself another girl. She's fourteen, just a year older than I was when that dead boy came after me, wanting to—to have a child, some sort of child, by me. She's to be his bride, since I fled."

"My granddaughter, that is," said Trelawny. "Rose, Rose Olguin. I will—*not* have her digging her way up out of a grave and"—he added with a shudder—"and having *congress* with that dead thing."

"You said your children were in America," protested Johanna's mother.

"Argentina," said Trelawny impatiently, "one of them. Others stayed here and died. Of course. But the daughter in Argentina moved back to London two years ago, in spite of my warnings, and now her fourteen-year-old daughter—"

Johanna noticed that the Larks had disappeared over a low wall to the left; and a moment later the roof moved sideways under her boots. She hopped to keep her balance, but her father sat down and her mother crouched and braced one hand against the roof surface. Patches of snow slid down all the roof slopes, and she heard a low rumble roll across the City.

And then something buzzed past her ear, and when she jerked back, she saw a wasp swinging away through the moving veils of snow.

A wasp, she thought, in the middle of a snowstorm? Only after that did she think: An earthquake? In *London?*

"Follow me!" yelled Trelawny, moving now away from the way McKee and Crawford had come, toward the roof-edge wall beyond which the Larks had disappeared.

The roof was still swaying, and Johanna helped her father to his feet, waving away another wasp, and before hurrying after Trelawny she glanced back the other way.

A figure stood now beside the chimney where her mother and father had first appeared; its face under a tall silk hat was shiny black, and at the end of each of its long arms it waved a thin bamboo stick as if conducting an enormous orchestra.

"Where where where?" it called, in such a melodious voice that Johanna thought it had begun to sing.

A loud, hard pop shook the air, and the figure bowed and thrashed its sticks wildly but didn't lose its balance; looking the other way, Johanna saw Trelawny lowering a smoking pistol.

"*Mere de Dieu!*" she exclaimed, halting. "What are you doing?"

"Get over here!" yelled Trelawny, tucking the pistol away.

Johanna hustled her father to the far edge of the roof where Trelawny was waiting impatiently, and then the four of them climbed over the low wall and dropped six feet into a narrow snow-filled gully between two projecting gables.

The footprints and handprints of the Larks were visible in the snow to the left, and had presumably extended up the shingle slope on that side before the shaking of the earthquake, but Trelawny led them through the knee-deep snow the other way, up and between a pair of cupolas and down into another snow-choked trough, this one thickly hazed with black smoke from a rank of chimneys at the downhill end.

Crawford was coughing before they had moved three paces, and when Trelawny stopped, Johanna yelled, "Get us out of this smoke!"

"In a minute," the old man called back hoarsely. "The smoke will repel the wasps, and they're how he sees."

From somewhere behind among the slopes and peaks and chimneys, Johanna heard again the nearly musical *Where where where?* Had Trelawny's pistol ball missed the man with the sticks?

"Christina Rossetti—" began Trelawny, then paused to cough himself before going on, "blinded him seven years ago."

Crawford managed to choke out, "Can we—get down this way?"

Johanna could hardly see her companions through the stinging billows of smoke.

"We can get farther away," said Trelawny. "I don't know about down. Follow me."

Beyond the next gable ridge, blessedly out of the worst of the smoke now, they found a row of windows overlooking Whitefriars Street extending away to their right, and the sills were a foot-wide stone ledge over the sheer drop. Trelawny began shuffling along it, facing the building and edging to his left, gripping the eaves that projected at shoulder height above the windows. Over the sighing of the wind, Johanna could faintly hear the rattle of wagons and carriages eight floors below.

Johanna quickly unstrapped the wobbly pattens from her boots and saw her mother doing the same. They wouldn't fit in the pocket of her coat, so she dropped them on the roof.

Then, her ears ringing with fright, she shuffled out onto the ledge after the old man, her gloved hands holding tightly to the eaves and her boots scuffing in the tracks Trelawny's had cleared in the snow. Her father was right behind her.

"Hang on," she said to him over her right shoulder, earnestly and unnecessarily. "Walk carefully."

"You too."

The wind was from the north, sweeping straight down Whitefriars Street, and it kept funneling between her torso and the window lintels and trying to push her outward. Every new grip on the eaves shingles was tight enough for her fingers to feel the grain of the wooden ridge through the leather of her gloves, and she scraped her boots slowly along the ledge, very aware of the glaze of ice.

"Who," she panted through clenched teeth, speaking mainly to distract herself from the abyss an inch behind her heels, "is he? The blind wasp man?"

Trelawny's snow-dusted hat twisted around, and for a moment she caught the gleam of one eye above the scar-twisted lips.

"You should know him," he said, looking forward again. "He's the dead boy who hoped to have his way with you."

"But—he's a blackamoor now!"

"It's paint."

Johanna looked back to her right and was relieved to see the silhouettes of her father and mother slowly shuffling single file along the ledge behind her.

"Why is he—here?" called Johanna.

"Speaking of *hear*," growled Trelawny, "he's not *deaf*."

Polidori used to call me Josephine sometimes, she thought. That was my grandmother's name, and she was supposed to be a particular favorite among his victims fifty years ago, though she got away from him in the end.

I'll bet Polidori—and his dead boy—would rather have me than Trelawny's granddaughter, if given a choice. All things considered! I'm in what Polidori would think of as his chosen family, and she's not. He might let the granddaughter go, if he had me.

"Is that why you called me here, in the dream?" she asked, speaking into the wind in a normal tone so that Trelawny might or might not hear.

But he had heard. "Would you have stayed in France, either way?"

She shuffled along after him, tense and careful, without answering.

No, she thought, even if I'm just back here to be a red flag to distract a devil bull from a young girl, I'll do it, I'll be that. I can't bear to think of another girl going through what I went through.

"You're still a bastard," she said.

"Now and forevermore," Trelawny agreed. He had halted, his cape blowing around him more violently now. "We're at the corner," he said. "We can't go any farther."

At that, Johanna's resolutely sustained control deserted her. *Can't go any farther?* Her arms and legs tingled with sudden fright, and the ledge seemed narrower—the way back to the gable roof and the smoky chimneys seemed impossibly long and precarious, and her mother and father were blocking the way and might panic and refuse to move—!

And what if the earthquake wasn't quite finished?

Breathing rapidly, she gripped the slanting eaves in front of her with no intention of ever letting go.

"So," said Trelawny, "we'll take the stairs down." He swung one leg back, out over Whitefriars Street so far below, and then drove his knee forward into the top of the windowpane in front of him.

It shattered inward, the noise muffled and blown away by the wind.

Johanna realized that the first person to climb in would have no one to grab his hands and clothes while he crouched, but Trelawny let go of the eaves and squatted on the icy ledge with no evident qualms, and in the moment before he would have tipped over backward he reached out with his right hand, broke a wedge of glass out of the window frame, and then gripped the frame just as his weight came on it. Then his left hand gripped the opposite side and he hiked his legs forward into the dark room beyond. He disappeared inside, and she heard his boots knock on a wooden floor.

A moment later his squinting white-bearded face and one hand were back out in the wind.

"A little farther, child," he said.

"I'm right behind you," came her father's strained voice.

In her panicky state it seemed suicidal to release her iron grip, but Johanna exhaled and took a deep breath, and was able to let go of the eaves she was clinging to and reach out to take hold of the one over Trelawny; the move made ice water of her guts, but she gritted her teeth and followed it with a shuffle forward, and then Trelawny had a firm hold of her waist.

"Lift your feet," he said.

She did, and a moment later she was standing beside the old man in an unlighted slant-ceilinged room, hugging him and trembling.

"Still a bastard," she whispered. He patted the top of her hat and then turned to the window to help her father in.

When all four of them were safely in the room, peering nervously at the cobwebby banks of wooden filing cabinets that hid all the walls, her father finally took off his hat and glared at Trelawny.

"Did you mean to trade Johanna for your granddaughter?"

"Keep—your voice down," said Trelawny, panting. "We're trespassing here, wherever this is." He flexed his shaking fingers. "No, you fool, I don't want that thing to have any bride at all. You think I want London destroyed? But I'm eighty-four years old—I can't sprint across rooftops anymore, or swim the river, or—and your daughter knows his places."

McKee went to the short door and opened it; after peering into the hallway beyond, she shut the door and stepped back to the middle of the room and sat down on the floor. "Nobody about. But do let's be quiet." She turned to Trelawny, and the expression on her narrow face was one of concern. "You love your granddaughter."

"I wouldn't go that far," said the old man. He lowered himself carefully to the floor and stretched his legs out. "Ah! I've only seen her twice, and the second time was when her mother was ordering me out of her house. Still, she's a nice child." He sighed. "It's more that she's *my* granddaughter, you see."

"You . . . care about her, then, as much as you care about anything."

Trelawny shrugged and nodded. "That sums it up."

"Let my husband cut that stone out of your throat."

Trelawny smiled at McKee. "No."

"You'll be saving two girls, Johanna here and your granddaughter, this girl Rose."

"There's *other* ways to stop Polidori," said Trelawny irritably, "without killing me."

"My husband is a skilled surgeon—"

Trelawny raised a hand to interrupt her. "And we need to *find* Rose in any case," he said. "We can't leave her clean but down a well somewhere." He sighed and rubbed his eyes. "We need to get hold of the damned Rossettis again."

Johanna sat down too. "I *am* helping in this," she told her parents as she brushed out her short brown hair with her gloved fingers. "I can't not."

Crawford sighed and joined them on the floor. "The Rossettis? Are they still alive? What can they do?"

Trelawny lowered his hands and stared at the dim ceiling. "Five years ago!—I gave William Rossetti a protection. He had put together a book of Shelley's poems, and I knew Shelley, and I helped William with the book and got to know him. I admire him, he's a friend. And he was thinking about asking a woman to marry him, and he had . . . no conception of the peril he'd be putting her into, much less any children they might have. His brother and sisters knew, and I suppose they tried to tell him, but he was *skeptical. Scientific.* So I gave him my piece of Shelley's jawbone, scorched from the funeral pyre. It deflects the attention of . . . those things."

Johanna blinked at him. "You never offered *me* that."

"I thought you were off to America. If you'd all just go to America and *stay* there, I wouldn't have all these problems."

"*You* wouldn't have problems!" said Crawford, and he began coughing again.

"So William has the Shelley jawbone?" said McKee quickly.

"That's right. He gave it back to me at first, after showing it around to his friends as if it were a—a morbid relic or *souvenir*—he told me he really had no use for it. It was *unsanitary.* But three years ago he finally did get married, and his wife started having nightmares, when she could sleep at all, and their first child miscarried, and her brother whom they were both fond of flopped down dead at the age of nineteen—and William came back to me *then,* and begged me to give it back to him! I did, and now his wife's recovered and he's got a baby daughter who seems healthy."

"'London destroyed,'" echoed Crawford belatedly. "How would the dead boy destroy London, just by getting a bride?"

"The *dead boy* is a child, or product, at any rate, of Miss B.," said Trelawny. "You remember her, I'm sure! She had largely assumed that poor woman Rossetti married, Dizzy or some such name; you remember her funeral. And if Polidori can raise up from the dead a girl who's a member of *his* family—and he's choosy about that!—the two can, if we stretch the term, marry."

McKee started to interrupt, but Trelawny frowned and went on, "The thing that is Miss B. is British, as British as the Cotswold Hills; in a sense she *is* the Cotswold Hills! And the thing that is Polidori is European, specifically Alpine. The offspring of their families, of their continents, would exert an actual physical tug across the Channel." He nodded at Crawford. "Earthquake."

"To *destroy London*?" said Crawford. "There are never earthquakes in London." He paused. "Well, until today."

"A minor local one," agreed Trelawny, "just from your daughter and the dead boy being in *proximity*. And Rossetti's house shook, if you recall, when they were briefly in proximity in his bedroom seven years ago! And she, Miss B., destroyed London with an earthquake eighteen hundred years ago, when her resurrected British daughter gave birth to a child, so to speak, by a resurrected Roman soldier. She'd very much like to do it again."

"Did the . . . child live?" asked McKee.

"The child was the earthquake," said Trelawny. "It lived less than a minute."

Johanna could see that her parents didn't believe this story, but she remembered a vision she'd had seven years ago, in which astronomically vast wheels had pulled a city apart, rupturing underground rivers and toppling towers.

"I don't have those hide shoes anymore," she said. "Let's get this jawbone before sundown."

CHAPTER TWO

Venus-cum-Iris Mouse
From shifting tides set safe apart,
In no mere bottle, in my heart
Keep house.

—*Christina Rossetti, "My Mouse"*

IN THE DIMMING daylight to the west, Christina Rossetti could see the Charing Cross Hotel and railway station, and she remembered the Hungerford Market that had stood where the hotel and railway station were now.

Her dress, shawl, and bonnet were black.

"Oh, I've outlived my London," she said, turning to William, who was holding her elbow. "With Maria gone, I feel like a ghost myself. This modern London is for people like your new son, not for me."

They were here so that she could show him the spot where she had talked with their father's ghost fourteen years earlier, and the two of them were standing below the central arch of the York water gate—but the stairs that had once led her down to the watermen's shed on the river shore now ended, after only two steps, at a wide gravel pavement, beyond which stretched a broad landscape of snow-covered lawns and paths. The new Victoria Embankment had pushed the river shore a hundred yards out from this spot, and from here she couldn't see the water at all.

"It was . . . there," she told William, pointing at the snowy ground to her right, "about twenty feet below the surface now, where I talked with the watermen. I wonder if their shed is still down there, buried!"

She remembered the old waterman, Hake, telling her, *We're well after being ghosts ourselves,* and she shivered now in the cold.

"And I saw Papa . . . a bit farther on."

She hobbled down the steps, leaning on William's arm as he matched her pace. After walking several yards through the snow, she stopped and pointed down.

"About here."

William obediently stared down at the frozen grass for a moment, then peered around at the leafless trees and lampposts standing up from the whiteness.

"I expect he's at peace now," he muttered.

"*He* was, from the moment of his death," said Christina. "I'm sure he went directly to Heaven. But I trust his ghost has dissipated by now—certainly I don't sense him at all here. One of the watermen told me it was remarkable that Papa's had lasted eight years—and it's been nearly a quarter of a century now."

William steered her back toward the arch. "Thank you for showing it to me," he said, "but we should find a cab and get you home. This winter doesn't seem as if it ever means to make way for spring."

Christina sighed and nodded. William had brought this outing on himself, by quizzing her this afternoon about what dangers their uncle might still pose to his growing family. Only two days ago his wife, Lucy, had given birth to their second child, a healthy boy they had named Gabriel Arthur Madox Rossetti.

The discussion had started with Maria's ghost.

Their sister, Maria, had died three months earlier, of cancer, at the All Saint's convent in Margaret Street, and the sisters had refused permission to Christina and her mother to view the body in the coffin, or even to enter the convent mortuary. Christina assumed it was because the sisters recognized the ineradicable Nephilim mark on her soul and therefore feared that she would try to capture Maria's ghost—and in fact Christina *had* worried about Maria's ghost, cut off from the Heaven-bound soul and perhaps swimming about disconsolately in the cold river. *All fear one another,* her father's ghost had told her, fourteen years ago; *river worms now . . . Ugly, crushed, blind . . . this waits for you all too, remember.*

Christina had no doubt that it waited for herself and Gabriel and William, but she had been unable to bear the thought of even a half-sentient fragment of gentle Maria drifting fearfully in the cold river at night, part of what they had called the Sea-People Chorus . . .

And so she had been inexpressibly grateful when poor, silly, gallant old Charles Cayley had, on New Year's Day, given her Maria's captured ghost.

Cayley had said, with fastidious embarrassment, that he was distressed to see Christina so unhappy, and that he had learned from her that there was another London behind the one he had grown up in. And so he had consulted a series of "spiritualists" who had pointed him eventually to one of several magicians living in the sewers—and, through a hired intermediary, Cayley had had to deliver several cages full of songbirds to the magician in exchange for the peculiar sea creature that contained Maria's ghost.

Cayley had given it to her preserved in a wine bottle filled with brandy. It was a kind of worm called a "sea mouse," or more properly an example of *Aphrodita aculeata.*

It was a little oval thing no bigger than a baby's shoe, furred with fine crystalline hairs that shifted from blue to green to red as one turned the bottle in the light.

Cayley had provided the magician with various items to draw the ghost to shore, where it could be netted—a copy of a book Maria had written, *Letters to My Bible Class,* and an old hairbrush of hers, and a sliver from the wooden floor of the old family house on Charlotte Street, which was now a City Registrar's office—and Cayley had not been cheated. Though the creature itself was dead, swirling in the amber brandy, Christina could clearly feel her sister's presence when she held the bottle.

Christina kept the bottle in her bedroom, and sometimes read Tennyson to it by candlelight when the night beyond the windows was especially cold and stormy.

This afternoon in Christina's parlor, William had again obediently held up the bottle and peered into it, though he never sensed any presence of Maria in it. Then he had asked her whether a captive ghost—"I mean a contained and protected ghost," he had added hastily, putting the bottle down—might be a protection for his new family against the lethal attentions of their uncle. Christina had for three years known about the piece of Shelley's jawbone, which seemed so far to be effectively serving that purpose, and William had wondered aloud whether its evident power might derive from some fragment of Shelley's ghost still adhering to it.

Christina had told him that ghosts weren't supposed to last nearly that long, and she had described her nighttime river-side encounter in 1862 with their father's ghost; and William had said, "I'd like to see that spot sometime."

Intrigued by the idea herself, she had got up and fetched her overcoat and shawl and bonnet, and within minutes they had been in a cab bound for the Victoria Embankment.

And in the end she had been able to show him only expanses of frozen dirt where the river shore had once been. Feeling antique and irrelevant now, she let him lead her back to the cab rank by Gatti's Restaurant on Villiers Street.

"I wish your friend Trelawny had more bits of Shelley to give away," she said as a sedate old hackney coach bore them back up Tottenham Court Road toward the house Christina now shared with her mother and two aunts. The streetlamps were already lit and made passing halos on the coach's window glass. "I believe that to some extent our terrible uncle is punishing Gabriel and I for our renunciation of him."

Six years earlier, Christina had nearly died of some ailment that had swelled her throat and made her eyes protrude and permanently darkened her skin; it was tentatively diagnosed as Graves' disease, and she had somewhat recovered since, though her hands shook almost too badly to write, and she still had little energy. The following year Gabriel had tried to kill himself with an overdose of laudanum, perhaps in mimic expiation of his guilt at Lizzie's death; and though he had not died, he now believed that enemies were perpetually spying on him, and he had built partitions in his studio to keep them from peering in at him while he worked. And he took ever-increasing doses of chloral hydrate in brandy in a vain attempt to be able to sleep more than a couple of hours a night.

William was still as responsible and competent at forty-seven as he had ever been, and he was a devoted husband and father—but Christina sometimes sensed a wistful sadness in him, as if he too had chosen to make some never-referred-to but profound sacrifice for the sake of his family.

"I'll ask Trelawny," said William now with a gentle smile. "He always speaks highly of you. He calls you 'Diamonds.'"

The coach had turned in to Torrington Place, and lights glowed in the windows of most of the houses in the row; Christina and her mother and aunts had moved here six months ago, but Christina still sometimes had trouble identifying which of the similar steps and doors were hers.

This evening she was able to tell immediately. "I think you can ask him right now," she said, suddenly very tired.

Four people stood in the lamplight on her doorstep. Though they were shapeless bulks of winter clothing, the white-bearded one was clearly Trelawny himself, and she was pretty sure that two of the others were Adelaide McKee and her husband.

The cab slithered to a stop on icy cobblestones, and William climbed out and helped Christina step down; and he kept hold of her elbow as they nodded to the visitors and made their way carefully up to the lamplit door.

After unlocking it, Christina turned to McKee and said, "I'm afraid I'm not up to guests at the moment, Adelaide. If you would write to me tomorrow—"

"Actually, Miss Rossetti," interrupted Trelawny, "it's William we came to see."

William glanced at his sister, and she sighed and nodded. "Do come in. William can be your host."

"Just for a couple of minutes," said William. "I've got to be getting home myself."

They all trooped up the steps and into the entry hall, where there was another little snowstorm as everyone unwound scarves and took off hats and shrugged out of overcoats, and then William had fetched in another chair from the dining room so that they could all sit in the parlor. Trelawny made quick introductions.

"I'll just join you all in a cup of tea," said Christina, "and then I'll have to ask you all to excuse me." She smiled at Johanna, who now looked very much like her mother did when Christina had first met her at the Magdalen Penitentiary, nineteen years ago. "It's so good to see you again, Johanna!" she said. "You were still a child when I saw you last."

Johanna, sitting between her mother and father on a sofa by the fireplace, nodded and returned the smile. "I remember that you fired two shots from a revolver in my father's surgery."

William, sitting closer to the fire, had clearly been about to ask Trelawny what his business was, but at this he turned to stare at Christina.

She shrugged. "It was a stressful afternoon. And the second shot was just because I dropped the pistol."

Trelawny stood up. "We've come," he said bluntly to William, "to ask you for that piece of Shelley's jawbone that I gave you three years ago."

William blinked up at him, his mouth open. "But—but Edward, surely you know why I can't give it back!"

"We were just talking about it," exclaimed Christina. "Did you know William's wife gave birth to a son two days ago?"

Trelawny bared his teeth in a pained grimace, but he went on, "It was a loan. I'm calling it back now."

William's eyes were wide, and his beard was shaking along with his chin. "I'd be killing my children—and my wife—if I gave it up! Just as I killed our first child, and my wife's brother, when I refused it at first, foolishly!"

"You've had benefit of it," said Trelawny. "Now my grandchild has been taken by *your uncle!*—the uncle *you*," he said, turning on Christina, "quickened!"

Christina's face was hot, and she took a breath but then couldn't think of anything to say.

McKee and her husband were looking away, but Johanna—who must be twenty now!—was listening avidly, her blue eyes bright in the glow of the gas-jet chandelier overhead.

"I thought," began Christina. William and Trelawny both swung to face her, so she went on weakly, "I thought we had reached a working truce. William had the fragment of jawbone to protect his family; you," she said, nodding at Trelawny, "were in a favored position; and Adelaide, I thought you three had fled overseas!"

"My idiot daughter moved back to England," said Trelawny, "and now her daughter is a captive of your damnable relative."

"As I was," murmured Johanna.

"As you're likely to be again," snapped McKee, "if we don't get you into a foreign-bound boat damn quick!"

"I *can't* leave," said Johanna, "while a fourteen-year-old girl is in the trap I was in." She gave Christina a look that was almost merry. "You're the one who saved me, with your mirror trick."

To Trelawny, Christina said in a whisper, "She's fourteen?"

The old man nodded grimly.

"I was fourteen too," Christina said softly, "when I fell into his trap."

"My *son* is *two days old*," said William, standing up.

"We've been friends, William," said Trelawny, "but I *will have* that bit of bone." He drew a revolver from under his coat, hesitated, then stepped to Christina's chair and pointed it diagonally down, straight at her face.

She found herself looking up the barrel, which was only inches in front of her nose—she noticed spiral grooves in the bore, and in that tense moment the only thing in her mind was remote curiosity about whether all guns had that feature.

Trelawny glared sideways at William. "The first incentive I offer," he said, "is the life of your sister. Forfeiting that, you'll find I can bring further incentives to bear."

"I have another idea," Christina said.

CRAWFORD HOPED SHE DID. The Rossettis' mother was in some nearby room preparing tea, and Trelawny might very well be capable of blowing Christina Rossetti's head off right here in the parlor.

Crawford's ears were ringing as if in anticipation of the shot, and Trelawny was too far away across the carpet for Crawford to hope to spring up from the sofa and catch the old man's arm before he could shoot, and William's chair was on the other side of the sofa from Trelawny.

"My sister, Maria," said Christina evenly, "died three months ago. Two months ago a friend acquired her ghost for me. It's in my room upstairs."

"And your idea is . . . ?" grated Trelawny, not lowering the gun barrel.

"Maria always claimed—that is, she never denied—that she had found a way, in her studies, to stop our uncle. She would never tell us what it was, because it apparently involved us committing some mortal sin, and she didn't want to be a party to us damning our souls."

William, almost as pale as his shirt, nodded jerkily. "That's right."

Christina's face had somehow darkened and sagged since Crawford had last seen her, but when she smiled, it was the face he remembered. "She had scruples, do you see?" she said. "While she was living. But ghosts don't have scruples."

For several seconds the clock on the mantel ticked and no one spoke. Then Trelawny lowered the pistol and tucked it back under his coat.

"Three months? Not too diminished, then. We'll bank on that, God help us, and I can certainly commit one more mortal sin." He frowned at Christina. "I could not have shot you, Diamonds. I abjectly apologize for pretending that I would."

The couch and chairs creaked as the Crawfords and Rossettis began hesitantly to relax.

Christina closed her eyes and breathed deeply. "You pretend very well," she said; then she opened her eyes and gave him a frail smile. "But I can respect your concern for your grandchild."

She got unsteadily to her feet. "I'll fetch the bottle," she said, and she made her way to the hall; soon they could hear her shoes bumping on stairs. Crawford reflected that she looked much older and gaunter than the intervening seven years could justify.

Johanna nodded. "A drink first would be a splendid idea."

"The bottle contains the *ghost*," said William, slumped back in his chair and rubbing his face. "Edward," he burst out, "all this will make further literary consultations between us mightily awkward."

"I don't see that as necessarily so," said Trelawny, who seemed shaky now himself. "Friends *do* have *disagreements*."

Crawford barely had time to dig out a handkerchief and wipe his forehead, and exchange wide-eyed glances with his wife and daughter, before they heard Christina clumping with painful haste back down the stairs.

"Paper and pencil, William!" she panted as she reappeared in the parlor doorway. She was holding a corked glass bottle full of some pale brown liquid. "I told Mama not to bother with tea, and that we're not to be interrupted."

William stood up from his chair and crossed to an old slant-front desk against the wall. A framed picture hung over it, and he muttered a curse and flipped it around to face the plaster, then grabbed a paper and pencil and hurried back to the others.

Christina had pulled the low table closer to her chair and more squarely under the chandelier, and now she took the pencil and paper from her brother and laid the paper on the tabletop beside the bottle.

She sat down and waved Trelawny into a chair, and then she started to write a series of capital letters on the paper; but her hand shook too violently, and she pursed her lips and gave the pencil to William. He hiked his chair forward and quickly finished the row of letters.

"Silence, now," said Christina, "everyone." Then she lifted the pencil and said, "Maria, are you there?"

Crawford jumped then, and felt Johanna beside him twitch too, for there was some furry little thing in the bottle, and it had moved. The half-dozen gas jets on the chandelier overhead made a fan of the bottle's shadow, and the thing in the bottle glimmered like mother-of-pearl.

But after a few moments, Christina frowned. "Are you there, Maria? We need you."

William was looking uneasy. "No knocks," he whispered.

The room seemed distinctly colder. Crawford exhaled but couldn't see his breath.

"Maria!" Christina went on. "Communicate with us, please! This is your sister and your brother asking!"

The overlapping shadows of the bottle on the table were waving slightly back and forth across the wood surface.

Johanna had shifted around on the sofa, and when Crawford glanced at her, he saw that she was looking toward the hallway arch.

Then she turned to Christina. "Did you lock the door?"

"Shh," said Christina. "Maria, let us know you hear us!"

A loud, wavering buzzing distracted Crawford now; looking up, he saw a wasp looping through the air around the gas flames, and the chandelier was swaying on its chain.

Trelawny saw the wasp and struggled to his feet, pulling the heavy revolver out of his coat again.

"What now?" exclaimed William, shoving himself back from the table in alarm.

"This time," Trelawny wheezed, "I blow off his damned block and tackle!" He took a step to catch his balance, bumping the table.

"Yes," agreed Johanna in a high-pitched voice as she stood up and drew a knife from inside her blouse.

Everybody was leaping up in confusion, and the table went over with a bang—the ghost jar was rolling across the carpet, and the swinging chandelier threw bobbing shadows across the walls.

"He can't actually get *in*," said Johanna, watching the windows. "He hasn't been invited."

The air in the parlor was now very cold, and drafty, and carried the smoke-and-horse smell of the street. Crawford heard scuffling in the hall and the clattering bang of a framed picture hitting the floor.

He shot a glance at Christina, and her brown old face was a mask of dismay.

"You *have* invited him in!" he exclaimed incredulously. He could see the steam of his breath now, and wasps were darting back and forth around the rocking chandelier and through the streaks of glowing dust sifting down from new cracks in the ceiling plaster.

"He was my," Christina choked, "his soul was *my* child, before it was Lizzie's!" She was wringing her gnarled hands and blinking around at her shaking house. "I *baptized* him!"

"You *blinded* me!" came a musical voice from the hall, and then the thing stepped into the parlor.

It was tall, and made to seem taller by the silk hat on its narrow black head, but its arms were so long and slack that its white-gloved hands crouched on fingertips on the floor like crabs. Its face was covered with tarry black paint, shiny in the lamplight, and its eyes had been painted over so thickly that there was scarcely any indentation between the eyebrows and the cheekbones. "I have to paint my face to hide the baptism stains!"

The floor was moving back and forth, and bits of plaster were falling from the ceiling now.

"You promised!" shrilled Christina, rushing at the thing. "You promised—"

William caught her around the waist and pulled her back, without taking his wide eyes off the intruder.

"You promised you'd only visit when I was alone!" There was an inarticulate cry from a nearby room, and Christina screamed, "Mama, *don't come in here!*"

Trelawny had aimed his pistol at the creature, then raised the barrel toward the ceiling when Christina had got in the line of fire, and now he aimed it again.

"I am welcome and assured of no harm in this house," sang the blind thing, its mouth open in a wide smile that bared rows of white teeth against the coal-black lips, "and I have come to claim my proper bride." He moved into the shaking center of the room with one rapid long-legged step.

Christina saw Trelawny's pistol and shouted, "No, I gave him my word—"

But Trelawny fired, the stunning explosion of the shot momentarily compressing the air. The front of the thing's trousers exploded in a spray of what appeared to be sawdust, and the figure bent double, still lunging forward.

"Gave me her word—!" it squealed, as William threw himself against the dining-room door to keep his mother from coming into the room.

Johanna struck one of its hands aside with a convulsive slash of her knife, and a finger, still gloved, flew through the dusty air and leaping shadows, and Trelawny fired again, and then once more, and Crawford thought the windows must break out into the street before the hammering blasts.

Johanna danced back away from the thing's tumbling hat, and with her free hand she juggled a little jar out of her coat pocket and flung it hard onto the floor, and it shattered right under the bent-over creature's face; the long-limbed thing recoiled away, and a moment later Crawford smelled garlic.

Trelawny caught his eye and jerked his head urgently toward the hall; Crawford nodded and grabbed McKee by the elbow and then caught Johanna by the shoulder and shoved them both toward the hallway door. Glancing back, he saw that Trelawny had paused only to bend and pick up the ghost bottle before hurrying after him.

The street door was wide open to the night, and the hall leading to it was a mess—either because of the earthquake or because of the blind thing's blundering passage through it—with furniture overturned and pictures knocked off the walls.

"Down!" Trelawny yelled loudly, and Crawford didn't have to push his wife and daughter to the floor, but simply fell on top of them.

Something rushed over his head, swirling the cold air and leaving a smell of clay and cologne in its wake—looking up cautiously after it had passed, he saw a contained black cloud rush out across the pavement of the street and sweep up out of sight beyond the door lintel.

A tangle of coats and hats and scarves was scattered across the floor. Hastily Crawford grabbed his own things and made sure that McKee and Johanna took somebody's.

Then they were out on the dark street, hurrying away on foot down

Tottenham Court Road as they hastily buttoned coats and pulled on scarves in the intensely cold wind.

Trelawny was moving more slowly than the other three, and panting. "Here," he said, thrusting the bottle at Crawford. "Get to Chichuwee—he can boil her out—that pencil-and-paper stuff, table knocking, that's—fine, if the ghost *wants* to talk to you." He stopped and leaned against a lamppost and bent over and gripped his knees as he blew out quick puffs of steam. "Boiling—*forces* 'em."

Johanna touched the old man's arm. "We'll get you into a cab," she said.

"No," snarled Trelawny weakly, "there's no time. The three of you—separate, now! Meet at dawn. All of us. At"—he glanced apprehensively into the sky before going on—"at the place where you were married." He straightened up and pushed away from the lamppost and began shuffling carefully away. "Don't die in the meantime," he added over his shoulder, "or I'll—have your ghosts for breakfast."

Two horses harnessed to an old four-wheeled clarence cab were clopping down the street in their direction, and Trelawny waved the driver toward the Crawfords.

"It's got a roof—and four walls!" the old man yelled.

"Right," snapped McKee, stepping into a patch of yellow streetlamp radiance in the cab's path and waving her arms. "We *cannot* be together under a night sky. In, quick."

The cab swerved to a halt, and McKee had opened the door before the old vehicle had stopped rocking on its springs, and she boosted Johanna inside and scrambled in herself and reached out a hand for Crawford.

Crawford was two steps away and hurrying forward when the thing struck.

CHAPTER THREE

Unripe harvest there hath none to reap it
From the watery, misty place;
Unripe vineyard there hath none to keep it
In unprofitable space.

—*Christina Rossetti, "A Coast-Nightmare"*

THE ABRUPT ROAR of it was like mountains crashing together at the end of the world, and the sheer sudden air pressure of the sound blew Crawford's hat away and drove him to his knees.

The cab slid away sideways across the shaking pavement, and the cab horses bolted, pulling the slewing cab after them in terrified acceleration down Tottenham Court Road.

Crawford rolled through the snow to the gutter, and he found himself staring straight up into the sky.

The stars were perceptibly moving outward from around a dark shape that was leaning down toward him; a number of wings or limbs radiated out from the central blackness of it, and it was rushing toward him at astronomical speed.

Instinctively he raised his arms to block it, and then he was seeing the thing over the top of the bottle that he still gripped in his hand.

The terrible roaring stopped so suddenly that Crawford almost felt weightless, and the bottle in his upraised hand was glowing now, blue and green and gold. He blinked against the dazzling light, but his view of the sky was now blocked by a broad figure in a black robe and a wide hood, facing away from him.

"I'm Clubs," said the figure in a clear, resonant voice, and Crawford dazedly realized that it was a woman—a nun, in fact.

Beyond her he saw a flickering in the sky, and the air seemed to shiver and surge.

"I belong to your family," the nun went on, "but not to you."

For a moment the air was still—and then a gust of wind whipped down the street, so strongly that it rolled Crawford over onto his face.

He hugged the bottle and scrambled to his hands and knees and scuttled across the pavement to an iron fence, and when he dimly realized that he was trying to crawl between the close-set iron bars he sat back, coughing and shivering violently, and quickly swung his gaze in every direction.

The sky was empty except for stars. More lights were on in nearby windows, but nobody had yet burst out into the street to see what the terrible noise had been, and though it should have frightened all the horses in this dozen streets, several cabs were wheeling along the street sedately enough. By the dimming glow of the bottle he still held, Crawford saw the round-faced nun standing near him in the street, and she smiled.

"Poor man," she said, and then as she sighed, he was able to see windows and walls across the street through the space where she had been.

Crawford got weakly to his feet, gasping and still shivering, for the cold wind had found his sweat-damp shirt and hair. Cabs and carriages whirred past, the horses' hooves clattering on the icy road, and the drivers were all too bundled up in hats and scarves to even glance at where Crawford stood.

The bottle had stopped glowing. He raised it against the glare of a streetlamp, and the furry little thing still bobbed inside.

He lowered the bottle and peered away through the traffic down Tottenham Court Road. The coach with his wife and daughter in it had at least apparently not capsized; and McKee knew where he would be going next.

Looking the other way, Crawford saw the high wheels of a hansom cab rolling in his direction.

He stepped out and waved, and the driver reined to the curb, but the man frowned at the sight of Crawford's disheveled clothes and bottle.

"It's not—liquor," Crawford managed to say. "Oh hell—five shillings if you'll take me to the—to the Spotted Dog in Holywell Street."

That was the way to Chichuwee's underground chamber, and McKee would know to meet him there.

HE REMEMBERED TO HAVE two pennies in his hand when he pushed open the door of the Spotted Dog, and he laid the brown coins on the counter of the little window in the entry hall and took his dented tin card before stepping through the open doorway into the remembered wide kitchen. And for nearly a minute he just stood on the flagstone floor and let the warmth sting his face and hands.

Under the glaring gas jets between the ceiling beams, men and women stood around the black iron stove in the corner or sat with plates on the shelf-like bench that ringed all four walls, and as he shuffled farther inside Crawford wondered if any of them might have been here on that night fourteen years ago when McKee had brought him to this place.

Again the room's warm air smelled of onions and bacon, and this time he crossed to the door in the far side of the room and hung his coat on one of the hooks in the hall beyond it, then shambled back into the kitchen, still holding the bottle, and joined the queue by the stove. He hadn't eaten since breakfast at a seaside pub in Southend, and McKee and Johanna would probably be arriving here soon.

He looked down at himself—the knees of his trousers were torn, and black stains mottled the front of his white shirt. With his free hand he tried to brush his hair flat.

A gritty voice behind him said, "When you going to open the bottle, then, eh?"

Crawford turned and saw a toothless old fellow already taking hold of the bottle Crawford held.

"It's not liquor," said Crawford hastily, pulling it away. "It's a, a laboratory specimen, in formaldehyde, a . . ." He glanced at the thing. "A platypus. A . . . baby one."

"A baby patty-puss!" exclaimed the old man, vastly impressed. "Can you shake it out?"

"No," Crawford said desperately, "it would—crumble on exposure to air."

"Those things dance, I've heard," put in a haggard-looking girl in front of him. "Make it dance."

"A dancing panda-puss!" said the old man, nearly beside himself now with excitement.

"Won't make much of a dinner," advised another man. "It'll render down even more when they cook it. Two bites and it's gone."

"It's a nun!" exclaimed a thin young girl in old leather trousers and a stained apron, who had crouched to peer at the bottle. "It's a baby nun! You can't cook her!"

Crawford was sweating in his damp shirt now. Why couldn't Christina have kept the damn thing in an opaque jar? He frowned and looked worriedly toward the street door. And what the hell had become of McKee and Johanna?

"It's not a nun," he said dizzily, "and I'm not going to cook it." Several pairs of bloodshot eyes were still looking at him hopefully, and he added, "And it doesn't dance."

One by one, the people ahead of him in line were served plates of some steaming stuff, and when it was his turn to stand in front of the stove he paid four pence for a plate of half-burned ham and potatoes with strings of onion all over it. A man next to the stove was tilting mugs under the open tap of a beer cask, and Crawford paid another tuppence for a filled mug, which he gripped in the same hand that was holding the ghost bottle. He found an empty stretch of the bench and sat down. Some of the people in the room were still staring at him, hopefully or disapprovingly, but he concentrated on his plate.

No one appeared to have any forks or spoons, so he set to with his fingers, and when he had wiped the plate clean and licked his finger and wiped his hand on his shirt, and drained the last of the beer, he wondered when he had ever found a dinner as satisfying—and then he remembered the ham and cheese and raw onion repast he had shared with Johanna in his basement on the first night he had met her. Met her to speak to, at any rate.

She and her mother should have got here by now.

Anything might have happened to them.

He carried the bottle outside to stand for several minutes shivering in the dark snowy street, but he saw no pair of figures approaching, and then since he had left his tin card in his coat in the back room, he had to pay another tuppence to get back inside, glad all over again for the stove-warmed air in the kitchen.

He resumed his place on the long bench, and after a few moments he tucked the bottle inside his shirt and leaned back against the wall.

Movement of the bottle against his undershirt brought him awake, and he caught the wrist of the person who had tried to steal it.

It was the girl who had thought the panda-puss ought to dance.

"Mine," he croaked at her, his voice still scratchy with sleep. Coughing as he looked past her, he saw several people watching, apparently hoping that she would succeed in getting the bottle. Clearly he hadn't slept for very long.

Crawford stood up, only clearing his throat now, and a couple of rough-looking men stepped toward the street-side door as if to block his exit. Crawford pretended not to notice, and he carried the bottle across the room away from them, toward the back wall, where he made a show of reading the posters tacked up on the white-painted wood.

Very aware of the doorway to his right, which led to the coat room and the remembered stairs that led down to the ancient well, Crawford absently read that Peter the Great Wikinsmill would soon be appearing at the Waterloo Music Hall, performing his signature song, "All Round My Hat, or Who Stole the Donkey?"

Christina had said that Maria had been dead for three months; Trelawny had said her ghost should not have diminished too much in that time—and certainly it had been solid enough an hour ago in Tottenham Court Road! But what if that appearance had nearly used her up? Maria's ghost was apparently their last hope for saving Johanna—and Trelawny's granddaughter—and the last shreds of the ghost's vitality might be evaporating right now!

After one more glance toward the street-side door—McKee and Johanna had still not appeared, and the bullyboys were still eyeing him—Crawford stepped through the doorway and grabbed his damp coat and walked directly to the wooden stairs and started down them. He remembered the smells of clay and smoke on the draft that welled up from the dimness below him. He recalled that there would be climbing to do, so he pulled on his coat and tucked the ghost bottle into a deep side pocket.

Soon he was in total darkness, but the echoes of the thump of his boots on the stairs told him that he was in a narrow stairway; after forty or fifty steps, the banister he had been alternately clutching and releasing ended in a ragged stump, and after that he proceeded more slowly, dragging his hand along the gritty bricks.

He was expecting it when the stairs ended and he found himself on a flat, slanted stone surface. His shuffling boots and panting breath echoed in a bigger space now—and after groping his way for several yards through the lightless chamber, he heard a distant windy groaning.

It's got some Latin name, he told himself firmly, it's just pressure differences equalizing in the uneven levels of remote tunnels; but his outstretched hands were trembling, and he didn't realize that he was holding his breath until he let it all out in relief when his palms brushed the rim of the old well.

He leaned over the edge, and the remembered smell like sourly fermented seaweed faintly stung his nostrils. He ran his hands around the curved inner surface and then he edged around the well until he felt the topmost iron rung. He sighed unhappily and swung one leg over the coping and carefully lowered his leg until his foot found the rung. There was a muffled clunk as the bottle in his pocket rapped the stone.

Only then did the lingering thought *Latin name* remind him that McKee had recited some kind of ritual phrase before entering the well.

He paused with both hands on the well rim and both boots on the rung, and across fourteen years he tried to remember what the phrase had been. There had been a mnemonic nursery rhyme to remind one of it, but he couldn't remember the nursery rhyme either. Something about frogs and snails? Sugar and spice?

For a moment he thought of climbing out again and waiting in the total darkness by the well for McKee to make her way down here, but the whistling wail sounded again, perhaps not quite so far away now, and he just gritted his teeth and lowered one foot to feel for the next rung down.

He had descended down six of the rungs, about twelve feet, when something stung him painfully in the neck. It jolted him, but he clung to the rungs as his face suddenly chilled with sweat; and a moment later his left hand was stung twice. He let go of the rung to swat at the fluttering insects, and in that moment he remembered the nursery rhyme.

"Oranges and—damn it—lemons," he gasped, turning his face away from another pair of invisible brushing wings. "Say the bells of St. Clement's."

And at that prompting the Latin came to him too. "*Origo lemurum*, you bastards!" he yelled.

He climbed down as rapidly as he dared, panting against the close brick wall, but perhaps the invocation had worked—he wasn't stung again.

But though his hands and feet continued to grip and press against the iron bars, his eyes gradually registered a glow that was not vision, for it was in front of him no matter which way he turned his head. He kept palpably climbing down the iron brackets moored in the brick wall as the sour draft from below continued to whisper up around him, but what he was seeing became a wide landscape—he saw a pillared temple and stone buildings with towers, surrounded by straight streets and low white houses with plaster walls and arched gateways and red tile roofs; there was a broad river, with a lone long timber bridge spanning it, and ships with short masts and curved sternposts were moored along wooden wharves. Smaller rivers slanted through the city, and boats with sails moved slowly up and down them.

Into his head came the thought that this was London when it was called Londinium by these invaders from overseas, before the tributary rivers were roofed over to become sewers. Farms stretched in green squares outside the city wall.

And now the fields were overrun by men in furs whose faces and arms were dyed blue and who carried black iron swords; the Romans fought them with spears and shields and short steel swords, but the wild Celts vastly outnumbered them, and the Romans fled; but the Celts retreated too—and then the city began to ripple like lilies on a disrupted pond. The towers and houses fell, and the river rose and swept the bridge away, and clouds of tan dust shaken up from the low hills mingled with black smoke as the broken city burned.

The vision faded, but he was dimly able to see his hand on the rung in front of him; and it occurred to him that the vision had been in his mind alone, not in front of his eyes, or he wouldn't have been able to see anything at all in this near-total blackness right afterward.

He held still, remembering having glimpsed fragments of this vision before. Clearly what he had just seen was the destruction of Roman London—by Boadicea in A.D. 60, according to Trelawny. And it had certainly involved an earthquake. *She'd very much like to do it again,* Trelawny had said this afternoon.

Crawford resumed climbing downward, and soon his reaching foot found no lower rung, so he lowered himself joltingly by his hands alone to the bottom-most rung, swung for a moment, and then dropped.

He fell about ten feet into damp sand and managed not to fall over or bang his chin on his knee, and he patted his pocket and was reassured to feel that the bottle was still there. When he straightened up, he could see the faint round-topped vertical glows of at least four arched doorways around him—he had forgotten that there were more than one, and he didn't have an ave to guide him.

He paced from one arch to another in the near-total gloom, listening carefully for the chirping of birds. At one arch he heard a distant susurrus like rushing water, and at another the remote windy groaning, and so he brushed his hair back from his face with both hands, took a deep breath, and ducked into one of the silent tunnels.

It curved to the left, which was familiar, but soon, instead of the broad glow of Chichuwee's chamber, he saw a dot of yellow light ahead. It seemed some yards away at first, but quickly dropped in apparent height as he approached it, and when it disappeared in the moment before his groping hands brushed a wall of upright planks—and then his fingers felt down the length of it to a pitted doorknob—he realized that the tiny glow was a keyhole.

He crouched to peer through it and saw, perhaps twenty feet beyond the door, a lamplit row of high desks at which visored young clerks wrote with pens in big ledger books.

Crawford sat back on his heels, frowning. Could this be the deepest sub-basement of some enormous bank? He straightened up and tried to twist the doorknob, but it didn't move at all.

Crouching again, he put his mouth to the keyhole and called, "Hello! I wonder if any of you could direct me?"

Quickly he put his eye to the keyhole again, and he had to blink—this time the lamplight was much dimmer, and the clerks were bent with age, their beards long and white.

"Still here?" called one of them wearily. "On your way and face your sins, phantom, we can erase no names."

Crawford recoiled and sat down on the sandy tunnel floor, nearly losing the bottle, then got to his feet and hurried away, back to the central chamber below the well, and he made his way down another of the tunnels.

This one did not bend, but he didn't remember whether Chichuwee's did right away or not, so he followed it for a few yards before concluding that it wasn't the right one either; but ahead of him now he could see a faint vertical streak of emerald light that widened and narrowed, as if it were a gap between a curtain and a wall, and he stole forward to peek at what might lie beyond.

But as he hesitantly touched the curtain, a woman's voice said, faintly, "Oh, help me, please, brother!"

He froze, and a moment later shook his head and started to turn around, and then was appalled to realize that he could not in good conscience walk away from it; and so he braced himself and pushed the curtain aside.

The room beyond was wide and lit from some undetectable source in flickering green, as if it were under sunlit water. The floor was polished stone. Immediately in front of Crawford stood a glass table with a handful of black gravel and sand on it, and against the far wall was a long couch flanked by two chairs, with shelves above it.

At first he couldn't see the woman who had spoken. He took two steps forward. "Er . . . hello?" he said.

Then she spoke, and he saw that she was reclining on the couch amid a tumble of cushions. Her face, turned toward him, was narrow and youthful.

"Save me," she said, "please."

"How?" asked Crawford nervously. "From what?"

Then he jumped, for something had moved on one of the high shelves. He peered at it, and his stomach went cold when he realized that the object was a severed hand, pointing.

It was pointing at the table.

"Bless my broken body with some of your living blood," said the face on the couch.

Crawford's face was tingling, and he spread his hands and took a long, careful step backward, not looking at her.

Quickly she added, "You are Polidori's son; that's why he wants you. In the summer of 1822, in Italy, your mother, Josephine, belonged to him. Come to me, give me yourself."

He looked at her now—and he saw that there was no body reclining there, just the speaking head. Her eyes were enormous and glittered in the green glow.

With a choked shout, he spun toward the curtain, but a slim severed arm lay in the way now, and it immediately began a furious convulsing like an energetic fish hauled up onto a dock; the knocking of the elbow and the slapping of the hand against the floor were as rapid as a fast drumbeat.

He stepped back in horror, and, as other pieces of a woman's body stirred to life in various parts of the room, the head on the couch said, "My insect fingers permitted me to show you my one-time power. You would have seen more, been stung many more times, if you had not spoken to the Roman gods. I can save you and all you love. Only give me your blood."

Crawford had leaped to the side while she was speaking, the bottle swinging wildly in his coat, but the arm flipped over in that direction, blocking him. The fingers on the jumping hand were spasmodically curling and snapping out straight.

"Your blood already remembers the way," the woman said, speaking more loudly to be heard over the drumming of the arm. "My sweet

Swinburne is lost to me, and I hold all the verses he would write—he writes only dead lines now under his unkindly master. Heal me, join my family, kill my enemies."

Crawford hesitated, trying to place himself for a jump over the flailing arm, when she added, "You know the way back."

The way back—

And, as he sometimes did very late on sleepless nights in one French city or another, Crawford remembered how he had felt after McKee's common-law husband had bitten him seven years ago: light and restless, eager to be striding quickly down dark streets. He had had no responsibilities or worries, hardly even any thoughts.

No home waited for him now, up there on the surface. His wife and child were lost.

His relaxing hand brushed the bottle in his pocket, but it was the lively face of Johanna that sprang into his head. And he remembered her clapping her hands when McKee agreed to marry him seven years ago and saying happily, *Oh, well done, you two!* And on the day they married, she had said, *I'll kill myself before I'll let him have me again.*

He gripped the bottle and told himself, No—you can't relax yet.

He said, clearly, "No," and vaulted straight over the flexing arm into the curtain.

He ducked, hoping the fabric would slow his fall, but the green glow winked out while he was in midair and he landed hard on the sandy floor of the tunnel, clanking the bottle alarmingly.

He scrambled to his feet, wincing at new pains in his shoulder and hip, and looked fearfully behind him—but he could see nothing in the darkness, and there was no sound except for his fast breath echoing away in a void, and there was no curtain underfoot.

The creature was lying, he told himself. I am not a vampire's son. My parents told me that they had wondered about that themselves, and concluded that it was not so.

And even if I am—I will save Johanna from him.

He felt the bottle and exhaled in relief to find that it was not broken.

He limped back to the central chamber and blindly stumbled into the next tunnel; its low ceiling was familiar, as was the deeper sand underfoot, and it curved perceptibly to the left. As he trudged along through the unseen damp sand, the curve became more pronounced.

But he remembered seeing lamplight on McKee's hair as she had preceded him down the tunnel fourteen years before, and he remembered the chittering of birds; this tunnel was dark and silent, and the draft from ahead smelled of the river, not birdcages.

When the tunnel came to an end, and he felt the open doorway to his left, he almost stepped out onto the remembered floor, but something was wrong about the echoes.

He crouched and waved his hand past the lip of the tunnel, but didn't feel the floor boards; so he stretched his legs out backward and lay on his stomach and reached down as far as he could—and there was no floor.

Then he jumped and scuttled back, squinting, for a light had sprung up somewhere ahead. He peered out, and by the glare of a paraffin lantern on the far wall he saw that he was looking into a wide stone shaft that extended away into darkness above and below.

Crawford recalled Trelawny saying that he had consulted Chichuwee on Wednesday, two days ago; had he consulted him *here*?

Now Crawford could make out a small white face next to the paraffin lantern fifteen feet away across the abyss, and he recalled that there had been a boy attending the old Hail Mary dealer fourteen years ago.

"I—want to see Chichuwee," Crawford called.

The boy pointed downward, and Crawford automatically looked in that direction, into what seemed an infinite pit. He slid a little farther back into the tunnel.

"But two days ago," he called, "a man named Trelawny consulted him?"

The face nodded, and the boy said, "And then the big vampire. It stopped the dice."

Crawford squeezed tears out of his stinging eyes and felt like just throwing the ghost bottle down the shaft.

"But I've—your name is—" What had it been? "Sam! Right?"

"George," the boy corrected him. "There might have been a Sam once."

Of course, Crawford thought, impatient with himself, the boy we saw would be grown up by now.

"I've got a ghost," he said desperately, reaching back to be sure he still had the bottle in his pocket. "I wanted to get it . . . boiled, so I could ask it some questions."

The boy just pointed down the pit again. "The word is," he said, "all the great old Hail Mary artists got jacked Wednesday night."

The lantern was extinguished, and Crawford heard the boy scuffling away down the tunnel on the other side.

"Polidori doesn't want ghosts answering questions," said Crawford bleakly. In a louder voice, he added, "Specifically *this* ghost!"

He began to push himself backward, away from the open doorway to nothing, but the light on the other side of the pit flared back on again.

"What's your ghost?" the boy called.

"It's Maria Rossetti," Crawford answered. "Two arches to the right of this tunnel is the way back up, as I recall?—to Portugal Street?"

"If you're lucky. Who was Maria Rossetti?"

"She was the niece of Polidori. She knew of a way to kill him, but she was too religious to tell anybody because doing it would involve some dire sin. I hoped that her ghost could tell us the trick."

"Wait." The boy's face disappeared from the lantern glow, then after a few seconds was back again. "I'll throw something to you."

"Throw something? How can I—what is it?"

The boy was standing up in the opening on the other side, swinging his arm back and forth. The shadow swooped up and down the wall of the shaft.

"It's invisible," the boy called. "Drop it and there's no hope. Stand up."

Crawford got carefully to his feet, but he found it supremely difficult to stop looking at the abyss an inch in front of his boot toes.

"Look at me," called the boy.

Crawford made himself lift his eyes and squint steadily across the shaft.

"Can't you——" he began, but the boy had flung his arm up and opened his hand.

Swaying on the ledge, Crawford held his arms out over the drop—and a moment later something heavy bounced off his forearm and the inside of his elbow and he caught it in his hands before it could rebound away. He had begun to tip forward, and he flung out one hand sideways and clawed the rock wall to pull himself back, and he wound up sitting in the sand trembling and panting, still holding the thing the boy had thrown.

He could feel that it was round and rough, but when he looked down at his arms, he saw only his arms.

The light went out again, and he heard the boy say, "Good," before scuttling away down the other tunnel.

Crawford got wearily to his feet in the renewed darkness and, after taking anxious care that he was facing the right way, plodded back down the decreasingly curving corridor.

In the central chamber, he felt along the wall to the right of the tunnel he had just come out of, shuffled past the next open arch—from the depths of which he seemed to hear some distant but enormous person snoring—and then stepped through the next one. This tunnel widened out, and the sandy floor was indeed sloping perceptibly upward.

Behind him, distorted by echoes, he heard a voice call, *"Origo lemurum."*

He paused and turned back, glad now of the total darkness.

He could hear boots scuffing on the iron rungs; more than one set of boots. The sound grew louder.

He crouched, taking deep breaths to quell his noisy panting, and he clutched the thing that the boy had thrown to him, which seemed to be a light iron pot. In the darkness, he began to doubt that it really was invisible.

After listening, for a longer time than he would have expected, to the boots descending the rungs, he heard the hard chuff of someone dropping to the sand in the central chamber, and then he heard McKee say, hoarsely, "John? Are you down here?"

"Yes!" he said, aloud so that she would know it really was him, and not some lonely whispering ghost. He shuffled carefully back down the unseen slope to the dimly visible chamber of arches.

His groping hand found hers in the darkness, and a moment later another pair of boots impacted the sand and then Johanna had found him and was hugging him.

CHAPTER FOUR

And the old streets come peering through
Another night that London knew
And all as ghostlike as the lamps.

                       —*Dante Gabriel Rossetti, "Jenny"*

D IRECTLY BEHIND ME," he whispered, "is the tunnel that leads up to the surface. I just came back out of it."

"I heard you," McKee whispered back. "I can walk to it from right here. But you were leaving? What happened with Chichuwee?"

"Dead and gone—floor, wagon, and everything. But I've got his invisible boiling pot."

He felt her hand brush the thing and then jiggle the bottle in his coat pocket. "How—? No, later. Quiet now."

She started forward, taking his left hand—and Johanna's right hand, he gathered, for he could hear her footsteps now too—and soon the three of them were trudging up the inclined sand slope.

The sand underfoot was wetter than he remembered, and his right hip and both knees were soon aching at each labored uphill step. He was about to whisper a suggestion that they rest, when he gasped and involuntarily squeezed McKee's hand.

Someone else was stepping along, very lightly, a few yards to his right. And then he could hear the faint crunch and slither of other footsteps beyond those. None seemed to impose much weight on the sand.

McKee gripped his hand more tightly, clearly conveying *Don't pause or speak.*

He remembered encountering the ghosts of his first wife and his son Richard down here, last time, and, as sweat chilled his face and he forced himself to inhale and exhale evenly, he wondered if they were among the things pacing them here.

He could hear footsteps now on the far side of Johanna too; and ahead of them, and behind them. The windy *vox cloacarum* moaning started up, and it was faint only because the voices were very soft this time, not because its source was far away at all. Crawford could almost feel the mingled breaths from the cold throats on his right hand.

Pressure—differences! he thought furiously as his aching legs kept pushing him up the slope.

And then he was aware of weak plucking at his sleeve, and fragments of whispers: "whatcha got . . . lemme just . . . ye spare a bit of . . ."

These seemed to be a frailer sort of ghost than those of Veronica and Richard had been, perhaps because they didn't have any intrinsic psychic power over him from which to draw virtual substance, but there seemed to be hundreds of them.

And McKee was pulling him strongly ahead and up, and her grip on his hand was still tight.

Crawford's sleeve was snagged, and when he shook off the thing that clung to it, he felt a tug and heard cloth tear; then his boots were tangled in something that audibly gnawed at his boot before he could kick it away. He heard sharp breaths and scuffles from McKee and Johanna too.

We don't dare fall, he thought as the three of them kept plodding uphill, all of them panting audibly. How much farther?

Little cold hands were tugging at the bottle in his pocket, and the whispered voices were now saying, "Give us the nun, we need a nun . . . she's in brandy, we need that too . . . and your blood, your blood . . ."

McKee had just whispered, "If any of us falls—throw the bottle—" when a new sound intruded from behind them.

The sound struck Crawford as a very familiar one in a different context, and a moment later he recognized it as hoofbeats—striking more lightly than was natural in the wet sand, but unmistakable, and he heard the whicker of breath blown through a horse's lips.

The hoofbeats drew alongside, apparently trampling the human ghosts, to judge by the crackling and faint wails.

Crawford leaned to the right and reached out with the hand that held the pot, but encountered nothing, though the sound of hooves striking the sand came from no more than a yard away from his boots. He drew his arm back and found that he was only reassured by this new spectral escort. McKee seemed to feel the same thing and let their desperate pace slow to a fast walk.

In his exhaustion, Crawford almost imagined he could see the graceful creatures pacing on either side of his party—the rippling flanks and tossing manes and bright intelligent eyes.

The ghost horses paced alongside until the slope leveled out and the faint high arch showed in front of them; then the hoofbeats seemed to break into a barely audible gallop and diminish to silence ahead, where a mist briefly blurred the glow that Crawford remembered was reflected moonlight.

McKee led Crawford and Johanna around the left-side edge of the tall arch. Ahead of them, clearly visible in the diffuse white radiance after so much time in total darkness, the stonework wall of the fallen Roman building stretched up like a ramp.

"The light is coming in through a hole in Portugal Street," McKee whispered to Johanna as she started walking up the side of the building, skirting the long box that was a tilted balcony. "It's an easy climb up from here."

The three of them trudged up the slanted wall, sometimes using hands as well as feet in traversing buckled sections, and soon they were all seated on the rounded ridge that was a fallen turret. Wavering moonlight slanted in through the rectangular hole twenty feet overhead.

"Horses?" said McKee once they had all caught their breaths. "Horse ghosts?"

"Like the cats?" ventured Johanna. "Old friends?"

Crawford was surprised by the thought, and he hoped it was so.

Then his smile relaxed into a frown. "I met Trelawny's Miss B.," he said hesitantly, "in one of the other tunnels. She—"

"You went into another tunnel?" exclaimed McKee. It seemed to require an effort on her part not to draw away from him. "And you met *her?*"

"She was all—in pieces, and there were broken bits of black stone and sand on a table. Corresponding." His heart was thumping again just recalling it, and he peered nervously back the way they'd come. "You remember Christina said that Trelawny had shrunk and hardened her and put her in a box. I believe he broke her up with a hammer too. She wanted my blood, and I ran out."

"She must have been pretty sure she could talk you into it," said Johanna thoughtfully. "She wouldn't spend herself so much to become visible just on an off chance."

Crawford heard unvoiced insight in his daughter's remark, and he reminded himself that she too had experienced the dark elation of being severed from human concerns.

"She told me I'm Polidori's son," he said. "She said that in the summer of '22, my mother—"

"Josephine," said Johanna.

"Yes. I didn't believe her."

"Oh, why didn't you wait for us at the Spotted Dog?" asked McKee.

"I did, I even napped for a bit, but the tough lads started to want the bottle." He braced his feet on a window lintel and sighed. He thought of putting the pot down in some secure niche, then decided they'd have trouble finding it again. "I've never been so glad in my life as I was when you two dropped down the well back there."

"We were glad to find you," said Johanna. "Very."

"We caught another cab," said McKee, "right after that big boom, and went back to Tottenham Court Road, to—to see—" She paused and exhaled, shaking her head.

"We were sure we'd find you dead in the street," said Johanna in a small voice. "Smashed flat."

"Maria saved me," he said, touching the bottle that was still in his coat pocket. Nuns and horses, he thought.

McKee pushed her hair back with both hands. "We looked," she began, but her voice cracked; she took a deep breath and went on, "We *looked* around the area, but there was no sign of you."

"Nor of the tall black-painted thing," said Johanna with a shiver. "We kept our eyes out for it."

"Sister Christina was probably giving it soup," said McKee bitterly.

"But we—*met*—*Rose*," said Johanna. "She had followed that thing, and she jumped at us from out of an alley."

"Rose? Good God, Trelawny's granddaughter? Was she—alive, still?"

"Yes—same as I was, when you saw me at Highgate Cemetery," said Johanna. "Not dead and resurrected. And she—knows me, hates me. Tried to kill me."

McKee took her daughter's hand and said to Crawford, "She had a knife, but I blocked her first stab, and then we held her off with our own." She barked out two syllables of a strained laugh. "We didn't want to hurt her, but she surely wanted to hurt us."

Crawford anxiously tried to see the faces and hands of his wife and daughter. "Were either of you cut?"

"No," said Johanna, "nor her either. Well, maybe her hand. It was hard to see. There was no way to talk to her at all, much less *grab* her. We outran her—she's not very strong now. I remember how that is."

"Rose is," said McKee, "furiously jealous that . . . Christina's uncle . . . would apparently rather have Johanna. We really couldn't hope to capture her—so we just—left her there."

"And then we went off separately," Johanna added, "to meet up at the Spotted Dog. By the time we both got there, you had already gone below."

"Can I see the pot?" asked McKee.

"No, actually," said Crawford, carefully handing it across, "but you can hold it. His boy tossed it to me, across the pit where Chichuwee's place used to be. The boy said 'the big vampire' wiped out all the Hail Mary artists Wednesday night."

"The same night the Mud Lark man came to me in my dream," said Johanna.

"And William Rossetti's son was born on Wednesday," recalled McKee.

The glow from above was fading.

"Moon's moving on," said Crawford. "It'll get pretty dark down here."

"I think we're better off down here than out under the night sky," said Johanna.

"Too right," agreed McKee. "We'll climb out when we can see day-light. Here's the pot back," she added, handing the thing to Crawford and not letting go of it till he had both hands on it. "*Don't* lose that."

"I'm keeping my knife in my hand till dawn," said Johanna.

THEY HAD TO KNOCK so much snow aside to crawl out of the hole in Portugal Street next morning, and the sky was so heavily overcast, that McKee said they were lucky to have seen the daylight at all.

All three of them had lost their hats during the night's confusions, and McKee and Johanna had left their overcoats at the Spotted Dog, so Crawford gave Johanna his coat, and they were all shivering when a cab let them out at the corner of Bozier's Court.

"Good Lord, it's after seven o'clock!" said Crawford, peering down the street at the clock over the Oxford Music Hall.

"Hold your cab," came Trelawny's voice from the shadows under the pub awning. As Crawford waved at the driver, the old man hobbled out into the gray daylight and added, "It's nearly half past seven. I had to sit through dawn Mass." He wore no hat, and his collar was open.

"I wish we had," said Johanna.

"*Did* the ghost speak?" asked Trelawny, holding the cab door for McKee and Johanna as they climbed back in, and then he called an address in Pelham Crescent to the driver and got in himself.

"Not yet," said Crawford after he had stepped up last and sat down inside the cab next to Trelawny. The vehicle jolted into motion. "But we can boil it at your house. I've still got the ghost, and this," he said, holding up his two spread hands, "is Chichuwee's boiling pot."

Trelawny simply reached out and tapped the invisible pot, then nodded. "You *took* it?"

"His assistant threw it to me, over the pit where Chichuwee's chamber used to be. Polidori visited him right after you did. Lethally."

"*All* the old Hail Mary men," added Johanna.

Trelawny pursed his scarred lips, deepening the lines in his face, and Crawford reflected that the old man must be in his eighties by now.

Trelawny pulled the bell cord, and when the cab slowed, he half stood and pushed the door open, letting a gust of chilly air into the cab. "To the river, first," he called up to the driver. "Steps, we want to get down to the water."

He pulled the door shut and sat down again beside Crawford. "We need river water to boil," he explained.

Johanna squinted tiredly at the old man. "My mother and I saw

Rose last night, in the Tottenham Court Road. She's still alive, not resurrected."

Trelawny was still, staring at her. At last he said, "You didn't—catch
her?"

"We were lucky to keep her from killing us. No."

Trelawny closed his eyes and shook his head. "He's holding off,
then, in hopes of getting *you*. That's good—he'll be like the dog in the
fable, getting neither bone." He opened his eyes and looked warily at
Johanna. "No offense meant."

"And," Crawford said hastily, "I spoke to your Miss B., down the
sewers. She's in fragments, and wanted me to give her some of my
blood."

Trelawny looked at him, then looked away and sighed. "Poor old
girl, though I'm glad to hear she hasn't recovered. But she wasn't just
scattered in some mud puddle, I hope?"

Crawford blinked at McKee and Johanna, sitting across from Trelawny and himself. "No," he said. "Er . . . very nice room. Couch."

Trelawny nodded, squinting out the cab window at the white-
fretted buildings. "Can't help being a bit fond of her still."

Johanna's face was stern, and she looked older than her twenty
years when she said, "I bet you could help it, if you tried. I'm not fond
of mine at all."

The old man scowled at her, then grinned. "You've grown up since
I saw you last, my dear."

"You," said Johanna, "have not."

"True, true. Bit late to start, now. But perhaps the hour calls for one
truly immature soul."

At a set of marble stairs below Savoy Street the driver waited while
Crawford hurried down to the river shore and dipped the invisible pot
into the muddy shallows and then wrapped it in his scarf to keep the
river-side loiterers from becoming curious about it. Within five minutes
he was back in the cab, holding the thing in his lap.

It sloshed when the cab got moving again, dousing his trousers in very cold river water; soon the interior of the cab was steamy with a smell like the Billingsgate pavement at the end of a market day.

"Your cologne, sir—" began Trelawny.

"Could be yours too in a few seconds," Crawford said through clenched teeth.

Trelawny shut his mouth.

Johanna had been yawning, but now she abruptly giggled; instantly she stopped and waved her hand in apology, and then she was sobbing quietly, frowning as if disgusted with herself.

McKee patted her daughter's knee. "It would have been something to see those two splashing each other."

Conversation lagged while the cab wound through the already crowded streets of Soho and Mayfair and Belgravia, and then rocked along at a good speed down the King's Road to Chelsea, where it made its way up Sydney Street past the Gothic bell tower of St. Luke's to Pelham Crescent.

Trelawny unlatched the cab door when the vehicle creaked to a halt in front of one in the long row of imposing white houses.

"Hand me the pot," he said when he was standing on the street, and Crawford was glad to lean out and let Trelawny take hold of it. It now looked like a glass pot half full of muddy water. The cab driver looked on curiously but didn't appear to note anything unnatural.

"Bring the girls, living and dead," Trelawny said. "Luckily the neighbors are accustomed to seeing unsavory characters at my house."

"I hope you've got a fire going," said Crawford as he climbed out of the cab.

"I know how to boil water," Trelawny assured him testily.

"In the fireplace," said Crawford. He took Johanna's hand as she stepped down to the slushy pavement, then reached for McKee's. "The three of us are half frozen."

Trelawny nodded, conceding the point. "I'll lay on more coal."

Once inside, Crawford retrieved his coat from Johanna and they pulled chairs up around Trelawny's fireplace, where the flames waved tall and blue with a new shovelful of coal. The old man even provided brandy when Crawford asked if he had any, and Crawford and Johanna each gulped a glass of the liquor.

Trelawny's house was spartan, with only a few chairs and bookcases against the spotless white walls, and fussily clean.

After a few minutes, Trelawny said, sternly, "My granddaughter is almost certainly not having brandy by a fire. Adjourn we to the kitchen."

They all crossed through the dining room to the stairs, Trelawny carefully carrying the half sphere of brown river water, and when they had clumped down to the basement kitchen, Crawford was again struck by the old man's neatness. Somehow Crawford could not imagine that Trelawny employed servants, but the red linoleum floor of the kitchen was swept and dry, and there were no damp clothes hanging over the stove or dirty dishes in the scullery beyond; Crawford peeked into the pantry and saw dust-free glasses and china plates in neat rows, and the pantry sink's lead lining was undented. Small windows in the area-side wall, unsmudged by soot, let in gray daylight.

Trelawny knelt by the stove and opened the firebox door, and after dumping one small shovelful of coal onto the fire, he got to his feet with resolute ease and no grunt of effort. He retrieved the invisible pot from the kitchen table and placed it with a clank squarely on the front iron cook-lid.

He gestured toward the four wooden chairs around the table, and McKee and Johanna sat down.

"Give up the ghost," Trelawny said with a kinked grin as he held out his hand, and Crawford fetched the bottle out of the pocket of his coat.

Trelawny held it up to the window light judiciously. "Well, you've got the sediment roiled up—probably a good thing. I should remember her name."

"Maria," said Crawford, remembering that Christina's sister had been unfailingly kind to him when he had been so often imposing himself on the Rossettis in the spring of 1862, after McKee had disappeared; and last night her ghost had shielded him from Polidori.

The brown river water was already boiling and steaming, and Crawford remembered Chichuwee's claim that the pot was actually up in the Alps, where the air pressure was lower. Trelawny twisted the cork out of the bottle's neck.

"Intelligent woman, as I recall," he said, "and dead only three months—let's hope for the best."

Crawford stood beside him at the stove. "Let me talk to her," he said.

"As you please." The old man poured several splashes of the clouded brandy into the boiling water—and the steam immediately gathered itself in to form an oval.

"Maria," said Crawford to the steam. He glanced nervously at McKee, who nodded.

"Maria," he said again, more loudly. The kitchen smelled now of brandy and fish.

The bubbling of the water produced a whisper: "Where is Christina? She was reading 'The Lady of Shallot' to me."

"Christina is at home, and thriving," Crawford said, wondering how true that might be. "We need to know how to banish your uncle, John Polidori."

"We . . . stopped him with mirrors," said the bubbles slowly as the face in the steam bobbed. "I learned it from the . . . the old Jewish books. I can't remember their titles."

"That was good," said Crawford. Sweat and condensed steam beaded his face and tickled in his gray beard. "But that didn't work forever. We need to know how to stop him forever."

"Cut the stone out of Edward John Trelawny's neck," said the steam.

"Barring that," put in Trelawny.

"I gathered you know of another way," pursued Crawford.

"I might," spoke the slow bubbles. "'The mirror cracked from side to side; / "The curse is come upon me," cried / The Lady of Shallott.'" The bubbles seemed to sigh. "It would damn souls."

"How would it be done?" asked Johanna.

"I never would say, while I lived."

"But you're not living now," said Crawford gently. "You can say, now."

"I was in the river Purgatory for long cold days and nights. Catholics knew about that. Now I . . . live with Christina? An indulgence?"

"Yes," said Crawford. "We'll return you to her as soon as you've told us."

He hadn't anticipated being ashamed of questioning this ghost, but he found that he was. Maria had been a deeply devout Christian, and more intelligent than him, and nevertheless kind to him; and he was taking advantage of the limitations of this poor malodorous little fragment of her . . . which had stepped out to save him last night.

"I told you—I was in the infinite dark river, with the worms."

"No, when you've told us the *other* way to banish your uncle."

The steam said, "Oh—someone would have to cut Christina, so that she bled—she couldn't do it herself. She would have to appear to be threatened. And then she would have to call for him, our uncle, as if for rescue. She would have to invite him back to herself. She would not want to do that, because she has always wanted to do that."

The bubbles popped and the steam oval nodded.

"That—would *not* stop him," put in McKee.

"No," agreed the evanescent bubbles. "But he would come to her, in his human body—vulnerable, by daylight, not the . . . monster in the sky. And then there would have to be a death."

For several seconds no more words came out of the bubbling brandy and river water, and Crawford cast a worried glance at McKee and opened his mouth, but the steam spoke again.

"I don't want Christina to die," it said.

"Well—no," agreed Crawford.

"If she died there, and he were confined in the right sort of penta-gram in daylight, I believe he would die too. Blood relatives, and the diabolical link. But for this, if she is to be able to keep me, and read to me—"

Again there was silence, and Crawford waited it out.

"I believe there would have to be a murder," said the bubbles, and the emotionless monotone voice seemed grotesque now, "and Chris-tina could catch the new ghost and use its agitated mental strength to double her own—and, still linked with our uncle by blood relation and her will, she could then stop our uncle, hold him in his human form. Forcibly. For a little while. He wouldn't be able to fly away, as long as she was able to keep imposing his human form on him. He could still run—but I think he could be killed then, and stopped forever with silver and wood and cremation."

Crawford was feeling nauseated, and he realized that it was a reac-tion to having made this frail phantom violate Maria's principles by divulging this. But he remembered something McKee had said four-teen years ago: *People who have let themselves be bitten by these devils can sometimes catch a very fresh ghost, ingest it, and it supposedly gives them extra psychic strength—lets them control the people around them for a minute or so.*

"If it didn't work," said Johanna nervously, "we would—everybody present would be in big trouble." She blinked. "Even if it *did* work."

"'Who is this?'" whispered the steam, and before anyone could answer, it went on, clearly quoting again, "'and what is here? / And in the lighted palace near, / Died the sound of royal cheer; / And they crossed themselves for fear . . .'"

The steam oval dissolved in the air, and at the same moment Tre-lawny fumbled the bottle and got a fresh grip on it, as if it had moved in his hand. Crawford took it from him and shoved the cork back in the neck and set it on the table.

"We'll return that to Christina," he said.

"Yes," McKee agreed weakly.

Crawford and Trelawny sat down at the table, both of them staring at the bottle.

After a while, "How can we . . . *kill* a person, to do this?" asked Johanna. "Plain murder."

"I could do it," said McKee in an unsteady voice. "If it was a stranger, and—and if I was drunk again."

Crawford said quickly, "No, you couldn't, Adelaide."

Trelawny smiled at her, his eyes half closed. "I named you Rahab, not Jael."

Crawford recalled that Jael had been the woman who, in the Book of Judges, had saved Israel by pounding a tent stake through the head of a Canaanite general.

"I could—to save Johanna," McKee insisted. Her face was pale.

"And my granddaughter." Trelawny sat back and looked around at the cupboards and the boiler and the racked knives as if he couldn't recall how he had got here.

Johanna touched her mother's hand. "I'll do it. It won't," she added, staring at the bottle, "be the first time I've killed a person."

"Is it not a couple of wild Bacchantes!" said Trelawny, smiling crookedly. "Ready to tear the head off a stranger! But no, children— I'm—eighty-four years old, as of last November."

He stood up and crossed to the brick street-side wall and leaned against it between two of the gray-glowing windows, so that his expression was hard to make out.

"Have any of you read my book, *Adventures of a Younger Son?*" he asked. "No? Well, I never took you for a literate lot. It concerned my desertion from the British navy in India, and my subsequent career as a pirate on the Indian Ocean. In it I described my rescue of an Arab princess, Zela, and how I married her, and how she died in my arms. I know Byron always thought the whole thing was a bundle of lies."

He sighed. "And—though I can still call poor lovely, loyal Zela up in my memory more clearly than I can my last wife—" He paused and then laughed softly. "Byron was right! This is difficult for me to admit, even to myself, after all these years, but—I *didn't* desert the navy. I was honorably discharged at the age of twenty, in Bristol, because of having caught cholera. I was never a pirate, never met or married any Zela. I can hardly get my memory past the fictions now, all the sea battles and piracies, but I do know that they are fictions."

He laced his fingers behind his head and stared at the ceiling.

"*But* then in Pisa in '22 I met Shelley, and Byron, and became their friend. And after Shelley drowned, I sailed with Byron to Greece to fight for that nation's independence from Turkey. Byron died in '24, but I allied myself with a mountain bandit-king whose lair was a cave on Mount Parnassus. And I married his young sister—so in a way my imaginary Zela was really just a . . . premonition! And when we had a daughter, I named her Zella, slightly different spelling, to honor that dear figment.

"But—my bride's brother, the mountain bandit—was one of several powerful men vying for the leadership of Greece in those days, and he was resolved to establish an alliance with the—the stony children of Deucalion and Pyrrha."

Evidently stung by Trelawny's assessment of her literacy, McKee explained stiffly to Johanna, "In Ovid's *Metamorphoses*, Deucalion and Pyrrha survived the great flood by setting sail in an ark, and they repopulated the earth afterward by throwing stones behind them, and the stones grew into people."

"Into things that *looked* like people, sometimes, at any rate," said Trelawny, nodding. "Deucalion and Pyrrha resurrected the Nephilim, pre-Adamite godlike monsters. By 1824, the Nephilim had been banished, but this chieftain was determined to call them up again and become something like a god himself."

Trelawny rubbed one hand over his white-bearded face. "I—was young!—and I wanted the same, and I was willing to commit the large-

scale human sacrifice the Nephilim required. In Euboea I killed . . .
many Turks. Men, women, and children." For several seconds he was
silent. Then, "And I was betrayed," he went on. "I was shot in the back
with one of the living stones, so that I would merely become the bridge
between the two species. The ball was fired clay, and it broke against
my bones, but"—he paused to touch the base of his throat—"as you
know, it's been growing back, and with it the power of the Nephilim."

Crawford was sure the old man was about to volunteer to kill someone in order to perform the procedure Maria's ghost had described.

Instead, Trelawny stepped forward into the light and glared at him
and said, "Cut it out of my throat."

CHAPTER FIVE

And now without, as if some word
Had called upon them that they heard,
The London sparrows far and nigh
Clamour together suddenly . . .

—*Dante Gabriel Rossetti, "Jenny"*

C RAWFORD BLINKED, AND his mouth was open for several seconds before he spoke. "Very well," he said. "Where?"

"Right here in the kitchen. Where did you suppose, out in the street?
You've got hot water in the boiler, there's brandy in the cupboard—and
I can fetch my sewing kit for you to stitch me up with afterward."

Crawford pushed his chair back and stood up, wishing that he had
got some sleep last night. "You'll be fine," he said, with more confidence
than he felt. "I've cut around dozens of horse arteries without losing the
patient."

"Horse arteries," echoed Trelawny. "Excuse me while I fetch needle
and thread."

The old man turned and clumped away up the stairs, shaking his
head.

"It's brave of him," said Johanna.

"At this point," said McKee, "it would have been cowardice not to do it."

"Well, that's what I said. There's no neutral place."

Crawford had stepped across to the knife rack, and after looking over the variously sized blades, he just picked up a whetstone and was rubbing his thumb across it.

"Go through the drawers in the pantry too," he said. "See if you can find a knife with a short blade. These here are all for hacking joints apart."

"Well, that would *do*," said McKee, standing up and walking into the pantry.

Trelawny came downstairs carrying a small leather box. "I've got a pocketknife with a short blade," he said. "I'd just as soon not have you hacking joints." His voice was light, but Crawford saw the pallor under the old man's eternal tan. "I'm not afraid," Trelawny added.

"I'll go out and find a chemist's," said Crawford, "and fetch some ether. I'd rather use that than chloroform."

"It's not even half an inch deep!" said Trelawny scornfully. "Just cut, I promise not to flinch."

"No, cutting so close to the vein, I—"

"And what's happening to Rose, while we wait for you to find a chemist's? Just cut; I won't move."

Crawford frowned at the defiant old man, then shrugged.

"Would you," ventured Johanna, "like me to return a favor? I could . . . baptize you."

"Me loyal old Lark," said Trelawny, turning to her with a smile. "No, thank you, my dear, though I—" He shut his mouth, and after taking a deep breath and letting it out, he said, "I appreciate the thought behind the offer, more than I can say."

Crawford eventually settled on one of the short blades in Trelawny's bone-handled pocketknife, and when Johanna had lit a candle and brought it to the table, he held the blade in the flame.

"Open your shirt and lie down across the table," he told Trelawny. His eyes were stinging from not having slept last night, and he squeezed them shut and then opened them wide; he looked at his hands and was reassured to see that they were not trembling.

The old man took his shirt off, exposing a broad chest matted with white hair and shoulders still corded with muscle. He touched a spot on his throat just above his collarbone, on the left side. "Here's your target, Doctor."

The lump did appear to be firmly stuck in place, very close to the jugular vein.

Crawford took off his coat and rolled his sleeves up past the elbow. "Pour a lot of brandy over my hands," he told Johanna, "and then soak a towel in it and—"

"—Scrub where you're going to cut," said Johanna.

"That's it." He looked up at Trelawny's drawn face. "I'd really like to get some ether. This is likely to hurt quite a bit."

"I don't mind hurt," said the old man through his teeth. "Me and hurt go way back."

Crawford shook his head. "As you please. Just, whatever you do, don't twitch."

When Crawford had rubbed his hands in the sluicing brandy and Johanna had swabbed the old man's throat with the soaked towel, Crawford held the lump in Trelawny's throat with his left hand and reached out with the knife in his right—

—and the blade stopped abruptly, two inches above Trelawny's skin, and would move no closer.

Peripherally Crawford noticed that Trelawny's face was slicked with sweat.

The heady smell of brandy was overpowering. Crawford carefully increased the pressure against the invisible barrier, not wanting to spear the old man if it were suddenly to relent—but the blade simply skittered aside; as if, it occurred to him, he had tried to push it through Chichuwee's invisible pot.

"The blade," he said in a strained voice, "won't get close to your throat."

For a moment the old man just breathed in and out. Then he whispered, "Infirm of purpose, give me the pocketknife," and took it from Crawford's hand.

The blade was steady in Trelawny's hand as he pressed it to the base of his own throat, but again the metal was turned aside.

"What's this?" snapped the old man, sitting up and jabbing uselessly at his throat several more times. "I shave, sometimes!"

"Not with the intention of cutting the stone from your throat, though," said McKee. "The stone can evidently tell the difference."

Trelawny dropped the knife and it clattered on the floor.

"This is Polidori's protection," he said furiously. "It seems the Nephilim won't permit any human to cut the man who is the bridge between the species. But it shouldn't protect me from *me;* I'm not just *any* human." He glared around at the others. "I wouldn't have confessed my sins here if I'd thought I wasn't going to *die.*"

He picked up his shirt—which had got liberally splashed with the brandy—and tugged it on.

His face was grim as he added, "It seems we must rescue my granddaughter by Maria's means."

"And who'll commit a murder?" asked Crawford.

"Oh, who was *ever* going to do it?" grated Trelawny. "It will be me. I've got so many mortal sins on my soul that one more won't matter. I really thought—"

He finished buttoning his shirt and tucked it into his trousers. "I really *thought,* there for a moment, that the universe was offering me a noble death. Expiation."

He walked to the stairs and was halfway up when he turned. "Come along, my sad crew—I've got an errand to run, and you've got to go roust Christina out of her nest."

THEY BORROWED HATS AND two coats from Trelawny before getting into a cab in front of his house, so Johanna had a black bowler hat that made her short brown hair stick out to the sides and McKee wore a straw boater with a flower-pattern ribbon, surely something left behind at Trelawny's by a guest. Crawford was wearing Trelawny's Inverness cape and a tall brown beaver hat that had probably been fashionable in 1830.

None of them made jokes about the hats on the ride east past Green Park and up the Mall to Charing Cross Road. Crawford held the bottle with the sea mouse bobbing in it, and he tried to project a mental apology to the ghost but got no sense of acknowledgment.

"We can't let—" he began finally as the cab started up Gower Street, but McKee and Johanna both interrupted him.

"Certainly not," said McKee.

"*I* could—" said Johanna, but Crawford waved her to silence.

"*None* of us," he said.

His wife and daughter both looked at him uncertainly.

"If—" Crawford said, pausing to look around to be sure the cab had four walls and a roof, "if Polidori appears in vulnerable human form even for a moment, we must try to kill him in that moment. We can't let poor old Trelawny commit a murder—nor participate in one ourselves."

Both women seemed to relax, cautiously, though their expressions were skeptical.

"We'll fail," said Johanna.

"We can jump into the river," said Crawford, "if we fail."

"We'd be safe then," Johanna agreed, "as long as we remembered not to come up for air."

For a minute or so no one spoke, and Crawford stared out the window at the passing pillars and the high neoclassical pediment of the British Museum. Fourteen years ago McKee had told him about her father taking her there when she was eleven and about her fear that she might be in the room full of Egyptian mummies when the General Resurrection occurred.

"Christina won't be happy to see us," said Johanna, bracing herself as the cab was steered into Torrington Place.

"I don't believe she's *ever* been *happy* to see us," said McKee. "And small wonder."

Christina's house had muslin sheets across the lower half of the front window to keep soot from blowing in, but above it Crawford saw the curtain twitch as he climbed down from the cab; he waved the bottle as a placating gesture before helping his wife and daughter down and paying the driver.

Christina herself opened the door when he knocked—she was wearing a plain black smock, and her dark and prematurely sagging face was stern.

Without a word she took the bottle from Crawford, held it up to the daylight, and then held it to her ear.

She sighed in evident relief. "Thank you. I'm sorry I can't invite you in, but we have plasterers due to repair the ceiling—"

"We contacted Maria," interrupted McKee. "Her ghost, that is. She told us how to banish your uncle."

Christina shivered as she hugged the bottle to her chest. "You— *forced* her?"

Johanna said, "Trelawny's fourteen-year-old granddaughter is somewhere out in the City with your uncle right now. It's a cold day, and it'll be a colder night."

Christina sighed, and the steam of her breath whisked away on the chilly breeze. "Come in then, you punishments for my sins."

She led them into the entry hall, where Crawford noticed Johanna's coat still hanging on a hook from last night; God only knew whose coat she had left at the Spotted Dog.

The parlor still smelled of garlic from the bottle Johanna had broken under the nose of the monstrous black-painted thing, and by the gray daylight filtering in through the lace curtains he could see the new cracks in the ceiling. Christina carefully set the bottle on the table, which had been righted.

Crawford said, "I'm sorry we left so abruptly last night—"

"Say calamitously," said Christina, nodding.

"At least," he went on, "the thing followed us out."

"Yes, it did," said Christina. "Mr. Trelawny shot it—it might be dead now."

"Much luck," murmured Johanna.

A housemaid appeared at an inner doorway, and Christina asked her to bring a pot of tea.

"What is the required sin?" she inquired with a brittle semblance of cheer after the housemaid had withdrawn. "The one Maria's method calls for."

Crawford didn't look at his two companions. "You need to let one of us cut you," he said, "so that you bleed, and then you must summon him, call for rescue—invite him back to you."

He hoped that was enough—she would surely balk at the proposed murder of a stranger.

He could see a strong pulse in Christina's throat. "I—" she said. "This hardly seems—how would this aid in banishing him?"

Crawford cleared his throat. "Maria believes he will then appear, wholly, in his vulnerable human form. You're a blood relative of his, in, er, several senses, and you might be able to forcibly hold him in that form—by mental effort—for at least a few seconds."

"So that you can kill him," said Christina softly, "with wooden stakes and silver bullets."

"And cremation," added Johanna.

"I—don't think I can do it," said Christina.

Maria's ghost had said, *She would not want to do that, because she has always wanted to do that.*

"We need you to try," Crawford said. "Trelawny's granddaughter needs you to try."

"I—well, it would indeed be a sin. Even for a praiseworthy purpose, to call up a devil—invoke his love for me—"

McKee cocked her head. "Sister Christina," she said, "do you mean it would be a betrayal of your uncle? Do you mean it would be wrong to *trick* him?"

Christina frowned and shook her head impatiently; and then she stopped.

"I," she whispered, almost wonderingly, "think I do mean that! God help me—"

McKee leaned forward. "You trick a rat when you put bait in a trap."

"You put it so elegantly." Christina sighed. "That will be all, Jane, thank you," she added to the housemaid who had brought in a tray and set it down on the table.

There were eight flat biscuits in a tray beside the teapot, and Crawford made himself ignore them. McKee and Johanna each grabbed two.

"When did you people last eat?" asked Christina in sudden concern.

"I had supper last night," admitted Crawford.

"About twenty-four hours, for me," said McKee, and Johanna nodded to indicate the same.

"Good heavens. I'll have Jane prepare sandwiches—"

"Sandwiches would be good," said Crawford. "We can eat them on the way to the boat."

"I don't understand," said Christina. "Boat? You're . . . leaving the country?"

Johanna said, "It's a moored boat at the Queenhithe Stairs, by Southwark Bridge. I slept aboard it for a year or so, when I was a Mud Lark."

"It's where Trelawny wants to trap Polidori," said McKee. "And he wants to do it while it's daylight. It's cold out; you'll want to bundle up."

Christina lifted the teapot and filled one of the cups. "I think," she said as she picked it up in her shaking hand—and she took a careful sip before going on—"I must do as you say. I think I always knew the day would come when I must, for the sake of my soul, betray him."

There were tears in her eyes as she set the cup back down. It rattled against the saucer.

THEY ALL CLIMBED INTO a cab and took it to the river south of St. Paul's Cathedral, and in Upper Thames Street Johanna had the driver let them out at Bradburn Alley, by a row of tall brick warehouses just short of Queen Street.

"Better we approach along the river," she said as she and her mother helped Christina Rossetti down from the cab. They had eaten several cheese sandwiches on the ride and now brushed crumbs from their coats.

Stout wooden bridges connected the buildings on either side of the alley, and men leaned out of doorways high up in the walls and guided boxes and canvas sacks being raised and lowered on long ropes by pulleys. Crawford led the three women down the alley, around walls of stacked crates and casks, and several times waved them into recessed doorways when heavy-laden carts with chain traces creaked past behind horses in heavy leather collars. Smells of oranges and tobacco and quinine spiced the turbulent air.

At the far end of the alley they were out in the sea-scented wind, viewing the broad face of the river from an elevation only a few feet above the water, and out on the rippled expanse white sails and black smokestacks contrasted with the gray sky. Crawford helped Christina over a low wooden fence, which McKee stepped over and Johanna vaulted, and then they followed a set of narrow-gauge coal-wagon tracks that paralleled the shore, toward the northernmost arch of Southwark Bridge twenty yards ahead.

A chorus of shouts broke out in the alley behind them, and Crawford wondered if a broken pulley had dropped a load.

He was about to glance back when, ahead of him, Johanna jumped and nearly pitched off the tracks into a rowboat below.

She caught her balance and threw him a scared look.

"One wasp doesn't mean—" she began.

Two wasps buzzed between them, and Crawford heard McKee curse behind him.

He looked back at her. "You and Johanna run ahead to the boat," he said.

More shouting from the alley behind them was audible now over the wind in his face.

As McKee and Johanna sprinted away toward the shadows under the bridge, Crawford held Christina's elbow and tried to get her to move faster; finally he said, "Excuse me, it's an emergency," and picked her up in his arms and began striding between the coal-wagon tracks after his wife and daughter. He had to shake Christina's lavender-scented black veil away from his hat brim twice before she noticed and tucked it behind her head.

"Wasps," she said. "It's my nightmare son, isn't it?"

"So you said—last night," agreed Crawford breathlessly. "Can you—look behind?"

She shifted in his arms. "I see men running out of that alley. Some of them are jumping into the river. No sign of . . . him, yet."

Crawford's throat ached with panting, and his knees and hip jabbed him at every jolting step; he hoped he would have enough warning before falling to set Christina down first.

"I miscarried," she said. "To me he was born dead. But then his . . . soul? . . . his insistent soul went on to become the child of Gabriel and Lizzie."

"He—seems to have been—born dead—there too."

"That's true, poor thing."

The tracks curved sharply away inland to the left, and he stepped out from between them. He had reached the shadow of the bridge, and through stinging, watering eyes he saw Johanna and McKee on the deck of a low canal barge moored under the arching span.

"You—can walk, from here," he gasped, lowering Christina to the stone pavement.

Together they hobbled to the wide plank that was laid from the embankment masonry to the boat's gunwale, and McKee helped pull Christina across; when Crawford had limped across too, he lifted the plank and shoved it sideways so that it splashed into the river.

Trelawny's head was visible in the low cabin hatch, and he clumped the rest of the way up onto the deck.

"What," he said irritably, "something chasing you?" Then he squinted beyond them and swore. "Get below, quick," he snapped.

Crawford stole a glance over his shoulder as he hurried Christina to the hatch.

For a moment he nearly jumped into the river along with the dock-workers. Bouncing down the coal-wagon tracks toward the bridge came rushing a figure that at first seemed to be just two very long cart-wheeling gray arms, with rippling pennants of white cloth at the wrists; its black-clad torso bumped along behind, with one leg trailing and one twisted up around its neck, the toes of the bare foot holding a para-sol over the rolling black head. It seemed to be singing as it flailed and bounced rapidly toward them.

"Get below!" roared Trelawny, and Crawford nodded and hustled Christina to the ladder. "Grab the swords! Do it!"

The cabin belowdecks was nearly as wide as the barge, lit by an open porthole in the starboard bulkhead. Slanted vents at the bow and stern ends of the ceiling were apparently to let fresh air in and stale air out. A stove against the port bulkhead was flanked fore and aft by rows of floor-to-ceiling bunks, and the bow end was blocked by a sleigh so big that Crawford thought two horses must once have been required to pull it.

And a short, stocky man with a drooping mustache stood halfway down the cluttered deck, staring at the newcomers in surprise.

"He's still got the sleigh!" whispered Johanna. "I used to sleep in it."

Christina was just blinking around in evident alarm.

The stocky man looked past them at Trelawny, who had pulled the hatch closed and was now scuffling down the ladder.

The man called, angrily, "One, you said! Not . . . four! Not women!"

Crawford noticed the hilts of two slim rapiers standing in an elephant-foot umbrella stand by the ladder, and he snatched one of them up and held the hilt of the other out toward McKee. She took it with a quick nod.

"Shut up, Abbas," said Trelawny tightly, striking a match to a lantern bolted to the wall by the ladder. "I'll—explain."

Crawford reached up to take off his ludicrous beaver hat, but he saw Trelawny draw a pistol from under his coat—and he realized that this man Abbas was the person the old man intended to kill, to fulfill the conditions Maria's ghost had described.

Thumping and sliding sounded from the deck overhead, and then someone was pounding at the hatch and a girl's voice was screaming words Crawford couldn't catch.

"That's Rose!" whispered Johanna. "I know her voice!"

Trelawny took an uncertain step toward the ladder. "She *follows* that thing," he said; then he shook his head and spat out an obscene monosyllable and turned toward the others, raising the pistol. "Abbas," he said.

Crawford leaped at him, striking the pistol aside with his free left hand and aiming a punch at Trelawny's chest with the sword's basket hilt; but Trelawny tried to block the blow, and the hilt was deflected upward and rebounded at the old man's face.

The flare and hard bang of the pistol shot flung Trelawny and Crawford apart; Crawford slammed against the port bulkhead, and Trelawny tumbled limp to the starboard-side deck.

Above and behind Crawford the hatch cracked and blew in splinters down the ladder, and a moment later a cloud of wasps swept buzzing and looping into the cabin, followed by two huge gray hands and a gleaming black head that bobbed in the air. One of the hands was missing a finger.

"Where where where?" sang the thing, twisting the eyeless face back and forth on its snakelike neck and sniffing loudly.

The bullet from Trelawny's deflected gunshot had apparently still whistled very closely past Abbas's head, and now the man had drawn a revolver of his own.

"Call me here to *kill* me?" he screamed, and, still screaming but without words now, he rushed forward and began firing indiscriminately as wasps fastened on his face and hands.

The noise of the shots was stunning in the close cabin, and Crawford's eyes were dazzled by the fast muzzle flashes. But through the smoke and wasps he saw Johanna step into the man's path, crouching, her knife held low for an upward thrust; Abbas saw her too, and he swung the barrel of his revolver toward her.

Crawford lunged forward, spun her aside with his left hand, and with his right he drove the rapier blade into the man's belly.

He was face-to-face with Abbas now and their eyes met, both squinting with nearly impersonal exertion; Abbas tilted the gun barrel up, and Crawford caught the wrist with his left hand, then shuffled forward to drive the blade farther in. *Liver,* he thought crazily, *peritoneum, superior mesenteric artery, spinal column.*

The gun fired into the ceiling, and Abbas folded, his knees knocking on the deck.

Crawford had to brace his boot against Abbas's chest to tug the blade free; he spun to face the others, and immediately he slashed at one of the snakelike gray hands that was groping toward Johanna. It contracted back, and the shiny black head twisted toward him. Suddenly wasps were clinging to Crawford's face, and points of sharp pain flared in his cheek and forehead.

"I take my bride, oh yes, sir!" sang the wide mouth in the coal-black face.

McKee chopped with her own sword at the long gray neck, and the head whipped around toward her. A girl's voice was screaming back by the hatch.

Christina Rossetti pushed past Crawford toward the ladder, and as he slapped at the stinging insects on his face, he glimpsed a young girl standing at the base of the ladder, backlit in the gray daylight slanting down the hatch.

Crawford's sword blocked Christina's path, and he twisted the blade so that she hit the edge with her hand. She gasped and paused, looking down at the blood that was already dripping from her fingers.

Crawford caught her shoulder and turned her around to face him. There were no wasps on her.

"I cut you!" he shouted. "Summon him now!" He pulled her back across the deck with him to Abbas's sprawled body, and he crouched to lift the man's limp hand and then wrap Christina's bloody fingers around it.

"Catch this man's ghost, catch his strength, and call Polidori!"

With her free hand she brushed at the wasps that still clung to his face, and tears were running down her cheeks, but she nodded. For a moment she squeezed the dead man's hand, and then she let it fall and took a deep breath.

The girl, Rose, was rushing across the deck now at Johanna, who raised her knife.

"Uncle John!" Christina called softly.

And the air seemed to twang.

There was another man standing in the bow end of the cabin now, beyond Abbas's body, and Crawford recognized the curly dark hair, and the mustache, and the deep alien eyes; McKee knew him too, and sprang at Polidori, driving her sword toward his chest—

But the blade flexed as it met a barrier a few inches away from Polidori's white shirt, and the torqued blade was twisted out of McKee's hand.

It clattered to the deck as McKee retreated a step, and Polidori stepped back and stood up straight—then paused, flexing his white-gloved hands in front of his face.

He looked at Christina. "Let go of me," he said in a voice like rocks shifting at the bottom of a well.

"Hold him!" said Crawford. He glanced anxiously back at Johanna—she had wrestled the thrashing Rose to the deck and was fending off the gray hands and the black face with kicks and swipes of her knife.

"I will!" wailed Christina. Her fists were clenched and her eyes were shut.

"*Et tu, Brute?*" said Polidori to her, and then his human body crouched and picked up McKee's dropped sword.

With no more now than a desperate hope to distract him, Crawford sprang forward in a lunge, and Polidori straightened and parried the thrust away.

"My son!" he said in his rumbling voice.

Thumps and curses and musical hooting from behind Crawford let him know that McKee had joined Johanna's fight.

"I'm not," panted Crawford. "I'm Michael Crawford's son." And he lunged again, this time disengaging his blade around Polidori's parry.

But Polidori easily countered and parried it again and drove his left fist hard into Crawford's chest.

The force of the blow punched the air out of Crawford's lungs and flung him backward across the cabin; he hit the deck and slid on his back until his head collided with the aft bulkhead.

Colors spun in his vision, but he dimly saw Trelawny snatch up his hat, and then the old man had rolled him over and yanked the Inverness cape off his shoulders.

Struggling to pull air into his stunned lungs, Crawford managed to get to his hands and knees. And he saw Trelawny, wearing the beaver hat and the cape now, snatch up Crawford's sword and advance quickly on Polidori.

The light from the porthole and the lantern were at Trelawny's back—Polidori would see only Trelawny's backlit silhouette in the hat and cape and must suppose it was Crawford.

"I threw you aside," said Polidori, crouching again into an en garde, "to live, if you cared to."

Crawford saw Trelawny lunge.

Polidori parried the thrust and riposted with a lunge of his own—

—and Trelawny caught the vampire's darting blade on his, but instead of parrying it away, he simply nudged it upward and canted his head to the side.

And Trelawny's head jerked as the vampire's blade tip snagged his throat.

Then the old man had toppled backward onto the deck, and Crawford was crawling toward him, still not able to breathe.

Trelawny was breathing, though, in great gasps, and each time he exhaled, the air in the cabin rippled like heat waves over noonday pavement.

Several wasps pattered dead to the deck by Crawford's sliding hands.

The upright figure that was Polidori was flickering in and out of visibility, and his great voice was audible only in chopped fragments: "—*Trelawny—him up!—stone must not—bridge—*"

Crawford glanced to the side and saw that the spidery figure of the dead boy was appearing and disappearing too—he saw Johanna drive her knife into the thing's forehead in a moment when it was present, and when it reappeared again two seconds later, it was hunching backward away from her with dust shaking out of a hole above its gaping left eye.

McKee was kneeling on Rose, holding her wrists.

Crawford had reached Trelawny, who rolled his eyes up at him.

"Get it all the way out," the old man whispered through blood-stained teeth, and his opened throat hissed with his words. "His protection—you see—didn't protect me—from himself."

Fresh blood was puddling under Trelawny's ear and shoulder and soaking into his tumbled white hair, but it wasn't spurting as if from a major vessel, and Crawford peered at the wound. The gash in the old man's throat had exposed part of the trachea—air was blowing a narrow bloody spray out of a cut in it as he breathed—and a walnut-sized cyst hung between the thyroid cartilage and the jugular vein. The cyst was partly cut free, flapping back and forth with each breath.

"Johanna!" Crawford managed to gasp, and when his daughter looked up he beckoned.

She scrambled up on the other side of Trelawny, and her eyebrows went up nearly to the sweat-spiky fringe of her hair when she saw the cut.

"Give me your knife, quick."

He forced out of his mind the otherwise disabling comprehension that this was a man, not an injured horse.

The intermittent figure of Polidori was flashing closer, and before its flickering, groping hands could reach him, he took Johanna's knife and held his breath—and with the point he carefully cut along the narrow strip of scar tissue between the pulsing jugular vein and the cyst.

The cyst was lying bloodily across his fingers now, and he traced the knifepoint around the far side of it, freeing it from the thyroid cartilage.

The thing fell into his palm, and he could feel the heavy, nearly round stone inside it.

Polidori collapsed in a thumping swirl of dust that did not flicker away. The dead boy squeaked shrilly and then was just a puff of smoke, slowly dissipating as it drifted under the ceiling toward the stale-air vent.

"Not even anything to cremate," said Johanna in an awed voice.

Crawford pushed the knifepoint into the cyst, and the steel grated against the fired clay.

AND THROUGH THE KNIFE'S tang in his palm, Crawford was drawn into a vision of the woman in fragments in the green-lit chamber, and he saw the separate hands and arm and wide-eyed face collapse as siftings and spillings of black sand, and the green light faded to darkness, and for a moment he saw bare trees shaking in a gust on the distant Cotswold Hills;

He glimpsed the thing that had been Polidori too, moving like a mountain through the sky, retreating east to the snowy airless heights where nothing organic could live;

And in a house in Holmwood forty miles west of London, Algernon Swinburne dropped his glass of brandy and staggered to the window, but when he had fumbled it open and thrust his head out into the cold wind, the fresh air couldn't provide the sustenance he was now deprived of;

In Chelsea, Gabriel Rossetti stepped back from his dark, cramped painting of *Astarte Syricaca* and blinked around bewilderedly at the partitions that blocked his view of the garden, and then he sat down and was sobbing because he couldn't remember why he had ever nailed them up;

William Rossetti looked up from his desk and stared through his office window at the gray walls of King's College, and, for just one fleeting moment before returning his attention to the petition at hand, he tried in vain to recall any of the verses he had once been shown, verses that he might have written;

In Christina's bedroom in the house in Torrington Place, the bottle on the bedroom shelf vibrated faintly, and the furry sea mouse slowly sank to the sediment at the bottom;

And across the bridges and rooftops and steeples of London, all the songbirds burst into wild chirping and trilling.

WHEN THE VISIONS ABATED, no time seemed to have elapsed; Crawford was still holding the knifepoint pressed against the stone.

He shook his head and handed the knife back to Johanna, then pulled his handkerchief out of his pocket, folded it, and gently laid it across the hissing gash in the old man's throat.

"Pressure," he told Trelawny, whose hand wobbled up to hold the handkerchief in place. "Not too much."

"Let—me up," whispered Trelawny. His face was pale under his tan and slicked with sweat.

"No! Your larynx would probably fall out on your chest." Crawford looked across at McKee, who had wrestled Rose into a sitting position on the deck. The girl was panting and grinding her teeth.

"She'll be pretty wild for a while yet," commented Johanna. "As I recall."

Christina Rossetti was gripping her cut hand. "I think she'd benefit from staying at the Magdalen Penitentiary," she said.

"It saved me," agreed McKee.

Rose made a sullen suggestion about what Christina might benefit from.

Christina sighed and looked down at Trelawny. "Someone should tell her parents, soon, that she's well."

"I'll do it myself," croaked the old man on the floor, but Crawford frowned and shook his head.

"I'll send Johanna for medical supplies, and I'll clean out the wound and sew you up. But you're going to be living right here for a few weeks, if you live at all. And I mean *right* here, on the deck—I don't think even a pillow would be a good idea for a few days. Swallowing is likely to be difficult—can your Larks cook soup?"

"My Larks," gasped Trelawny, "are going to be busy tonight disposing of a body."

"I can cook soup," said Johanna. "I can stay here with him." She looked down at the old man. "Who's sleeping in the sleigh these days?"

"I'll turn 'em out," whispered Trelawny. "It was always yours."

Crawford got to his feet, wincing at the pains in his knees and hip. He dug some coins out of his pocket and handed them to Johanna.

"Alcohol," he said. "Carbolic acid. There's a stove here? Good. Water. A sewing kit. Thread. Bandages." He glanced down at his scowling, sweating patient; the handkerchief Trelawny was pressing to his throat was already completely blotted and gleaming with blood, and the red puddle on the deck seemed wider. "I'd advise a Bible too, and a priest," Crawford added uneasily.

Christina nodded. "A Catholic priest, I think, when it's something important." Then she bit her lip and looked down. "I'll even—say a rosary."

"Don't talk more foolishness—than you need to, Diamonds," whispered Trelawny. "This is just the . . . last stage of the assault I survived fifty years ago. I'll go on surviving it."

"No priest?" said Christina. Her eyes were anxious.

"No priest," echoed Trelawny in a hoarsening whisper. "I married my Zela and loved her without a priest's consent, and when I *do* die, it will be without one."

Christina gave him a wan smile and then looked at the scattered dust on the deck by Abbas's corpse. She sighed, and said, perhaps to herself, "I only loved one man, and it was my misfortune that he died nine years before I was born."

Crawford stared at her and opened his mouth, then shut it and turned to Johanna. "You'd better hurry up getting those supplies."

Johanna nodded and started toward the ladder. "He won't die of this," she called back over her shoulder. "He'd scorn to."

"She was always the best of the Larks," whispered Trelawny.

EPILOGUE

April 14, 1882

I want to assure you that, however harassed by memory or
by anxiety you may be, I have (more or less) heretofore gone
through the same ordeal. I have borne myself till I became
unbearable to myself, and then I have found help in confession
and absolution and spiritual counsel, and relief inexpressible.

—*Christina Rossetti, in a letter to Dante
Gabriel Rossetti, December 2, 1881*

THE OLD FIELDSTONE All Saints Church at Birchington-on-Sea,
east of the Thames Estuary in northeast Kent, was separated from
the North Sea only by a gently descending mile of sand and sparse
weeds, but the churchyard was bright with flowering irises and lilacs,
and Christina Rossetti had brought woodspurge and forget-me-nots.
The angular gray stone steeple was the only interruption of the bright
blue sky.

Gabriel had died five days earlier, on the evening of Easter Sunday,
at the age of fifty-three. The cause of death had been kidney failure, or a
stroke, or the ravages of breaking a chloral hydrate addiction by switch-

ing to whisky and morphia. A local doctor had pronounced that Gabriel had simply not wanted to live any longer.

Birchington was a long train ride from Victoria Station in London, but Gabriel had been staying out here in therapeutic retreat, and he had been adamant that he was not to be buried at Highgate Cemetery with Lizzie and his father. No one had argued with him.

The coffin had been carried from the church down to the grave on the shoulders of William Rossetti and five men Crawford didn't recognize, and the priest was now praying over it. The walls of the grave were straightly cut down into the chalk.

Swinburne was absent—at forty-five he had reputedly become something of a penitent hermit, living out in Putney and forswearing drink. Of course his poetry was technically competent but uninspired these days, but he seemed grateful for his deliverance from it; it was said that he even remembered Trelawny fondly.

Trelawny had died only last August, at the age of eighty-eight, having lived actively for four years after Crawford cut the stone ball from his neck.

Christina, at least, had apparently noticed the four figures hanging back by the church porch, and she hobbled up the path to where they stood.

"Adelaide!" she said, squinting in the sunlight but not cringing from it. She touched an old scar on her hand. "And Mr. Crawford. Your beard is white now! And—Johanna . . . Foyle, is it, now?" When Johanna nodded, Christina turned to the fourth person in the group, a diffident and clean-shaven man of about thirty. "And Mr. Foyle himself?"

"Yes, ma'am," he said, bowing.

"I'm sorry I was too ill to attend the wedding . . . two years ago already?"

Crawford nodded. "At the church in Bozier's Court."

"I remember it well."

"Trelawny was there," said Johanna. "Muttering heresies."

"And his granddaughter? Rose? Was she at the ceremony?"

"No," said McKee. "I gather she stayed on at the Magdalen house, working there now."

"Ah. I haven't been back there in years." Christina shook her head, and her gray hair blew around her face as she turned to look back down the shallow slope to the churchyard. Absently she blew aside a stray lock.

"No mirrors in Gabriel's coffin," she said, "and William has three children now, the youngest a two-year-old girl. All well, and I don't know if he even remembers now where the bit of Shelley's jawbone is."

Christina glanced at Mr. Foyle and seemed reassured when he nodded, clearly acquainted with the whole story.

"I've—been to Confession," she said, "at a Catholic Church, though it was hard. I truly think you three would benefit from doing the same." She sighed and looked at Crawford. "But if it weren't for your actions, I believe we would all be very different people now, and incalculably worse, living in a London like Dante's *Inferno*."

"Or dead under an inverted London," said Johanna.

"That too, that too," Christina said distractedly, staring again down the slope at the mourners and the coffin. "I should rejoin the others." She blinked, then focused again on Crawford. "I'm glad you have your spouse and child," she said, and Crawford could hear the effort it took for her not to emphasize some of the words. "And I . . . truly do forgive you for the . . . sometimes stressful changes you brought us."

Johanna's brown hair was longer now, pinned back against the wind. She cocked her head and smiled at Christina. "We forgive you too," she said, "for the same."

Christina blinked. "Oh, yes. That's—yes, thank you. And may the— the Father forgive us all."

She shivered in the sunlight and then began hobbling back down the path to her brother's burial.

About the author

About the book

Read on

Insights,
Interviews
& More...

Meet Tim Powers

Serena Powers

TIM POWERS is the author of numerous novels including *Hide Me Among the Graves*, *Last Call*, *Declare*, *Three Days to Never*, and *On Stranger Tides*, which inspired the upcoming feature film *Pirates of the Caribbean: On Stranger Tides*, starring Johnny Depp and Penelope Cruz. Powers lives in San Bernardino, California. ∽

Questions for Discussion

1. When Adelaide McKee re-enters John Crawford's life, he is uncomfortable with her, and only gradually admits to himself that he loves her. Of course prostitutes were considered lost souls in Victorian England, but is there more than that behind his initial reserve?

2. William is strongly tempted to accept Polidori's offer. What makes him ultimately refuse it?

3. Edward John Trelawny puts his own life at risk, twice, to free his niece and Johanna from Polidori—but before that he is willing to kill a stranger to accomplish the same thing. Did you find him an admirable character, or a villainous one, in the end? Why?

4. Maria knew for years of a way to kill Polidori, but for religious reasons she never revealed it while she was alive. Was she right to keep the secret?

5. Dante Gabriel Rossetti blamed himself for his wife's suicide. Was he right?

6. Both Christina Rossetti and Johanna became victims of the vampire Polidori at an early age, but, after their liberations from his control, Christina remained reluctantly attracted to him while Johanna hated and feared him. What was ▶

it in the character of each of them that led to this difference?

7. What was the basis of Algernon Swinburne's relationship with Lizzie Siddall? What might have happened if she had agreed to "marry" him, on that night out at sea?

8. Christina's father caused all the trouble by saving the little statue and then tempting Christina with it. What do you think his core motivation was in doing that?

9. Christina's poetry became mundane and uninspired after her connection with Polidori was broken. In the terms of the novel, was this entirely a good thing?

10. Trelawny says that ghosts "are ashamed of being dead." Why might this be? ∼

More from Tim Powers

ON STRANGER TIDES

Aboard the *Vociferous* Carmichael puppeteer John Chandagnac is sailing toward Jamaica to claim his stolen birthright from an unscrupulous uncle when the vessel is captured . . . *by pirates*! Offered a choice by Captain Phil Davies to join their seafaring band or die, Chandagnac assumes the name John Shandy and a new life as a brigand. But more than swashbuckling sea battles and fabulous plunder await the novice buccaneer on the roiling Caribbean waters—for treachery and powerful *vodun* sorcery are coins of the realm in this dark new world. And for the love of beautiful, magically imperiled Beth Hurwood, Shandy will set sail on even stranger tides, following the savage, ghost-infested pirate king Blackbeard and a motley crew of the living and the dead to the cursed nightmare banks of the fabled Fountain of Youth.

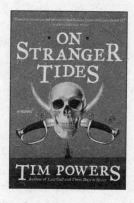

"Powers writes action and adventure that Indiana Jones could only dream of."
—*Washington Post*

More from Tim Powers *(continued)*

Read On for a Sneak Peek at *On Stranger Tides*

Prologue

Though the evening breeze had chilled his back on the way across, it hadn't yet begun its nightly job of sweeping out from among the island's clustered vines and palm boles the humid air that the day had left behind, and Benjamin Hurwood's face was gleaming with sweat before the black man had led him even a dozen yards into the jungle. Hurwood hefted the machete that he gripped in his left—and only—hand, and peered uneasily into the darkness that seemed to crowd up behind the torchlit vegetation around them and overhead, for the stories he'd heard of cannibals and giant snakes seemed entirely plausible now, and it was difficult, despite recent experiences, to rely for safety on the collection of ox-tails and cloth bags and little statues that dangled from the other man's belt. In this primeval rain forest it didn't help to think of them as *gardes* and *arrets* and *drogues* rather than fetishes, or of his companion as a *bocor* rather than a witch doctor or shaman.

The black man gestured with the torch and looked back at him. "Left now," he said carefully in English, and then added rapidly in one of the debased French dialects of Haiti, "and step carefully— little streams have undercut the path in many places."

"Walk more slowly, then, so I can see where you put your feet," replied Hurwood irritably in his fluent textbook French. He wondered how badly his hitherto perfect accent had suffered from the past month's exposure to so many odd variations of the language.

The path became steeper, and soon he had to sheathe his machete in order to have his hand free to grab branches and pull himself along, and for a while his heart was pounding so alarmingly that he thought it would burst, despite the protective *drogue* the black man had given him—then they had got above the level of the surrounding jungle and the sea breeze found them and he called to his companion to stop so that he could catch his breath in the fresh air and enjoy the coolness of it in his sopping white hair and damp shirt.

The breeze clattered and rustled in the palm branches below, and through a gap in the sparser trunks around him he could see water—a moonlight-speckled segment of the Tongue of the Ocean, across which the two of them had sailed from New Providence Island that afternoon. He remembered noticing the prominence they now stood on, and wondering about it, as he'd struggled to keep the sheet trimmed to his bad-tempered guide's satisfaction.

Andros Island it was called on the maps, but the people he'd been associating with lately generally called it Isle de Loas Bossals, which, he'd gathered, meant Island of Untamed (or, perhaps more closely, Evil) Ghosts (or, it sometimes seemed, Gods). Privately he thought of it as Persephone's shore, where he hoped to find, at long last, at least a window into the house of Hades.

He heard a gurgling behind him and turned in time to see his guide recorking one of the bottles. Sharp on the fresh air he could smell the rum. "Damn it," Hurwood snapped, "that's for the ghosts."

The *bocor* shrugged. "Brought too much," he explained. "Too much, too many come."

The one-armed man didn't answer, but wished once again that he knew enough—instead of just *nearly* enough—to do this alone.

"Nigh there now," said the *bocor*, tucking the bottle back into the leather bag slung from his shoulder.

They resumed their steady pace along the damp earth path, but Hurwood sensed a difference now—attention was being paid to them.

The black man sensed it too, and grinned back over his shoulder, exposing gums nearly as white as his teeth. "They smell the rum," he said.

"Are you sure it's not just those poor Indians?"

The man in front answered without looking back. "They still sleep. That's the *loas* you feel watching us."

Though he knew there could be nothing out of the ordinary to see yet, the one-armed man glanced around, and it occurred to him for the first time that this really wasn't so incongruous a setting— these palm trees and this sea breeze probably didn't differ very much from what might be found in the Mediterranean, and this Caribbean island might be very like the island where, thousands of years ago, Odysseus performed almost exactly the same procedure they intended to perform tonight. ∽

More from Tim Powers *(continued)*

LAST CALL

Onetime professional gambler Scott Crane hasn't returned to Las Vegas, or held a hand of cards, in ten years. But troubling nightmares about a strange poker game he once attended on a houseboat on Lake Mead—a contest he believed he walked away from a big winner—are drawing him back to the magical city. Because the mythic game did not end that night in 1969. And the price of his winnings was his soul. And now a pot far more strange and perilous than he ever could imagine depends on the turning of a card.

"A thrilling tale of gambling, fate, and fantastic adventure."

—*Los Angeles Daily News*

Read On for a Sneak Peek at *Last Call*

Leon had wanted an excuse to stop by the Flamingo Hotel, seven miles outside of town on 91, so he had taken Scott there for breakfast.

The Flamingo was a wide three-story hotel with a fourth-floor penthouse, incongruously green against the tan desert that surrounded it. Palm trees had been trucked in to stand around the building, and this morning the sun had been glaring down from a clear sky, giving the vivid green lawn a look of defiance.

Leon had let a valet park the car, and he and Scott had walked hand in hand along the strip of pavement to the front steps that led up to the casino door.

Below the steps on the left side, behind a bush, Leon had long ago punched a hole in the stucco and scratched some symbols around it; this morning he crouched at the foot of the steps to tie his shoe, and he took a package from his coat pocket and leaned forward and pitched it into the hole.

"Another thing that might hurt you, Daddy?" Scott asked in a whisper. The boy was peering over his shoulder at the crude rayed suns and stick figures that grooved the stucco and flaked the green paint.

Leon stood up. He stared down at his son, wondering why he had ever confided this to the boy. Not that it mattered now.

"Right, Scotto," he said. "And what is it?"

"Our secret."

"Right again. You hungry?"

"As a bedbug." This had somehow become one of their bits of standard dialogue.

"Let's go."

The desert sun had been shining in through the windows, glittering off the little copper skillets the fried eggs and kippered herrings were served in. The breakfast had been "on the house," even though they weren't guests, because Leon was known to have been a business associate of Ben Siegel, the founder. Already the waitresses felt free to refer openly to the man as "Bugsy" Siegel.

That had been the first thing that had made Leon uneasy, eating at the expense of that particular dead man. ▶

More from Tim Powers *(continued)*

Scotty had had a good time, though, sipping a cherry-topped Coca-Cola from an Old Fashioned glass and squinting around the room with a worldly air.

"This is your place now, huh, Dad." he'd said as they were leaving through the circular room that was the casino. Cards were turning over crisply, and dice were rolling with a muffled rattle across the green felt, but Leon didn't look at any of the random suits and numbers that were defining the moment.

None of the dealers or croupiers seemed to have heard the boy. "You don't—" Leon began.

"I know," Scotty had said in quick shame, "you don't talk about important stuff in front of the cards."

They left through the door that faced the 91, and had to wait for the car to be brought around from the other side—the side where the one window on the penthouse level made the building look like a one-eyed face gazing out across the desert.

The Emperor card, Leon thought now as he tugged Scotty along the rain-darkened Center Street sidewalk; why am I not seeing any signs from *it*? The old man in profile, sitting on a throne with his legs crossed because of some injury. That has been my card for a year now. I can prove it by Richard, my eldest son—and soon enough I'll be able to prove it by Scotty here.

Against his will he wondered what sort of person Scotty must have grown up to be if this weren't going to happen. The boy would be twenty-one in 1964; was there a little girl in the world somewhere now who would, otherwise, one day meet him and marry him? Would she now find somebody else? What sort of man would Scotty have grown up to be? Fat, thin, honest, crooked? Would he have inherited his father's talent for mathematics? ∿

DECLARE

As a young double agent infiltrating the Soviet spy network in Nazi-occupied Paris, Andrew Hale finds himself caught up in a secret, even more ruthless war. Two decades later, in 1963, he will be forced to confront again the nightmare that has haunted his adult life: a lethal unfinished operation code-named Declare. From the corridors of Whitehall to the Arabian desert, from postwar Berlin to the streets of Cold War Moscow, Hale's desperate quest draws him into international politics and gritty espionage tradecraft—and inexorably drives Hale, the fiery and beautiful Communist agent Elena Teresa Ceniza-Bendiga, and Kim Philby, mysterious traitor to the British cause, to a deadly confrontation on the high glaciers of Mount Ararat, in the very shadow of the fabulous and perilous Ark.

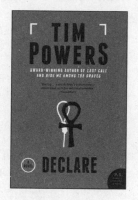

"Dazzling . . . a tour de force, a brilliant blend of John le Carré spy fiction with the otherworldly."

—Dean Koontz

More from Tim Powers *(continued)*

Read On for a Sneak Peek at *Declare*

Prologue

Mount Ararat, 1948

> *. . . from behind that craggy steep till then*
> *The horizon's bound, a huge peak, black and huge,*
> *As if with voluntary power instinct,*
> *Upreared its head. I struck and struck again,*
> *And growing still in stature the grim shape*
> *Towered up between me and the stars, and still,*
> *For so it seemed, with purpose of its own*
> *And measured motion like a living thing,*
> *Strode after me.*
> —William Wordsworth, *The Prelude*, 381–389

The young captain's hands were sticky with blood on the steering wheel as he cautiously backed the jeep in a tight turn off the rutted mud track onto a patch of level snow that shone in the intermittent moonlight on the edge of the gorge, and then his left hand seemed to freeze onto the gear-shift knob after he reached down to clank the lever up into first gear. He had been inching down the mountain path in reverse for an hour, peering over his shoulder at the dark trail, but the looming peak of Mount Ararat had not receded at all, still eclipsed half of the night sky above him, and more than anything else he needed to get away from it.

He flexed his cold-numbed fingers off the gear-shift knob and switched on the headlamps—only one came on, but the sudden blaze was dazzling, and he squinted through the shattered windscreen at the rock wall of the gorge and the tire tracks in the mud as he pulled the wheel around to drive straight down the narrow shepherds' path. He was still panting, his breath bursting out of his open mouth in plumes of steam. He was able to drive a little faster now, moving forward—the jeep was rocking on its abused springs and the four-cylinder engine roared in first gear, no longer in danger of lugging to a stall.

He was fairly sure that nine men had fled down the path an

hour ago. Desperately he hoped that as many as four of them might be survivors of the SAS group he had led up the gorge, and that they might somehow still be sane.

But his face was stiff with dried tears, and he wasn't sure if he were still sane himself—and unlike his men, he had been somewhat prepared for what had awaited them; to his aching shame now, he had at least known how to evade it.

In the glow reflected back from the rock wall at his right, he could see bright, bare steel around the bullet holes in the jeep's bonnet; and he knew the doors and fenders were riddled with similar holes. The wobbling fuel gauge needle showed half a tank of petrol, so at least the tank had not been punctured.

Within a minute he saw three upright figures a hundred feet ahead of him on the path, and they didn't turn around into the glow of the single headlamp. At this distance he couldn't tell if they were British or Russian. He had lost his Sten gun somewhere on the high slopes, but he pulled the chunky .45 revolver out of his shoulder holster—even if these survivors were British, he might need it.

But he glanced fearfully back over his shoulder, at the looming mountain—the unsubdued power in the night was back there, up among the craggy high fastnesses of Mount Ararat.

He turned back to the frail beam of light that stretched down the slope ahead of him to light the three stumbling figures, and he increased the pressure of his foot on the accelerator, and he wished he dared to pray.

He didn't look again at the mountain. Though in years to come he would try to dismiss it from his mind, in that moment he was bleakly sure that he would one day see it again, would again climb this cold track. ◠◡

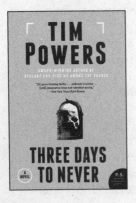

THREE DAYS TO NEVER

Albert Einstein's groundbreaking scientific discoveries made possible the creation of the most terrible weapon the world had ever known. But he made another discovery that he chose to reveal to no one—to keep from human hands a power that dwarfed the atomic bomb.

When twelve-year-old Daphne Marrity takes a videotape labeled *Pee-wee's Big Adventure* from her recently deceased grandmother's house, neither she nor her college-professor father, Frank, realize what they now have in their possession. In an instant they are thrust into the center of a world-altering conspiracy, drawing the dangerous attentions of both the Israeli Secret Service and an ancient European cabal of occultists. Now father and daughter have three days to learn the rules of a terrifying magical chess game in order to escape a fate more profound than death—because the Marritys hold the key to the ultimate destruction of not only what's to come . . . but what already has been.

"A genre-bending thriller . . . endlessly inventive . . . [with] imaginative leaps and relentless pacing."
—*New York Times Books Review*

Read On for a Sneak Peek at *Three Days to Never*

Prologue

Sitting on a bank,
Weeping again the King my father's wrack,
This music crept by me upon the waters.
                    —William Shakespeare, *The Tempest*

The ambulance came bobbing out of the Mercy Medical Center parking lot and swung south on Pine Street, its blue and red lights just winking dots in the bright noon sunshine and the siren echoing away into the cloudless blue vault of the sky. At East Lake Street the ambulance turned left, avoiding most of the traffic farther south, where reports of a miraculous angel appearing on somebody's TV set had attracted hundreds of the spiritual pilgrims who had come to town for this weekend.

At the Everett Memorial Highway the ambulance turned north, and accelerated; in five minutes it had left the city behind and was ascending the narrow blacktop strip through cool pine forests, and when the highway curved east the white peaks of Shasta and Shastina stood up high above the timberline.

Traffic was heavier as the highway switchbacked up the mountain slope—Volkswagen vans, campers, buses—and the shoulder was dotted with hitchhikers in jeans and robes and knapsacks.

The red-and-white ambulance weaved between the vehicles on the highway, and it was able to speed up again when the highway straightened out past the Bunny Flats campgrounds. Three miles farther on, the parking lot at Panther Meadows was clogged with cars and vans, but the hospital had radioed ahead and Forest Service officers had cleared a path to the north end of the lot, where trails led away among the trees.

In the clearings around the trailhead, people were strolling aimlessly or staring up into the sky or sitting in meditation circles, and the woods were noisy with ringing bells and the yells of children; two white-clad paramedics got out of the ▶

ambulance and carried a stretcher through a sea of beards and gray ponytails and pastel robes, with the tang of patchouli oil spicing the scent of Douglas fir on the chilly breeze—but they didn't have to hike far, because six people had already made a stretcher of flannel shirts and cherry branches and had carried the limp body most of the way back from the high glades of Squaw Meadow; the body was wrapped in an old brown army blanket and wreathed with Shasta daisies and the white flowers of wild strawberry.

The paramedics lifted the old woman's body onto their aluminum-and-nylon stretcher, and within minutes the ambulance was accelerating back down the mountain, but with no siren now.

Back in the clearing up on Squaw Meadow, the people who had not carried the stretcher were dismembering a swastika-shaped framework of gold wire, having to bend it repeatedly to break it, since none of them was carrying a pocketknife. ◠